THE SONGS WE HIDE

THE SONGS WE HIDE

Connie Hampton Connally

Connie H. Connally

cp
coffeetownpress

Seattle, WA

coffeetownpress

Coffeetown Press
PO Box 70515
Seattle, WA 98127

For more information go to: www.CoffeetownPress.com
www.ConnieHamptonConnally.com

Cover design by Lance Kagey, www.rotatorcreative.com
The Songs We Hide

ISBN: 978-1-60381-631-1 (Trade Paper)
ISBN: 978-1-60381-632-8 (eBook)

Library of Congress Control Number: 2017962923
Printed in the United States of America

To Rory, with love and gratitude

Author's Note and Acknowledgments

SINCE I FIRST began writing *The Songs We Hide*, I've often been asked if I'm Hungarian. I'm not. My interest in Hungary's turbulent history grew out of my love of music. Through music I discovered the story of Zoltán Kodály, a twentieth-century Hungarian composer who spread music in his nation despite totalitarianism and two world wars. Kodály's example gripped me. What would it be like to offer beauty in a milieu of crushing fear? I began researching Hungary. In its tense national narrative and the poignant stories of its people, *The Songs We Hide* took root.

I didn't know at the outset how hard it would be to write about a time, place and culture not my own. As I spent endless hours reading, interviewing, listening to Hungarian music, negotiating the streets of Budapest, and especially writing draft after draft, I struggled not only with understanding it all but also with setting aside my modern American assumptions. Whether we recognize it or not, Americans are optimistic and entrepreneurial, counting on opportunity. We take pride in speaking our minds and making our own choices. But what if, as in Cold War Europe, opportunity barely existed? What if speaking up meant endangering not only ourselves but others as well? What if social constraints were so tight that every choice carried a high cost?

As I wrote *The Songs We Hide*, I had to think with the guardedness, and sometimes bitterness, of post-war Europe. The mental adjustment wasn't easy. Still, at some point my frustration turned to understanding. I learned to appreciate dark Hungarian humor. I've come to love Hungary's beautiful folk heritage and especially its rich musical tradition. This culture that is not my own has nonetheless become part of me, and that's been my greatest reward in this project.

Writers of historical fiction seek stories among fact, and as I researched Hungarian history, some facts were much easier to uncover than others. Quite a bit of information exists in English about Hungary during World War II, especially the last terrible months. Detailed accounts have been written about Hungary's 1956 uprising and the Soviet Union's subsequent clamp-down. The other Cold War years receive less attention, and accounts in English are scarcer and less detailed. Yet as I interviewed Hungarians who lived through this era, I sensed that the early 1950s were some of the hardest years, with ordinary citizens feeling constantly silenced, threatened, hemmed in, and watched. Compelled by the stories I heard and read, I decided to set my novel in 1951.

The Songs We Hide is a work of the imagination and the characters are fictional, but the conditions described in the book are based in fact. The execution of László Rajk is a matter of historical record, and so is the forced relocation of "class *x*" families to the countryside. I have depicted 1951 Budapest to the best of my ability, based on what information I could find about war damage and post-war reconstruction. The Pest Music Academy in this novel is modeled after the actual Liszt Academy but not identical to it. Likewise the villages of Kőpatak, Mezősárgás, and Háromkeresztes are fictional, but they are based on research into Heves County's agriculture, sociology and way of life. Several Hungarians now living in the U.S. have read the manuscript for historical and cultural accuracy, but any errors in the story are mine alone.

I'm indebted to many people for their help. Márta Boros Horváth, author Helen Szablya, and Zoltán and Mária Kramár told me their stories, answered countless questions, checked the manuscript, and offered their insights. Writers Gina Ochsner, Bruce Holland Rogers, and Scott Driscoll gave helpful critiques at different stages of the writing. Ruth Tiger, a close friend and fellow writer, helped me persevere when the project was most difficult. Jay Schaefer's editorial comments were invaluable. In addition, my book club read the manuscript, and their enthusiasm gave me confidence to seek publication.

Special thanks to Lance Kagey of Rotator Creative for designing the cover. I could not ask for a more beautifully evocative representation of the story's themes. I'd particlarly like to thank my publisher, Coffeetown Press. Editors Jennifer McCord and Catherine Treadgold caught the vision of the story and sharpened it. Jennifer especially contributed to the penultimate chapter and Catherine to the musical references.

I'm grateful for the support of my family. My sons and their wives gave me tremendous encouragement during the research, writing, and revision. Most of all, I want to say thanks to my husband, Rory Connally. Literally and figuratively, he journeyed with me through it all: traveling three times to Hungary, deciphering Central European history with me, and reading early and later versions of the manuscript. Rory kept me anchored when I felt overwhelmed, and he never quit believing that *The Songs We Hide* was a story worth telling. Although other people have strengthened my writing craft, no one has done as much to strengthen *me*. For this great gift, my deepest thanks.

Chapter One

～〜〜〜〜〜

The Train to Budapest
Hungary, 1951

Six years after the war was lost, the spring harrowing still turned up bullets and mortar-shell pieces in the fields every March. The farmers of Heves County had grown used to this happening. The war's detritus was easier to live with than the shortages that should have ended by now, easier to deal with than the produce quotas for the good of the people.

Péter Benedek, twenty-two years old, kicked away a gray shell fragment as he led two plow horses up the long, narrow field of newly sprouted wheat. His father paced behind, anchoring and guiding the weed harrow. Not loudly enough for his father to hear, Péter sang to the mare beside him. She was temperamental since the war, and today she was teamed with a borrowed gelding. Péter's breath turned to vapor in the morning cold as he sang. The mare's left ear turned toward him. Then it pricked forward toward the road.

Péter eyed the source of the noise at the field's far end. With a muddy rumble, a black motor car pulled into view. A State car: there was no other kind here. Péter stopped singing.

He looked over his shoulder at his father. "Apa." With a small pitch of his head, Péter indicated the road.

They watched the car pull aside and brake. The doors opened and three figures climbed out. Péter halted the horses. His right hand gripped the reins too tightly and he made himself ease up for the sake of the mare.

"Three of them this time," Apa muttered. His eyes slitted behind his high cheekbones as he squinted toward the road.

The men crossed the field, a grim triangle, their forms blurring in the mist, then sharpening as they drew closer. Péter envied them their long warm coats. He recognized all the men—in back, the squat deputy who had once been police chief here, and then the hulking younger man who had taken his job. In front walked Tamás Márton, the local Party secretary who ran the communal farm. He was a little older than Apa, with red hair gone wash-water gray and a brown mole under his eye. Péter remembered when the man used to sharecrop barley.

The three stopped a few meters away. Márton touched one hand to his fur cap and gave a nod in greeting. "Freedom!"

Péter glanced at his father. Apa only brushed a finger over his graying mustache. He had not shaved this morning, and a sprinkling of stubble showed in the hollows above his jaw. Apa's gaze moved between the three men.

The police chief set his hands on his service belt and drew back his shoulders. Péter tried to catch Apa's eye. *Speak!*

Apa did not speak.

Péter lifted the brim of his cap and summoned the saliva to his dry mouth. "Good day, comrades."

Tamás Márton threw Péter a look but turned back to Apa. "Jancsi Benedek." Márton swept a gloved hand in a downward arc, left to right. "This is not your land."

Péter's chest pulsed hot.

Apa's hand dropped from the harrow. "What?"

Márton gestured toward the west. "The fields there belong to the collective farm."

"I know."

Márton pointed toward the stream to the east and the field that lay this side of it. "And also there."

"No," Apa said. "That's Jakab Kozma's land."

"Kozma joined the collective yesterday. *He* is supporting the economic plan."

Apa stared at Márton.

"So you see, there is collective property on either side," Márton said. "The economic plan calls for communal farms to have contiguous land. The collective will work this land now." He jerked his thumb toward the lower field that had belonged to Jakab Kozma. "There is yours."

Péter had walked that land: a good third of it was nothing better than pig mud.

His hand closed taut on the reins. The mare tossed her head; the gelding sidestepped; the harness jerked.

Péter clutched the mare's halter. *"Ho!"* he ordered the horses, hearing the choke in his own voice.

Apa grasped the harrow again. "My son and I already planted this field," he said. "We have work to do here. Péter, forward. Go."

But the big police officer in back pulled the billy club out of his service belt and thumped it in the palm of his hand. "Work this land if you want to, citizen, but the harvest belongs to the collective."

The three turned and walked away, with only the short deputy turning once to look back.

Péter did not move the horses forward. He stood with his father among the green shoots of this lost land. He knew its every ridge and pit, knew the desperate hopes that he and his father and his grandfather had sown here year after year. Beside him, his father gazed over the field in silence. Péter wanted to speak, but the words would not come. When the car drove off and the drone of its engine faded, there remained only the sounds of a distant crow, and now and then, the stamping of the horses.

THAT AFTERNOON THEY paced the contours of the plot they could not stop calling Jakab Kozma's. On the higher stretches, the winter wheat had spiked through the surface of the soil, though it was not as far along as their own crop. In the muddy lower reaches, close to the stream and the reeds, Kozma had not planted at all. Péter sifted a handful of the soil in his fingers, examined it with his glasses lifted, then showed it to his father, though they both already knew this field was a loss. The family would have to supplement their income by doing more day labor and even then, they would probably come up short. They weren't the first. It was happening all over the country, people were saying, when they dared speak of it.

"This land won't feed us," Apa said. He motioned in the direction the car had driven off. "The bastards don't want it to. Collective farm, economic plan, faugh. They're trying to turn us into serfs."

Péter glanced around to make sure no one had overheard.

With the toe of his boot, Apa pushed at the muddy soil. "They say this field's ours. Maybe they don't mean it, but we're not giving it up."

"No," Péter said, for if they had any stature, any protection, any future at all, it was in the land.

The next day they drew the weeding harrow over the upper stretches of the new plot. That night, after Péter's grandfather and brothers were asleep, Péter and his father began discussing Budapest. In whispers, they formed a plan: Péter would go to work in the city. He'd come home on some weekends and at harvest, and they'd try to make up for what they'd lost. Maybe they'd get lucky and there would be another regime change—good God, didn't the regime seem to change every two weeks? One way or another, they'd hold on to this scrap of land. And no matter how many other farm boys had gone to the city for good, Péter would come back. How they were going to manage this, or even if they really could, Péter wasn't sure; but he knew his father could bear no other possibility.

THREE WEEKS LATER at the end of March, Péter made ready to leave Kőpatak, the village where he'd lived all his life. The Saturday morning was softly cool, the apricot trees blossoming. In the distance, the vineyards, not yet green, stretched into the Bükk Hills. Feeling the melancholy of the goodbye, Péter took his time with the milking and threw extra corn to the chickens and the pregnant sow. In the barn, he gave the horse a conciliatory apple from cold storage, stroked her black neck, and sang softly to her. Though he never let others hear him sing, the horse was used to it.

"You'll have to get along without songs now, Zsuzsi," he told the mare. "Be good to Apa. No skittering. No teeth."

Péter joined his brothers in the cow's stall, where they shoveled manure and spread straw.

Tibi and Gyuri were ten years old, twins but not identical—mismatched socks, their mother used to say. The light at the glassless barn window fell across the boys' bobbing heads and gangly arms as they worked.

"I don't know why you have to go to the city, Péter," Tibi grumbled. "It's terrible that they made us trade our fields and—"

"Quiet!" Péter grabbed Tibi's forearm. "You don't talk like that. You don't say things are terrible."

Tibi jerked away. "But they are."

"You don't *say* it!" Péter yanked the shutters closed and thrust a finger toward the blinded window. "Not on the road, not in the square, not at school, never out there. Do you understand?"

Both boys whispered yes.

"You have to be careful," Péter breathed. "You have to."

When the twins left the barn, he watched and waited until they disappeared into the house. Then he walked outside to the back of the barn and down the stone steps to the cellar. He tugged at the padlock to make sure it was snug. It was.

He and Apa had done things carefully, inconspicuously, yes, even invisibly. They had taken every precaution. Péter leaned against the cellar door, reminding himself of this, and he yanked once more on the lock. It held.

IN THE EARLY afternoon, Péter collected the items he would need in Budapest: a few changes of clothing, his razor, his toothbrush, and a wooden comb. Combs had never done much good with his curly brown hair, but he had not quit trying. He pushed everything into a rucksack, then checked his corduroy jacket for the letter from his Budapest uncle. Yes, it was there in the breast pocket, along with his red identification booklet. His ID made it plain he was not a Party member, and he wondered how many times in the coming weeks he would have to hand it over.

Under the reed-thatched eaves outside the door, Péter said goodbye to his grandfather and brothers. The old man patted him carefully, keeping one hand on his whittled cane. The twins stood close. Péter grasped them around the shoulders, and Tibi buried his face in Péter's shirt.

As he left for the train, his father walked with him. They did not speak, did not wave to the Kozmas next door, did not meet the gazes of others they passed. Beside them, ducks swam in the ditch water that ran past the adobe houses, past the milk jugs upside down on the fence posts. In the town square, Péter and his father walked silently past the stone marker commemorating the Kőpatak men who had died in the Great War of 1914-1918. There was no memorial to the recent war, unless it was in the barn stalls without animals, the empty yards where houses had burned or—for Péter—the wooden marker at his mother's grave.

They kept silent as they passed the large house that until three years ago had belonged to the town's wealthiest peasant. The man was either dead or in a work camp now, and his house and land belonged to the collective farm. At this moment, Tamás Márton was standing on the porch of the house, looking over the square. Apa prodded Péter's elbow and they hurried on.

At the Kőpatak train stop, a bare concrete platform, Péter raised the lever arm on the signal post. Apa turned his head in a quick surveillance.

"It's not what I wanted, you going off to the city," Apa said. "You know that, don't you?"

"Yes."

It was not what Péter had wanted, either.

Apa reached inside his jacket pocket and handed him a small, rough linen pouch with seed peas in it. "In case you find somewhere to plant them," Apa said.

The earth trembled beneath them, and the train bore in from the horizon. Apa clasped Péter's shoulder as the train hissed to a stop.

"I'm sorry, son," he said.

Péter threw one arm around his father, and Apa's roughly shaven cheek pressed against his neck.

"*Viszlát*," Péter said in a hoarse goodbye.

"*Isten áldjon*," Apa whispered, using the old parting blessing that had gone out of favor with the State.

Péter ran to the train. From the ladder steps, he looked back to where his father stood watching him, alone, lifting his hand in its frayed glove.

Be careful, Péter wanted to say. Oh God, Apa, be careful.

OUTSIDE THE STREAKED train window, the kilometers of Heves County rolled past. This was the western stretch of the *puszta*, the great, spreading Hungarian plain. The sprouting crops tinged the cold soil with a fine green cast that dented down in places where the war's bomb craters were not yet filled in. Péter thought of the sorry new field back home, and of the wheat and the piglets that would grow while he was in the city, with all its concrete and soot.

And its strangers. He watched a soldier across the aisle chatting up a pretty girl. Péter had never been good at chatting up anyone, and now he'd be among thousands of blank faces.

The train shuddered onward and soon groaned to a stop at Háromkeresztes. Rucksack over one shoulder, Péter walked into the small station where he was to catch the westbound train for Budapest. After wiping his glasses on his shirt, he willed himself to read the schedule board. He found a B. B-U ... Bu-da-pest. Budapest, Track 2. DELAYED.

The woman at the ticket counter said it could be two or three hours. Péter sat down on a bench under one of those electrical lights that hadn't yet come to his house in Kőpatak. He wished he had brought something to eat.

On the stained plaster above the ticket window hung the two portraits displayed in every classroom, train station, post office, and courthouse across Hungary: Josef Stalin and Hungary's national Party Chairman, Mátyás Rákosi. The Old Mustache and the Bald Murderer, people called them, but only among safe company. Péter thought of the obscenities Apa spat out regarding both these men when Gyuri and Tibi weren't around.

A long time passed. He ran a song through his head to entertain himself, but finally, restless and hungry, he headed into town. By now the sun was dropping.

From somewhere, he heard music. He turned and followed the sound down a line of shops. Soon he stood before a restaurant door, and from it wafted the scent of peppers and the melody of a violin. Food and music—they pulled him in.

The place was a step up from Kőpatak: red-checked tablecloths, artificial flowers, floorboards that someone had actually swept. The women wore clean blouses and the men had shaven well, and here he stood with his old cap and rucksack. He would have retreated out the door—but, oh, that music!

Two Gypsies in wide sleeves and black vests were working magic. One sat at a cimbalom striking the strings with little hammers. The tinkling tones rose and fell as the other Gypsy paced with a violin, sweeping the bow over it like wind across a wheat field. An aching, tender melody poured forth. Péter stood, transfixed. His mother used to sing that song.

Then the violinist saw him and crossed the room, playing as he came. The fellow looked so eager, so expectant. *I have no money,* Péter was going to have to tell him; but he could not say it, for the music was wrestling and stirring within him—reaching, tugging, turning.

The song spilled off his tongue.

The Gypsy's dark eyes widened. "Louder. Sing louder!"

Péter stopped. All eyes in the room had turned to him.

"No," he mumbled to the Gypsy. "I can't sing so well."

The Gypsy lifted his hands, the bow in his right and the violin in his left, in a grand shrug to everyone listening. "This fellow thinks he can't sing."

A gray-haired woman at a nearby table raised her wine glass to Péter. "I heard you, and I'll buy you supper if you sing that song louder."

"So sing it!" the Gypsy urged him. "Supper, and she's paying. Don't you want to eat?"

The cimbalom player shouted, "Come back here, boy, and I'll sing it with you!"

The violinist pulled him by the elbow across the room. By the time Péter stood next to the cimbalom, his hair stuck to his forehead in damp rings. Good God, he was only used to singing around horses and cabbage plants, and now all these cleaned-up people were waiting with upturned faces. He dumped the rucksack on the floor and pulled off his cap. The violinist touched his bow to the top string and drew out a sliding, sentimental introduction. The cimbalom player stood up and sang, nodding fiercely at Péter to join in. Péter opened his mouth to sing along, but the words stuck. *Jézus Mária.* He tried again. The song shook. He shut his eyes and imagined he was behind the plow. There was Zsuzsi, tail swishing, the thirsty earth, the lonely *puszta* sky weeping rain. He began to sing: "*Fölszállott a páva.*"

The cimbalom player quit singing, gestured Péter on. As if by its own strength, the song lifted, grew, and overflowed. At the tables, all was silent. The song carried on, relentless, to the last tone. The violin hushed. Péter bent his head in astonishment, eyes on the floorboards.

Applause. Whistles. Cheers.

"I'm finished," he told the violinist, and he walked on trembling legs back to the door.

But that gray-haired woman kept her promise. A waiter nudged him, picked up the rucksack, and beckoned him impatiently into the kitchen. Amid the dirty dishes, Péter sat at a work table and ate bread and goulash.

Soon the violinist walked in, sat down, and lit a cigarette. For the first time,

Péter really looked at him. The fellow seemed not much older than himself, though his dark face was etched at the eyes and mouth.

"You should go out there and crow again," the Gypsy said. "Those people like you. Maybe they'll stuff your pockets."

Péter did not answer. His hands had not stopped trembling.

"We'll be back tomorrow, my brother and me," the Gypsy said. "Want to sing then?"

"I won't be here."

"Where are you going?"

Péter hesitated. Was this a Gypsy's business? Was it anyone's business? "To Budapest," he finally said.

"Everybody's either going to Budapest or getting thrown out of Budapest. I lived there at the end of the war. I swear on my grandmother's grave, that place was butchered. It was a city with its guts falling out. Met some good musicians, though."

Péter leaned in closer. "Yes?"

"They might still be there." The Gypsy tapped his cigarette ashes onto a dirty plate. "Name is Varga. Antal and Katalin, brother and sister. In Pest, Terézváros neighborhood. Antal—now there's a damned fine violinist. And the girl, she was just a filly, a young thing when I knew her. But listen to me: when she sings ... oh, you go weak in the knees."

"Terézváros?"

The violinist smiled around the cigarette. "North past the operetta theater a few blocks and turn right at the tobacconist shop. Halfway down the block or so, gray building. Above the front door there's a little statue, fat baby angel with a wing broken off. At least, there used to be. That family—Katalin, Antal, their parents—good people in a miserable world."

He stood up and finished his cigarette. "My name is Miklós Kolompár. Good luck." He turned out of the kitchen.

In the dining room the music began again. Péter stayed in the kitchen, listening as the violin and the cimbalom spun on. And from somewhere, a trembling—

The train! Holy God, had he missed it? Péter jumped to his feet, grabbed his rucksack, bolted out of the restaurant and onto the street. He didn't stop running until the train whooshed into the west. Without him.

Furious at his own empty-headedness, he dragged himself, out of breath, back to the station's schedule board and muddled through, reading it again. No more trains for Budapest until tomorrow. He threw his rucksack down on the bench and there, under the electric light and Stalin and Rákosi, he tried to sleep. It was hours before he dozed off. The lonely misery appalled him, except for one puzzling memory: he had sung for a roomful of strangers, and they had not laughed.

PÉTER HAD BEEN to Budapest before, but most of what he knew about the city he had learned in the Kőpatak school, or from hearsay. Budapest had once been two cities, with Buda on the west bank of the Danube, and Pest, larger, on the east. Most Hungarians simply called the city Pest. All its bridges had been blown up during the siege of '44-'45, and the people of Kőpatak had talked about it, aghast. Péter himself remembered the wartime talk only vaguely; he had been barely sixteen at the time, his mother two months dead and his house full of Russian soldiers. Most of the bridges had been rebuilt since then. People said you had to give the communists credit for that.

It was late morning when he arrived at the Budapest East train station, neck and shoulders hurting from his bad night. On the station steps, he pulled out the letter from Béla Matai, his mother's uncle. Béla's letter was a reply to the inquiry his father had dictated to Gyuri, who at ten years old read and wrote better than the rest of the family. Uncle Béla said that of course Péter could stay with him and was probably needed in the print shop where he worked as a repairman. Uncle would recommend him. Péter checked the address on the letter, oriented himself west, and started walking.

The fine city was like a crippled baron. Once-stately buildings four or five stories high stood with window ornamentations shot off and walls sprayed with bullet holes. In some places, new buildings had been shoved together, plain and angular and already dingy. Péter walked on, past a wall where huge black letters had been slap-painted: *"Le az amerikai imperializmussal!"* Down with American …. He didn't bother with the long last word.

He hadn't been here in at least three years, and it was harder than he expected to remember the way to his uncle's apartment. Noon came and went before he finally found the old building, recognizing it by its muddy-yellow color. He climbed the interior stairs and walked down the dim third-floor corridor to Uncle Béla's door at the end.

He knocked. There was no answer.

He knocked again. Nothing.

Well, Uncle must be out. Péter went back outside and waited in a small square, watching the pigeons and the unsmiling pedestrians. After about an hour, he tried the apartment again, but still no one answered.

He returned to the square and once again waited, longer this time. Last night's sleeplessness on the station bench wore on him, and his neck muscles hurt. He had eaten almost nothing today. Rain began to fall. It was late afternoon when he went a third time to Uncle Béla's apartment.

Again he knocked, and this time the door opened halfway. A wrinkled woman in a housecoat peered out. "What do you want?"

"Ah," his voice faltered, "I'm looking for Béla Matai. My great-uncle."

"He doesn't live here."

"But ... what?" He showed the woman the envelope with his uncle's address.

"Yes, that's this flat," the woman said, "but I don't know who that man is. My son and I moved in three days ago. That's all I know." She started to shut the door.

"Wait!" he pleaded. "Comrade!"

The woman frowned through the slit of the doorway.

"Please ...." His neck had cramped, and he shifted the rucksack. "Please, is there someone else here who would know about him?"

"Maybe. I don't know who." The woman shut the door hard. The lock clicked.

Na, what was he going to do now? He hated talking to strangers, but all he could think of was to pound on more doors. He went to the next apartment. Hesitated. Knocked. The door did not open.

He tried another apartment, and there asked a tight-lipped woman about Béla Matai. She shook her head firmly and shut the door.

The ache in Péter's neck was radiating into his head. He hesitated longer now, much longer. Finally he knocked at a door across the hall, and an old man in suspenders answered.

"Excuse me, I'm looking for my great-uncle. Béla Matai."

The old man looked him over and glanced into the hallway, lips twitching. "Your uncle," he said quietly.

"Yes. Matai."

The old man set his finger to his lips and shuffled closer. "Matai is gone."

"Where?" Péter whispered. "What happened?"

"I don't know where he is. He left. In the night."

"With... ?"

Before the man shut the door, he gave the smallest hint of a nod. Péter understood: the *Államvédelmi Hatóság,* the secret security police, had come for Uncle Béla. There among the closed doors, Péter hunched his shoulders and walked back up the dim hallway and down the decrepit stairwell, where a single lightbulb glowed a sickly yellow.

HE SPENT A long time in a small diner, eating potato fritters and cheap ham, looking through the café window at the traffic and the rain. He now had nowhere to stay. And what about work tomorrow? As for that whole plan that he and Apa had worked out in whispers, what now? Maybe he should telephone Apa—but no, the only telephones in Kőpatak were in the post office, which was closed, and in the police station. He couldn't call and couldn't go back. Lord, was he going to have to spend another night on a train station bench? Did they throw people in jail for that here, just like they had dragged an old repairman out of his apartment?

Then the words of the Gypsy came back to him: good people, musicians, near the operetta theater.

But wasn't it stupid to trust a Gypsy's word? And anyway, if he did manage to find these people, why would they trust *him*? What was he supposed to say? *I'm Péter Benedek and my uncle has disappeared ....*

No.

I'm Péter Benedek and I'm from Kőpatak ....

Kőpatak, where his father was not supporting the economic plan. No.

Yet he pushed aside his empty plate and unfolded the Budapest map he had brought. The light here was so poor and the lettering on this map so small, damn it: *á* looked like *ó* looked like *ő* looked like *ö*.

"What are you trying to find?" someone asked.

He looked up at the middle-aged waitress with her hair in a careless bun. The way his mother used to wear hers.

"The operetta theater," he answered.

"It's off Stalin Avenue, between the Oktogon and the opera house." She explained the subway route and then asked, "Is something wrong?"

"I ... I hope not."

When he left the café, she thrust a paper parcel into his hands. He opened it on the crowded subway and found two rolls and four slices of cheese. Tomorrow's breakfast, if he could hold out that long. He wished he had thanked her. And the woman who bought his dinner last night, he hadn't thanked her, either. He couldn't go on like this, walking off with people's gifts as though they meant nothing. But he was so unused to gifts.

AT THE OPERA house stop, he surfaced into the rain and trudged around until he found the operetta district, throbbing with pedestrians and taxis. He walked on for more than a kilometer, looking for a tobacconist shop, and then remembered wearily that the Gypsy had been here during the war. Every store, even every window could have changed since then.

He went back and searched for anything that might have been a corner tobacconist shop at one time. Well, here was a drugstore, diagonally across from a bombed-out building. He turned onto the intersecting street, looking for a broken angel.

Music. From somewhere, a violin and a piano. The Gypsy had said the people were musicians. Péter clutched his cap and his rucksack and ran, following the music until he stood beneath a lit window. And the statue ... yes, above the building's front entry sat a fat baby angel with one wing.

He made for the door.

And stopped. This was a bigger, grander building than his uncle's, with curlicue flourishes on the bullet-dented window frames. Maybe this building had a concierge, some comrade who would ask questions.

Wait, now he heard singing. Yet it did not come from the window above, but from farther up the street. Péter peered through the night as a female silhouette moved toward him. She carried a load on her hip. It was a baby, he realized. On long, soft tones, she was singing to the child, following the violin's melody.

"Sweet God," he murmured, for the song flowed, soothing and pure and good, quiet but full, richer than spring cream. He listened almost guiltily as though stealing nourishment from the child and stealing joy from heaven. A person could die happy in the presence of such music. Was this the singer the Gypsy had spoken of?

Her song ended, and her footsteps stopped in front of him. In the light above the door, he saw the starkly shadowed face of a pretty girl-woman in a rain-flecked blue scarf. She looked at him with large brown eyes and did not smile. Neither did the child.

She reached for the doorknob. "Excuse me."

"Wait!"

Her brow creased.

"Eh ... pardon me ...." He touched his cap and prodded himself to speak, using the polite, formal *maga* for *you*. "Are you ... is your name Katalin?"

She hugged the child closer and took a step back. "Yes."

"And your brother ..." Péter stopped, unable to remember the brother's name. "He's playing the violin?"

"Yes, that's him."

The child bleated. Katalin shushed it. "I'm sorry, if you'll excuse me—"

"Wait. No! Katalin ... I ... my name is Péter Benedek, I'm from ... east of here, and ... you see, a Gypsy told me to come see you."

She laughed abruptly. "What? A fortune teller?"

"No, listen ... a violin player. His name is Miklós. Miklós Kolompár, I think."

Her laughter cut short. "You know Miklós?"

"I met him."

"I haven't seen him in years."

"Yes, he ...."

She was waiting for him to go on, but the beautiful curve of her lips unnerved him, and he stood in desperate wordlessness. The baby thrashed in

Katalin's arms. Now she was turning toward the door. If she walked through it, all would be lost. He shoved aside everything he had ever been told about manners and blurted out, "Could I please come in? I need to talk to you."

He saw her eyes flicker over his rucksack and his unshaven chin. She set her hand on the knob.

"Please," he said.

Above, the violin kept singing.

"Wait here," she said.

Chapter Two

~~~

The Stranger the Wind Blew In

H AND ON THE doorknob, Katalin looked down the street past this stranger who had come in on the night wind. No one seemed to be following him. From his lost look and the way his corduroy jacket tugged across his broad shoulders, she guessed he was from the country.

In the entry passage, she glanced at the concierge's apartment door. Right now, mercifully, it was shut. Carrying her daughter, Katalin climbed the main stairs to the second floor and hurried along the walkway. The family apartment would be full of musicians and listeners, as it always was on Sunday evenings.

She waited outside the apartment door as her brother and the pianist, Ildikó, finished a Handel larghetto. During the applause, Katalin stepped inside, tightening her hold on Mari to keep the child quiet. Her parents, standing near the tile stove, looked her way. Her father smiled at Mari and took the girl into his arms. Katalin's eyes swept over the gathering. Her brother stood in the piano's curve, violin in hand, gesturing in acknowledgment of the accompanist as the audience of about twenty people applauded. Most were friends. Not all. At the far wall, in a verdigris jacket, stood the concierge, gripping that notebook of hers and scanning the crowd.

Katalin waited for her brother to look her way, then made a small movement of one finger toward the door and lifted her eyebrows. He gave the barest nod.

A few minutes later, she stood outside on the walkway with him. Antal leaned over the railing to peer into the courtyard. It was empty.

"There's a fellow, Péter or something, waiting by the front door," she told Antal quietly. "In some kind of trouble. He said Miklós Kolompár told him to come here."

"Miklós?" Antal's angular brow puckered. "He told this fellow to come here?"

"That's all I know."

Antal looked down into the courtyard again, and they walked downstairs together. Katalin crossed her arms against the chill in the building's entryway, which connected to both the courtyard and the street. Antal opened the front door and called out into the dark, "Good evening. I'm Antal Varga."

This person named Péter stepped into the entry, shook the rain from his cap, and tried to stroke down his hair. It bounced up again like rough brown coils. His eyes were deeply set behind prominent cheekbones and oval wire glasses. He was taller than Antal, and he slipped his rucksack off his shoulders with a motion that was at once effortless and very tired. Antal had asked him something, and Péter, faltering, answered, "The Gypsy just ... he said ... he told me you're good people."

Antal gave a short laugh. "Not the sort of thing he used to say."

Péter's eyes slitted behind his glasses. He seemed to be trying to smile.

"What do you want, and why are you here?" Katalin asked him.

"I was going to live in this city with my uncle," he said, barely above a whisper, "but he is not here."

Katalin and Antal glanced at each other.

"Do you know what happened to him?" Antal asked Péter.

A long pause. "Eh ... I have the usual worries."

Katalin watched as Péter stood motionless, cap in hand. How much desperation had it taken for him to tell two strangers that he was related to the wrong side? For good or for ill, he had come here trusting them to understand. She thought of Mari's father, Róbert, as she did countless times every day. Róbert was on the wrong side.

"I understand," she murmured.

Péter looked at her gratefully. "And I ... I need a place to stay tonight."

Hearing footsteps on the stairs, Katalin turned and saw Erika Jankovics, the concierge, descending with her notebook. Her gray-brown hair frizzed around her jacket collar.

"Tessék." Erika frowned. "May I help you?"

Katalin took a step forward. "Our comrade here needs a place to stay tonight."

Erika extended her hand to Péter, palm up. "Your identification, please."

He reached into his breast pocket and handed her the red booklet. Erika leafed through it, compared his face to the photo, grunted. "Why are you in the city?"

"For work."

"What?"

"Work, comrade."

"Follow me, then." Erika gestured impatiently toward her flat, pulled a key from her jacket pocket, and opened her door.

Péter turned to Katalin and Antal. "Should I go with her?" he mouthed.

After a long moment, Antal nodded and led Péter into Erika's apartment. Katalin watched the door close. This was only a lodgings discussion, but her stomach roiled, the way it had for the last two years, as though this were an interrogation.

When she returned to the apartment, the musicians and guests were dispersing. Two of them reproached her teasingly on their way out, "Why don't you ever sing for us anymore?" "How long have you had laryngitis now? A year? Two?"

Katalin raised her eyebrows and did her best to smile. "See you next week."

The apartment had grown stuffy while the crowd was here. Katalin opened one of the tall window-doors in the main room and stepped out onto the tiny front balcony, letting Mari toddle beside her and peer between the railing slats. The girl had just had her first birthday and was recently walking, occasionally surprising everyone with a burbling attempt at a word.

Katalin was twenty years old and had always lived in this neighborhood that pulsed with music and commerce. In the time it took the phonograph to play the first movement of Beethoven's Seventh, she could walk to the operetta theater or she could run to the opera house, the music academy, or the best sheet-music shop in the city. She used to circulate among those places all the time and still could if she wanted to, but she seldom did. When people asked her why not, she told them it was hard lugging Mari along.

Here on the balcony, the night was chilly. Katalin gently pried Mari's hands off the railing posts and carried her into the tiny bedroom the two of them shared. Sitting cross-legged on the bed, she snatched up Mari's favorite blanket and played peek-a-boo with her. She tousled her daughter's fluff of hair, which like her own was just a few shades short of black. Everyone said Mari looked like her, but Katalin saw more. The rise of Mari's brow, the lay of her eyelids: these were Róbert's.

A knock clattered on the bedroom doorframe. Antal strode in with Ildikó Brauer, the pianist. Mari grinned at them. Ildi lifted Mari, laughing as the child tugged on her red-blonde hair.

"That fellow Péter is staying here a few nights," Antal told Katalin. "Erika said he could sleep in the cellar for now. I gave him some blankets and sheets." Antal handed Katalin a slip of paper with an address on it. "That's near where you work, isn't it?"

"Yes, around the corner."

"He'll be working there. Assuming he gets the job, now that his uncle is

God-only-knows where. I told him maybe he could ride the tram with you tomorrow. And did you know he sings? He didn't tell me much—believe me, he isn't much of a talker—but he sang with Miklós, that much he said."

Ildi swung Mari into the air and the girl squealed in delight. Ildi bounced her again. Mari crowed.

"This little one has a *voice*," Ildi laughed. "She's a singer. Like her mother."

Katalin's eyes turned to a small photograph on her corkboard. *Like her father.*

"Like her mother used to be," Ildi corrected herself, eying Katalin.

"I still sing," Katalin said. "To Mari. And to the children at work."

"You know what I mean. Performing." Ildi gestured toward the main room where the musicians had gathered. "People want to hear you. If you're a little weak, well, so are the rest of us sometimes."

"I need to put Mari to bed."

"Katalin," Ildi insisted, "if you never sing, you're going to lose what you have."

Antal touched Ildi's elbow, his *enough* signal, but he gave Katalin a pointed look. The subject had come up before. It would come up again.

Katalin waited for them to leave, then began the nighttime routine. She diapered Mari, dressed her in her nightgown, and softly sang the major and minor scales into her ear. Carrying the child to the corkboard, she pointed at a photograph of a smiling man with thin white hair and a cup of coffee.

"Your great-grandfather," she told Mari. The man had died less than a year ago, and Katalin missed him deeply.

She then touched a second photo, a snapshot of a young man glancing up from a piano keyboard as though someone had just called his name: *Róbert! Here!* Katalin had long since memorized every centimeter of the photo: the open collar, the lean chin, the half-smile, the narrow nose, the straight hair falling careless and perfect over the forehead, and the shadowed eyes, gray in the photo but blue in her memory. This was her only picture of Mari's father.

"Your *apuka*," she murmured to Mari. "Someday he'll meet you and he'll love you. When he comes back."

She said *when* every night. She did not say *if*.

Laying Mari down, she turned out the light and stood quietly beside the crib, her hand on her daughter's back. Róbert had been gone almost two years now. Where was he? The prison in Vác? Or in Recsk? The mines of Tatabánya? The quarries of Hortobágy? Months and months ago, she had marked up a map of Hungary, circling the locations of political prisons and work camps.

Not long after Róbert disappeared, Katalin had gone across the river and inquired at the prison on Fő Street, but he was not there. Her mother, when she found out what Katalin had done, told her *absolutely, under no circumstances* should she make further inquiries: it would draw police scrutiny, and weren't things hard enough already, her being pregnant by a vanished man?

Yet there had to be a way to find Róbert. There had to be a day he'd be released. He was no capitalist, no fascist, only a music student. He would come back. He had to.

When, not if.

THE NEXT MORNING Katalin collected her diaper bag and the old guitar her cousin had left when he fled to America. She picked up Mari, said goodbye to her parents drinking coffee, and went to the cellar. From the top of the wooden stairs, she could see Péter shaving without a mirror at the laundry sink. It seemed to embarrass him to be caught in the act of shaving.

"Oh," he said, seeing her. "Hello, sorry, just a minute."

He pulled his corduroy jacket on and hurried up the stairs two at a time. On the walk to the tram stop, she tried to coax conversation out of him, but besides offering to carry the guitar, which she let him do, he said little. It all felt very stiff to Katalin. He did smile at Mari now and then.

They squeezed into the aisle of the tram between silent passengers who smelled of cigarette smoke. Outside the windows, trucks and horse wagons rolled by. Shop workers were setting out produce bins and hand-painted signs, some of them in front of windows still boarded over from the war. At an intersection, Katalin caught Péter's eye and pointed east.

"Police station that way," she mouthed.

He would have to go and register where he was staying, even temporarily. Péter nodded.

At their stop, the tram bell clanged. They pushed their way to the front and stepped off, and she led him up the street.

"Excuse me, I'm sorry," Péter said as they walked. "Who is the child?"

"Mária. We call her Mari." Katalin pushed past the momentary hesitation that always arose. "She's my daughter."

"Ah." Péter's face clouded in confusion. "Antal—he's your husband? Your brother?"

"My brother."

Katalin let this drop, for the question of *husband* had been raised. She pointed out a brick building across the street and told him that was the place he was looking for. She thought he sighed. If he was reluctant, she didn't blame him, for it would be horrible to go looking for work after leaving your home behind, finding your uncle gone, and sleeping in somebody's cellar.

"Good luck," she said.

He handed her the guitar and she turned to leave.

"Katalin?"

She turned back. "Yes?"

"Eh … thank you. I mean, for everything."

She nodded and hurried away.

KATALIN'S WORKPLACE WAS a child-care nursery that served a clothing factory. Inside the front door, she pushed through a throng of kerchiefed women heading for a vast room of sewing machines, and she took the stairs to the nursery on the upper floor. She had started working here three months postpartum, when her parents told her to look it in the face that Róbert was gone. Against every pull of her own heart, she had weaned Mari from the breast and taken a job. Dropping off her daughter in the infants' room each morning was still hard. Today Mari cried.

Katalin gave the child one last hug, then went down the corridor to the room where she worked with the four-year-olds. They were called the Happy Squirrels, after a communist children's song: "Like the squirrels in the trees, we are very happy." At present, there were fourteen Happy Squirrels. Katalin was an assistant here, settling disputes over toys, taking the children to the toilet, walking them to the small courtyard playground, and keeping watch. But each Monday, she brought the old guitar and taught the children songs and musical games.

At music time, she arranged the children in a circle and pulled up a chair for herself. The portraits of Rákosi and Stalin, ever-present, hung on a wall behind her. She plucked a guitar string. "What sound is my guitar making? Can you sing it? So-o-o-ol."

"So-o-o-ol."

Their pitch was improving. After some songs, she led the children through a musical game, with the children marching around and pairing up until one child was left over as the "goose." The game was from somewhere in the country. Maybe Péter knew it.

Thinking of Péter, she recalled Miklós, who had sent him. She had not seen Miklós since '45, and she now realized she was very glad just to know he was still alive. She no longer took survival for granted. And thinking of *alive* or *not alive* brought to mind Mari's father, and once again the old, sad dread rose in her. But she could not let herself think this way, not now, not here, not under Stalin and Rákosi, not around the children.

Chapter Three

～～

State Printing Office No. 8

Péter pulled open the door of State Printing Office No. 8. The smell of gear oil and metal hit him harder than the smell of any threshing machine ever had. In front of him hung a sign, and he made himself read it: *This is your factory! You are working for yourself!* He was not at all sure how to get this work they said was for himself. He had planned to pull out Uncle Béla's letter as a recommendation, but now he didn't dare.

From down the corridor, he heard indistinct voices. He headed that direction and peered through an open door. In a large room, about a hundred people sat at long tables, some in jackets or office dresses and some in chambray or work aprons. He hoped that by some crazy luck Uncle Béla would be there, but he didn't appear to be. At one end of the room, a man in a work shirt read aloud from the Party newspaper, *Szabad Nép* (Free People). Péter had heard that in the city you couldn't escape *Szabad Nép* any more than you could escape Rákosi's photo. The man in front was reading something about Yugoslavia, and he stumbled on a word. The poor bastard. What kind of workplace was this, that you had to stand and read to a hundred people?

A woman in an office blouse took the newspaper from the man and held it up. "The weather forecast is for more rain," she cried. "But bad weather will not keep us from our task. Only with diligence can we finish the State Railways manuals by the end of March and meet our quota. And let me also state our stern agreement with what our comrade has read. Yugoslavia is no friend of Hungary."

She went on: Yugoslavia's Tito was a running dog, a pawn in the hands of American imperialists, abandoning the wise guidance of Comrade Stalin.

At one of the tables a man stifled a yawn. Next to him, a girl in a kerchief chewed at a fingernail. Péter heard a chair scrape the floor. A balding man in back stood up and looked at him. Now the man was walking toward him. Péter's knees stiffened.

The man stepped through the door and beckoned Péter to the side of the corridor. *"Tessék?"* he hissed. "What are you here for?"

"A job, comrade."

"What?"

"Work. I hope."

"Your name?"

"Péter Benedek."

The man glanced around. "Béla Matai's nephew?"

Péter's cheeks flashed hot and his hands clenched, knotting up like the *yes* he could not speak.

The man looked to be about the age of Péter's father. He was not smiling— did anybody in this city smile?—yet maybe there was a faint softening around his eyes. Péter gambled on it, not knowing what else to do, and nodded.

"Come with me," the man said.

The man said he was Frigyes Molnár, the production manager. Péter followed him up some stairs and into a small office, and they sat down on either side of a cluttered desk. Péter was suddenly conscious of his wrinkled shirt, which had spent the weekend crammed in his rucksack. He handed over his red identification booklet and Mr. Molnár turned its pages.

"I see you're from Heves County," he said.

Last night the Comrade Concierge had asked Péter why he had left Kőpatak instead of working on one of the fine collectives there. He had stammered out something about wanting to serve the economic plan in Pest, then felt like a fish off the hook when she shrugged and let him sleep in the cellar. Mr. Molnár did not ask. He lit a cigarette for himself and offered one to Péter, and though Péter was indifferent toward smoking, he accepted it with relief.

"Béla Matai doesn't work here anymore," Mr. Molnár said.

Péter watched the cigarette smoke rising and asked, carefully neutral, "Where is he?"

"I don't know."

Mr. Molnár reached into a desk drawer and pulled out a form. "You've come at the right time, end of the month, the quota due Saturday. We need the help. You're used to hard work, I suppose."

"Yes."

"And your uncle said you can do heavy lifting. Do you know how to drive?"

"Horses, not motor cars."

"Can you read maps?"

Péter hesitated. "I can."

"We need someone for loading and deliveries. We have a truck, but it's not running right now, and we have a draft team."

"I like horses."

"Well, wait until you meet ours. You might change your mind."

Mr. Molnár began talking about the work hours and rate of pay. Péter sat in silence. The pay was lower than what he and Apa had anticipated. The job would keep him alive, with only scrawny leftovers for the family. But maybe this was what the pay was like all over the city. He couldn't risk walking out of here with nothing, then getting questioned for indigence. He had a father who'd refused the collective and an uncle who'd been taken away.

Somewhere below, machinery had begun throbbing and vibrating like a great drum. Mr. Molnár ignored this as he wrote on the form and pushed it across the desk for Péter to sign. Péter looked it over, deciphered the first and last sentences, and underneath scrawled *Péter Zsigmond Benedek.*

"All right, then." Mr. Molnár leaned in, speaking barely above the machinery noise. "I'd keep it quiet that you're Matai's nephew."

Péter clenched his hands in his lap and nodded.

Mr. Molnár then showed him the press room. Banging and whirring, a huge train of machinery pulled paper, beat, inked, and threw it. Péter's joints shook. Suddenly the press jammed and a buzzer rattled. The workers stood back and lit cigarettes. Mr. Molnár and another man began checking over the press. Péter looked warily around at the great wheels of paper and at the workers hoisting lead plates. A man could break his back here.

Finally, the press was roaring again. Mr. Molnár took Péter outside to the loading dock, a cobbled lot big enough to back in a truck or turn around a wagon and team. There Mr. Molnár introduced him to a square-shouldered man named Csaba Pál who looked to be about thirty-five.

"Benedek here knows horses," Mr. Molnár said.

Csaba's broad face broke into a grin. "Thank God."

Over the next hour Péter and Csaba carried boxes full of pages from the press room to the loading dock. Then it was time to cart the pages to a bindery half a kilometer away. As they walked down the street to the livery stable for the horses, Csaba told him about the truck that wasn't running, about the replacement parts on order—he seemed to smirk at this—and about the horses.

"The gelding, Karcsi, he's not too bad," Csaba said, "except that he has to walk around with that mare. Kisbarna's her name. And she's like a bad wife, would make a drunkard out of anybody."

The stable stank of horse piss. Csaba led Péter to the mare's stall door.

Péter stopped outside it. "So here we are," he said to Csaba, just so the horse would hear his voice. No surprises. He leaned on the door, taking his time as he had always done with irritable Zsuzsi back home.

"Good morning, Kisbarna," he said. He opened the door and sidled along the stall wall with the bridle, avoiding the mare's hind feet. She swung her head toward him. He lifted his hand slowly and patted her neck.

"My name is Péter," he murmured, "and I don't let horses throw me in the gutter."

He began to sing, barely loud enough for the horse to hear. Kisbarna's ears turned. Péter eased the bridle onto her head, prodded the bit into her mouth and backed her out of the stall. So far the horse was cooperating.

Csaba fetched Karcsi, and in single file Péter and Csaba led the horses to the loading dock. There they yoked them into the shoulder harness. Csaba hitched the harness to the freight wagon while Péter adjusted the horses' blinders. Suddenly Kisbarna flung her head toward Karcsi, teeth bared.

"None of that!" Péter thrust his elbow between the horses' heads. The mare's nose struck it. She pulled back, startled.

But Karcsi was unhurt, and Csaba was nodding in approval. Péter exhaled in relief. Since leaving Kőpatak, this was the first time he'd known what he was doing. They loaded the freight onto the wagon bed and climbed onto the drive seat, where Csaba handed him the reins. He steered the horses between trucks and pedestrians, between taxis and beer wagons, between the war-pocked old buildings and the new apartments thrown together cheap and out of square.

"Rabbit hutches," Csaba said, as he pointed one out. "So young couples can make babies. Boost the birth rate, you know—it's part of the plan."

It was raining again. The rain smelled different than on the *puszta*, Péter noticed; here it mingled with smoke and gasoline. Csaba went on talking.

"It's not always this busy at the shop," he said. "The first half of the month, we blab and smoke. And we didn't used to have to lift so much. For a while we had a dolly to wheel things around. But it disappeared. I suppose somebody took it home. It happens, you know. People take things home, use them, take them apart, sell them. We had one fellow that made off with parts from the press, built a hot rod for his boys."

"Did he get sacked?"

"He left. I didn't hear why. I don't ask too many questions. *Na*, the press slams on the brakes several times a day. And the fellow who was best at putting it right, I hear he's gone. Older man named Béla."

Péter took a breath, kept his eyes locked on the road and the horses. "What happened?"

"I don't know, probably just the same damned story. Maybe he laughed when he wasn't supposed to. Maybe he told the wrong person that the pay stinks."

At midday Csaba took him to the large room where *Szabad Nép* had been read, which was the lunchroom. Csaba introduced him to other workers as they stood in line for pea soup and bread: "This fellow throws freight around like it's chaff in the wind. And he can handle horses, even that brainless mare. I'm telling you, send me ten more from where he came from."

The server ladling soup was the girl Péter had seen biting a fingernail this morning. She handed him a bowl. "So where *are* you from?" she asked irritably. "The country, like everybody else lately?"

"East," Péter mumbled, and he took the soup and turned away.

HE AND CSABA made several more trips to the bindery in the afternoon. At quitting time he was unhitching Kisbarna when Mr. Molnár approached across the loading dock. With him was the woman who'd led the *Szabad Nép* meeting.

"We are asking that you give another hour or two," the woman said to Péter and Csaba. "For the success of the economic plan this month."

Péter was sweaty and hungry and tired, but he worked with Csaba for another hour and a half, telling himself it was extra money to send home. Csaba then told him in an aside that they would probably not be paid. "That's how it goes," he said. "You heard the woman say *give*."

When the day finally ended, Péter stopped at the police station on his way home. He handed over his identification booklet and explained where he was working, and at least for now, where he was living. The desk clerk made notes and handed the booklet back. It then occurred to Péter that if anyone had information on Uncle Béla, it would be the police.

"Eh ... pardon me," he began to ask, then stopped.

"Yes?" the clerk prompted impatiently.

I'd keep it quiet that you're Matai's nephew ....

Péter shook his head. From the wall behind the clerk, Stalin and Rákosi looked on.

Back at the apartment house, the concierge stopped him as he crossed the courtyard and asked if he'd been hired. Asked if he'd been to the police. Asked what he was going to do for living space.

"Could I just stay here, comrade?" He made himself hold her gaze. "In the cellar is all right. With the housing shortage—"

"There is no housing shortage. You may stay at least for now. I collect the rent on the first of the month."

"Eh, I don't get paid until the tenth."

"You will pay me on the eleventh then. How much you will pay is to be decided."

She wrote in her notebook and walked away.

* * *

THE REST OF that week, the workers at State Printing Office No. 8 were told each morning in the *Szabad Nép* meeting that they were to push on, to struggle against all frailty and laziness, to find new strength in their mighty cause. The message was clear enough: meet the damned quota. But the week ended, the month ended, and the quota was not met.

"Just wait," Csaba said. "Next week they'll be trying to sniff out saboteurs."

Sometimes at night when Péter lay on his thin bedding under the cellar stairs, his new life in Budapest seemed to him a great, endless void. He was alone—no brothers here, no father, no grandfather. Whatever home this place was, it was empty. His wallet was almost empty. Back home the family's pantry and stores of grain would be emptying, too. He and his father and Csaba and everybody else could all work themselves to exhaustion and still be called saboteurs.

But in all his disheartenment, now and then two memories would interrupt, blurting out a strange, inexplicable hope. He remembered that a girl named Katalin had sung to her baby with an unfathomable beauty. Maybe she would sing again. And he remembered that one evening with a Gypsy in Háromkeresztes, he himself had sung, too. This was a wonder.

SUNDAY, THE DAY after they'd missed the quota, Péter woke as dawn broke gray and thin between the iron bars of the cellar window grate. Today he had no cow to milk, no fields to tend, no boxes to load, but since he was not used to sleeping past dawn, he rose and dressed under the stairs. The cellar was not private, and fairly often the residents came downstairs for coal, firewood, or other things they kept in the back storage compartments. But the cellar was livable. The front area contained a laundry sink, three benches, three lightbulbs hanging from the arched brick ceiling, and a pot-bellied stove with a pipe extending out the window.

Péter went outside to the loo that served the poorer apartments, then took a look around the courtyard. None of the residents had begun stirring yet. The four-story building stretched up on three sides with a walkway connecting the apartments at each story. Often, in the evenings, Péter had seen the residents smoking and chatting beside their painted doors or spreading laundry on the wrought-iron railing. On the fourth side of the courtyard stood a wall a little taller than he was, and in front of it an unpaved patch of weeds. It was a sunny spot, and he had seen a spade in the cellar.

He spent the next hour or so digging out weeds, overturning the earth, and planting the seed peas his father had given him. This was home now and he would have to make the best of it. He had little privacy and he didn't like that concierge, but Antal seemed like a nice-enough neighbor. His sister did, too. Péter wondered, not for the first time, where her husband was. If she had a husband. He didn't think that bourgeois girls, as they were called here in the city, usually had babies without husbands, but then what did he really know about them? This place was not Kőpatak.

In the afternoon, Péter pulled up a bench under one of the cellar light bulbs to labor through writing a letter home. *Family of Jancsi Benedek, Kőpatak,* he wrote on an envelope, and on a sheet of paper, *Dear Apa, Nagyapa, Gyuri & Tibi—*

Apa had insisted on letters. But for Péter, every word of this was a dilemma. What could he safely say about Uncle Béla? The letter would be read by a State censor. Once it reached home, Péter's brother Gyuri would probably read it to the family, and God only knows what the boys would say around town. Besides, the news about Uncle would infuriate Apa, and that made nothing easier.

"I have a job," Péter eventually wrote. "I help somebody named Csaba drive horses and load boxes. The job is at Uncle's work place but Uncle isn't there anymore. I live in a basement."

The door at the top of the stairs opened, and Antal stepped in with his violin case, music stand, and satchel. "Hello, Péter," he called. He did this frequently, practicing in the cellar when he thought the sound would irritate his neighbors.

Péter welcomed it. He folded the letter, stuffed it in his hip pocket, and sat down on the bottom stair to listen in rapt silence. Antal played for a long time, swaying and dipping with the bow as though dancing with a beautiful girl. The low tones seeped into Péter, flowing and spreading. The high ones beckoned him as they sang and called and whispered. The violin spoke so many messages in its secret language: *Don't be afraid,* maybe it said. Or *My heart is broken.* Or *I still believe.*

When at last Antal laid the bow on the music stand, he said, "You're a better audience than most people who pay to listen."

"Your music is …" Péter groped for the words, pressing his palm to his heart. "It's from inside."

"You can say things in music you could never say in words." Antal glanced at the window above the laundry sink. "You should come to the music session in our flat tonight."

Péter hesitated. He would feel like a mule among Lipizzaners there. "I don't have a suit to wear," he said.

"Most people don't. At least not a suit that's less than twenty years old. Come anyway."

"Eh … will your sister sing?"

"I'm sure she won't. She used to, but not anymore. We've coaxed her, we've tried. But my sister is as stubborn as a Calvinist." Antal laid the violin in its case. "So you're a singer, too. You must have some talent or Miklós never would have shared his stage with you, believe me. Have you had training?"

"There's *training* for that?"

"Of course. Voice lessons. My mother teaches singers. Maybe she could teach you …. Well, no, she probably doesn't have time." Antal closed and latched the violin case. "But you know, I wish Katalin would do it. It would be good for her. If you want voice lessons, ask her, see what she says."

Antal departed up the stairs.

For the rest of the day, the violin's voice kept returning to Péter, and so did Antal's words. *You can say things with music … ask her ….*

The girl was bourgeois. Pretty. How could he ask her for anything?

But wait, he already had, the night he had begged her to open the door. And she had opened it. If she said yes to him once, maybe she would say it again.

Maybe she would sing. Maybe *he* would. Maybe in this terrified, silenced world, music had its own voice.

Ask her ….

The thought of that possibility, or impossibility, would not leave him.

Chapter Four

~~∽~~

Pain and Pleasure

IT WAS SUNDAY night, and as the weekly music gathering was going on, Katalin listened from the dining table. Here she could keep an eye on Mari, who was sidestepping around the table legs. From where she sat, Katalin saw Péter-from-the-cellar, standing next to the tile stove in his brown corduroy jacket. Exactly when he had arrived, she wasn't sure; he had such a way of going about unnoticed. He turned a little and his eyes met hers. He lifted his hand slightly as though in greeting, but his face looked so anxious or hopeful or puzzled or *something* that there had to be more on the poor fellow's mind than simply hello.

Katalin's mother stood in front of the group, singing Henri Duparc's "*Chanson triste*" as Ildi Brauer accompanied on piano. Katalin knew the song well. Under her mother's coaching, she had studied its long, sensuous lines and ecstatic climax to a high A. Then came the crackdown of 1949 and all that had broken with it. Katalin left flights of ecstasy alone now.

Her mother finished, and the next performer was one of Antal's violin students, a fourteen-year-old boy. He played a violin scherzo very well. Nearby, Antal nodded in approval. After the applause died down, he invited the audience's comments. Two of Antal's orchestra colleagues complimented the boy on his tone and interpretation. The boy smiled. So did Antal. Then a cello player gave a cough: a little faltering in the stop-bow section, just a little, barely noticeable, the cellist said.

Katalin winced. Barely noticeable. So couldn't the cellist just overlook it, give the boy credit for beautiful work? She had never liked that cellist anyway, the way he tended to look her over and smile lazily. But people said that was the kind of thing that happened when you had a baby and no husband.

After a flautist had played the night's last piece, Katalin helped her mother serve schnapps. She avoided the cellist—*let him get his own liquor!*—and poured a glass to take to Péter, who was standing apart as though unsure what to do. But the concierge, Comrade Erika, stepped up to her, took the glass, handed it to the thick-jowled man that had been coming and going from her apartment lately, and then held out her hand expectantly for her own drink. Katalin poured another glass for Péter. But Mari began banging on the piano keys, and by the time Katalin pulled her away, Péter was slipping out the door.

"Good night, Péter," she called, but the door was already shut.

After all the guests but Ildi had left, Katalin sat down on the old Turkish carpet in the main room, bouncing Mari on her knees. Ildi and Antal joined them, sitting down on the folding sofa that doubled as her parents' bed. The family had only recently bought it; they were still trying to replace the furniture that had been destroyed in the shooting and shelling of 1945. For two years after the war, the only cushioned chair in the house had been a seat they had removed from a disabled army truck.

Ildi crossed her long legs. "That concierge sets my teeth on edge," she said. "I can't believe you *invite* her to these things, Antal."

"She would come anyway, invited or not," Antal answered. "If I invite her, she knows that everything we say is above board, that we're not ..."

Ildi pushed her hair behind her ear with a jerk. "Not plotting a counterrevolution."

Katalin touched her finger to her lips, hushing Ildi. The walls had ears, as people said. Katalin understood what Ildi's family had endured, though. Her father's broken career had been as an officer in the Hungarian Army. He had dreaded Hungary's entrance into the war, disagreed with the government's decision to side with Hitler, then had to carry out orders anyway. When the Soviets rounded up prisoners at the end of the war, he was in the hospital with an abdominal injury, and only this good luck had kept him from being shot or sent to Siberia. The family lived with a fascist stigma now, classified *x* in the State files. Because of the *x*, Mr. Brauer now made a meager wage in a chemical plant. Because of the *x*, Ildi could not attend music academy. The family still had their once-comfortable house, but the State had moved renters into several rooms. Ildi was fairly sure at least one of the renters was watching them as a favor to the ÁVH, the State security police. Everyone in Katalin's family knew all this. When Ildi was here, they let her speak or change the subject as she chose.

"So," Ildi asked Katalin, "did you do any practicing this week?"

Without waiting for an answer, Ildi went to the piano bench, lifted its lid, and sorted through the sheet music there. She pulled out a song folio and handed it to Katalin. "This song was running through my head a few days ago. I bet you could still sing it. Want to give it a go?"

Katalin knew almost by the feel of the paper what it was. Mari made a grab for it. Katalin pulled it away and gave it back to Ildi.

"Kati, this is such a waste," Ildi said. "With all the talent you have—"

"She never says yes, Ildi," Antal broke in.

Soon Antal left with Ildi. He would see her home on the tram and then return. It wouldn't take long: he always accompanied Ildi home on dark evenings but didn't linger over goodbyes with her. Katalin suspected Ildi wished he would.

Katalin touched Mari's soft shock of hair. Antal was wrong, thinking she never said yes. Having Mari was a *yes*. From the first twinges of pregnancy, she could have arranged a *no*, but she had pushed the *no* aside at every turn.

"Oh, girl," she whispered, and the child lay down in her lap.

Katalin reached for the song folio that Ildi had left on the sofa, and within her the slow, familiar melody formed around the pained Italian lyrics: *Caro mio ben, credimi almen, senza di te languisce il cor.* My dear beloved, believe me at least, without you my heart languishes.

KATALIN COULD NOT begin to guess how many times she had sung *"Caro Mio Ben"* two years ago in the spring of 1949. She was eighteen then, about to finish preparatory school and intent on following Antal to music academy. Her grandfather, still alive at the time, called the song her best yet. Her mother said the time had come for Katalin to receive wider exposure, and she arranged for her to sing in a joint student recital at the academy.

It was April, and the Sunday afternoon of the recital was warm. Katalin stood on stage in the curve of the piano, wearing the slim black dress that had fit her then. Behind her hung the chamber hall's green velvet curtain. Someday, God willing, she would sing in the great auditorium with the pipe organ behind her, and after that—why not wish?—in the opera house with a chorus behind her.

"Good afternoon," she said to the recital audience. She breathed slowly and smiled to trick her nerves into loosening. "My name is Katalin Varga, and this is my accompanist, Ildikó Brauer. I am going to sing Giuseppe Giordani's 'Caro Mio Ben.'" She lowered her head in concentration then raised it again, signaling Ildi to begin playing.

The tension of weeks of practice eased away. The song's slow melody rose within her, its anguish growing sweet on her tongue. As she sang, her gaze moved over her listeners and came to rest on a young man in the fourth row. He sat forward in his chair, watching her with one hand lifted to his chin, his lips moving.

He hears me. He is with me.

She let her song soar, crying out in all its good and passionate sorrow. *Without you my heart languishes.* The young man closed his eyes.

She held the song's final word into a long hush: *cor ... heart.* The piano notes faded.

The audience applause rose—a trickle, then a roar. Katalin smiled, threw back her head and grinned, bowed, bowed again, and looked again toward the beautiful listener. His eyes locked on hers.

In the lobby afterward, Katalin's parents and grandfather said she was breathtaking. Ildi hugged her and laughed. Among the art-nouveau pillars, Antal spun Katalin in a waltz flourish. Suddenly he stopped mid-beat and dropped her hands.

He nodded to someone behind her. "Hello, Róbert."

Katalin turned. There he was, the one from the fourth row: a lean face with probing blue eyes, straight brown hair fringing his forehead.

"*Szevasz,* Antal," he said. "Is this your sister?"

"Yes. This is Katalin."

"Katalin," the stranger said. "I'm Róbert Zentai. Piano and voice student here, final year."

Here under the chandeliers, he wore no jacket and his shirt collar was open. She offered her hand. He held it longer than the handshake and his gaze did not waver.

"Your singing," he said. "The Giordani piece. Beautiful work. Beautiful."

Róbert turned, or maybe she had turned, or maybe all of life had shifted. Antal and the rest of the world had vanished.

"You don't attend the Academy, do you?" Róbert asked her. "I would have seen you."

"No." It was difficult admitting how young she was. "I hope to attend next year."

"I'll be done by then."

"I'm sorry."

"Your smile lights up the stage," he said. He did not smile.

They drifted out the lobby door and wandered into the square. The air hung motionless under the sycamores, the hammer-and-sickle flag limp on a balcony across the street. Róbert told her he would be finishing his music studies in June, with his final recital at the end of May.

"About an hour's worth of music," he said, "mostly piano, and a few voice pieces. There's a baritone and soprano duet I was planning to do, but the soprano canceled." He looked at her. "Would you consider it?"

"Of course," she said, and they arranged it: Mozart. Wednesday after classes. Third floor, south practice room.

A hint of a smile parted his lips. "Let me hear it again," he said. " '*Caro mio ben …*' " He began to sing softly, his tones rich and silken. She sang with him, and by the time she reached the end he had dropped out and stood listening in silence.

"You're an astonishing singer," he told her, "the way you mix pain and pleasure."

He had used *te*, the close, familiar form of *you* when he said this, although she had not invited him to. Not yet. But she would have.

"Goodbye, Katalin."

The sun stroked light across his hair as he walked away, and pleasure shivered through her.

But over the next few days, every now and again like a sudden twinge, the song's sad echo returned to her, and she recalled the solemnity of his face.

Now two years later, it was growing harder day by week by month to recall his smile, which even on better days only broke momentarily, or his rare laugh. Wherever he was, behind bars or barbed wire, did he ever laugh at all?

Oh, my beloved ….

Katalin pulled Mari close, whispering to her. She could not sing.

TUESDAY EVENING AS Katalin came home with Mari on her hip, she was heading along the second-floor balcony when she heard someone call her name. Looking over the railing into the courtyard, she saw Péter Benedek standing beside a dirt patch where two short green rows had sprouted. He lifted his cap to her. She would have simply waved and walked on, except that he was regarding her worriedly, and after glancing around, he beckoned. She carried Mari down the back stairs and joined him. Above, the early evening sky misted a cold gray.

"Is something wrong?" she asked.

He gripped the handle of a hoe. "Katalin … eh … Antal said … maybe you could help me sing? Lessons?"

"I don't know why Antal told you that. I've never taught singers before."

"But would you? I mean … please?"

She had never known Péter to look directly at her for longer than half a second; now it seemed those hazel eyes behind the wire glasses would stare at her until next October if it took her that long to answer.

"I would pay," he said.

Katalin thought his worried look deepened. She could not imagine that Péter, coming from Lord-knows-where in the country, had any money to spare.

"How would you ever practice?" she asked. "Where?"

"I don't know, maybe in the cellar."

"It isn't private."

"I know."

"And voice lessons can be embarrassing. You have to make ridiculous sounds, buzz your lips, sing nonsense. And I can't promise that my family won't hear you. And the neighbors. And do you smoke? If you want to be a good singer, you can't smoke. My mother has been saying that all my life."

"All right. I won't smoke."

Mari was clinging to Katalin's arm and regarding Péter as though he were a great mystery. And maybe he was. Katalin could not understand how this quiet fellow could be coaxed to sing loud enough for anyone to hear him.

"You don't really want to do this, do you?" she asked.

"But yes."

"Why?"

He shifted the hoe to his other hand, and his answer was slow to come. "Some days ... many days ... singing is the only pleasure, you know? And also ... Antal said sometimes music works even if talking doesn't. Or something like that."

Maybe it was Antal who had said it, but it sounded so much like Róbert. Katalin was going to tell Péter that this just wouldn't be possible, she didn't have time, she wasn't a teacher. But when she looked at him again, none of those words would come.

She relented. "We could start Thursday night."

He squinted a little, broke a smile, almost laughed. "Good!"

"As for pay," she said, "when you go home, if you find something that's hard to get in Budapest, bring it. We're always running out of soap. Where is home, by the way?"

He took a step back, looked away. "I will try to find some soap," was his only reply.

THAT NIGHT SHE told her mother about Péter's lessons as they finished bathing Mari in the kitchen sink. Her mother wrapped Mari in a towel and held the squirming bundle against the bodice of her peplum-style dress. She asked Katalin in rapid-fire words what this Péter Benedek's background was, and whether it was a good idea for this unknown person to be coming into the flat, and whether Katalin understood the male singing range.

"Yes, yes," Katalin sighed.

"I'm surprised you agreed to this."

"Maybe I felt a little sorry for him."

"That's your weakness."

Katalin glared at her.

"Maybe I'd better play piano at these lessons," her mother said.

"No, I'll do it."

"Don't you need help?"

"I said *I'll* do this."

Her mother tossed her head of dark bobbed hair and gave a small, triumphant smile.

"Well, then. See that you do."

Katalin spent two hours that night sorting through her mother's music books and reading vocal pedagogy. It all made sense. Except that there was nothing about untrained teachers coaching peasants.

ON THURSDAY, WHEN Péter was expected, the family retreated to the bedrooms, Katalin's mother with Mari. Katalin opened the door to the sight of Péter in a waistcoat. Stepping in, he was nervous about treading on the Turkish carpet in his heavy boots, which were scuffed and battered but not dirty. Katalin wanted to tell him that the carpet was too threadbare to worry about anyway, but it would probably make him even more self-conscious. She sat down on the piano bench and asked him to sing something so she could hear him on his own. Any song, she told him, it didn't matter what.

He stood next to the treble keys, clenching and unclenching his hands. "Any song?"

"Anything."

He put his hands in his pockets, turned his head, and sang very softly:

> *Madárka, madárka, csácsogó madárka …*
> Birdie, birdie, chattering birdie,
> Deliver my letter, deliver my letter
> To my beautiful homeland.

His pitch was flawless, but she could barely hear him. She leaned forward, straining to listen. As their eyes met, his tone shook.

"Turn around," she said. "Go stand at the window and pretend I'm not here. You're singing the song to the little bird, and you want him to be on his way."

Péter stood by the old lace curtains, his back to her, and began again.

"The bird can't hear you," she interrupted him.

He started over, barely louder.

"The stupid bird is hard of hearing," she called.

A short laugh. "*Madárka, Madárka …*."

Péter's notes rose, each glowing and smooth at the center, some rough at the finish, but the roughness was lovely, like wood grain. The same texture, she realized, had been there in his laugh. He finished another verse. Then silence. He turned to her anxiously.

"I like what I hear," she said.

"You do?"

"Yes. It's beautiful."

He dropped his gaze and smiled.

"We just have to make it stronger," she said. "Come over here, let's check your range."

She played an arpeggio and sang it, demonstrating: *do-mi-sol-mi-do*. Péter sang after her. Whether by knowledge or by instinct, he lowered his chin instead of raising it. She nodded and played the pattern again and again, each time a half-step higher. He naturally shaped each set with a crescendo and taper until, at the top of his range, the tones strained and choked. She led him through descending patterns then, his notes rounding into the bass range until finally he shook his head.

"Well, you're a lower tenor, I think," she said. "Very nice. But let's work on your breathing. Try this. Pull in a breath—no, not a gasp, just a breath—but instead of lifting up here," she pointed at his chest, "fill up below." She pointed at his abdomen.

He stared at her, bewildered.

"Here." She placed her hand on his stomach and was surprised by its firmness. "Sorry, do you mind?"

Blushing, he shook his head.

"All right, now breathe in. But instead of pulling your shoulders up, try to push my hand out."

"With what?"

"With your abdominal muscles." Katalin looked away from him and just said it. "It's like you're in the loo."

"Oh." His strong middle turned solid.

"All right, good, but you didn't breathe with it. Try it again … no … again. Yes. Good!"

"Yes?" he asked eagerly. "That was right?"

"Very right." She smiled. "It takes a little longer before you can breathe that way consistently and really connect that breath to the sound."

She put on the glasses she used for reading, handed Péter a book of folk songs, and asked him to choose one. Péter turned the book's pages, furrowing his brow and blinking. He raised his glasses to the top of his head, brought the book close to his face, ran his finger under a song title, then moved the book farther back again.

"Péter," she pulled off her glasses, "try these on."

"I have my own."

"I know. But just put these on and then look at the book."

Péter put his oval glasses in his chest pocket and snickered a little as he slid Katalin's feminine frames onto his angular face. Peering through the strange lenses, he read the title out carefully and correctly: "*Mikor Gulyásbojtár Voltam*." He turned to Katalin, his lips parted in surprise.

"My God," he murmured, "the words aren't jiggling."

LATER THAT NIGHT, Katalin went to her ophthalmologist father and told him she thought Péter needed bifocals.

He laid aside the magazine he'd been reading. "Katalin, why has this young man suddenly become a family project?"

"He's a singer," was all she could say, and when her father answered wearily that he would think about it, she wandered off to bed.

She lay awake long into the night with the sound of Péter's sweet rough notes hurting inside her. *Oh.* The beautiful things of men—a deep, warm voice, a muscular stomach, a sleeve rolled up on a strong arm—would they ever stop leaving her so lonely?

Chapter Five

～～～

"Either We're Crazy, and We'll All Be Lost, or...."

IT WAS WELL into April now, and in the patch of broken paving in the courtyard, Péter's peas were sprouting and growing. When he had nothing to do, he dug in the soil, but not too deep: Antal had told him that during the siege they had buried a German soldier there. Sometimes in the evenings Péter would lean against the laundry sink in the cellar and try to practice his vocal exercises. But too often one of the residents would trot down the stairs with a coal bucket, or the building's old laundress would pick her way down, or Comrade Erika would simply step through the door and stand at the top of the stairs as though on sentry duty. With each interruption, Péter would close his mouth and pull in his arms.

So it was a great moment when he found the print shop's boiler room.

On a Monday when his shift was over, he was walking through the press room when he noticed an old door, ajar, and behind it a shabby flight of stairs. Curious, he descended.

At the bottom stood a boiler, its ducts sticking out like the pincers of a huge crayfish, and around it sat crates and sawhorses. No one seemed to be down here. In the back wall was a narrow door. Péter opened it and stepped into a broom closet, empty except for a few rags and cans of paint. Overhead the press pounded, whooshed and roared. It occurred to him that if he sang here, no one would see him or hear him. He tried it: *sol-mi-do*. Liking the feel, he closed the door and sang over and over. *Sol-mi-do. Sol-mi-do. Madárka, madárka.*

EVERY WEEK PÉTER worked all day Monday through Friday plus half of Saturday, and he put in extra hours when he was told to. On a Saturday afternoon late in April, he stuffed his pay in his pocket and left for Kőpatak. He knew it would be a weekend of work in the garden, the barns and the fields, but he hoped he might also find some soap to pay Katalin for the lessons.

When he stepped off the train and turned up the dirt road toward home, he wondered fleetingly what she would think of this place. After Budapest, Kőpatak looked smaller to him, muddy and crooked, with its geese and weedy ditches and picket fences made of sticks.

Just before he reached his house, the stout neighbor girl called to him from her front garden. It was her father's land—pig-strip, reeds, run-off slope and all—that had been exchanged for his father's on the day the police appeared.

"Your family's laundry," Ági Kozma shouted.

She ran into her house and back, her thick hair flying and her skirt bouncing around her beefy knees. Over the fence she handed him a pillowcase stuffed with shirts, trousers, socks, and underwear. He had always hated this laundry arrangement, his family's personals being handled by the noisy girl next door. It was just another of the small but endless miseries of his mother being gone.

"You're supposed to say thank you, Silent Peti," Ági said. "But never mind. So you went to Pest. I've only been there twice, but …." Her chatter shifted to an upcoming wedding, flitted to a sheep-shearing, darted to a movie she'd seen, drifted to the collective farm. "Your father should join. If we get enough members, we can have a tractor. That's what Comrade Márton said—"

"If you have any soap," he interrupted, "could I buy some?"

"The city is always running out of soap! What do people do there, eat it? Well, wait here, I'll get some for you."

Péter paid her for the soap and went on to his house next door. The chickens scattered as he opened his gate and banged it shut again. On the earthen porch under the house's reed eaves, his grandfather was sitting in his old chair with the rush seat. He half-smiled, half-grimaced at Péter. His hip must be hurting again today.

"Peti," he said, "you've been gone so long."

"I work in the city now, Nagyapa. Remember?"

Before anything else Péter gave Nagyapa a little *pálinka,* a strong brandy made from last year's apricots, to ease the pain. Péter would have liked a happier welcome. But this was home.

THAT EVENING PÉTER lit the iron cook stove and prepared supper. He was not good at cooking, but the family had quit expecting good meals after his mother died. He set potatoes, bacon fat, bread, and the kerosene lantern on the table in the cramped kitchen and pulled up chairs. There was a better table in the larger room that fronted on the street, but they seldom ate there.

It was growing dark at the windows when the family gathered: Nagyapa easing into his chair with his cane, Apa throwing aside his felt work hat, Péter's brothers elbowing each other. The twins hardly resembled each other—Tibi, like Péter, had inherited Apa's eyes and cheekbones, and Gyuri had the darker, heart-shaped face of their mother. At the table, Péter sliced the bread, as he had been doing since he was fourteen and became strong enough for a full day of scything. Like smoking in public, cutting the family loaf was a privilege of manhood.

Supper was noisy. Nagyapa dropped the bowl of potatoes. Tibi accused Gyuri of taking more than his share of the bacon drippings. Gyuri retorted that he had not, and that Tibi would grab the whole world for himself if he could.

"Tibi got in trouble at school yesterday," Gyuri told Péter. "He didn't stand up when it was time to clap for Comrade Stalin."

Tibi slammed down his fork. "I didn't hear the teacher tell us to!"

"That's because you weren't paying attention. You never do!"

"Oh, Lord," Apa sighed.

"I don't think the boys should clap for that Russian monster," Nagyapa said.

Apa gripped his father's wrist. *"Psss!"*

"I don't like school," Tibi stated.

Péter wanted to tell Tibi that school would get better, but he couldn't. His head was clogged with memories of being scolded, swatted, and sent to the corner. When he was called upon to read aloud in class, he stood in agony as the words in the primer he held blurred. As a small child, he cried. In later years, he lapsed into voiceless anger. "Silent Peti," the neighbors had called him. If it had been legal to leave school at Tibi's age, Péter would have. Only the force of law had kept him there through eighth grade.

"Tibi," he said, "just try to put up with it."

Apa changed the subject and asked Péter about the city. The twins jumped in, full of questions: Were there really bullet holes everywhere? Was it true that people waited on the corners to steal your clothes? Did Péter get to use a flush toilet?

"And why was are you living in a cellar," Gyuri asked, "instead of with Uncle—"

Apa held up his hand. "Gyuri, Tibi, finish supper and go outside."

When the boys left, Apa pushed the door shut. He helped Nagyapa light his pipe, pulled out his cigarettes and offered one to Péter. Péter shook his head.

"No?"

"I'm taking voice lessons," he said. It was strange how hard it was, admitting to something that no one in Kőpatak ever did.

"What's wrong with your voice?" Nagyapa asked.

"I mean, singing lessons."

Apa lit his cigarette. "But you already know how to sing. Why are you taking lessons for something you already know?"

"Sing for us," his grandfather said.

Péter stared down at the shadows cast by the kerosene lamp. "I still don't know where Uncle Béla is," he said. "When I got to the city, he was gone." Péter dropped his voice. "Somebody said it was the ÁVH. I don't know what he did. If he did anything. My boss told me not to tell people I'm related to him."

Apa shut his eyes and rested his forehead on his hand. "Christ and his seven bleeding wounds."

PÉTER'S HOUSE, LIKE so many in Kőpatak, consisted of three whitewashed rooms: a pantry in back, a kitchen, where most of the living was done, and the *tiszta szoba,* the "clean room" with windows on the street. There had been a time when the clean room of his house actually was clean, kept clear of the mud and straw and manure that stuck to their boots. When his mother was alive, she had swept the earthen floor daily, even at the edges of the hive-shaped clay oven. She had kept the ornamental guest bed piled high with a display of good linens and pillows. Though the linens were worn and stained now and the extra pillows gone, still, by long tradition or habit, the family did not use the ornamental bed. Apa slept on a plain bed near the door in the *tiszta szoba.* The twins slept near him in trundlers they were supposed to roll under Apa's bed and the guest bed every morning. In spite of his bad leg, Nagyapa used a mat on the pantry floor. Péter slept in the *pitvar,* the space between the front door and the kitchen work table, on a mat that he stowed in a large basket by day. He was used to this, going without a mattress. During harvests he had sometimes slept in the fields, and while the Russians were here, he had slept in the barn.

His first morning back in Kőpatak, he awoke in the *pitvar* as the Kozmas' rooster was blasting raucously next door. Péter groaned. The damned bird needed voice lessons. He rose when he heard the shrilling of the cowherd's pipe.

While milking the cow, he practiced his vocal exercises. He thought about Katalin, how she had set her hand on his stomach. "Do you mind?" she had asked. Remembering it made him laugh. Did he *mind?* Did children mind chocolate? Did sunflowers mind the sun?

"Íí-á-á-á-á-á," he sang, but broke off when he heard his grandfather's uneven footfall.

Nagyapa limped into the cow stall and leaned against the rough boards. "What were you singing, Peti?"

"Just mouthing around," Péter hedged, "like Kozma's rooster."

"We have Kozma's land now. I hope Jancsi didn't pay much for it."

Péter wanted to say that his father had not bought it, that the State had simply switched it out, willy-nilly, but the family no longer tried to explain these things to Nagyapa.

"I want to see that field of Kozma's," Nagyapa said.

Péter was fairly sure his father had already shown Nagyapa the field, but after the milking, he hitched the mare to the wagon and drove his grandfather to see it again. The field lay on the other side of Rock Creek, *Kőpatak*, for which the village had been named. As the wagon clattered toward the creek, Nagyapa began talking about the pole bridge and how they'd had to throw it together fast. He didn't seem to remember that Péter had been there. At age sixteen Péter had helped build this bridge to replace the one the Germans blew up. They used telegraph poles, the transmitting wires having been cut long before.

"We bought our first field after the war," Nagyapa reminisced. He always talked like this, saying "*the* war" to mean the one that was lost in 1918. "The land cost us, we went hungry, we took it out of our bellies, but we bought it. And then we got some more—devil take it, I can't remember, when was it? Back when they split up the old baron's land."

"It was in '45."

Péter remembered the hubbub that spring when the new government dispossessed the aristocrats of their land, cut it into parcels and offered it for sale, cheap and on easy credit, to the peasants. Apa said it was the first thing the Bolsheviks had ever done that he liked. The news even made him laugh. Apa bought a field the family had been sharecropping, just behind the one Nagyapa had bought years before. The village had lost most of its animals to the war—draft horses requisitioned, pigs and cows eaten by the armies—and Péter's family was down to one horse. So they paired Zsuzsi with a borrowed mule to plow the new land. Apa laid out the plan: they would work this land and the old field as well, and they'd keep doing day labor for other farmers. They'd scrimp. They'd take it out of their bellies; and as soon as they could, they'd buy another horse so they had a team. Someday they'd buy another field. And then another. No matter how much time and sweat it took, they would become independent farmers. By God, they would do this.

At the edge of the new field, Péter reined in the mare and let his grandfather look out over the land.

"Muddy," Nagyapa grunted.

Péter was silent, thinking of what they had risked, what they had lost, and what they had hidden.

On the way home, as they re-crossed the bridge, he looked off toward a clump of willows in the bend of the stream. There, in the last winter of the war, he and his grandfather had hammered two wooden crosses, one small and one tiny, into the half-frozen earth. The crosses had disappeared not long after, probably carried off as firewood; that winter had been desperately cold. Still, whenever he crossed the bridge, his eyes turned toward the spot where his mother and the child within her—whom he always imagined as a girl— had died among the November snows.

THERE WERE THINGS Péter and his father never spoke of around Nagyapa and the twins and hardly ever spoke of, even to each other. In the early afternoon, when Péter was sure he was alone, he lifted an old crockery beer stein from a kitchen shelf and curled his fingers around the key beneath it. Taking a lantern with him, he walked to the back of the barn and down the stone steps to the root cellar and unlocked the door.

He lit the lantern and shut the door behind him. In this small space, hardly more than three paces in any direction, his family had waited out the worst of the wartime shooting, sitting on the cold earth and eating dried maize they had grown for the pigs. The gun blasts had terrified the twins. From a few old covered bowls on a narrow shelf by the door, Péter now took some vegetable seeds and put them in his pockets for his Budapest garden. Then he shone the lantern on the horizontal boards of the back wall.

He nudged a board and tugged at it. Finally it came away, exposing a hole in the wall. The boards above and below it would do the same thing: lift out five of them, and he could clamber through to the low crawl space on the other side. During the war, they had hidden barrels of wheat, baskets of maize, and jars of lard there, away from the hungry Russians and Germans.

The barrels were still there. Last summer after harvest, he had helped his father hide wheat here again, holding it back to grind in a hand quern and sell for cash under the table, instead of selling it to the State at less than the cost of growing it. So they had not met their produce quota for the State.

When they had hidden the grain, Péter asked his father, "What if they find this?"

"I can't give them any more," his father answered. "What do they want— my hands and my feet and my liver?"

Now there were too many stories circulating of barn searches and loft sweeps. Péter stood peering at the barrels. Then he pried out the remaining boards of the false wall, set them quietly on the dirt floor and crouched through the small opening. His hands trembled as he lifted a barrel lid. It was empty. Opening the others, he found them empty as well. The grain had been used up. No evidence remained. He blew out his breath in relief.

But another harvest was coming.

PÉTER WENT BACK to Pest with five balls of soap from Ági Kozma, four of them for Katalin and one for himself. On Thursday night at his lesson, he gave her two. She was delighted and said that she and Mari were going to have the bath of their lives. He blinked and tried not to dwell on this, the stirring image of Katalin in the bath.

She handed him a business card. "This is from my father. If you go to him at that hospital address, he'll try to get you some glasses that work better. But don't tell anyone. There are people who have been waiting two years for lenses."

He thanked her in astonishment and followed her to the piano. It still amazed him to see a piano in this flat, especially the big kind. None of the houses in Kőpatak had any kind of piano. Katalin's flat also had a telephone in it, and a toilet—he knew because he had once heard it flushing—and in front was a balcony with a wrought-iron railing. It was a very small balcony, true, but still a balcony, and there were none of those in Kőpatak, either.

Katalin seated herself on the piano bench. "I've been meaning to mention that we might as well stop saying *maga*," she said, for in all their conversation they had been using the formal word for *you*. "You can say *te* with me. Almost everybody does. Did you practice?" she asked, using *te* instead of *maga*.

"I did. In a broom closet at work. Under the noisy press."

"Smart!"

As she led him through vocal warm-ups, she watched his jaw, his lips, his chest, his stomach. He was trying to get used to this, but he felt like a horse for sale.

"Knees looser, please," she said. "Jaw looser. Tongue lower. Keep it down behind your bottom teeth. And more space in the back of your mouth … no …."

This was working against nature, like sneezing backwards. He tried again.

"Yes," she cried. "Very nice."

"I don't know what I did."

"Never mind. You're getting it."

Katalin pulled out the same book they had used before, but this time she didn't hand it to him. She flipped the pages. "Do you know 'Fölszállott a Páva'?"

His hand clenched. "Yes."

"Do you like it?"

His mother had sung the song. So had he, on that night in Háromkeresztes with the Gypsy. The song was in him. It was not a question of liking or disliking it, any more than he liked or disliked his own blood, his own heart.

"I'll sing it," he said.

She played through the slow, sad melody that had been born among the rivers and fields of the Magyars, played by shepherds on their lonely long flutes. Péter began to sing, but the tones cowered back.

"Sing out," Katalin said.

He tried again, louder. "*Fölszállott ….*"

"Tongue down," she reminded him. "Throat open. Hold the vowel for the full length of the note. You're clipping the vowels. You can do that on some folk songs, but not this one, it's too slow for that. And when we get into classical pieces, you can't do it at all. Try again."

He began again. She interrupted, correcting him. He tried, she stopped him; he tried again, she stopped him again. "No, Péter, I said hold the vowel."

"I don't know what you're talking about. If I'm doing it wrong, then sing it for me the right way."

Katalin sat with her eyes on the spread pages of music.

"Please," he said, "just let me hear it."

Finally, she pressed several keys, withdrew her hand from the piano, and sang. "*A szegény raboknak szabadulására* … for the freedom of the poor prisoners." Her music hovered like the night stars. He listened without moving, almost without breathing.

At the end she looked up at him. "So, do you see? That's what I mean by holding the notes."

"Sing more," he said. "Please."

"No, this is your lesson time." She touched the keys again. "Sing it. And don't clip the vowels. This time I won't interrupt you."

"All right." Péter counted the piano beats, pulled in a low breath, closed his eyes, and began: "Fragile, proud peacock, make your dazzling feathers let it be known: all will be different tomorrow." He tried to hold out the notes of this melody that had been part of his home and his bread and his rising and sleeping, back before the chopped telegraph poles and the grain hidden in the root cellar and the wooden crosses by the stream, and oh, what if it were true, that all could be different tomorrow.

On the piano keys, Katalin's fingers tripped up. She put her hand over her mouth, circled her wrist in a gesture for him to continue.

"New winds will make the old Hungarian trees moan," he sang.

He stumbled on the words. Katalin gestured again, eyes closed, and he pressed on, "Either we're crazy, and we'll all be lost, or our belief will come true …."

"Keep going," she said.

He sang to the end, "For the freedom of the poor prisoners."

"Good job, Péter," she said. She pulled off her reading glasses and brushed at her eyes. "Really good. Let's go back to … let's …."

She shook her head and lifted one hand, signaling for him to wait. With the other hand she covered her face.

"Katalin! What's the matter?"

She turned away and her shoulders trembled. "Let's go back to the beginning. More open … back of your throat."

"But what's wrong?"

She shook her head again, and though he asked her a third time, she would not answer, only placed her hands back on the keys and told him they were going to do the song again, and this time, even if he couldn't remember to hold any other vowels, would he please—she waited through a break in her voice—at least hold the *ö* in *fölszállott.*

Chapter Six

⌒‿‿⌒

Give Me Your Hand

Two years earlier, the country had gone through *the change,* as it came to be called. The radio said change was bracing and brave. In 1949, when Katalin was eighteen and finishing high school, she did her best to stand square-shouldered and earnest like the industrious women on the work posters. She wanted to trust, although she knew that Ildi Brauer had been kept out of music academy because of the change. She wanted to believe all was for the best, although the businesses of her parents' friends had been appropriated. Her father was still practicing ophthalmology—doctors were too badly needed to be seriously harassed, people said—but he did it in a State hospital now, not on his own, and he came home at night tired and taciturn.

Still, things were getting better in some ways, weren't they, if you took the long view of it? There were arrests, yes, seemingly senseless ones, and she herself had recently seen a man beaten for resisting arrest. But when the fascists were in charge, Germans and Hungarians both, they had tied Jews together and shot them into the Danube. Anything was better than that, wasn't it? She would rather have 1949 than 1944.

"At least the communists aren't fascists," she said to her family one night.

"I forget what the difference is," her father answered.

A snappish defense rose inside her, but she swallowed it back, for her family did not know she was falling in love with a communist.

She had begun meeting Róbert Zentai at the music academy to rehearse Mozart's *"Là ci darem la mano"*—There You Will Give Me Your Hand—for his graduating recital. He played piano and sang the part of Don Giovanni while she sang Zerlina's part. It was a flirtation song, and he teased her about it the first time they tried the song together in a small practice room.

"You have to fall for me," he said. "That's what the song is for."

He smiled, lips first and his eyes lagging an instant behind. He played through the piano introduction and sang his opening lines, but when she entered on her part, he stopped her halfway through.

"It needs more fullness," he said, "the way you sang 'Caro Mio Ben' at your recital. Your voice is beautiful. Just open up and pour that beauty into your part. You're holding back."

"But aren't I supposed to seem scared? Or worried? That's in the song's story, I mean."

"You can do both. Fear and beauty." With his left hand, he fingered a bass chord. "We're Hungarian musicians. We do both all the time."

So they began doing both fear and beauty all the time. After school, while her father was working at the hospital and her mother was away teaching voice late into the day, Katalin would head for the music academy and dart through the halls, hoping not to be seen by Antal or his friends, and meet Róbert to rehearse. His was a fearfully beautiful voice. After the singing, she would linger with him while he practiced piano. Often he walked her home, always stopping half a block from her apartment building, never seeing her completely to the door. On one of their walks homeward, he mentioned his roommate Gyula, a friend of his in the Party.

The Party. She tried to let her uneasiness pass.

She had been making trips to the academy for several weeks when she finally told her family about the singing. Over midday dinner on a Sunday, she tried to describe it in the professional terms her mother would have used. Her mother set her damask napkin on the frayed tablecloth and looked at Katalin. "We've not met him," she said pointedly.

"Antal has."

Antal took a sip of his wine and said nothing.

Katalin's grandfather peered at her in that gentle way he had, eyelids sagging, then turned to Antal. "Do you know this Róbert?"

"I don't really know him. He plays piano well." Antal rose, switched on the radio and waited until a dance tune began jangling. "He's a Party member, or soon to become one. I'd rather keep my distance."

"I think Antal has the right idea, Katalin," her father said. "I'd rather you kept your distance."

"But we're just singing. And if he's a communist, what of that? Everybody's turning communist."

Her mother thrust her finger to her lips and her eyes flared toward the neighboring wall.

Two hours later, Katalin left the flat in her favorite skirt without telling them where she was going and met Róbert on the Danube promenade. Hand in hand, they walked, looking over the river as it rippled beneath the barges and swirled around the huge stand posts of the Chain Bridge. It was only in the last year that the bridge had been whole and standing straight again since the siege. Across the river on Castle Hill where the final battle had raged, Buda Castle still lay as a charred, bony dome atop a field of rubble. Róbert slipped his arm around her waist, and for a long time they stood looking toward the ashes of Buda. She would never forget the horror of that winter—the smoke, the gunfire, the cold, the hunger, the dead soldiers in the snow.

"I remember how terrible the siege was," she murmured. "And then afterward there was this, the bridge crushed, the castle burned up. And the hammer-and-sickle flags everywhere ...."

No. He was in the Party. She bit back her words.

The sun had come out from behind a cloud bank, lighting the edge of Róbert's cap and the fringes of his soft, loose hair. He raised his eyes across the river.

"I grew up not far from the castle," he said. "But the apartment house is gone now."

"So were you there during the war?" she asked. "I mean, *there*, in the middle of it?"

"For most of the war. Not during the siege. I left."

"With your family?"

He shook his head. "My father, he sympathized with the communists during the war, and ...." Róbert coughed, paused.

Katalin laid her hand on his forearm. "And?"

"And the fascists killed him. My mother sent me to live with relatives in the country, near Győr. And she was going to come later with my younger brother. But they never came."

"And were they ... were they killed, too?"

"Yes."

She could barely speak. She murmured that she was sorry, very sorry.

He touched her cheek. "I know you are."

Under a tree still scarred by the fires of war, he kissed her for the first time. It was a sad, soft kiss, his embrace tentative and careful. Then he pulled back and held her fingers loose and tender in his hand.

"You're kind," he whispered.

PERHAPS IT WAS because of that kindness that he began to tell her more. She went to the academy on Tuesday, Wednesday, and Friday of that week and simply sat with him, doing her homework while he practiced piano. On

Friday after the practice session, they sat in the square in front of the academy, and he told her of his father, who had taught him to play piano. She listened quietly while he told her his father had been very talented but not successful. When she touched the tendons of his hand and waited, he went on.

"My father was in debt when the fascists killed him," Róbert said. "I didn't know how bad things were, not until after he was dead. My relatives gave me his composition books, and inside one of them were some notes. Like a diary. I doubt that my relatives had seen the notes. I'm sure my mother hadn't. He wrote about a Jewish woman he was in love with. The fascists came in; she took cyanide. My father was thinking of doing the same. That's what he wrote. But the fascists got him first. I was a teenager at the time."

Behind them the sounds of the traffic on the avenue rose and fell.

"I'm sorry," Róbert said. "This is a burden you don't need."

The intensity of his voice both drew her and frightened her.

"Your family is strong," he said. *"Alive.* Mine is gone. Because of the fascists. That's why I joined the Party. I had to. Inside me there was no choice. Can you understand that?"

Katalin wanted to say yes. But against the *yes,* there rose up memories of Ildi's father's friends who had been taken to Siberia and never returned, memories of drunken Soviet soldiers and of hiding under her bed while her father and Antal bolted and blocked the apartment door, memories of hangings, of police questioning neighbors, rumors of priests and nuns being arrested. And Rákosi calling Stalin the great father.

"But the Party," she whispered, "Rákosi …."

Róbert's gaze fastened on hers. "That's Stalinism, not Marxism. It's Soviet domination. We have to break away."

Katalin gripped his hand. She remembered how the State's furious denunciations and threats had poured out from every radio station when Yugoslavia broke with the Soviet Union.

"Hungary needs its own socialism," Róbert told her. "And I'm not the only one who thinks so. My roommate Gyula, he's been speaking with others. It's a spreading wave. Things have to change. Even László Rajk says so."

László Rajk. Katalin groped for what she could recall of him: a Party favorite, charismatic, praised over and over in *Szabad Nép*. He had organized the secret police and now was foreign minister.

"If Rajk and others like him are pushing for change," Róbert went on, whispering, "it could happen. There's strength in numbers."

She wasn't sure. Wasn't there risk in numbers?

"I don't want them hurting you," she said.

"Are you worried?"

"Isn't that obvious?"

"It's been a long time since anyone worried about me."

"You shouldn't be so alone, Róbert. Please."

"But I *am* alone."

"No, you have friends."

"Friends come and go."

"Not all of them. There's me."

He touched her hair. "You're too young to take on my worries. Too happy."

She pulled back. "You think I'm a child."

"I don't."

"Then don't treat me like one."

He bent his head and she trembled inside over this fragile promise she had made. When they left the square and walked toward her home, they turned down side streets, slipped close together without speaking. At a narrow passage between buildings, he pulled her into the shadows, touched her back, and drew her to him. His kiss closed her in, closed the world out. Katalin ached within and without. When their lips parted, she leaned on his shoulder, shaken and silent, then lifted her face for another kiss. And another. Hours later, the aching lingered.

As MAY WENT on, Katalin drafted her application letter to the music academy and practiced voice and piano. In preparation for her final exams, she memorized Hungarian poetry and re-read sections of her textbooks. It was all laborious. On days apart from Róbert, she counted the hours until she could see him again.

Once, she rode the tram south with him and climbed the old back stairs to his attic flat. In the tiny kitchen, his bearded roommate, Gyula Kardos, stood over a basin washing dishes.

"Ah, you must be Katalin the diva," Gyula teased.

He set three shot glasses on the cluttered table and poured vodka into them. She tasted it, and Gyula laughed when she grimaced.

"A little strong for you, eh?" Gyula drained his glass, wiped his mouth with the back of his hand, and rose. "I'm off to …." He cocked his head, looking at Róbert as though this were all understood. "Coming?"

"Maybe later," Róbert said.

It all seemed too clandestine. When Gyula left, Katalin begged Róbert not to go to wherever it was that Gyula had gone. Róbert stayed with her, and they sat in the window seat, kissing softly, kissing hard.

ON THE EVENING of Róbert's recital, Katalin's family and Ildi attended the recital to hear her sing with him. She sat in the auditorium with them during the piano portion, while on stage Róbert bent over the piano keys in concentration, hands flying. Katalin then left her seat and went backstage as Róbert stepped forward to sing his two vocal solos, one of them very difficult. From the wings, Katalin breathed, tightened, and relaxed through the rises and falls with him. Fear and beauty. They were doing both tonight. When the moment came for their duet, she joined him on stage, and he strained a smile at her.

"*Là ci darem la mano,*" he began, singing as Giovanni and reaching for her hand.

As Zerlina, she hesitated. The music tugged between them. He offered. He coaxed. She turned, gave him her hand. The song reached into her and filled her. Zerlina acquiesced. The piano notes faded. The applause rang out. Róbert kissed her hand.

"Gorgeous," he whispered. "Gorgeous, Katalin."

IN JUNE, RÓBERT finished his studies at the academy. Antal, who was one year behind him and had friends in Róbert's class, went with Katalin to the graduation ceremony. On the walk there, Antal told her to quit pretending to the family that she and Róbert were just friends.

"Well, you and Ildi pretend you're just friends," she retorted.

"As a matter of fact, we *are* just friends, and that's not the point. If you're going to be with Róbert, quit sneaking around."

A few days later, she took the public step of asking Róbert to her own graduation ceremony the following week. It would be the last thing her Catholic school would do as a religious body; the headmistress nun was being fired, and so were all the church-going teachers. Róbert, an atheist, told her he would come.

FOUR DAYS LATER the news broke: a conspiracy of the worst kind had been unearthed.

Katalin learned of it when her history teacher read out the report, thrusting his index finger into the air for emphasis. Within the government, *right there in the Hungarian government,* a ring of spies had been discovered. These spies selling their souls to American imperialism, these pathetic dogs trotting at the heels of Tito and his feckless Yugoslavs had forgotten the great debt of gratitude they owed to the Soviet Union and Comrade Stalin. In nationalistic hubris, they had forsaken the true flock of honest Hungarian communists led by Comrade Rákosi. The ringleader—make no mistake about this— was that unparalleled quisling László Rajk. But Hungary would stand fast in solidarity with the Soviet Union and with other members of the Eastern bloc. Communism of any other kind was not true communism. Those like

Rajk who advocated such false doctrine would be dealt with as the traitors—*traitors*—that they were.

Katalin sat gripping her pen, her hand shaking. She had to warn Róbert. As soon as school ended, she bolted for the tram, jumped off at his stop, and tore through the humid streets and up the back stairs of his house. Panting, she pounded on Róbert's door.

The door opened and Róbert stood with his hand on the knob. "Katalin! What—"

She stepped in, threw the door shut behind her, and locked it. "They've arrested László Rajk," she panted, "and they're going after nationalistic communists. I heard it at school."

He looked at her, troubled eyes narrowing. "I heard, too," he whispered.

"Is Gyula here?"

"No."

They sat pressed together in the window seat. Knotted up in his arms, she told him everything.

There was no missing the tension in his voice as he tried to soothe her. "I mostly kept my opinions to myself," he said. "I'm just a music student. Not that influential. No. Not like Gyula. I didn't tell many people what I really think. You didn't tell anyone, did you?"

"No, never!"

"The people that knew—oh, damn—they're trustworthy, I think—"

"They have to be."

In the heat of the day, he had taken off his shirt. She rested her head against his collarbone and wept.

"Katalin," he pleaded, "don't cry. It kills me."

"But what if they take you away?"

"They won't," he said. But she heard his fear.

"If it happens," she said, her voice breaking, "you have to come back. You have to."

He lifted her chin, searching deeply into her eyes. "Will it matter that much to you?"

"How can you doubt it? I love you!"

"*Jaj,* Katalin, I don't deserve it."

She clung to his sheltering chest while he told her it would be all right. Somehow it would be all right. Somehow they would stay together.

"We have to," she said.

"We will."

"Róbert," she whispered, "I'm afraid."

"Shhh, my dove."

It was a long time that he held her and kissed her, stroking her throat and speaking tenderly. Her fingers caressed his warm stomach. He opened her blouse, kissed her shoulders, unclasped her bra. She caught her breath, yet her arms pulled hard at the curve of his back and her breasts spilled against him. When she lifted her hand to touch his cheek, he enclosed her fingers in his and murmured, "Katalin. Come with me."

She followed him to the side of the bed. There she hesitated. But he kissed her again and their fire leapt. Sinking onto the bed, she reached for him, and he eased down beside her. Nakedness. Through the slats of the window blinds, the afternoon sun blinked.

Like song: a rise, a swell, a falling.

After the crescendo, after the descent into the final hush, she gazed at his face, his eyes closed against the sun at the window, and she touched his soft, limp hair.

"Róbert," she whispered.

He opened his eyes and turned to her.

"I'm afraid."

"No." He gathered her close. "No."

But the fear would not leave her. When she could no longer delay going home, she rose and dressed. She told Róbert not to see her to the tram stop.

"Lock the door," she said. "Don't answer unless it's me. I'll tap the rhythm to '*Là ci darem*.'"

As she made her way home by herself, a loneliness followed her, greater than any she had ever known.

SOMEHOW KATALIN PASSED her exams. On the evening of her commencement exercises, she sat among the graduates and looked for Róbert, but he was not there. Through the ceremony she waited and watched, but he did not come. Afterward her family said she seemed remarkably subdued compared to the giddy girls around her; they wondered if something was wrong. She shook her head.

In the morning, she left home without explaining herself and went to Róbert's attic flat. She knocked, rapping out "*Là ci darem*" with her knuckles. There was no answer. She rapped again, louder, faster.

The old landlady appeared on the landing beside her. "I haven't seen your boyfriend for two days," she said.

"Where … where is he?"

"I don't know, but the roommate's gone, too."

Katalin's knees trembled. Radio harangues. ÁVH sweeps. She began to cry, and the landlady told her she was sorry.

* * *

IN THE LONELY two years since the sun blinked between the window blinds, Katalin had never found out what happened to Róbert.

Chapter Seven

Living Space

THE FIRST OF May was Labor Day, a Soviet holiday, so it was a holiday in Hungary as well. Péter looked forward to a day off until it was explained at work that on this holiday they were all to show solidarity with the proletariat of the world. At City Park near the statue of Comrade Stalin. Be there.

So on May 1, Péter and the other workers from State Printing Office No. 8 assembled near Stalin's huge bronze boots. Péter stood with Csaba and they waited. And waited. All around them, machinists, electricians, and dock workers lined up, and teachers tried to arrange school children into parade formation. Young Pioneers in their red ties waited with banners. A loudspeaker somewhere blared the Internationale: *So comrades, come rally, and the last fight let us face ....*

Finally the parade moved out and Péter fell into step next to Csaba. In front of them plodded some press operators from No. 8. Somewhere a crowd was cheering, but only a sparse thread of onlookers lined the street.

"Nobody's watching the parade, because everybody's in it," Csaba said. "I hear there's free beer and sausage at the end."

They trudged past the statue and kept following the press operators, as the same hurrahs rang out over and over.

"It's the loudspeaker," Csaba said, "pre-recorded excitement." He pitched his thumb toward Stalin's statue. "I hope the Old Mustache is satisfied with this ridiculous show, because I sure don't want to do it over again."

Péter stifled a laugh. He hoped no one had seen Csaba's thumb. After the parade, he and Csaba stood in a long line for sausage and beer, but by the time they reached the front, the beer had run out. Someone jostled Péter and splattered mustard across his shirt. Chagrined, he had to wear the yellow streak home on the tram.

Back at the apartment, he trod down the wooden cellar stairs. Mrs. Kovács, the old laundry woman, was finishing the day's wash at the cellar sink. The creases of her mottled face deepened as she smiled at him. She had liked him ever since she found out he came from the country.

She pointed at his mustard stain. "Give me your shirt, before I drain the water."

As he waited, Mrs. Kovács washed his shirt and hummed "Lili Marleen," a German song heard everywhere during the war. She was—he tried to remember Katalin's words for it—off key. He couldn't help it: he hummed with her, and she corrected herself. He felt a small pride in this.

AT THE END of work the next day, Péter went to the hospital where Katalin's father worked. He had gone there last week, and in a small room Dr. Varga had checked his eyes with a contraption that looked like the face of a giant fly. Afterward, he had measured the frames of Péter's glasses. Today at the hospital, Dr. Varga had an assistant fit new lenses into Péter's frames.

On his way out, Péter picked up a copy of *Szabad Nép,* angled it in his hands, and watched the letters come into focus—not just the headlines, but even the small print: *e. gy. á.*

God almighty, he could *see* it.

That evening, he walked up and down the city streets, looking at things near and far, as long as the sky held light. It was late when he came home and entered the foyer. Erika Jankovics stepped out of her flat wearing a night robe and holding a shot glass. With her stood a jowly, bald man.

"Benedek," Erika called, "before you go downstairs, I'll just warn you there are people down there. My sister and her children moved in. Everybody has to take turns with the stove and the sink."

Erika handed off her glass to the man, walked ahead of Péter into the cellar, and turned on the light. On the floor near the bottom of the stairs, several benches had been pushed together, and blanketed bodies lay on them. A stiff-haired woman sat up, blinking and frowning.

"This is Péter Benedek," Erika told the woman. "He sleeps under the stairs. He leaves early for work."

The sleepy woman nodded, and Comrade Erika left.

Péter undressed in the dark under the stairs. Why didn't that Erika woman take these people into her flat instead of sending them down here? Maybe that man with the jowls had something to do with it.

The next morning, as Péter made ready for work, a child from one of the benches woke up. Péter climbed the stairs. The boy, who looked a little younger than Péter's brothers, padded after him in his stocking feet and nightshirt. He followed Péter into the loo and stared.

Péter waved him off. "Turn around and leave me alone."

The boy just scowled and trailed Péter back into the cellar.

"Who are you?" Péter asked at the bottom of the stairs.

"Rudi."

On the benches, another lump wriggled under the blanket. By the time Péter left for work, three children were watching him. Their mother slept on.

THE TOPIC OF the *Szabad Nép* meeting that morning was living space. If Péter recalled correctly, *living space* was what the German fascists had said they needed when they stomped all over other people's countries; but today the Party rep was talking about the metrical allotment of home that the State deemed necessary for each citizen. She explained it: to occupy a large house or flat without sharing it was to thwart the forward march of the people.

The Party representative was a small, fairly young woman who made herself seem bigger by raising her voice and constantly stretching out her hands. "It may be that you have more living space than you require," she blared. "You may be asked to share your living space—which, after all, does not belong only to you but to the people."

Péter shifted on his metal chair and thought of the boy who had followed him into the loo. Apparently privacy was bourgeois. The lack of it was embarrassing as hell.

Later on, at the loading dock, Péter and Csaba tied twine around boxes of revised history textbooks, and Csaba was not silent on the topic of living space. "My neighbor, she's a single lady, has this little flat. Tiny. All of a sudden the concierge tells her, 'Tomorrow you're going to have a roommate.' So tomorrow comes. A roommate? No. *Four* roommates. A young couple with a little boy and a baby. So my neighbor, she's sleeping on the kitchen floor now, and the baby sleeps in a basket on the dining table. Oh, did I say 'sleep'? Pardon me. Nobody sleeps. Last night the baby cried half the night."

Péter and Csaba walked a box of books up a plank ramp into the wagon. The motor truck was still out of service until a replacement starter could be found. Péter gave a nod and they squatted to set the box down. By now their work was perfectly synchronized.

Csaba straightened up. "No housing shortage," he said with a snort. "Just like there's no shortage of replacement parts. We all have everything we need. That's because nobody's allowed to need anything. That asshole Rákosi ...."

Péter grabbed Csaba's wrist. "Stop it, Csaba," he hissed. "Good God, shut up!"

Csaba stood motionless. "Yes, sorry," he breathed.

They worked on in silence.

PÉTER HAD FOUND a place to take showers: the locker room of the thermal pools in City Park. He went there after work at least on Thursdays before his voice lesson; he didn't want to look and smell like a swineherd next to Katalin's shiny piano. This Thursday after he paid the entrance fee, however, he had no subway change, so he walked home, passing the ÁVH headquarters on Stalin Avenue. Csaba had said it used to be the Nazi headquarters—same factory, different bosses. There were gallows in the basement, people said.

As Péter walked by, two officers came out of the building in their tunics, service belts, and flat hats. Péter turned his head and stepped faster.

When he reached home, the boy Rudi was throwing rocks at a trash bin in the courtyard. Rudi's two younger sisters were playing tug of war with an old clothes line. The smaller one fell into Péter's garden where he had just planted cucumbers.

"Here, stop that!" Péter shouted at her.

In the cellar, the children's mother, whose name he had learned was Irénke, was standing at the potbellied stove cooking beans. She watched Péter as he came down the stairs. "You have soap," she said, and it sounded like an accusation. "My children told me. Sell me some. "What do you want? I have beans and sauerkraut. Tomorrow I'll make dumplings—"

"I need the soap. It's not for sale."

"You're one person. Me and my children, there are four of us. How can you need soap as much as we do?"

Péter had not argued with a woman since his mother died, but damned if he was going to hand over his soap. "Irénke *néni*," he said, trying to sound polite by calling her aunt. "I can't sell it to you. I owe it to somebody."

"Paying gambling debts with soap?"

"I'm paying for music lessons."

"Music lessons? When you live in a hole?"

He turned his back and ducked under the stairs. There was no door to slam. In his hole, as she called it, a soap ball lay broken on the floor. He picked up the broken pieces and shoved them down into his bedding, hiding them. The other soap balls he carried with him upstairs to his voice lesson and saw to it that he placed them into Katalin's hands. He sang the best he could, and at the end, just before she saw him to the door, Katalin gave him a music book.

"A better folk song collection," she said. "More suited to your voice. Keep it. It's for you. Look through it, bring it with you next time."

He turned through the clean, smooth pages of music, words and even pictures: a tree by a brook, a shepherd with a flute, a flock of geese.

"Thank you," he murmured. "No one's ever given me a book before."

"A new book to go with your new lenses," she said. "How are they? Better?"

"Yes, better, very good."

On the open page, the word *szép*, "beautiful," took shape before him. He looked at Katalin. She smiled and pushed back a strand of dark hair that had fallen from her barrette. *Yes, beautiful.* He smiled back.

When he left the apartment, Comrade Erika met him in the courtyard and handed him a letter. "From your home, I assume," she said. "Oh, and I understand you've been taking your laundry to Mrs. Kovács."

He nodded, for it was true, but how could she possibly care who washed his clothes?

"My sister could do your laundry," Erika stated. "It would be convenient for you. She's right there in the cellar. Next to you. You might as well ask her."

Péter half-nodded. He had every intention of continuing to take his laundry to Mrs. Kovács. Was this now an act of rebellion?

The envelope contained two pencil-smudged papers, which he examined under the electrical light at the cellar door. One was a letter from Gyuri, the other a child's pencil drawing of five cats. Péter held Gyuri's note close, then farther off, adjusting it until his eyes focused through the bottom half of his new lenses:

> Dear Péter,
>   A cat came in our barn and had kittens! We looked under their tails and they are all girls! Here is a picture Tibi drew.
>   School is boring. Please come home.
>   Your brother,
>
> *Gyuri*

Tibi's drawing showed one big cat and four small ones, all with long eyelashes. Girl cats. The mother cat wore an apron and a kerchief. Péter had long ago guessed that his brothers were fascinated with mothers—those warm, helpful beings that other families had and theirs did not. Sometimes, in the market or on the road, it seemed the twins looked at women wistfully.

His father did. There was no question of seeming. Péter knew.

He refolded the letter and the drawing, and once again he turned the pages of the book from Katalin. He would read this gift. Every song, every page. No matter how long it took, he would do it.

Under the electrical light, he worked through the first page, and that night he slept with the book beside his bed. In the morning he hid it between his blankets. As he left for work, the boy Rudi followed him up the stairs again.

"Stay out of my living space," Péter told him.

* * *

AT WORK, PÉTER looked for Csaba in the *Szabad Nép* meeting. Csaba wasn't there. When Péter went to the loading dock, Csaba wasn't there either, but the production manager was, and next to him stood a lanky, pale man with a brush mustache hanging over his lips.

"Péter, this is Lajos Szabó," Mr. Molnár said. "He'll be working with you."

"Where is Csaba?"

"He's not here today."

"When will he be back?" Péter asked.

A pause.

"Lajos will help you," Mr. Molnár said.

Péter could not help noticing, or maybe imagining, a slight sighing inflection in Mr. Molnár's voice. Péter said a disheartened good morning to Lajos. The man did not answer.

As the press slammed and rolls of paper whizzed and the operator's bell clanged, Péter and Lajos boxed up flyers and loaded the boxes onto a handcart. Each time the cart was full, they would wheel it to the loading dock and lift the boxes onto the wagon bed. Lajos lagged and his eyes wandered. Péter would shout, "Here!" or "Careful!" and Lajos would say nothing. The work progressed much more slowly than it would have with Csaba. Sometimes Lajos would stop and turn his back, and after this had happened twice, Péter realized the fellow was taking furtive swallows from a flask he kept in his jacket.

Mid-morning, the Party representative appeared on the loading dock. "Comrade Benedek," she called, "may I see you upstairs?"

Upstairs. God, what had he done?

With quick, emphatic steps the small woman led him up the stairs and across a large room full of desks and typewriters. Women were reading long ribbons of paper. The Party rep opened a door into a narrow office, pointed him to a chair, and closed the door.

"My name is Tünde Fodor, and I am a copy editor." She sat down at the gray metal desk. "Our comrades in State Security have asked for some information, and I hope you will help us."

Péter tried to smile at the woman but could only manage a pull of the lips.

"I would like to talk with you about your acquaintance with Csaba Pál," she said. "It has come to our attention that Comrade Pál was negative toward the work here. Did you see evidence of that?"

Péter's mouth was parched.

"Well? Did you?"

From somewhere within him he dredged up words. "Comrade Pál is a good worker."

"But it has been said he complained and made comments that would demoralize other workers."

"No … no, he didn't demoralize me."

"But you aren't the only worker here," she pointed out. "Csaba Pál has been reassigned. Make your truthful confession. Did you hear him complain about equipment breaking down?"

Péter's gaze fixed on a floor stain and blurred.

"Comrade?" the woman prompted.

Speak.

Péter said, "He—Csaba—he joked about it, about things breaking—"

"To laugh about the work shows disrespect, doesn't it?"

"No, comrade!" Péter blustered along, hardly knowing what he was saying. "I laugh about the company's mare because she's so hard to harness up, but I like the mare. I respect her."

The woman leaned across the desk toward him. "Did you hear Csaba Pál make insulting remarks about Comrade Rákosi?"

Péter's cheeks burned, and he wanted to bolt from the room. "No," he lied.

"Are you sure?"

"Yes, comrade."

Tünde Fodor lifted a typewritten sheet and skimmed it with her finger. "I understand that you live in a cellar," she said, a little more softly. "And that your accommodations are rather primitive."

The accommodations were less primitive than the privy and the well back home in Kőpatak, but he kept silent.

"You're a good worker, Comrade Benedek," she said, "and certainly the State believes in rewarding diligence. If you can supply us with more information about Csaba Pál, we might be able to help you find a more comfortable place to live."

In his lap, his hands knotted. "My place is good enough. Comrade, please, may I go now? Lajos needs help, new on the job and all, I don't want to leave him on his own. Please."

She made notes on a steno pad and finally gestured toward the door. "That will be all."

Face sweating, Péter returned to the shipping boxes, where Lajos said nothing to him.

THAT NIGHT, AFTER work, he plodded down the wood stairs into the cellar. Comrade Erika and her sister, Irénke, sat on a bench, talking and smoking. They barely nodded to him and didn't pause in their conversation. He could hear the children squabbling. He made his way back to his space under the stairs … and stopped.

The boy named Rudi was rolling in the blankets. Péter's clothes and razor were strewn over the floor, and the pillowcase was gashed where the children had tried out the razor. The two sisters pulled on opposite edges of the book Katalin had given him. The younger girl screamed. A page ripped.

"Stop it!" Péter yelled. "Let go of that."

The children stared. The book fell to the floor. Péter snatched it up and fanned through the pages. They were dirty, ragged, and scribbled over in pencil.

"Irénke *néni!*" Péter strode back to where the two women sat. He thrust the book, open to a violated page, in front of Irénke. "Why did you let your children do this?"

She glared at him as the smoke rose from her cigarette. "They're just children."

"They don't belong in my space. In my bed."

"You'd better calm down, Benedek," Comrade Erika said.

"But my things are none of their business."

Comrade Erika shifted her bored eyes.

Péter stared at her, and the reality sank in: this woman could do as she liked here, and if she or her relatives wanted something, sooner or later they would probably get it. Not even his skimpy pile of worldly goods really belonged to him. He was not just living under an old set of stairs; he was living, as the saying went, under the frog's arse.

He stamped out of the cellar with the book and ran up the back stairs two at a time to the Vargas' apartment. When Katalin answered the door, he held out the book to her. "Look what those brats in the cellar did."

"Shhh, shhh." She beckoned him in and closed the door.

While her mother washed dishes and the baby played with some blocks on the floor, Katalin sat down with Péter at the table and turned the pages. With mending tape, she repaired the rips as best she could, erased the scribbling, and tried to smooth the crumples. There was grace in the movement of her fingers, kindness in the way she spoke to him, and by the last page, he was calmer.

She handed the book back and looked at him, her brown eyes probing. "Are you all right, other than this?"

"It was a bad day. I work—*worked*—with a nice fellow named Csaba, and he got sacked."

"Oh, no."

Péter leaned closer, spoke low. "They say he's 'reassigned.' God only knows what that means. I liked him. But isn't that the way it is? Just when you get to like somebody," he jerked his thumb over his shoulder, "out they go."

"I know." She rested her forehead on her palm, and her eyes turned to her daughter. "Oh, Péter, I know."

Chapter Eight

~~~

Caro Mio Ben

JUST WHEN YOU *get to like somebody, out they go .... Just when you need somebody ... just when there's no going back ....* The cold recognition hung on Katalin that evening as she sat on her bedroom floor, playing the family's old zither. Mari squatted in front of her, one hand clutching her yellow blanket, the other probing the zither strings. With the sound of footsteps in the passage, Mari turned.

"An-an," Mari said.

Antal stepped through the door. He had been out tonight, and as he bent to tousle Mari's hair, he told Katalin quietly about his evening. A few had gathered at Ildi's to listen to a black-market record.

"American jazz," he said. "Fitzgerald? I think that's the singer's name. We had to turn it off when the renters came home. Contraband capitalist music and all that."

He straightened up and pulled off his jacket, hooking it on one finger over his shoulder. "I don't know if you want to hear this, but there's somebody Ildi wants to introduce you to."

Katalin snorted. "And does that 'somebody' know I have a daughter?"

"Probably not."

"I'm not exactly free."

"But you're not married, either." Antal glanced in the direction of Róbert's photograph on her corkboard. "How long are you going to wait?"

Her eyes drifted to the calendar on the dresser. The wait had already been long, the fear and grief terrible, but worse than anything was the doubt.

To Antal's question, she could only answer, "I don't know."

* * *

RÓBERT HAD ONCE said that Hungarian musicians were used to mixing fear and beauty. But how they made music while terrified, she could not understand.

Two years ago, in July of 1949, Katalin had been eighteen. On a warm, humid morning after a night of little sleep, she sat on the edge of her bed and waited for the waves in her stomach to level. After a few minutes, she shuffled across the floor and steadied herself against the dresser, eying the letter she had left lying there.

> Dear Katalin Varga,
>
> Congratulations on your excellent performance on the Pest Music Academy's tests of sight reading and musical knowledge. The final step in your application is your voice audition ....

She looked at the little calendar propped next to the letter. The audition was today. Her hand hesitated, then flipped the page back to June. Five weeks since she last saw Róbert. Seven since her last menstruation. She pressed her hand over her lips, closed her eyes, and swallowed hard.

A rap sounded through her bedroom door. "Katalin," her mother called, "are you up?"

"Yes."

"Come, have some breakfast. Ildi will be here soon."

Katalin managed to eat some bread and salami. Maybe it helped, maybe it didn't. When she did vocal warm-ups at the piano with her mother and Ildi, she could hear the pallor in her own voice.

"Don't lag, Katalin!" her mother exhorted.

At the keyboard, Ildi pursed her lips.

Katalin's head hurt.

LATER THAT MORNING in the music academy auditorium, Katalin waited in the curve of the piano while Ildi sat down on the bench and spread out the sheet music. Katalin's mother sat midway back with Antal in the mostly vacant auditorium. In the sixth row, just behind where she had first seen Róbert last March, two men and a woman from the faculty bent, heads together, over some paperwork.

One of the adjudicators, a tall man with a mustache, called to her to begin when she was ready. Katalin wiped her palms on her black dress. Cheeks too warm, she ran her tongue over her dry palate, swallowed, and introduced "*Chanson triste.*" She signaled Ildi and counted through the piano's waltzing introduction.

Her opening was passable. The range of the song was not too high. All right.

Her hands began to loosen. She gestured with the song, spreading her arms to relax her upper body, and when it was time for the high A, not a sustained note, she was not unhappy with the result. From out in the house, her mother smiled and Antal nodded. The faculty members listened attentively. When the song ended, they made notes. Katalin clutched her hands behind her back.

"Continue," the woman said.

Katalin pulled up her ribcage and went on to *"Non so più cosa son cosa faccio"* from *The Marriage of Figaro*. "I don't know anymore what I am, what I'm doing. One moment I'm on fire, the next I'm cold as ice."

Struggling somewhat to keep her breath under her, she sang on: "A desire, a desire I cannot explain …." She closed her eyes and willed the final, slower notes to blossom, but they had sounded fuller on other days. At the close of the piece, she quavered.

No. Maybe the quaver was undetectable. Wasn't it? She smiled at the adjudicators, waited while they whispered and wrote. Then the mustached man waved.

"My final piece," she announced, "is *'Caro mio ben'* by Giuseppe Giordani."

She had sung this song so many times, she reminded herself. It was not considered a difficult piece. Yet she knew how hard it was to sing it well. There was no way to cover flaws in technique or breath control. If only she felt better.

She swallowed and tried to focus. Easy now. Soft power. She listened to the tender piano introduction and took in a strong, quiet breath. *"Caro mio ben,"* she began. On the first note she felt the barest crack, but she sang on. The lovely melody began to rise within her. It spun forth, reached from her, flowed on, as natural and unstopping as the wind, as the full brooks in spring, as a kiss arching into love's passion.

As a kiss ….

As passion ….

Her stomach twisted. She reached for breath but could not catch it. A high note and then another escaped her, choking off in her throat.

The piano notes slowed a little. "Keep going," Ildi whispered.

Out in the seats, her mother and Antal sat forward, expressions startled. The faculty members glanced at one another. The woman was frowning. The mustached man held up his hand. The piano stopped.

The man rose from his seat. "Would you like to begin the song again?" he asked.

Katalin nodded.

She attempted the song twice more but could go no farther than the second line either time. Her eyes filled. Finally she shook her aching head and stepped to the edge of the stage. "I'm sorry," she said hoarsely. "I can't."

Afterward, she walked out of the building with her mother and Antal and

Ildi, and they stood in the scant shade of the entrance's stone archway.

Her mother was blinking back tears. "Katalin, what happened? You've always been able to sing."

"I don't feel well."

"Then let's go back and tell the adjudicators that," her mother pleaded. "Maybe they'll let you schedule another audition."

"It won't do any good. I can't sing."

Antal clasped her forearm. "This is ridiculous! What do you mean, you can't sing? You're an excellent singer. You know it, all of us know it, and I think the adjudicators know it, too."

"Kati, this is your future," Ildi said. "Swallow your pride and go back there and ask for another audition."

Katalin sat down on the stone stoop and lowered her pounding head to her knees. How could anyone sing here, in this city where people were followed and grabbed, and lovers were torn from each other, and the innocent were undone?

"I can't sing," she repeated.

ABOUT A WEEK later she received a letter from the music academy, thanking her for applying but stating that regretfully the school was unable to offer her admission. The letter shook in her hands as she read the *no* that stamped out years of work and hoping. It was signed by the woman adjudicator from her audition. At the bottom, the woman had scrawled, *How can you be a singer if you can't hold yourself together?* Katalin tore the letter up and threw the pieces in the trash. Her music books, which had been lying on her dresser, she threw under her bed.

THE SPINNING IN her stomach had not stopped, and her menstruation had not returned. Now her breasts hurt as well. On a mid-August morning when she was alone in the apartment, she carried one of her father's medical books to the sofa and read about early pregnancy. It would not be impossible to undo this. The act wasn't legal, but her father would know someone who could do it.

She looked at the series of drawings showing fetal development. There was the nine-week diagram, the portrait of the tiny being inside her. Fishlike, froglike, but frighteningly childlike as well, it had huge, other-worldly eyes. She felt such a being could see into its mother's very soul. *The poor thing. The poor, dear thing.*

On the lamp table next to the sofa, a newspaper caught her eye—*Szabad Nép,* which her parents didn't usually bring home. The front-page article was more of the same that had been thrown at the public all summer: scathing denunciations of László Rajk and of those in his following. In the photo of

Rajk, he looked haggard and appallingly older than in last year's news shots. Rajk would be hanged. Or shot. Katalin had no doubt of it.

Oh, God, if only Róbert had never sided with him.

But he hadn't sided loudly, had he? Not beyond a few friends? His friend Gyula was more outspoken, but Róbert himself was reserved. Almost withdrawn at times. Katalin repeated this to herself. Róbert would come home soon. After the Party chiefs had proven their point, they would let an ordinary music student go. They had to. They simply had to.

She used to sing to make herself feel better. She tried to sing now, but the tones shut down in her throat. "God," she whispered, and she crossed herself and buried her face in her hands.

ALTHOUGH IT ONLY made things harder, Katalin found herself returning again and again to the pictures in the medical book. The little balled-up creature was all she had of Róbert. By the middle of August she still had spoken to no one of her pregnancy, had not asked her father to arrange an abortion. She could not do it. Maybe she had looked at the pictures in the book too often to carry out such a thing, just as a farmer who petted and coddled a lamb too often could not slaughter it.

Her family had noticed her moods. Her father asked why she had been so tired lately. Antal told her to start singing again, never mind the wrecked audition, and for God's sake to get out of this *funk* she was in. Her mother coaxed her to the piano to sing, but when she touched Katalin's abdomen for a breath check, Katalin jerked away like a scared rabbit.

It was her grandfather to whom she finally confessed. He walked into the apartment while she was looking at the medical book, and when he asked her kindly if she was ill, she broke down in tears and pointed at the eleventh-week diagram. He sat down and listened as her story tumbled out.

"This is a very hard thing for you to face by yourself," he said to her. "If Róbert were here, your father and I would pay him a visit, and there would be a wedding. But in this case, we can't do that."

"He'll come back."

"Little heart, maybe he can't."

"He will!"

Grandpapa looked at her grievingly and did not reply.

She touched her stomach. "I know the family will be upset and embarrassed. Antal thinks I'm too loyal to Róbert, I know that. And Papa and Anya will want me to get rid of the baby. I don't think I can do it, Grandpapa."

She began to cry again and could not stop.

Her grandfather spoke her name as she wept, took her hand, waited, finally raised his voice and commanded her, "Katalin! Listen to me. Listen.

You're not alone. Even if Róbert doesn't come back, you're not alone. It's true that your parents will be upset by the news. I am. Antal will be. Of course. But don't underestimate us. There is enough love here for you and your baby both. Do you hear me? Katalin!"

He stood up, set his hands on her shoulders and held her until she stopped shaking.

Two nights later, she and her grandfather told the others. Anya, her mother, sat white-faced with her hand over her lips. Papa slumped against the arm of the sofa, eyes shut. Antal swore under his breath. On the mantel of the tile stove, the clock ticked.

Katalin tried to speak firmly. "I think Róbert will come back. I really think he'll be released. This can't go on forever, can it? He'll come back. And we'll get married."

"Oh, my God." Her father rubbed his eyes with the heels of his hands.

Grandpapa was sitting next to Katalin, and she gripped his hand. "Róbert's only a music student," she told them all. "There's no reason for them to keep him very long."

"And what under God's heaven does 'There's no reason' mean?" her mother asked. "When have they ever needed a reason?"

"Are you completely sure you're pregnant?" Papa asked.

Face burning, Katalin described the doings of her body. Her father nodded grimly with each symptom. Her mother bit her lip.

"I love Róbert," Katalin said.

Her father rose and paced to the window, parting the curtains and looking out into the blackness. "And you're waiting for him to get lucky and come back," he said over his shoulder. "People don't get lucky anymore."

"Katalin, you shouldn't be having a baby," Anya said. "You're in no position to be a mother. This is such a mistake."

What was it that the Party had been saying to counter the hopeless drop-off in the birth rate? For a married woman to give birth was duty, but for an unmarried woman to give birth was glory.

"It's ... glory," Katalin mumbled.

Antal, Papa, and Anya stared at her, and Grandpapa shook his head.

"You don't really believe that, do you?" her father asked.

She was trying to believe it.

OVER THE NEXT weeks she endured her mother's sudden tears, her brother's alternating silences and outbursts, her father's stoicism, and her grandfather's pained glances. Her parents tried to speak to her of abortion, but Katalin had taken to walking out on these discussions. In September, when according to the medical book her walnut-sized baby had arms and legs and its own tiny budding of sex, Katalin told herself Róbert would be home in a couple of months. After the László Rajk trial.

The subject of the trial had been blaring nonstop from the radio. At the height of the trial, Rajk himself was given the microphone. Katalin and her family crowded around the radio to listen. In a hollow, impassive voice, Rajk said he was guilty of all the charges brought against him. His motivation, he confessed, had been to enslave Hungary to Yugoslavia and to its reactionary, capitalistic leader, Tito. He himself was an agent of imperialism and a common spy. His accusers were to be congratulated for finding him out and stopping his treasonous plans.

Katalin's pressed her hands over her growing belly. What threats had it taken to break Rajk like this? What privation? What torture? And what was happening to his followers? Oh, God, Róbert didn't do anything! God, Jesus, Mother Mary, he was only a music student.

IN OCTOBER, KATALIN plunked around on the piano a little, now and then toyed with the zither or the guitar, but she did not sing at all. That month László Rajk and two of his codefendants were hanged at night in a prison cellar. Others were locked up for life. Katalin was washing her nylons in the kitchen sink when she heard the radio announcement. She set her palms on the bottom of the porcelain sink and her elbows buckled.

Late that night when she lay in bed, she felt within her a tiny flutter. She waited, felt it again. *Róbert, our child is dancing.* She longed to place his hand over the ripple. But she was alone.

WORD SPREAD. IN December, Grandpapa set the matter straight with acquaintances: yes, Katalin was pregnant, he said, and she would have been married if she had not unfortunately been separated from the baby's father by circumstances neither could control. Hopefully the young man would be able to return. And Katalin would like her privacy respected.

It was about this time that she worked up the courage to stop in at the small music shop her family had frequented for years. The manager, Mr. Boros, was a pianist and had owned the shop before the State appropriated it. Several times Katalin had been in the store with Róbert for piano music.

Mr. Boros, a rather short man with thin hair, smiled at her today from behind the counter.

"Katalin. To what do I owe this pleasure? How may I help you?"

She glanced around the shop, waiting until the single customer walked out. "Róbert ... Zentai," she whispered. "No one has seen him since June. Have you?"

Mr. Boros sucked in his breath and shook his head. "Taken?" he mouthed.

She lowered her chin in a slight nod. "If you find out anything—*anything*—please tell me." She added, knowing she had to get used to saying it, "I'm expecting his child."

He nodded. Perhaps he had already heard.

"Let me give you something." He rummaged among some boxes behind the counter and handed her a snapshot. "This was pinned up on our notice board when Róbert gave his recital."

The picture showed Róbert's handsome face looking up from a piano keyboard. Katalin held the photo in her palm, her fingers slowly closing over the beloved image. That night she pinned it on her corkboard. His music came to her and she began to sing, but with the song came a shaking in her jaw, then in her shoulders, then throughout her being, and she silenced herself.

THE BABY GREW, kicking and tumbling. In February, Katalin's father bought a crib. Her mother ordered a set of diapers, began rather awkwardly to say, "our grandchild," and talked to Katalin about singing to the baby early on. *Ear training*, she called it.

And on the morning of March 20, 1950, Katalin rested her sore, exhausted body against her hospital pillows and gazed at her daughter, the miraculous mingling of flesh and spirit that had grown within her since the slanting of June's sun. The baby's forehead beneath her dark hair was marked red from the fight of birth, but that would fade. The child had Róbert's eyelids and was as lovely as sunlight and music and the touch of love. Smoothing back the cotton swaddling, Katalin let the tiny girl grip her finger.

A small, cat-like cry rose from the baby. Katalin pulled the shapeless hospital gown off her shoulder and nudged the baby to her naked breast. The child squirmed, turning her face, missing the nipple and finding it again. Her little lips pulled. Katalin winced and laughed.

They were so new at this, both of them, but the baby seemed to have found her way.

Katalin named her Mária Jozefa, the second name after her grandfather. When he came to see her during Sunday visiting hours, Grandpapa smiled at the tribute. He looked around the large room, up and down the row of metal-frame beds where other new mothers rested or talked with visitors. In a lowered voice, he asked, "Have you thought about having Mária baptized?"

"Is baptism all right anymore?"

"If you want it done, we'll have it done. It doesn't have to be in our own parish."

Katalin nodded. She understood: her family would not want to be recognized at a church now, jeopardizing her mother's teaching job and perhaps Antal's teaching prospects as well.

And she thought of Róbert, who did not believe in God. But Róbert was not here.

"I want her baptized," she said.

That evening, after Mari had nursed, Katalin held her and hummed to her. The baby opened her mouth in an O that was not quite a yawn. Vocal position. As if the child wanted to sing.

"Caro mio ben," Katalin sang softly. *My dear beloved.* She let the melody go on, singing the child's name instead of the sad words, but when old memories tightened her throat, she finished with humming again.

"There's music in you, Mari," Katalin murmured. "In us. We can't help it."

Two weeks later, Katalin and her family rode the tram to a church across the river in Buda. The church was a lonely, dark place since the war and the communist incoming: the communicants sat sparse in the pews between the broken, boarded-over windows. With the taste of the Eucharist on her tongue, Katalin thought of Róbert and hoped he was not starving. At the baptismal font, the priest touched sacred water to the baby's head in the name of the Father, and of the Son, and of the Holy Spirit. Katalin bowed her head and closed her eyes.

The next month, a sudden stroke killed her grandfather. The family and friends gathered in Kerepesi Cemetery, and with surreptitious glances over shoulders, a quiet blessing was spoken in the name of the Father, Son, and Holy Spirit. Anya sang at the burial. Katalin had wanted to sing with her but could not. She clutched Mari and wept. That night she began what would become a bedtime tradition, showing Mari Grandpapa's photo, then Róbert's.

"Your *apuka,*" she said each night as she touched Róbert's photo, even if the baby was asleep in her arms. "Your *apuka.*"

And now Mari was more than a year old, walking, beginning to speak, fascinated by Antal's violin, unaware of anyone named Róbert Zentai except from one small photo. Katalin still told Mari every night that the handsome young man in the picture was her *apuka,* her daddy, and when he came back, he would love her.

If he came back, he would love her.

If he came back.

Chapter Nine

~~~~~

Loosen Your Jaw and Tighten Your Belly

B y MID-MAY, Péter's days had settled into a dull, lonely pattern: rise early, go to work, eat supper by himself, perhaps weed his courtyard garden, stay out of the way of Irénke *néni* and her children, and go back to bed under the stairs. He didn't like this Lajos he worked with now, the way the fellow drank and hid it and grew surly with the horses, the way he said almost nothing except "yes," "no," and "fuck it."

Péter missed Csaba, missed the way his jokes and his friendliness had made this dismal place more bearable. Someone said Csaba had been put on a night job somewhere, working by himself because his chatter was considered dangerous to worker morale. Péter's own morale had plummeted since the incident. He often thought about the day the Party rep had questioned him. The other workers must have seen him with her, and he wondered, gut searing, if they thought he had snitched on Csaba. He still wondered what had ever happened to Uncle Béla, but after the trouble with Csaba, he was even less inclined to inquire.

Yet in the middle of all this, there fell a shocking stroke of good luck. One Monday, Péter guided Kisbarna into her stall, and in the straw at her feet she pawed up a fifty-forint bill. More than a day's wages. Briefly as a candle's flicker, Péter thought of handing it to the stable hand on duty—but what would the stable hand do with it, this fellow that let the stable stink and didn't even check the horses' hooves? The man would claim it, whether or not it was his, and he'd drink it off. Péter stuffed the bill into his pocket.

Before going home, he practiced his singing in the boiler room's broom closet again. The exercises Katalin had assigned him this week were bigger vocal jumps, and his throat strained at the top. *Loosen your jaw and tighten your belly.* That was what she kept telling him. *You can do this, Péter. Loosen, tighten, and go on.* He hardened his middle as though lifting a hay bale and tried to go slack-jawed. It wasn't easy. But at least he had fifty extra forints in his pocket.

After the singing, he sat down on a wooden crate under a steel light fixture in the boiler room, opened his rucksack, and pulled out the book Katalin had given him. He had been bringing it to work to keep it away from Irénke *néni*'s children. He was determined to read through the lyrics of all forty songs in advance preparation for his voice lessons, because he hated standing in Katalin's stylish flat staring blankly. Today he was on song number six. Péter adjusted his gaze through the lower surface of his glasses and worked through the first pencil-smudged line. Then the second. He blinked, looked up, shut his eyes, opened them and tried again. Third line. Fourth.

The song was about kissing the miller's daughter beside a stream. The word *csókolt*, kissed, kept repeating. This needled him, damn it, because he had never kissed any girl, anywhere. He flipped back through the previous pages, but in song number three, a swineherd boy was playing with his bride under a bush. Well, wouldn't that be something, to have someone to play with under a bush?

And how in God's wrath was he supposed to sing these songs around Katalin?

Giving up, he went back upstairs to the lockers at the end of the lunchroom. He opened his locker for his supper pail, for today at lunch he had bought extra stew and noodles to take home. Someone called his name. The low, bored tone sounded familiar. He turned.

The tall serving girl from the lunch line approached, smoking. She had very straight brown hair that he had never seen uncovered. Until now she had always worn a kerchief and a work apron. He didn't know her name and was surprised that she knew his.

"This is a strange place for a song book," she said.

She lifted her cigarette and leaned forward a little, her blouse gapping open. He could see the undulation of her cleavage. It was fascinating and troublesome, and the girl needed to put her apron back on.

"I hear you're a singer," she half-laughed. "Lajos says you sing to horses."

His gaze fell to the tile floor. "It works."

"It works?"

"I mean it calms them down. The horses. They calm down when I sing."

"So I've had a bad day. Sing something. Calm me down."

Péter shook his head and blushed as her cigarette smoke twirled.

"What's the matter?" she asked. "If you sing for horses, why can't you sing for me?"

"Horses are more polite." He pushed past her and made for the door.

The tram was long in coming. As he waited at the stop, he realized he had left his locker open and his supper pail of noodles and stew there in front of that lunch girl with the cigarette and uncovered flesh. He couldn't get her out of his mind. He didn't like her, but it gave him an excited, sweaty feeling to know that he had fifty extra forints in his pocket and that a girl had told him to calm her down.

AT HOME THAT evening as Péter weeded his courtyard garden, the boy Rudi hovered nearby, throwing dirt clods onto the pavement to watch them burst. Péter glanced up at Comrade Erika and Irénke *néni* on the second-floor walkway. Why didn't they do something about this public nuisance of theirs?

"We're going to have a better house," Rudi bragged to Péter. "An apartment. A real one, not in the cellar. My aunt Erika said so."

Péter stopped the hoe mid-stroke. *Oh, to have this mosquito and his family out of the cellar.* The boy ran off in great buzzing circles around the courtyard, almost knocking into Mrs. Kovács, the old laundry woman.

"Watch where you're going!" Péter shouted.

Mrs. Kovács came and stood at the side of Péter's garden in her housecoat and apron. "Tasty peas," she said, for the plants were bearing now, and he had given her some last week to pay her for washing his clothes. "I hope you'll have plenty for yourself."

She turned her head and spat, and with a bitterness Péter didn't expect, she added, "You'll need it. No one gets paid enough for a chicken to live on, I don't know how a young body like yours doesn't starve."

"Psss," Péter murmured, shushing the old woman, and looked up at the second floor just as Erika looked down.

THE NEXT DAY at work he found his supper pail, emptied and washed, in his locker. Next to it lay a note: "You forgot your supper. I'll give you more today if you want it. I am more polite than a horse. Dóra." Péter threw the note in the trash can.

In the lunch line that day the girl, whose name apparently was Dóra, handed him a bowl of *lecsó,* full of peppers and onions, skimpy on sausage. One corner of her mouth turned up. "Are you going to want to come back for seconds to take home?" she asked. "Since yesterday's didn't make it?"

Remembering what lay under her work apron, remembering the fifty extra forints, Péter felt befuddled, wondering if he was supposed to wink and tell her that *of course* he wanted seconds.

"Move on," someone from behind him shouted.

* * *

HE WENT TO see an opera that night. Katalin had told him, without explaining why, that she did not go to the opera these days, but that he should—it would be good for his education as a singer. Antal, who played in the opera company orchestra, found him a ticket and told him the show was about a beautiful Spanish Gypsy who made her lover so jealous that he killed her. *What a terrible notion.* Péter watched from his seat in a high balcony as the immense curtain opened. There on the stage, Spain had been propped up: arches, fake trees, a fountain without water, an old building front, Spanish soldiers standing around. Then a string of girls filed out of the building, their bodices low and tight. They sidled over to the soldiers, singing and smirking and waving cigarettes. Péter thought of Dóra.

On stage, a chesty black-haired woman in a flaming red dress stepped forward. The chorus girls parted as though for royalty. The woman was too old and thick to really be beautiful—*but, oh, the way she moved.* She sauntered among the soldiers, twiddling one's hair, lifting another's chin. She began to sing, her voice lifting, plunging, and teasing. She draped her arm over the shoulder of a corporal, and the bewitched soldier stared at her. She threw a flower at his feet. The man stooped for it. Péter dug his hands into the armrests. *Look out.*

PÉTER AND HIS father had never spoken of such things—of what women held and men longed for. No, except for that one moment when Péter was eighteen, leaving for his stint in the army. The war was over by then, but all the Hungarian young men had to train anyway. Another big one might be coming up, this time against the American capitalists. Péter and Apa stood on the Kőpatak platform together in the November cold, awaiting the train that would carry Péter off to the military base. The base was not far from Kőpatak, but somehow very far from home.

"Péter." Apa coughed. "Look, I know the army. I've been in it. There'll be some carousing, maybe much. Go easy on drink, and you'll come through better than some men do."

It was not lost on Péter that his father had said *men* and not *boys.*

"And another thing." Apa recited a saying Péter had heard before. "A kiss you pay for is no kiss. Son, don't pay women. It's only bribery, just lonelier. And there's more than one way of paying. Some women take advantage of shy fellows. So look out. Come home when you can."

The stint was to last two years, a term of drilling, shooting, running in the mud in full gear and gas masks, standing in the rain, sitting through political dogma classes, shoveling gravel, hoisting sandbags, bunking in rows, wearing faded second-hand uniforms, eating bad food, going hungry. In the two years, there was one thing to be grateful for: the army issued him glasses. He had never known he was half blind.

Entering his platoon, Péter found that the other boys—or men, if that's what they were now—had come from the same region as he had. They had all grown up with the same yearly rhythm of calving and butchering, sowing and reaping: peas, cherries, apricots, wheat, sunflowers. One of them was from Kőpatak and called Péter "Silent Peti," but here the name didn't stick. Here he was simply Benedek. Some Saturday nights, Péter would scrape together the pocket change that was called his salary and would ride the train home. Other times, when some of his bunkmates headed into town on a Saturday night, Péter joined them, but he remembered his father's words and felt like a bystander.

Two months after the beginning of his hitch, he walked with some others through the snow to a tavern. A soldier named Polcz led a drinking song. Péter and the others joined in. Polcz suddenly stopped, turned, and thrust up his hand.

"What do we sound like when we sing?" he shouted. "Hogs at the trough." Through the falling snow, he pointed at Péter. "What does Benedek sound like? Music. Music! Benedek, why is this the first time we've heard you? You should have been singing for us from the moment we arrived in this shit-hole."

Péter had no words. Was he supposed to apologize? Explain? Thank Polcz?

"I like Benedek," Polcz announced, then moved on to telling a joke about a donkey and a whore.

At the tavern, Péter ordered a shot of plum *pálinka* and sat nursing it as the group joked and pounded the table. On the radio, some impassioned male was crooning. Suddenly Péter felt Polcz nudging him.

"You sing better than that, Benedek," he said.

The others at the table roared. Péter smiled, but he wasn't sure what was so hilarious.

How many drinks had gone down at this table? The group had changed. It had begun as five soldiers but now included only three. And two girls sat among them, one next to Péter. Her arm brushed his. She flashed him a waxy-red smile and said something, but in the buzz here he couldn't make out what.

"Didn't you hear me?" she giggled. "I said you should sing something. They say you're a singer."

"I'm ... I'm a farmer."

"No! That's so ordinary. You should say you're a singer. That's more dashing. Anyway, you don't look like a farmer. You have glasses. You look like you work in a post office."

She smoothed her short blonde hair. Péter couldn't take his eyes off her.

She was young, too young to be drinking with soldiers. Embarrassed and confused, he felt he should tell her.

"I think," he began, "I think this isn't a good place for you."

She frowned a moment, then laughed. "If this isn't a good place, why are you here?"

"I mean ... I don't think ...."

Polcz gave Péter an older-brotherly nod. "It's all right. She can look out for herself. Can't you, Gizi?"

Gizi only laughed.

Polcz winked at Péter, then turned to the girl. "His name's Péter. Do you like him?"

Gizi leaned close to Péter, eying him. He pulled back.

"I like him," she said, "if he likes me."

The others laughed. Polcz slapped the table and flipped his thumb toward the corner, where a warped wooden staircase ascended. "Want to?" he mouthed to Péter. "Go on. Our treat."

Their treat? Péter stared at the old steps, then at Polcz, and his chest tightened.

The radio sang on. Péter felt something touch his thigh. The girl Gizi had let her hand rest there. He looked at her fingers curling on his uniform trousers like soft fishhooks. Now she rested against his shoulder, too. Everything within him throbbed. His forehead sweated, and he was paralyzed by the excruciating pleasure of her touch.

"It's all right," she whispered with her little laugh.

He looked at her face, at her round cheeks covered in that pink powder that women liked.

A kiss that you pay for is no kiss.

But he didn't have to pay for this. Polcz had just said so.

"It's all right," Gizi repeated.

It was all right. The girl had just said so.

He touched one finger to the girl's cheek. The pink powder felt like dust. Barn dust. Even in his own heat and bleariness, it seemed a terrible sham for a girl to cover herself with dust.

"Come," she said, scowling a little. Maybe she was losing patience. Her hand traced warm circles on his thigh. "You're so shy."

Some girls take advantage of shy fellows ...

Damn his father.

So look out ....

Damn his father.

Bribery ... just lonelier ....

Péter shoved the girl's hand away and stood up. The table bumped and teetered. A glass of beer crashed over, drenching the girl's skirt. He reached into his pocket, threw money onto the table for his *pálinka,* and yelled, "Go to the devil!" He didn't even know who he was shouting at, whether the girl or Polcz or the army or this whole bastardly world.

"Benedek!" Polcz shouted. "Fuck it, what's wrong?"

Péter strode across the clay floor puddled with melted snow and jerked open the door.

AFTER THAT, ON the Saturday nights when he didn't go home, Péter usually played cards with the married soldiers. It was lonely, but at least it wasn't lonely bribery. One night over cards, a married soldier told him he was famous. Word had spread with gusto that Benedek of Kőpatak had pitched beer into the face of a whore and thrown over the brothel tables.

"That's a drunken story," Péter said. "I spilled somebody's beer because I was clumsy."

The married soldier just laughed and laid down his winning hand.

FOUR YEARS LATER, here he was, waiting in a lunch line the day after an opera about a sexy Gypsy. He did not look the serving girl named Dóra in the eye as she held out a bowl of soup to him. She spoke his name with a little laugh. He moved away and sat down at a table with a press operator and a few gray-haired women. They ignored him. Péter ate his soup, and by the time he had finished it, he realized that although he didn't really want to say anything to these people or to Dóra, he wished that somebody would say something to *him.* That was the best thing Csaba had done, simply talking to him. Péter was so tired of his shyness, this unwelcome companion that had always come between him and everyone else.

SO MAYBE THERE was a reason he worked an extra hour that day, and when he went to the tram stop, he let two trams go by without him. And finally Katalin walked toward the stop with Mari in her arms. She wore a simple blue dress and a kerchief like the girls of Kőpatak. He wasn't used to her looking so workaday, but he didn't dislike it. Katalin could wear a horse blanket and still look better than the Kőpatak girls. He waved to her.

"Péter!" she called.

They squeezed into the tram together and stepped off again at a corner near home. On this corner stood a cheap diner where he had meant to eat tonight, since he hadn't bought any supper from Dóra. He felt himself in a sudden quandary: since Katalin was with him, wouldn't it be rude not to invite her? But he had been in this diner before and knew it was … well … unwashed. Across the street was a *rathskeller.* He calculated momentarily whether his clothes were clean enough and decided to take his chances. He fingered the fifty forints in his pocket. What else had he been keeping this for, really?

He turned to her and his jaw clenched.

Loosen your jaw and tighten your belly.

"Are you hungry?" he blurted.

She cocked her head as though startled.

"I mean," he gestured toward the *rathskeller,* "do you want to eat with me?"

She hoisted up Mari on her hip and for what seemed like a whole crop season she considered, looking up and down the street, looking at Mari, feeling around inside the big handbag she carried.

"Yes, let's," she said at last.

In the bunker-like brick cellar room, they sat at a corner table. Katalin pulled off her kerchief and settled Mari onto her lap. He watched the soft tuck of Katalin's lips as she kissed the child, the fall of her hair when she bent to read the menu. As they waited for their food, she spoke of his voice lessons, the exercises they would do, the songs they might try. The last evening light filtered through the dust-speckled window above them. When supper arrived, Katalin tore *lángos* into tiny pieces for Mari and let the child feed herself the fried bread. Sometimes Katalin spooned a little of her own soup into her daughter's mouth.

"I'm glad to see her eating regular food," she told Péter. "Every time Mari does a little growing up, I think, 'Oh, good, she's going to be all right.' It's silly of me to worry, I guess."

Péter smiled. On his palm he offered Mari a short string of sauerkraut. The child plucked it up, sucked it a moment, and spit it out. They laughed.

"Where I work, the children don't like sauerkraut, either," Katalin said. "But did I tell you they like to sing? Only four years old, and they're right on pitch! Not difficult songs, of course—but still, that's good, don't you think?"

"Yes!" Péter said, although he didn't know.

She told him she had first been hired at the nursery school because one of her father's patients knew someone there. "After Mari was born I knew I had to work, because her father was … gone. So I wanted to work in a place where Mari would be near me."

Mari grew restless, banged a spoon, dropped a fork onto the floor, stretched toward Péter's beer glass. Péter picked up the fork and moved the beer out of reach. Katalin sighed and pulled an embroidered yellow blanket out of her handbag for Mari. The child held it to her cheek as she sucked her thumb. Katalin signaled Péter with a finger to her lips, and for a long time swayed side to side with the child. Slowly Mari stilled and fell asleep.

"You're very patient," Katalin told Péter quietly. "Are you going to come to our flat for the music on Sunday night?"

"I can't. I'm going home this weekend, and the train gets back late."

"Péter, where's home?"

It was such a simple, natural question, but he had been dodging it ever since he arrived here, keeping silence about the place where his father was said to be sabotaging the economic plan. Yet how long could he go on being nobody, from nowhere? If there was anyone in Budapest he wanted to trust, it was Katalin.

"I'm from Kőpatak," he finally said. "It's a village south of Eger."

"And why did you come here?"

"My family needed me to work here and send money home."

"A farm family, then?"

"Yes."

"So how did you learn to sing so well in Kőpatak?"

He told her of how his mother sang when she sewed or worked in the garden, how he had sung with her as a child, how she had coaxed him into joining the children's choir at the church, and how he had left the choir when his voice changed.

"Did you join an adult choir?" she asked.

"No. My mother was in one, and I went to one of their practices with her, but I didn't go back."

"Oh? Why not?"

She had opened a story he didn't know how to close. "The choir director gave us music on paper," he said, "and I couldn't read it."

"Well, that's not unusual. Many people can't read music. You would have learned the music by listening. I've noticed that you learn really fast that way."

"But ... no ... I couldn't read the words, either."

"When did you get your glasses?"

"Later. In the army."

"Oh. That's probably why you couldn't read back then."

He leaned forward across the table. "How do you know?"

She shrugged. "My father's an eye doctor. But it's no secret. Everybody knows that a child who can't see can't read."

"But now I have glasses and it's still hard for me to read."

He didn't know why he was arguing with her, maybe because he wanted so badly for her to prove herself right. She shifted Mari in her arms and pulled a pencil and scrap of paper out of her bag. She wrote something and pushed the paper across the table to him.

"What does that say?" she asked.

He studied the markings. *Okosabb vagy mint gondolod.* "Well, it says, 'You're smarter than you think.'"

"There. You read it. So."

The waitress approached their table, lifted their plates, and glanced at the note. Péter snatched it away and crammed it into his pocket.

"And after the children's choir?" Katalin asked him. "Did you still sing?"

"Just when no one else was around. In the barn, in the fields."

"But your mother? Didn't you sing with her anymore?"

"No." His breath faltered. He tightened his stomach. "My mother was killed during the war."

"*Jaj*, no," Katalin murmured.

The nearby tables had emptied and their corner of the room had quieted. Péter rested his forearms on the table and would have said nothing more if she had turned away or spoken of something else. But her large brown eyes stayed with him, and she waited.

"My mother was pregnant," he said, although he didn't know why he began there. "November of forty-four. The Germans were in Kőpatak. And we knew the Russians were on the way—the radio was saying it; the next village was saying it. But we didn't know they were so close, right there at the edge of town. We should have been more careful, but we didn't know. And we didn't have enough to eat. We were trying to hide our food from the Germans. And my father, he'd had to leave with the army. He was up near Czechoslovakia, and ...."

Péter's voice suddenly quavered. He had never told this story through before. Even when he'd had to explain it to Apa, he had broken down in horrid chokes and blinding tears, and his grandfather had had to finish it.

"And ...?" Katalin prompted.

"And then the cow went missing, and my mother went out to look for it. And we never saw my mother alive again. She went down by the creek, and the Germans were there, waiting for the Russians, and then ... then one of the neighbors found her later. With a bullet in her back."

Katalin put her hand to her lips.

"My grandfather and I had to go get her," he continued. "My little brothers were only four, and they were so upset, so scared. All they knew of death was when we slaughtered animals, and they couldn't understand why anybody would shoot our mother. And we had to send word to my father." He breathed roughly. "That's what happened."

"Oh, Péter, how awful."

He sat still and waited for the tremor inside him to subside.

"And your father," she asked, "he lived through the war?"

"Yes."

"And has he remarried?"

The tremor again. "No," he said. "There was a time my father wanted to, but ... no." He looked at her, at the way the lamplight touched her cheek. "This is nice of you," he said, "to listen to such an unhappy story."

"We all have our unhappy stories."

Perhaps he was stumbling into that territory that was no one's but her own, but he asked, "And you? I mean, you have a baby and ... no husband, right? I'm not finding fault. I just think it's sad—isn't it?—that there's no husband helping you and Mari."

Katalin was quiet. She rose carefully with the sleeping child in her arms, and one-handed, pulled her chair around the corner of the table. She sat down close to him.

"Péter, there's something I need to tell you. No, two things." She bent her head, and a twirl of dark hair fell along the line of her jaw. "The first is that I'm not really a teacher. Not compared to what a teacher should be. I don't really know what I'm doing, I'm just trying to figure it out as I work with you. I wanted to tell you that because at some time you would have realized it anyway, and I don't want you to think I'm shamming you." She nudged Mari's drooping head into the crook of her arm. "And the other thing ... about Mari's father, Róbert."

She pressed her lips together, paused. "I really loved him. It wasn't a casual thing. I would have married him if I could."

Her eyes swept the restaurant and she spoke in a hush. "But then there was the Rajk trouble and the crackdown, and Róbert was gone and I was pregnant. I haven't seen him since. He's probably in prison. Or maybe dead." She looked at Péter. "I think this is the first time I've actually said it, that he might not be alive."

"God grant that he is," Péter said—trying, for her sake, to mean it. "You haven't given up?"

"Oh, God, no."

"Ah."

"And I suppose I'm telling you all this," she said, "because your respect is important to me."

"I do respect you."

Her eyes lowered to her daughter, and she looked thoughtful, almost reverent, like Mary in the old portraits that the communists had torn down. Péter watched her, and there rose in him a great ache to hold her and never again hear of that other man.

On the way home, he carried Mari with her yellow blanket. Katalin told him the blanket had been one of the few baby gifts she received. It was from the laundress, Mrs. Kovács.

"I heard that she was an unmarried *anyuka* back when she was young, too, so she understands," Katalin said. "Thank you for carrying Mari, Péter."

"Of course."

"She's growing and active, and sometimes I get so tired."

"Of course," he repeated.

She smiled at him. He didn't know what else to say, but for the first time, he felt that it didn't matter. Somehow, he had said enough.

HE AWOKE IN the middle of the night. From the windows above the laundry sink, an unfamiliar glow filtered through the weave of the blanket he used as a door under the stairs. The glow changed and moved. Outside in the courtyard, footsteps. Voices.

Péter sat up and listened. He heard the word *jössz,* come. The light turned. The footsteps faded. Darkness. Silence, except for a rustling among the benches, and then one of Irénke *néni*'s children whimpered.

THE NEXT DAY when Péter came home from work, the boy Rudi was standing in the doorway of Mrs. Kovács' ground-floor apartment.

"This is my house now," he shouted to Péter. "The old lady went away with the police. She was saying bad things. She was a bad citizen."

Péter bolted over to Rudi, and if it weren't for the fact that Irénke *néni* and Comrade Erika were somewhere around here, he would have grabbed the boy by the collar and thrown him across the courtyard. He pulled Rudi's chin upward to look him in the face. Then Péter shoved his hands into his pockets so he wouldn't slug the boy.

"You shut up," Péter whispered. "Just shut up *now.* If you say anything more, even one word, you're a bad citizen."

The boy's eyes widened.

"And stay the hell out of my garden."

Péter tightened his jaw and turned away.

Chapter Ten

⌒⌒⌒

Class Aliens

KATALIN HEARD ABOUT Mrs. Kovács' arrest from her parents, who were sure that Erika Jankovics had called the ÁVH on the old woman to get an apartment for her sister. Papa said it wasn't the first time he had heard of things like this. Katalin found herself spending extra time just holding Mari in the yellow blanket Mrs. Kovács had embroidered. There were things that Katalin did not want to explain to Mari for a long, long time, like the injustice of old women being carried away in the night. Or of music students disappearing. She tried not to dwell on what she had told Péter in the *rathskeller*, that Róbert might not be alive.

Péter. Ever since their talk together, her mind drifted to him more often. When she'd come home that night, her mother had asked her what that peasant boy was expecting. She had told Anya the whole thing was really nothing. But she knew the untruth of it: when someone told you how his mother had died, it was not nothing, and when you told someone that your child's father vanished during the Rajk troubles and might be dead, that was not nothing, either.

It was almost the end of May, and with the long daylight hours, it was harder to put Mari to sleep at night. Katalin ended up extending the bedtime routine—singing a few more children's songs for Mari, clapping rhythm patterns into the child's little hands, holding her close to the corkboard to see Róbert's picture, then Grandpapa's picture, then a newspaper photo from 1945, six years ago. The news photo had been there so long, Katalin wouldn't have noticed it anymore if Mari hadn't taken to pointing at it. The photo had been published in a small newspaper from a town to the north. It showed five teenagers, one of them herself, making music in front of a stone cross in the town's market square.

On a Sunday after the music gathering, Katalin again held Mari in front of the newspaper clipping. "There's your anyuka," she said, pointing out the narrow adolescent singer. "That's me. A long time ago." She touched the image of a dark-haired seventeen-year-old boy playing violin. "Uncle Antal."

Mari grinned and reached toward the picture.

Katalin showed her the Gypsy violinist. "That's Miklós. Your friend Péter met him." Then she pointed out the guitarist. "And our cousin Sándor. And there's the guitar he left."

There was one more person in the photo, a pretty cello player standing next to Antal. Katalin didn't name her to Mari. She was Márta Hanák, the daughter of a journalist hounded by both the fascists and the communists. Márta had fled Hungary with her family a few months after the photo was taken. Katalin had never been exactly sure what the situation was, but she remembered that Antal had taken things very hard. And though in the intervening years he often went with girls to dances or concerts, it seemed he held himself distant, even with Ildi. He had once said that violin performance took all the nerve he had, and there was nothing left over for falling in love. Maybe so, but Katalin understood that sometimes you said things to head off other questions.

Mari was beginning to sag into Katalin's shoulder, so Katalin laid her carefully in the crib and covered her with the yellow blanket. She then joined her family and Ildi in the front room. They had pulled their chairs up close and sat taut-faced as the radio played. Antal beckoned Katalin over, and she sat down among them on the Turkish carpet.

Antal turned to Ildi. "Tell them what you told me."

"There have been deportations." Ildi looked around at each of them and twisted a lock of her hair. "Relocations, as we're supposed to say. You know my family's class *x*."

Tonight there was none of Ildi's usual irony, no roll of the eyes as she spoke the *x* by which the State designated former military officers, businessmen, and intellectuals.

"Something's going on," she said. "My younger brother says two students from his school disappeared this past week. They're class *x*, too."

"*Teenagers* are disappearing?" Katalin asked.

"Whole families," Ildi said. "My parents made some careful inquiries. Class *x* men and women are being moved to the countryside to do farm work. They lose their houses and their property. Their families go too, no questions asked." She knotted her fingers in her lap. "And there's good reason to expect the same thing is going to happen to us."

Antal rested his elbows on his knees and stared at the floor. Anya shut her eyes.

"What is the rationale they're giving for this?" Papa asked.

Everyone sat without answering while the radio played Tchaikovsky. The rationale, Katalin knew, would be something about re-education, something about leveling society, something about leaving the old system of haves and have-nots behind, something about stripping reactionaries of power so the forward march of the people could really begin. She used to try to understand these things, back before Róbert was taken away.

"I don't know what the rationale is," Ildi said. "My father says they just want houses for Party leaders." She paused, breathed roughly. "Maybe he's right—I don't know. But they can do it. So they do."

Katalin and the others asked Ildi more questions, but she had few answers, and after a long while Antal saw her home. Katalin waited up for him. When at eleven thirty he still hadn't returned, she went to bed but couldn't sleep. Finally she got up, went to the kitchen, and drank a little milk. The clock said ten minutes past two when the apartment door opened and Antal walked in.

"What are you doing up so late?" he asked, whispering because of their parents asleep in the main room.

"What were you doing out so late?" she asked in reply.

He beckoned her outside onto the walkway. Under the dim balcony light, Antal's face was haggard. "I was with Ildi," he said. "Kati, I'm going to marry her. On Wednesday."

"You're going to *marry* her?"

"On paper. If she's part of our household, part of a doctor's family, the State will probably leave her alone, let her stay in the city instead of making her leave with her family."

"Wait—"

"So she'll live here. But not in my bedroom. She'd move in with you and Mari. I hope that's all right."

"All right?" Katalin echoed. She clutched her bathrobe around herself in the night chill. "What are you doing? You'll be married, but you won't? And after a while if things blow over and the deportations stop, you'll get a divorce? From the marriage you didn't have? Is that all right with *you?*"

"It's not all right with me for the ÁVH to drag her out of here."

"So she'll be living with us," Katalin went on, "and we'll be calling her your wife, but she isn't really, and she won't be sleeping with you. And what if Comrade Erika comes by and—"

Antal thrust his hands up. "I don't know what then! *Jézus Mária,* this was only dropped on me tonight!"

"Antal—Mother of God!—do you love her?"

"I don't dare! If you love somebody who's been blacklisted, they get jerked away from you. You know that." He turned toward the door. "It's too late to go on standing here. I'm going to bed."

They walked inside together, and at his bedroom door she stopped him with a hand on his arm. "Congratulations anyway," she whispered.

ON TUESDAY WHEN Katalin came home from work, some of Ildi's belongings had arrived: clothes, piano music, some books, and a few framed photographs. In Katalin's room, Antal and Papa had set up bunk beds, with the upper one to be Ildi's. Katalin made space in her dresser and armoire for Ildi's clothes.

On Wednesday afternoon, Katalin left Mari in the care of her co-workers at the nursery school and rode a bus to the office of a notary magistrate, a man her father knew. Her parents, Antal, and Ildi were already there when she arrived. Ildi's family, keeping their heads low, did not come.

The notary had Antal and Ildi sign some forms. Katalin's parents testified that the two were of sound mind and free to marry. The notary then rose, and Antal and Ildi stood together in front of the desk, she wearing a rose pinned to her dress, he a suit and his best tie.

"I, Antal László Varga," the notary prompted.

Antal pulled in a quick breath and took Ildi's hand. "I, Antal László Varga, take you, Ildikó Erzsébet Brauer."

His angular brow weighed down as he pledged Ildi his love and fidelity until death. Lips trembling, Ildi promised him the same. Antal placed on her finger the gold wedding band that had belonged to his grandmother.

"For you," he whispered.

A hesitation, then he slipped his hands around the back of Ildi's neck and kissed her, gently, twice. She rested her head on his shoulder and began quietly crying. This seemed to startle Antal. For one sharp instant, he drew back to look into her face; then he pressed her close, his eyes squeezed shut, and his lips caressed her forehead.

THE FAMILY, ILDI included, was eating supper together that evening when a knock clattered at the apartment door. Antal went to answer it and Katalin held her silverware silent.

"Well, and am I to congratulate you?" Erika Jankovics' voice asked.

"Yes," Antal said, evenly enough. "Would you like to greet my bride?"

"The pianist, I assume. I've met her already. Has she informed the police that she's moved here?"

At the table, Ildi put her face in her hands.

"I'll tell Ildikó to speak with the police," Antal said.

"Good. I will make a note that an additional person is living in the flat."

Comrade Erika's footsteps clicked away. No one spoke. Anya finally rose and poured champagne into glasses.

"Because there was a wedding," she said as she lifted her glass to Antal and Ildi. "Never mind the circumstances."

Later Ildi went out somewhere with Antal. Later still, when Katalin was lying in bed, she heard the two saying good night to each other in the passage and turning separate bedroom doorknobs. A rustling of clothing as Ildi undressed for bed, and then she climbed into the top bunk. It was all so lonely.

As that loneliness weighed on her the next evening, Katalin sat on the Székely rug on her bedroom floor. She spread out the Hungarian map she'd studied so many times and passed a finger over the places she'd marked, the locations of prisons, work camps, and hell-holes. In one of these places Róbert lived. Maybe. Or had died.

No.

The next day during a break at work, she telephoned the office of the music academy, just in case, not for the first time.

"I'm calling to inquire about one of your 1949 graduates," she said, perhaps a little too brightly. "Róbert Zentai. Do you have an address on file for him?"

The office clerk told her to wait. When the clerk returned a few minutes later, her voice was cautious and removed. "I'm sorry, nothing on record since he graduated."

Katalin answered with the same caution, "I see. Thank you."

ILDI AND ANTAL had gone to the notary none too soon. Friday morning before they left for work Ildi's father telephoned. The night before at four a.m. the ÁVH had pounded on the family's door and handed him a note: within twenty-four hours he and his family would be picked up for relocation to the countryside, destination undisclosed. They were to take only what they could carry.

After Katalin finished work that day, she rushed with Mari to the tram, rode to the Brauers' neighborhood and hurried up the walk to the large stone house they were being thrown out of. The front door was ajar. Inside, dishes, pots, phonograph records, silverware, clothes, papers, and suitcases lay on the floor, the tables, and the sofa.

Ildi's mother knelt on the floor, rolling up a rug. "Katalin, take some of these things for your family," she begged. "Or the ÁVH will just make off with them."

Behind Mrs. Brauer, her pale husband stood agonizing over the hundreds of books on the parlor shelves. "What am I to do with these?" he asked. "I can't leave them here. The renters will burn them for fuel."

Katalin took Mari into a bedroom where Antal and Ildi were helping

Ildi's teenage brother sort through his bureau drawers and shelves. With the Brauers, Katalin folded, sorted and packed until Mari was too tired to hold out any longer. When Katalin prepared to leave, Ildi handed her a duffle bag with a comforter in it.

"Give this to Péter Benedek," Ildi said. "For his bed in the basement."

THAT EVENING, KATALIN saw Péter hoeing his courtyard garden and took the duffle bag down to him. In the most neutral terms she could find, she told him where the comforter had come from and that the Brauers were leaving town.

Eyes carefully fixed on his garden as though they were discussing pea vines, Péter asked, "This was required? For them to leave?"

"Yes." She stepped closer. "Ildi lives with us now. She and Antal are … married."

He looked at her. "Married?"

"Yes," she repeated, though she wanted to tell him that it wasn't real—it was only paperwork. It galled her to lie to Péter. She said goodbye and left, telling herself that it would embarrass him anyway to hear about the sleeping arrangements. She climbed the exterior stairs, and at the door of her flat, she looked back over the railing into the courtyard. Péter was watching her, leaning on the hoe. She would have expected him to look away, avoiding her glance, but he did not, and for a few transparent seconds there was something bold in the lift of his eyes to hers, something at once masculine and pained and hopeful. A jolt of clarity nerved through her: he was not just her shy student, he was a lonely young man.

And she had once torn her life in pieces comforting a lonely young man.

Chapter Eleven

The *Tiszta Szoba*

Tʜᴇ sᴇᴄᴏɴᴅ ᴡᴇᴇᴋᴇɴᴅ in June, Péter rode the train home again to Kőpatak. The wheat was high and turning yellow. In a few weeks it would need harvesting, and he would have to ask for time off work to help his father bring in the crop. He would be glad enough to leave the print shop for a while. The truck was up and running again, and Péter didn't like the way Lajos drove it, jerking the brakes and blasting the horn. He hadn't grown used to the girl named Dóra, either, and the way her eyes caught him sideways.

He walked from the Kőpatak train platform toward home with the book from Katalin under his arm. Recent car tracks showed in his stretch of the dirt road. The State had been here. As he passed the neighbors' house, Ági Kozma called to him and trotted to her gate.

Grinning, she gesticulated toward his song book. "Peti! Look at you, back from the city with a book. Such a scholar. Didn't you used to hate school? And your brother does, too. Did you hear about Tibi running away from school?"

Warily Péter stopped. "No, I didn't."

"It's true. The teacher took the children outside, and he just disappeared. Ran off." She leaned toward him over the top of the gate. "By supper time, your father and Gyuri were knocking on doors all over town. Then I found that little devil in our barn. Not that I'd blame him if he left town and kept going. Who wants to stay here? Nothing but cabbages and chicken shit. My boyfriend is on Csepel Island."

Ági crossed her arms as though emphasizing that she now had a boyfriend. The poor girl had been of courting age for years. People used to say a fellow would have to be deaf to fall in love with Ági.

Péter shifted the book to his other arm. Listening to this girl was tiresome, but sometimes he found out more from Ági than from his father.

"My boyfriend's a lathe-turner," she said. "He went to a training school. Did you know there are training schools that give you top pick if your father's a peasant or a proletarian? Finally, you don't have to be rich. Maybe you should try to get into one of those apprenticeships, Peti. Well, no, you're probably not eligible. Your family should have joined the collective. Really, people have told your father that. My father told him to join. Comrade Márton told him. Honestly, we've tried to help your father out, but he is so stubborn! Oh, and your family's laundry is almost ready."

Overhead, the densely humid sky bore down. Péter told her it didn't matter when she brought the laundry, and he left. In the city, he had started washing his own clothes as a small, lonely protest against Comrade Erika's sister receiving Mrs. Kovács' apartment and laundering job.

Péter stepped through the gate of his yard. His grandfather was sitting under the eaves in his rush chair, and a woman with a long, graying braid handed him a cup. It was Mrs. Donáth, an old friend of Péter's mother and the director of the now disbanded children's choir. Her daughter Panni stood nearby with her little girl on her hip. Péter thought of Katalin and Mari. The women waved to Péter.

His grandfather turned toward Péter as he stepped on the porch. "Jancsi," he said.

"I'm Péter, Nagyapa. Not Jancsi. That's Apa."

"Péter's home for a visit," Mrs. Donáth told the old man.

"Well." Nagyapa shifted in his chair with a wince. "How was the army?" he asked Péter.

"I finished that two years ago. Remember?" *Remember* was more a plea than a question. "Now I work in the city."

"Ah."

Mrs. Donáth stepped close to Péter and touched his elbow, turning him aside. "The pain in his hip has been worse this week," she said. "I've been stopping by while your father is out in the fields. We gave your grandfather some willow bark tea. There's more on the stove if you need it for him." She smiled at Péter, her tired face creasing. "And your father told me about your voice lessons. I think that's marvelous."

"So do I," Panni said.

Nagyapa groaned and shifted on his chair. "Damned hip."

Péter had a feeling it wasn't just the damned hip anymore, maybe the damned heart, too, or the damned lungs. With Mrs. Donáth's help, he tucked a folded blanket behind his grandfather's back to help his posture, and he murmured his thanks to the women. Péter told Panni her little girl was cute.

He couldn't remember the last time he had spoken to Panni. She was a couple years older than he was, graceful and pretty, and as he was growing up he'd noticed her silently.

Once the women had left, Péter opened the door into the kitchen. Unwashed pots, dishes, oil rags, a shirt of Tibi's, and a muddy trowel littered the table. His grandfather's nightshirt lay on Apa's bed near the kitchen door. Apa must have traded beds with Nagyapa, taking the old man's mat in the pantry so that Nagyapa could rest his bones on a real bed. Péter could only imagine the fit of pride his grandfather would have thrown because of the switch. And what a mess the house was. Péter felt hot with embarrassment that two women had just been in here. His mother would never have permitted this chaos. She would have set things right.

But that was before the war, with its filth and blood and sorrow.

PÉTER WAS TWO months shy of sixteen when he and his grandfather pulled his mother's body out of the snow, carried her home in the wagon and told the local officers. His father was called home from military duty. Five days after the family buried Péter's mother, a Soviet officer informed the family in broken German that some of his men would be billeted in the house. Arriving shortly.

"Oh, God," Apa groaned after the officer had left. "Is it not enough that my wife is dead? Must the devil's miserable friends now move into my house?"

Péter and Apa and Nagyapa swept through the house, grabbing food and their few valuables, and carried everything to the hiding spot behind the false wall in the root cellar. The last thing Péter and his father salvaged was an old steamer trunk. Into it they jammed Péter's mother's handwork and clothes. Later that day the soldiers moved in—eight Russians and two Ukrainians, if Péter understood right. Some took the beds—the guest bed, almost virgin until now, seemed to be the favorite—and some threw down their own bedrolls, spreading them through the main room, the kitchen, and the cold storage pantry.

Péter and his family moved to the loft until the noise, stink, crowding, and drinking drove them to the barn, and there they lived mainly on what they had stowed in the root cellar behind the false wall. The strangers slaughtered the sow and the few chickens that the Germans had not already taken. The mare Zsuzsi, who had somehow survived her months of servitude with the Germans, was given to another Russian group billeted up the road. Sometimes Péter would see her hauling guns and supplies in wagons requisitioned from other farmers.

Over the winter months, he watched the soldiers. They were not heartless. Loud, yes; testy, yes; drunk, fairly often; lewd, yes, when they were drunk;

but heartless? No, not really. They offered cigarettes to Apa and Nagyapa and Péter and gave the twins extra bread. At times, Apa and one of the Ukrainians communicated a little in broken German. When the Russians came to understand what had happened to Péter's mother, they swore that the shot had come from the German fascists, not from their side. They liked mothers.

And maybe that was all true, Apa would tell Péter and Nagyapa, but they were still enemies. The Russians were sieging the capital and any day now it would fall. And what then? Germany had dragged Hungary into this hell-cauldron, and now Russia would burn them all up and help herself to whatever was left. Péter shivered in the barn and wished his father would shut up.

And as if things weren't bad enough, the daily habits of Péter's heart kept waiting for his mother. When the barn door would creak, he expected her to slip through it, looking for them: "Boys? Jancsi?" When the straw crunched, wouldn't her footstep follow? When the twins cried, he expected her voice, just for a moment—no, for the shadow of a moment—and then he would remember.

That February when the Russians took Buda Castle, the last fascist holdout in the capital, things began loosening in Kőpatak. In March, Zsuzsi wandered home. Péter was overjoyed to have the bony, dirty mare back, though she often bared her teeth now, as if threatened. The next day the soldiers left the village.

Péter and his father and grandfather paced through the barn, the shed, and the house. The spades, hoes, plowshares, and the harness had disappeared. The house's roof had thinned, for great bunches of reeds had been pulled out and burned as fuel. Much of the wood furniture was gone as well. The bedding, the clock, the pots, the dishes, and flatware had all been carried off. Even the curtains were missing.

"Goddamn it, what the devil do they want with our curtains?" Péter asked. He had begun swearing that winter.

Apa opened the door of the main room. The ornamental bed lay stripped. The straw mattress was so badly matted and crushed, there was nothing left to do but burn it. The floor throbbed with ants surrounding spilled gruel, curdled milk, and blood and bones from a chicken that had met its end here. The corner near the clay oven stank of piss. Apa ordered Péter to fetch some water and carbolic.

But Péter did not. He bolted past Nagyapa, out the door, past the gate, down the road, not stopping until he fell panting and sobbing at the edge of the stream where his mother had died.

That spring the family tried to make do without her. They patched the roof and kept Tibi and Gyuri within sight. Péter woke with Apa when the twins cried in the night. A few times, in sleepy confusion, Péter had first called to his mother to sing to the boys and comfort them—but no, he began to sing to them himself. And gradually the sad adjustment happened inside him: he quit thinking he saw her out of the corner of his eye and quit listening for her voice. She was gone. He was growing used to it, he told himself. He thought Apa was growing used to it, too, until one night, Péter overheard him talking to Nagyapa on the porch.

"I still miss Margit every hour of every day," Apa was saying. "I hate seeing Péter work so hard, I hate having the twins grow up with no mother, and I hate being a man without his woman. This is no life."

"I know, son," Nagyapa answered.

Across the room, Tibi groaned in his trundle bed and called Péter's name. Péter stepped across the darkness. Squatting beside the boy's bed, Péter whispered to Tibi that things would be all right.

But maybe they wouldn't.

SIX YEARS LATER, he still wasn't sure.

After supper, Péter and his father helped Nagyapa into his nightshirt and into bed. Nagyapa protested that this was not his bed, and where was his mat? Apa reminded him that they had traded. The old man sighed but rested quietly.

Péter lit the kerosene lamp that hung above the good table in the main room. On the table, he spread open the music book from Katalin. Of the forty songs in the book, he had now made his way through thirty-three. He polished his glasses on his shirttail and tried to focus on song number thirty-four. Tibi wandered over and stood next to him, peering curiously at the pages. Péter thought of Ági's story about Tibi's run from the schoolyard, and he turned back to an earlier page.

"You've seen music pages before?" Péter asked Tibi.

"Yes."

Péter pointed at the song title. "Can you tell what this says?"

Tibi shrugged, but when Péter ran his finger under the title and waited, the boy's lips began to move silently, and then he spoke: *"A jó ... lovas ... katonának."*

Gyuri and Apa were watching from the bench of the clay oven. Gyuri came over now and peered at the book.

"You got it right," Péter told Tibi. He showed him the first line of words under what Katalin called a staff. "Can you read this?"

"Gyuri can."

"But I asked you."

Tibi leaned close, pulled back, turned his head, scooted the book and began speaking the words slowly. After the first line, Péter coaxed him on to the second and onward. It was tedious work, and repeatedly Péter had to stop Gyuri from blurting out the words for Tibi. Péter took off his glasses and handed them to Tibi. The boy hooted when he put them on, but at Péter's insistence he worked his way through six lines. Apa joined them at the table.

"Keep going," Péter urged Tibi.

"I don't want to. Let Gyuri do it. He's smarter."

"No, you can read it."

Tibi pointed at the faint lines where Katalin had erased the scribblings of the children in the cellar. "What are these marks? Who did this?"

"Read some more first," Péter said.

"Sing me the song."

Nagyapa spoke up suddenly from the bed by the main room door. "Yes. Sing."

Péter sighed and shook his head. "Some other time."

AFTER THE TWINS had gone to bed, Péter went out to the porch, set the lantern on the work table, and sat down on a stool. His father joined him, taking Nagyapa's rush chair. The night had cooled and a cricket chirped. Apa lit a cigarette.

"Ági Kozma told me about Tibi running away from school," Péter said.

"Yes, and I told him no matter how much he hates school he still has to go. But I don't know what good school is doing him, with all the time they waste on political blather."

"I think Tibi needs glasses. You heard him try to read."

"He can read. Not as good as Gyuri, but—"

"None of us read as good as Gyuri! A whole houseful of people, and the only one who isn't scared of words on paper is Gyuri."

From somewhere up the road, a car engine droned. Two headlights shone, growing as they approached. A State car braked in front of the gate. The motor stilled. The headlights flicked off. Péter looked sidelong at his father, who was sitting bone-rigid. Two car doors swung open.

"Bring that lantern over here!" a familiar voice shouted from the car.

"My God," Apa breathed.

Péter and his father walked out the gate to the car, Apa carrying the lantern. In its glow Támas Márton and the police chief opened the back doors of the car.

"Out," the chief ordered.

A fleshy, balding man in a rumpled business jacket bent through the left door and stood. On the right, a tall gray-haired woman climbed out, clutching a shopping bag crammed full. They looked around as though lost, like the war refugees Péter had seen in photographs. The chief opened the car trunk.

"Here now," Márton shouted to Péter, "there's work to do."

Péter lugged two suitcases toward the house while his father carried two baskets and a box. Behind them, Márton and the officer prodded the disoriented couple along.

At the house door Apa stopped and turned to Tamás Márton. "I would like to know what is going on."

"Open the door, Jancsi," Márton said.

"I asked you what is going on."

At the sound of Apa's strident tone, Péter's fingers dug into the suitcase handles.

"We've brought Ottó and Bori Zöld," Márton said. "Class x. Removed from Budapest. They'll work on the collective farm. Here in time for harvest."

"And why are these unlucky people and their suitcases here at my house?"

The unshaven chief waved impatiently. "There is more room in your house than your five people need. Four people, now that your son here is usually in the city. State standards."

"If this is a hardship, Jancsi," Márton said, "remember that you ignored advice to join the collective. These two will live with you." He turned to the haggard man named Zöld. "Comrade Kozma next door can show you where to report for work Monday morning."

"And as you know from the trip here," the chief told the city couple, "four other class x families arrived today. You are not to associate with any of them."

Márton and the chief turned and walked back across the dark yard. The car doors creaked and slammed, and the car sped off.

Mr. Zöld rubbed his forehead. "Well, this is a predicament."

Apa looked in the direction of the car's disappearance. "They like predicaments."

"Your names?" the woman asked, gravely polite.

"Jancsi Benedek. And my son Péter."

The city people nodded.

Apa led the couple inside. The woman in her hose and pumps stepped carefully onto the dirt floor of the kitchen. Péter followed with the suitcases, trying to think where these people could sleep. Next to Tibi's trundler, in the old guest bed, which was missing both sheets and a mattress?

Standing in the kitchen, Péter heard Apa tell Nagyapa to stay in bed. "No! Don't try to get up. It's visitors. I'll explain in the morning. Lie back down."

The barefoot twins padded out to the kitchen in their nightshirts, blinking and staring.

"I'm sorry about the mess," Péter said to the Zölds. "And there's not much privacy—"

"Please." The man raised his hand. "We'll manage. This is a great inconvenience to you."

Wearily, they all decided to work out the permanent arrangements the next day, but for tonight the newcomers would sleep on the guest bed. The twins would join Apa in the pantry, and Péter, as usual, would throw down his mat in the entryway of the kitchen. Péter and the twins carried in straw for a makeshift mattress.

"I should have thought to bring sheets," Mrs. Zöld said. She opened a suitcase and spread dresses and shirts over the straw.

In the middle of the night Péter wakened on his mat as the woman stepped past him to go outside—probably to use the privy, which would be impossible to find in the dark. She would have to skip it and just pee in the yard. Péter wished he or Apa had thought to give these poor exiles a chamber pot.

THE NEXT MORNING, Péter rose early to milk the cow and feed the chickens and pigs. The sow had born nine piglets in April, and in other years a large litter had always been a good sign for the winter: lard for the kitchen, meat for the table, bacon and sausage for the smokehouse, and some of everything for market. But now Péter wondered how many of the pigs his father would be forced to sell without profit. And there were two more mouths to feed here. If these city people were going to work on the collective, they probably wouldn't be paid until after harvest, and even then they were likely to receive no better than soldier's pay.

It was still early, the day cool and dewy, when he saw Mr. Zöld make his way to the privy in his wool trousers and city shoes. After that, the man walked around, taking in the barn, the shed, the fruit trees, and the well. Finally he came over to Péter.

"I wonder if you might show my wife and me how to help with the gardening," he said. "Or something else if you'd rather, but we ought to help in some way. It's quite an imposition on your family, us being here."

Péter thought of the manuring that had not been finished in the garden, but he couldn't ask this soft, tired man to do it. The work on the commune was going to flatten him.

"My brothers are supposed to look after the garden," Péter said.

"I see."

Péter felt for these people, so regretful of their own uselessness here. He said, "If you really don't mind, you could help with the cooking. My grandfather has done it ever since my mother died, but he's too old now."

The man gave a polite nod. "Thank you. We will see to that."

A little later Péter found the man in the kitchen squatting in front of the wood stove, the grate open. His wife stood at his side. Nagyapa leaned on his cane and watched them.

"We'll have this lit in a minute," the woman said. "I'm sorry, we're used to a gas stove. We had a wood stove once. But you see, back then we had a servant."

At breakfast the coffee was weak. Péter suspected that the stove had not been hot enough. Instead of eating in the kitchen, they all sat down together at the corner table in the main room. Everyone passed around the bread, *pálinka,* and raw, smoked bacon that was the usual breakfast. Mr. and Mrs. Zöld raised the *pálinka* to their lips once, but after that their shot glasses sat untouched on the table. In the lagging conversation, Apa told the man and woman that Péter worked in Budapest during the week. The twins watched the newcomers as though they were stray animals that had been let into the house. Tibi whispered something to Apa.

"My son wants to know if you have children," Apa said to the Zölds.

The man nodded once. "We have two sons. One is married, and he's in Buda. The younger one is nineteen and he … he is in a military camp."

The wife set down her bread and pressed her hand over her eyes. She rose suddenly and hurried out of the room.

"Please excuse us," the man said, and followed her out.

Nagyapa watched them leave. "Why are those people here?"

Mute, Apa traced his thumb over the side of his shot glass.

"Well, why?" Tibi asked, and Gyuri eyed Apa as well.

Apa mumbled, "It's the damned—"

Péter kicked his father's ankle under the table. Apa glared at him. He glared back.

Péter turned to Gyuri, Tibi, and Nagyapa, and spat out the only words that he knew would be safe: "The man and the woman are here for the good of the people."

AFTER BREAKFAST THE Zölds walked into town. While they were gone, Péter, his brothers, and his father tried to turn the *tiszta szoba* into something like a bedroom for them, although Nagyapa would have to stay there, too. The family moved Tibi's mattress and Gyuri's into the now-crowded pantry. Gyuri swept the dirt floor. Tibi polished the windows with vinegar. Péter and Apa carried out tools to the shed and burned old papers, and at the foot of the now scratched and dented ornamental bed, they uncovered something almost forgotten: the steamer trunk that Apa had saved in the cellar and brought out again after the war.

"It's a treasure chest!" Tibi said.

"What's in it?" Gyuri asked.

Péter shushed the twins. Apa knelt beside the trunk. Nagyapa stood with his whittled cane and they all looked on as Apa raised the lid in silence.

Red. Sudden blue. Green, alive and joyous. Memory jarred Péter: his mother wore color. Here atop the trunk's contents lay a red kerchief, a grass-green dress, a skirt blue as the August sky. Péter's eyes suddenly stung.

Nagyapa limped closer and looked into the trunk. "Margit's clothes."

"Who's Margit?" Tibi asked.

"Oh, God, Tibi," Péter cried, "don't you know? Margit was our mother!"

In a small, slow movement, Gyuri folded his hands in front of him. Apa bent his head over the trunk. Péter reached into it. His hand rested on the unfinished pink lace, still on the crocheting hook, that had been his mother's last evening project. She used to sing, voice lilting, as her hook pulled at the thread. Péter swallowed hard and lifted away the lace and then a blouse underneath it, exposing a cream-white quilt embroidered with red and blue stitching. The quilt used to lie on the bed his parents had shared. Apa, catching sight of it, turned aside with his face in his hands.

"Apa?" Gyuri asked.

Péter whispered to the boys that Apa was just sad. Things would be all right, he told them, fighting back the ache in his throat. The twins tiptoed out with Nagyapa.

Péter knelt beside his father. Apa laid his hand on the folded bed quilt. Péter did not speak, for he had not forgotten the night sound of his parents' hushed laughter and rustlings under the quilt. Péter waited with his father until together they closed the trunk's lid.

BEFORE PÉTER LEFT Kőpatak that day, he rode Zsuzsi to the stream. He looked across the water to the field that was his family's now, and beyond to the higher, better land that had once been theirs. The wheat in both fields rippled with the wind, but Péter, in an old loyalty, thought the upper reaches more beautiful. He slid off Zsuzsi's back and led her down the bank to drink. Glancing upstream to the willows, he lifted his right hand in the sign of the cross.

He touched the rough strands of Zsuzsi's mane and began to sing one of his mother's songs. He could not finish it. But Zsuzsi turned to him and bobbed her head.

"I still miss her, Zsuzsi."

The horse blinked.

Péter waited, listening to the wind and the water, and when the song stirred in him again, he did not hold back.

WHEN HE LEFT the house that day to return to the city, a gaggle of neighbors stood clustered in the road. They broke their circled stance as he opened the gate. Péter glanced at each one, but his gaze settled on Ági Kozma.

He crossed his arms. "What's the matter?"

She shuffled a little and turned to her father.

The man's eyes were lined pink, as they so often were after a Saturday night's drinking. "We heard that a class enemy and his wife are staying with you," he said.

"The people are polite," Péter said, and he pushed past the neighbors and strode off toward the train station. But he knew what this meant: if it was at all uncertain before, the village now had no doubt that his family was on the wrong side.

Chapter Twelve

~~~~~~~

Intermezzo

IT HAD BEEN a couple of weeks now since Ildi had moved in. Katalin felt for her, the way she lived as an awkward attachment to the family, hanging about after supper and playing piano until the neighbors pounded on the walls, then sitting up waiting for Antal to come home from orchestra performances. Ildi stayed out of his bedroom. Now and then Katalin saw the two of them hugging each other tentatively, as though the terms of their arrangement hadn't quite been worked out.

Katalin was more aware than she wanted to be of the sharp words between those two. It seemed to distress Ildi when Antal came home late—which he frequently did, because of his job. Katalin had heard him impatiently telling her that there was nothing he could do about it. Recently they'd been arguing about whose turn it was to practice in the flat. On a Tuesday evening, Katalin was in the kitchen with Mari when she overheard them squabbling again, Antal telling Ildi he was tired of going to the cellar, "performing for Péter," as he put it.

"Well, *I* can't practice down there," she retorted, "and I can't go home to my own piano. I can't go home at all."

Ildi walked out of the apartment. Katalin went to the front room where Antal sat on the piano bench, tightening his violin bow with quick jerking twists.

"So you won, did you?" she said.

He set his violin upright on his knee. "Did anyone ask you to butt in?"

"Can't you be nicer to her?" Katalin glanced at the neighboring wall and dropped her voice to a whisper. "How do you think she feels, pretending to be married to you and sleeping in a bunk in my room?"

Antal stood up, his hand choking the violin neck. "That's my business and hers. No one else's."

"Well, here's something you'd better know. Other people are *making* it their business. Today the woman next door told me Erika Jankovics was asking if you two have consummated your marriage. So I lied, and I said of course you have, and what a ridiculous question."

"And the neighbors are supposed to be reporting on what goes on in my *bedroom?*"

"You're surprised?"

"I'm not surprised, I'm sick."

"I don't like it either, but honestly, Antal—"

"Is it too much to ask that I be left alone on this?"

He grabbed his bow, and when she didn't leave, he emphatically changed the subject. "In my hours playing in the cellar, I've been getting to know your student's musical tastes. He likes the intermezzo from *Cavalleria Rusticana*. Maybe you should teach him the *Ave* that goes with it." Antal lowered his voice. "If you can risk a religious song."

Throughout the evening and in stray moments the next day she thought about her brother's suggestion. She loved the *Intermezzo*. It would certainly be work for Péter, and maybe it was too much. But maybe not. And it wasn't as if things were going perfectly, anyway. Last week when she had tried to explain what it meant to interpret a song—"Breathe with it, feel it"—he had said that all he felt was tired. Might as well try something else.

WHEN PÉTER CAME for his voice lesson on Thursday, he brought her the last of the pea crop from his courtyard garden. He inquired how the newlyweds were doing and then asked carefully if Ildi's family had gone to a farm village somewhere. Katalin nodded. He asked if by chance there had been word from Mari's father. She said no, and it dampened her spirits.

She was teaching Péter harmony. Last week in the lesson she had made him hold out *do* while she sang *mi* and then *sol*. Tonight she had him sing *fa* and *la* while she sang *do*. She then took Péter through extensive vocal exercises, encouraging him to sing two notes higher than he ever had before. His chin trembled and his throat strained.

"Relax your throat and give more effort below," she urged him, touching her belly. "And try to picture the sound rolling around up here." She patted her cheekbones.

"I don't understand," he said irritably. "Why are you making me sing this high?"

"If you work on these high notes, the ones under it will be stronger, too. I want to give you some harder music. You can do it if you work up to it. Let's try it again. No screeching. Shoulders and face loose. But really firm through your middle."

She sang *la* as a starting pitch for another minor arpeggio while she set her right hand on his hard, flat stomach, her left hand on his back. At his lessons she had been touching him to check his posture and breathing. Péter never seemed to mind. In fact, he usually smiled.

They'd been working on an old song from the Hungarian uprising against Vienna. It was within his best range, the lines fairly short and not strictly rhythmic. They used no accompaniment for the song, and she urged him to sing it freely. He nodded as though he understood, but he stood stiff as he sang, hands at his side, eyes on the tile stove, the notes of the song measured and careful.

"Relax with the song," she told him. "It will be beautiful in your voice if you just *let* it be. Quit locking your knees. Try it again."

He began again, voice tight again.

"Move around while you sing it," she said.

He sang a line. Took a step. Sang another line, which stuck in his throat.

"Stop." She rose from the piano bench and grabbed his hand. "Follow me, and *sing*."

Startled, he gripped her hand.

She led him pacing around the room in the slow meter of the song, and he sang in the rhythm of their steps: *"Duna, vized miért olyan keserü?"* Danube, why are your waters so bitter?

"Let's keep going," she told him.

His grip eased as they walked. *"Árkod miért van tele?"* Why is your river bed full?

Yes. She could hear the song opening in him.

"Good," she said. "You've got the idea. Now do it without me leading."

She had meant for him to go on without her, but he did not drop her hand. Instead he moved in front of her, tugging her along with gentle insistence. Together they walked the song's current and Péter's voice rose, strong like the pulse of the river, warm like dawn edging up into the night sky.

THE NEXT DAY after work, Katalin stopped into Mr. Boros' music shop with Mari. On the shop phonograph, a Mozart symphony played, making Mari bounce in Katalin's arms. Mr. Boros greeted them with his deep-creased smile and pushed aside a clutter of sheet music on the counter. Katalin asked if he had a mid-range male vocal arrangement of the *Ave Maria* that was set to Mascagni's Intermezzo.

"What are you doing singing mid-range male?" he teased.

"It's for a student of mine."

"You're teaching?"

"Just one student."

"Still, that's good."

He climbed a step stool to a high shelf behind him and handed down a music folio. "It's an old edition," he said.

Katalin was just glad it was available at all. She read through it at the counter and paid for the music.

"You have a pretty little girl there," Mr. Boros said.

"Thank you. She does this bouncing and swaying whenever she hears music. A musician," Katalin added quietly, "like her father."

She stood aside as a customer approached and bought clarinet reeds. They waited until the man had left.

"Katalin," Mr. Boros said, "have you ever had any word from Róbert?"

"No. Never."

Another customer approached the counter, and Mr. Boros switched to talking about the Mascagni piece. Though Katalin did, too, it was the *never* that stayed with her.

However irritated Antal might have been on Tuesday night, by Wednesday he was offering Ildi the piano. On Thursday night, he took her out for a drink before his performance at the opera house. Very early Saturday morning, Antal and Ildi left together for the weekend. Ildi's family had been lodged with some peasants in a small settlement in the lonely eastern reaches of the plain. To travel there, Ildi and Antal would have to spend most of the weekend riding the train, waiting at transfer platforms, and buying rides from farmers with hay wagons.

With Ildi away, the piano became more available. Saturday night Katalin played through the Mascagni music and hummed along with it, writing in a few adjustments so Péter could sing it. When her mother realized what Katalin was doing, she sat down on the piano bench to help her. Together they devised a new ending. Instead of climbing to a high, sustained and very difficult final note, it hushed to an *amen* one octave lower, comfortably within Péter's range. Katalin supposed there had been times when Anya had changed music for other students, but she couldn't remember Anya ever revising musical scores for her.

The next afternoon, Sunday, was warm and languid. Katalin left Mari napping with Anya and went to the cellar to show Péter the new song. She stood on the rough landing inside the cellar door. Daylight shone through the iron-barred window above the laundry sink onto the brick-walled space below, where a man's laundry hung from a plumbing pipe. Péter sat on a bench, bare-chested—a beautiful chest, she couldn't help noticing. He held a book.

Seeing her, he snapped the book shut and jumped to his feet. "Katalin."

"Oh … excuse me … I'm sorry," she stammered.

"No, no, come in, just a minute."

He dropped the book onto the bench, yanked the laundry off the plumbing pipe, and threw it into his space under the stairs—all except for a chambray shirt, which he put on, hastily fastening the buttons. Flustered, Katalin almost told him she had seen men shirtless before, but she shut herself up and stepped down the wooden stairs.

She now saw that his book was one she had read as a school girl, a story about an American Indian named Winnetou. "You're reading a Karl May book, I see," she said.

"Yes, I found it in a back corner down here with some other books. I'm not good at reading—you already know that. I'm trying to get better."

"You must be making progress. Last time I talked to you, you were working on the lyrics in the song book."

"I finished with that." He pointed at the Winnetou book. "I like that story, but it's taking so long to read. I'm not good at it."

"Quit saying that, Péter. Lord, you work so hard." She sat down on the bench, pushed aside the book and patted the space beside her. "I've brought you some new music. It's a piece you've heard Antal playing."

He sat down beside her and she opened the folio. "It's religious," she said, realizing that she was cautioning him. "The words are Latin. '*Ave Maria, gratia plena* ….'"

"*Dominus tecum*," Péter continued.

"You know the prayer, then?" She lowered her voice on the word *prayer*.

"Yes. From school. Church. When I was little." Péter, too, was almost whispering.

Outside the window, which sat at ground-level in the courtyard, a woman's feet passed by. Thick ankles, gray felt slippers: Comrade Erika. Katalin kept silent and waited to see if the door would open. It did not.

"Listen," she told Péter, "when you practice the song at work—in your janitor closet, that's where you practice, yes?—don't sing the words, all right? Not yet. Just the pitches. Around certain people, you're not singing 'Ave Maria,' understand? You're singing the intermezzo from *Cavalleria Rusticana*. By Mascagni."

Péter looked up at the arched brick ceiling. "Mascagni."

"Yes. The intermezzo from *Cavalleria Rusticana*."

He shook his head and shrugged with an impatience she wasn't used to. "And what is an intermezzo?"

"It's music that's played between acts in an opera. Classical. So remember—hold the vowels. Nice, long, smooth notes. Think of Antal's bow. Do you want the sheet music? Or shall I keep it for your lesson?"

"Keep it. I can't read Latin. I can't read music. It's hard enough just to read Hungarian. Sing me the song. Let me hear it."

Of course, she had known she would have to sing it. How else could she teach him the song? But these days she rarely sang anything harder than children's songs. Her face muscles felt suddenly rigid.

"Please?" Péter asked.

Katalin coughed and began singing, not very loud, and felt the notes wobbling. She needed to gain control of her nerves and support the tone. She tightened her stomach like she'd been telling Péter to do and loosened her jaw. The music's sweetness filled her mouth. *Oh, just to taste a song.*

"Pain and pleasure," Róbert had said.

She kept singing.

"Never," Mr. Boros had said.

She caught her breath and sang on.

How can you sing when you can't hold yourself together?

She tightened her arms around her middle and kept singing. Breathy. The closing faltered, buckled, faded. Weak. She looked at the floor.

"Beautiful," Péter he said softly.

"But it wasn't strong enough."

"I didn't notice."

She sighed. "The ending is different than what Antal plays. Did you hear that? My mother and I rewrote it a little, so that you can—"

"So that I can sing it. Yes. Could I hear it again?"

She stood up, a little shakily, and began the song again, a half-step lower. He walked to the stair rail and leaned on it as he listened. When she finished, he asked her to sing it again, and then a third time and a fourth. Sometimes he closed his eyes. Sometimes he watched her face, sometimes the floor.

"Thank you," he said at the end.

"Forgive my choking up," she said, "and my mistakes."

"Mistakes?" He spread his hands, scowling. "What you just did—the way you just sang—you call that choking up? Mistakes?"

Katalin clasped the music folio to her chest. "My voice closes up on high notes. I can't sustain long ones. I'm very out of practice."

"Katalin …." He shook his head. "When you sang that song just now, or when I hear you singing to Mari, even when you just show me how to sing *do-mi-sol*, it's … oh God, I don't even know how to say it! I don't like it that you keep on saying you're weak, you're choking up, and la la la. That's like a rose saying, 'I'm just an old thorn bush.' "

"You're kind, Péter," she said.

"It's not kindness, it's true. Don't you know what you have?"

A silence throbbed. The furrows in Péter's brow eased, his expression gentling as he looked at her. It had been so long since someone looked at her softly like that. She stepped toward him. His hand rose and his fingers opened, and she remembered how they had reached to each other at his lesson and paced the music's current. She lifted her hand, and her fingertips met the callused surface of his.

And what compelled her, she did not know, but she drew close and touched her lips to his cheek. She sensed the fine scratch of a few unleveled whiskers, the hardness of his jawbone: the feel of a man. Inside her something hurt. She stepped back.

From above, she heard a click. A hinge squeaked. The door at the top of the stairs cracked ajar.

"Katalin?" her mother called out, "are you down there?"

Katalin dropped her hand to her side. "Yes," she called back.

"You have a phone call."

Katalin turned to Péter. His eyes searched hers. She climbed the stairs. At the top, she looked back over her shoulder to where he stood next to the stair rail, eyes upturned to her.

"Goodbye," she whispered.

IN THE APARTMENT, she picked up the telephone receiver.

"Katalin, something has come up," Mr. Boros' voice said. "Today I was opening some mail that had accumulated, and there was an order for piano music." He paused. "From Róbert Zentai."

She could not speak. She turned her back to the family in the front room and carried the telephone into the kitchen as far as the cord would reach.

"Are you there?" Mr. Boros asked.

"Yes."

"Róbert sent a postal money order for some Chopin music," Mr. Boros said.

Her hand sweated on the receiver. She placed her other hand over her lips and the mouthpiece. "Are you sure it's him?"

"It's him. I have his address here. Do you want it?"

"Yes." She reached for a pen, dropped it, picked it up again, and grabbed the nearest slip of paper, a grocery receipt. As Mr. Boros dictated, she wrote down the address: Gold Harvest Farm, Mezősárgás, Heves County.

"I've never heard of that town," she said.

"Neither have I."

"And why …." She took a breath and started over. "Does he say why he's there?"

"No."

"Or how long he's been there?"

"No."

"When was the letter sent?"

"A week and a half ago." Mr. Boros sounded apologetic. "It's just a music order, Katalin. But I thought you would want to know."

"Yes. Thank you. My God."

After she hung up, she carried the slip of paper to her bedroom, where Mari was asleep in the crib. Katalin lay down on her bed and stared at the underside of Ildi's bunk.

Róbert was alive. He was here in Hungary. He had asked for piano music. He was alive, she repeated to herself. Thank God. He was alive and free.

And he had not come to see her. He had not phoned. He had not written.

Every possibility rose in her mind: he had only recently been released. Or it wasn't safe for him to send a letter to Budapest. No, that wasn't it—he had already written to Budapest for piano music. Maybe he didn't know her address, her phone number. He had never actually entered her building or telephoned her before he left, before he was taken.

But maybe he *had* written to her, and maybe some mailroom snitch had intercepted the letter and handed it to the ÁVH. *Oh, Holy Mother of God, please ....*

She looked again at the address on the paper. A farm. She couldn't imagine him living anywhere but the city, at least not willingly. Why was Róbert on a farm? She pictured him bent among the crops, sweating and sore and sunburned, his long piano fingers scratched and bleeding.

Piano. He had ordered piano music. She didn't think of farm villages as possessing pianos, but there were so many things she didn't understand.

Katalin glanced across at her sleeping daughter. Noiselessly, she rose and pulled the map of Hungary out of her dresser drawer. She spread it open on the floor, atop the old Székely rug. Running a trembling finger over the markings and town names in Heves County, she at last found Mezősárgás. It was southwest of the city of Eger.

In the crib, Mari squirmed. Katalin waited, still and silent, hoping the little girl would go back to sleep, but Mari began to cry. So Katalin rose and lifted her, kissing her warm head, shushing her gently, whispering over and over that Anyuka was here, Anyuka was here, soothing the poor child whose *apuka* was gone.

THAT EVENING DURING the Sunday music gathering, Katalin stayed in her bedroom until well after she heard the music start. Then, tiptoeing, she went into the front room and stood against the far wall. She could see the back of Péter's shoulders and his curly hair. Just this afternoon she had kissed his cheek, and oh, the way he had looked at her as she said goodbye from the stairs. Now his head turned, and his eyes lifted and caught hers. Troubled, she threw him a quick, tight smile and looked away; then she slipped off into the back bedroom again.

ANTAL AND ILDI didn't arrive back in the city until Monday morning, and Katalin didn't see them until that evening. In their bunks, Katalin and Ildi talked across the darkness. Ildi told her about the trip east to see her family: "They're so far out of the way, the State might as well have sent them to a TB sanatorium," she said. "They're living with a peasant family, and there's hardly any room. My brother hates the place, and my mother doesn't like the farm wife, and my father can't keep up with the work. Antal spent five hours bailing hay for him."

The upper bunk creaked as Ildi turned over. "Kati, I don't know what I'd do without Antal. We have our quarrels, but for someone with only a *pro forma* marriage, he's a very good husband."

A *pro forma* husband. Katalin didn't even have that. She had a baby and a distant, silent lover. She ached to tell Ildi that Róbert was alive. But Ildi would tell Antal. And Antal would ask the question Katalin kept wanting to turn aside, which was, why this news had come from Mr. Boros instead of from Róbert himself. She blinked back tears.

THE WEEK WENT on and she told no one what Mr. Boros had said. Thursday night, after everyone else in the flat was asleep, she rose from her bed and carried a flashlight, a pen, and stationery into the passage. She sat on the floor and started a letter.

> Dearest Róbert,
>   I love you and

And what? He needed to be told about Mari. She drafted the letter five times, crossing out whole paragraphs and crumpling pages, until in exhaustion she decided this was not a message for paper. She had to tell Róbert face to face. He had to see his beautiful daughter.

> Dearest Róbert,
>   After two years of missing you, I found out this week that you are in Mezősárgás. I thank God you are alive. I love you and want so badly to see you. Also, there is something I have to tell you. Please, could we meet? Tell me where and when and I will come. Please write me back

or telephone me as soon as you can.
With all my love,

Your Katalin

At the end of the letter, she wrote her address and phone number. She read back over what she had written and still felt unsatisfied, but the next morning she mailed the letter. He had to answer. So much depended on it.

Chapter Thirteen

Careful, Brother

Péter had never lived alone before moving to Budapest. On long evenings now, just to get out of the cellar, he walked or ran along the Danube embankment, passing the tugs on the quay and the geranium bed shaped like a hammer and sickle. Most evenings, he scraped a hoe through his courtyard garden. The year was at the zenith, the sun lingering late over the roofline of the apartment building, the earth warm where he bent to throw aside a stray upstart of crabgrass or chickweed. From time to time, the boy named Rudi still dogged him in the courtyard, bragging and blatting about the huge melons he would grow if that garden were his, but Péter found he could drive the boy off by simply raising an eyebrow and saying, "Why don't you shut up now, citizen." As for the garden, Péter tried not to let it bother him too much that the residents had begun pulling up radishes and making off with lettuce leaves. He had known that would happen.

As he gardened, he would often shoot an upward glance at the second-floor balcony, and with an inner longing, remembered Katalin's kiss to his cheek. She was keeping more distance now. At his last voice lesson she had spoken little, only saying enough to correct his mistakes and teach him the "Ave Maria" music. His disappointment was sharp, and he felt no better when he asked himself what he as a peasant's son could really expect.

When it grew too dark to work, Péter would retreat to the cellar, and under one of the hanging lights he would try to read the book about the Indian, or he'd leaf through some other books he had found in the cellar. One dealt with animal husbandry, although why such a book was here in the city, he had no guess.

The solitude of these evenings or Sundays was occasionally broken by

Antal coming to the cellar to practice violin. Péter would sit down on the bottom stair and stretch back to listen, resting his elbows on a step behind him. Antal's bow danced over the strings until the very air sang.

Sometimes, between pieces, Antal and Péter would talk a little. One Sunday afternoon Antal told him about waiting out the siege down here in the cellar, trying to stay out of the line of fire. Péter said the line of fire had been terrible back in his village, too.

When Antal took up the bow again, the music circled mournfully in the cellar's brick arch. Péter listened, remembering the purpled mangling of his mother's flesh where the bullet had ripped through. He shut his eyes and saw his father, who remained alone while other widowers remarried. Péter saw the lost field back home. He felt again the searing touch of Katalin's lips on his cheek, and against his will he thought of that other man, that ghost named Róbert who still seemed to shadow her. It was all there, in the music.

THE NEXT MORNING, the work day began as usual with a meeting in the lunch room. The Party rep yammered about a Russian worker who had produced seven times his quota. Péter had heard this story at least twice before, and his gaze wandered to the lunch girl named Dóra. That tended to happen at these meetings when he was bored. Lajos the drinker was sitting next to her, absently tapping one finger on the table in front of him. The man looked pale, and he had missed work twice last week.

Péter had been dreading asking for time off for the harvest, but during the mid-morning break that day he finally broached the subject with Mr. Molnár, asking for the first week of July. The man looked at a big wall calendar and gave his permission but repeated emphatically *July*, not June. The quota cycle, Péter knew.

He returned to the loading dock before Lajos came back from his break. Péter positioned the ramp board for loading the truck bed. Today's boxes of pages were smaller than usual, so he hoisted one and walked it up the ramp. Relieved to have the conversation with Molnár behind him, he began to sing a little.

"Show-off."

In all his life, Péter had never been accused of showing off. He turned. At the bottom of the ramp stood Lajos, his cigarette stump sticking out from under his mustache.

"Who do you think you're singing to?" Lajos muttered. "The horses aren't around."

"I wasn't singing to anybody. I was just singing."

Lajos squatted to lift a box, but the box teetered and toppled onto its side. Péter ran down the ramp, righted the box, carried it up the ramp, and rearranged the weight of the boxes in the truck. When he turned around again, Lajos was gone. This kept happening lately. Péter loaded boxes on his own until Lajos wandered back, sometime later.

"Come on, hurry up!" Péter shouted.

Lajos frowned.

Once all the freight was loaded, they drove the truck to the warehouse. Péter sat in the passenger seat and did not speak, and he certainly did not sing. God, he wished Csaba were still here instead of Lajos.

At the end of the work day, Péter watched to make sure Lajos had left. Then he went down to the boiler room, shut himself into the broom closet, and told himself that he was not a show-off. Lajos and his flask could go to the devil, who would be waiting. Still, Péter hesitated before beginning his scales, and he hesitated even longer before beginning his new song, this classical one that Katalin kept saying needed the vowels held.

THE NEXT DAY Lajos was absent. Again.

A temporary replacement turned up, the plant's white-haired janitor. The man couldn't have been younger than sixty-five. Though he was tall, one shoulder hung lower than the other, making him appear to lean to the left. Whatever was wrong with his back, lifting freight certainly wasn't going to help.

Péter and the janitor positioned themselves at either end of a box. "I don't want you to hurt yourself," Péter said.

"Well, it won't be the first time," the man said. A slight dimple formed at one corner of his creased mouth as though he were joking.

"I can take most of the weight if you just help keep the boxes balanced," Péter said.

The man nodded. "I thank you."

He said his name was Ernö Gárdonyi. They shuffled between the press and the truck with the boxes, Péter tipping the weight toward himself. The boxes of pages were to be driven to the bindery, Gárdonyi said between loads; he added that he usually was not permitted to drive, but today an exception had been made. He did not explain. After several loads, Gárdonyi was sweating and breathing hard. He lifted his hand in apology and went to stand in the thin line of shade next to the building. Péter called it a break and joined him.

"Very nice singing," Gárdonyi said as he rubbed his lower shoulder.

"What?"

"I've enjoyed your singing downstairs."

"You mean you can hear it?"

"You mean you didn't think anyone could?"

"But I only sing when the press is running."

As though in answer, Gárdonyi sang a line of the *Ave Maria*.

Péter's stomach clenched and he pushed furiously through his memory: had he really let loose with a holy song in this screeching, unholy place? Had he sung the words? This janitor who couldn't stand up straight, who probably owned nothing but the supper in his pail—what if he was a snitch? People said they were everywhere, those who told on neighbors and co-workers for a few more forints, a little more bread.

"Beautiful song, yes?" he rushed to say to Gárdonyi. Damn, what was it that Katalin called this music? "It's from an opera, eh …."

"Mascagni's Cavalleria Rusticana."

Péter felt himself buckling in relief, but he didn't know whether he should.

He almost skipped practicing at the end of that day, but the habit was so strong by now. He went downstairs, shut himself in the broom closet and sang his warm-ups at low volume. Overhead, the press roared. He did not sing Mascagni's "Ave Maria," not even on *da da da* as Katalin had said. He sang what he could remember from his previous lessons. The music smoldered within him—a small, watched ember that he could not allow to ignite.

During a lull in the press noise, he broke off singing and stepped out of the closet. Near the boiler with a mop stood that lunch girl who was careless about her blouse buttons. Today her work apron covered the little point of flesh that sometimes showed.

"You didn't sing very loud," she said.

"Some people don't like it."

"Some people don't like anything." The girl snickered. "But horses do. They're more polite. Isn't that what you said?"

Slow footsteps sounded on the stairs, and Ernö Gárdonyi walked in. "Here now, Dóra," he said, "are you bothering this young man?"

"I didn't mean to," she mumbled. She left with her mop, sidestepping between the sawhorses.

Gárdonyi waited until she was gone. "Forgive her. Sometimes she speaks before she thinks. But don't we all? Thank you for your help today. Perhaps we will work together again tomorrow, but I hope Lajos will be back."

Péter looked at the man's tilted face, his concerned brow. For all that the bastard Lajos didn't deserve it, it seemed Gárdonyi genuinely wished him well.

"Do you *like* Lajos?" Péter asked.

"I knew him when he was a less frightened man."

Overhead, the press banged into action again. Gárdonyi touched Péter's sleeve. He smelled like other old men Péter knew, probably having trouble with his teeth. "You are Béla Matai's nephew, yes?" he said.

Péter did not speak, only hoped desperately that this man was harmless.

"Béla told me he had invited a nephew Péter here," Gárdonyi said. "You look a little like him, I think. But maybe I'm imagining? Not related?"

"Do you know where he is?"

"He *is* your uncle, then." Gárdonyi's eyes traveled the room, the stairs. "No, I don't know. You don't, either?"

Péter shook his head.

"Listen. Your uncle worked here for years before the State took the company over. The old owner depended heavily on him. Treated him well, I hear. Béla was very loyal to the old owner. I suspect that was his only crime. But I think we'd best not speak of this again, for your sake more than mine. The boiler room is my domain, if it may be said that I have any in this world, and you are welcome to sing here whenever you like. Just know that people hear you more than you think. Be careful. You have a powerful voice."

"Holy Christ," Péter muttered.

"Indeed." Gárdonyi lifted his right thumb and two fingers toward Péter. "Don't stop singing, brother. We need good voices. There are so many evil ones."

Péter couldn't remember anyone calling him brother before; not even his brothers. The Hungarian fascists used to call each other brother. Wait, there was once a priest in Kőpatak who had called the men brothers and the women sisters. Who was this lopsided man, strangely strong in his mildness? As Gárdonyi plodded clumsily away, Péter watched him and felt a crazy rise of hope.

AFTER HE LEFT the print shop that day, Péter walked to his uncle's old district and asked around until he found the police station. The officer behind the front desk asked for his identification. Péter handed it over, then stood clenching and unclenching his fingers until the man gave it back and asked what he wanted.

"Eh … comrade … my uncle is … he is not at home. Not for three months. I want to find out where he is."

Péter gave him his uncle's name and old address and the officer disappeared into a back room.

After a long time, the man returned. "Relocated for corrective measures," he said brusquely. "Location undisclosed." He turned to the queue at the counter. "Next," he called out.

Péter walked to the tram stop and kept his gaze on the street ahead of him, away from all the oncoming faces. It was what you did when you had shown your ID with your name and your face on it and then you asked for a man who had been relocated for corrective measures.

ON SATURDAY PÉTER caught the train to Kőpatak again because there was much to do before the wheat harvest. He was growing very tired of these trips. It would help if Apa thanked him now and then.

When he arrived home late Saturday afternoon, he noted changes around the house. The porch showed the markings of two more people here taking up space: Mr. Zöld's trilby hat hung from a peg outside the door and Mrs. Zöld's dark-blue cardigan, newly washed, lay spread on the work table to dry. In the *tiszta szoba*, the ornamental bed had been covered with a tan blanket Péter didn't recognize. Folded up in the pantry were the mats and bedding that Apa and the twins used in that room now.

He found Apa in the little grove of five apricot trees behind the barn. This year's fruit was still green but abundant and growing heavy, and Péter helped his father prop up the branches with poles so they wouldn't break under the weight. They were still working and the sun was dropping a few hours later when the Zölds came home from the collective tomato fields. The two carried their hoes on their shoulders like the peasants here, but the angle was awkward. Apa said they came home every evening like defeated soldiers, with their steps dragging. Péter ran to the well, lowered the lever arm, and raised the bucket for them so they could drink and wash. They were sunburned in spite of the old straw hats they wore, and Péter winced as they splashed their faces.

Supper that night was late, with Nagyapa propped up in the bed near the door. Sitting beside him, Apa handed him berries, tore bread into small pieces for him, and lifted a shot glass of *pálinka* to his lips for the hip pain. After supper, Péter helped his grandfather into his nightshirt. He knew that the Zölds were wanting their bed in the opposite corner.

"Péter," Nagyapa said sleepily as he turned his head on the pillow, "when are you going to sing for us?"

"Another time, Nagyapa."

LATER PÉTER SAT with his father under the eaves as Apa carved a flour scoop in the light of the kerosene lantern. The street windows glowed at the Kozmas' house next door. There was a light wind tonight.

"Your grandfather's back and forth, good, bad," Apa said. "Next week he'll be better if he'll just stay off his bad leg for a while. He'll have to. I've asked Mrs. Donáth to look in on him during harvest. I can't be with him then, and neither can the twins—I need them out there with me. You too, more than anybody. When are you coming home?"

"A week from Monday."

"Monday?" Apa asked. "Why don't you come Sunday?"

This week at the print shop Péter would be lifting for two—unless Lajos came back, damn him. Then Péter would put in a long day on Saturday the thirtieth as well, since it was the end of the month. To get on the train again the very next day was more than he could stand.

"I can't," he said.

"Why not?"

"I just can't."

Apa pursed his lips.

"I tried to find out more about Uncle Béla this week," Péter said, and he told his father about the janitor's words and the trip to the police station.

"A man works and works," Apa muttered, "and look what happens. Corrective measures."

The gate next door banged, then the Benedeks' gate.

"Uncle!" Ági Kozma's voice shouted across the dark to Apa, calling him by the polite address of a younger person to an older one. "Peti! I'm going to get married!"

She ran toward them, the lantern lighting her billowing skirt. Apa rose, as he always did in the presence of women, whether or not he liked them or their fathers. Péter pulled himself to his feet.

"Well, aren't you going to say something?" she teased.

"Congratulations, Ági," Péter said.

"*Gratulálok,*" Apa said.

Ági grinned, lifting her heavy hair off her neck in the warm evening, as she talked about her apprentice lathe-turner on Csepel Island. "We don't know for sure when we can get married. We have to find a place to live, and what is there to find? Right now he lives in one of those men's dormitories. I can't live there." She burst out laughing. "So Dani's going to make a housing request, and I'm going to tell Comrade Márton, see if maybe he knows somebody on Csepel Island or if he knows somebody who knows somebody. You know how it is. But everything is so crowded, isn't it? On Csepel, everybody's crammed together like pickles in a jar. But out here it's bad too, with class aliens moving in."

Péter's shoulders stiffened. Apa stood still with the pocket knife dangling in his fingers.

"I mean, I'm sorry for you," she went on. "It must be horrible to have capitalists living with you, maybe even stealing from you. I couldn't take that. Oh, and do you know, I saw Tibi up in an apricot tree yesterday, wobbling the branches up and down like some huge wind was blowing them, and he yelled out, '*Sej,* Ági! Look, it's a storm.' Such a funny boy."

From the direction of town came the whirr of a car engine. The car pulled up at the gate, the lights flicked off, and the engine cut. Péter set his hands on his hips and his fingers bore into the fabric of his trousers.

Tamás Márton crossed the yard with an unlit flashlight and stopped just in front of them, his face pale in the glow of the kerosene lamp. He brushed across his cheek and the mole under his eye.

"Good evening," he said.

"*Jó estét*," Péter answered.

Ági Kozma straightened up as though at attention. "*Jó estét*, Comrade Márton."

Apa gave a short nod. "Márton," he acknowledged.

"Good news, Comrade Márton," Ági blurted out. "I'm engaged."

Márton smiled at her. "Well, Ági."

"My fiancé's a dedicated worker," she said, "and he's applied for Party membership."

"Yes, nice, good." Márton stepped onto the earthen porch.

"And we'll be making a request for a Csepel flat," Ági went on, "and we'd be grateful—honored—if you ... if you could pass our request along, maybe speak to someone—"

Márton raised his hand, stopping her, and turned to Apa. "Zöld and his wife have been staying within the confines of their relocation?"

Apa frowned. "Probably. I don't watch them."

"And you, Benedek. When will you be harvesting?"

Apa fixed his eyes on Márton's face. The night wind gusted.

"When will you harvest?" Márton repeated.

"When the wheat is ripe," Apa said. The pocket knife hung open in his hand.

"Close that thing," Márton commanded.

Apa looked at him, snapped the blade shut, and dropped the knife into his pocket.

"I asked you *when* you are going to harvest," Márton said.

"The same time as you, I suppose, unless your crop is late."

Péter touched one fingertip to his father's hand in warning. What was the point in this refusal? The whole village would see them harvesting.

Márton waited. The silence stretched on.

"When?" Márton repeated.

Apa stood with his arms crossed.

In the dense night, Péter looked at his father again and finally told Márton, "First week of July."

Apa's head jerked toward him.

"I'll inform the tax assessors," Márton said. "I hope you don't come up short like last year."

"I gave you what I had last year," Apa said, "and I don't want to discuss this in front of a neighbor."

Márton turned to Ági. "Leave."

Ági blinked wide eyes.

"You heard me," Márton said.

She ran away across the yard and out the gate.

"All right, she's gone now," Márton said to Apa. "You may say what you will."

"I have nothing more to say."

Márton walked back toward the car. Halfway there, he blinked the flashlight. A car door opened, and out stepped the tall police chief, then the deputy. The flashlight's ray circled and swung, and in the changing shadows it seemed that Márton had handed the flashlight to the chief. The light traveled again, shining onto the porch and into their faces, moving over the house, then the shed, then the sty and the chicken coop. The men padded across the dirt, grass and weeds toward the barn, circling it once, twice. Péter held his breath, knowing the men were passing the root cellar.

The light turned again as the men advanced toward the car. Its doors opened, the flashlight went out, and the doors slammed. The car's headlights came up. The engine ground. Péter watched the taillights disappear around a bend in the road.

Apa walked into the house with the lantern. Péter leaned against an eaves post and closed his eyes. His head hurt at the temples. The wind blew dark.

BEFORE HE LEFT Kőpatak the next day, Péter packed strawberries and eggs into a straw-lined bag to pay Katalin. Then he went into the pantry and scanned the shelves of jars and bottles. He found apricot *pálinka* they had made from their own fruit last year, and plum and cherry *pálinka* they had bought or traded for. Péter lifted a bottle of plum and one of apricot and dusted them with his sleeve. Behind him the door opened.

"What are you doing?" Apa asked. It was the first time Apa had spoken to him all day.

Péter held out the two bottles. "I think you'd better give these to Tamás Márton. To get him off our arses."

"Two bottles of liquor aren't going to do that."

"They might at least improve his mood. Do you want more of these little night visits? Did you see where that flashlight went?"

The creases of Apa's face hardened. "I've already given those snakes more than they'll ever deserve." He turned away.

On his way to the train platform, Péter stopped at the gate of the old kulak house where the collective farm was now headquartered. He called to a child chasing chickens and asked her to get Comrade Márton. The girl ran inside the house, and a few minutes later Tamás Márton stepped onto the porch, his colorless hair uncombed.

Péter gripped the bottles and thrust them toward Márton. "For you," he said, "from my father."

It was raining hard and blowing as his train pulled into the city. When Péter stepped off the tram near the opera house, the rain still pelted and water ran in the streets. He was soaked by the time he stepped into the apartment house foyer. He paused to wipe rain off his glasses.

"Péter." It was Antal who had spoken. He stood under the light fixture with his hair matted in wet hanks and his shirt clinging to his shoulders. "You didn't see Ildi, did you?" he asked.

"No. Why?"

"She went over to Buda to visit a friend. I expected her back two hours ago." Antal's eyes shifted uneasily to the door of Erika's apartment. "It isn't like Ildi to just … disappear."

Because of all the significance of the word *disappear* in this terrified city, Péter pulled off his rucksack and waited with Antal. Time went by. They walked out in the rain to the tram stop to look for Ildi but did not see her. It was Antal's third trip out.

Returning to the foyer, they sat down on the stairs and waited again in silence.

At last they heard a click at the front door. Antal jumped up and jerked it open. There stood Ildi, dripping and startled.

Antal pulled her in by the elbow. "Thank God! Where were you?"

"The electricity went out in Buda and the tram wasn't running," she said, shaking water from her hair.

"*Istenem*, Ildi, you scared me to death! I thought you were … in trouble …."

The hand in her hair stilled. "The telephones were out, too, or I would have called," she said softly.

Péter rose from the stair and left. He'd gone all the way through the courtyard and halfway down the cellar stairs when he realized he'd left his rucksack behind. He went back across the courtyard and opened the foyer door.

There under the dim lamp Antal and Ildi stood kissing, their rain-drenched bodies pressed tightly together. With the sound of the door they jumped apart and turned.

"No, no, excuse me, carry on," Péter mumbled.

He grabbed his rucksack and hurried out, the door banging shut behind him.

In his cellar corner under the stairs, a spread of moisture showed on the earth floor. Péter pulled the miserable heap of linens he called his bed farther off from the outside wall. He stripped off his wet clothes and tried to dry himself with the old towel he kept here, but by now he was damp to the bone, and cold. He lay down and shivered under the comforter.

Loneliness flooded him. He was a wanderer. He had pulled up stakes in Kőpatak but had nothing in Budapest. In Kőpatak he had fought with his father. He had no mother. And here …. If only there were someone to look for him, to want him and to warm him when it rained, someone to draw him into her own good heat, and with her lips and heart and body bring him peace. There were comforts only a woman could give, and he had none of them.

Chapter Fourteen

～～～

Caro Mio Ben, Reprise

IT WAS MONDAY, the day after a night of thunder and rain. Thunder always sounded like war to Katalin, and the pounding had wakened her and Mari through the night. In a blurred muddling of dream or half-wakefulness, Katalin had heard Ildi come in. And leave again, Katalin thought, but she didn't really know. In the morning Ildi's bed was made and she was gone. Katalin dressed herself, dressed her cranky daughter, and left for work. A bag of strawberries and eggs padded in straw had been set outside her door— from Péter, she supposed, and that was nice. The rest of the day was hard. The children at the daycare bickered, and one of the little boys wet his trousers.

Now Katalin stood in line at the butcher's, doing the family's shopping on her way home. Mari pouted in her arms. Once at the front of the line, Katalin asked the butcher if there was any chicken. The butcher in his blood-smeared apron shook his head.

"Beef?"

The man snickered as though she had asked for a Western car. "Kidney," he said.

Katalin hated kidney. "What else is left?"

"You should have come sooner."

She had heard this line before; it was the way the butchers and grocers and bakers and druggists spoke of shortages in this country where shortages were not to be spoken of. Katalin handed over her meat ration coupon for the kidney she didn't want, and after the butcher had wrapped it, she trudged down the street to the bakery. It was closed. Mari leaned toward the ground, wanting down. Katalin put her down; she wanted up.

"Enough of this, Mari."

She hoisted the child up and lugged her toward home. As they neared the apartment house, Katalin's back tensed up. Her neck, too. Inside the foyer she glanced toward Comrade Erika's door. It was shut. Good. Katalin stepped close to her family's mailbox and peered through the slot. Mari began to cry. Katalin anchored her more firmly on her hip, thrust her key into the mailbox door, and opened it with a twist. Inside were three white envelopes. Please, oh, please, one had to be from Róbert. She grasped the envelopes, fanned them out. Two for her father. One for her mother. And that was all.

"Na-ma," Mari wept.

"Mari, we'll be with your nagymama in a minute."

Katalin tried to stuff the letters into her bag but only dropped them onto the dirty tile below. She squatted to gather them. A door creaked on its hinges and footsteps clicked across the floor.

"Would you please hurry up and take her upstairs," a voice ordered. "Nobody wants to listen to a bastard brat scream."

Katalin lifted her eyes to Erika Jankovics, with that gray frizzing hair of hers and those eternal frown lines. Shoving the letters into her bag, Katalin choked back the fury that arose in her. She grabbed her overwrought daughter, pushed past Erika, and hurried into the courtyard.

Péter was out spading in his garden patch, his sleeves rolled up over his arms like a figure on a communist work poster. "Katalin?" he called.

"Thank you for the strawberries and eggs!" she shouted and ran up the back stairs. Guilt ripped through her. Except at his voice lessons, she had been avoiding this good soul ever since that day she had kissed him, the day Mr. Boros had telephoned and her world had convulsed.

"Pé-tó," Mari said, squirming to look over Katalin's shoulder.

When Katalin entered the flat, she found her parents, Antal, and Ildi in her bedroom. The mattress had been taken off Ildi's bunk, and Antal and Papa were carefully lifting the upper bedframe, disconnecting it from Katalin's. Ildi was pulling her lingerie out of a bureau drawer. She looked up and smiled at Katalin, and her cheeks colored.

"I'm moving in with Antal," she said. "We're married."

"That's right." Antal threw Katalin a grin then turned back to lowering his end of the bunk.

Katalin stood, open-mouthed.

"Step aside, Kati," Papa said.

He and Antal tipped the frame on its side and carried it down the passage. Katalin's mother took Mari into her arms and followed. Katalin turned to Ildi, who stood holding the folded lingerie.

"Married?" Katalin whispered.

Ildi nodded, her hand over her lips as though suppressing a giggle or a secret.

"So, last night?" Katalin asked. "It's real, then?"

"Oh, *very* real."

Katalin whooped, laughed, hugged Ildi hard, and laughed again. For in this world where over and over things went terribly wrong, last night during the rain and the thunder something had gone very right.

It was a relief that these two were sharing a bedroom now: the family could quit worrying about Comrade Erika nosing around. Over the next few evenings while Antal was at orchestra performances, Katalin helped Ildi fit out Antal's small bedroom. They pushed her bed and his bed together and spread a comforter over both. On the dresser they propped a photo of her family and set a vase of flowers Ildi had bought at the market. Ildi said she wished she and Antal could have some moments to themselves. Katalin told Papa Ildi's request. On Wednesday night, Antal didn't have to work, so the family left the apartment for two hours to give the couple a little privacy. When the family returned, Antal and Ildi were sitting on the sofa in their bathrobes, Ildi quiet in the shelter of Antal's arm. Her happy, married peace was suddenly more than Katalin could bear. She still had received no word from Róbert. It had been about two weeks since she had written to him, which maybe wasn't all that long, except when she wondered why Róbert didn't write to her long ago.

Later she reasoned that maybe she should write to him again. Wednesday night, she opened her box of stationery and lifted out the top sheet, but when she reached for a pen, something stopped her. Suddenly she was shoving the stationery back in her desk drawer and slamming the drawer shut.

The big calendar at the nursery school, like many Hungarian calendars, showed name days. The tradition of name days, she assumed, had begun by honoring saints on their feast day, but now each Hungarian name was assigned a day of the year, and small gifts and drinks were given to people bearing that name. When Katalin looked at the nursery calendar on Thursday, she realized the next day, June 29, would be the Péter day. She wondered if anyone had acknowledged the day for Péter Benedek.

After his voice lesson that evening, she invited him to stay and toast his day. Surprised, he thanked her several times. She poured pear schnapps into glasses, filled a bottle with milk for Mari, and the three of them drank together on the tiny balcony in front. Sometimes Péter squatted down beside Mari and let her investigate his hair and his glasses. At odd moments, she would point at him and say, "Pétó." The first time he answered, "Yes, good!" After that he would point back at her and say, "Mari," and it became a game.

He told Katalin he wouldn't be able to come to his voice lesson next Thursday. "I'll be in Kőpatak for the wheat harvest," he explained. "I leave Monday."

"Harvest. I've heard songs about how beautiful it is. Is it true?"

"In good years, yes, in spite of the work. In hard years, no."

"And which is this?"

"We'll see." Péter finished the schnapps and rested his hand on the iron railing. She thought he sighed. "Most years, I've spent all of July and part of August reaping, threshing, and clearing the land for another crop. Not just for our family. For others, too. But now, with my job here ... I can't be gone much more than a week."

She asked him about Kőpatak, and he spoke of the sweep wells and the fruit trees. When she asked him more, he told her how potatoes grew, and how bacon was cured, and how foals were born feet-first. There was so much she had never known. She thought of Róbert on that communal farm, and she almost asked Péter if he knew anything about that place. But she could not bring herself to raise the question. He might ask why she wanted to know.

The lowering sun burnished the outer strands of his hair. Next Thursday the evening would feel empty without him. Too empty.

THERE WAS GOING to be a party. In about two weeks the family would host a dinner at a restaurant to celebrate Antal and Ildi's marriage, and they were all to act as if it had been the real thing all along. Katalin's mother explained this to her on Friday evening, as they sat at the table with chicory coffee.

"Oh, and Ildi wants you to sing at the party," Anya added. "She wrote some Hungarian love lyrics for *Caro Mio Ben*."

"*That* song?"

"Yes." Anya looked at her pointedly and rose. A moment later, she laid the familiar music book on the table in front of Katalin and opened it to the song. New lyrics had been penciled in. Mari toddled over, and Katalin lifted the child onto her lap. She kept reading, whispering Ildi's new words of surrendered love. She would have whispered to Mari, "I can't do this," but something told her that if Mari heard "I can't" many more times, the girl would be saying it all her life.

Katalin joined her mother at the piano. Anya played the introduction and Katalin tried to sing. She felt her shoulders hunching forward, her lips pulling as she formed the new lyrics.

"It sounds tight," Anya interrupted. "Open up."

Katalin eased her tongue down, lifted her back palate, and kept singing.

"Better," her mother said as Katalin sang on. "Don't strain. Open up on the vowels. Give it some muscle below."

They repeated the song and began it a third time. Katalin's voice was scraping.

"It doesn't fit, not in Hungarian," she complained.

"But that's the way you've been asked to sing it. Start again and keep going this time."

"It's terrible."

"Katalin, you need to do this. It's your brother's wedding."

"I don't like this song anymore."

"That doesn't matter. Ildi asked you to sing it." Anya looked at Katalin over the top of her reading glasses. "And that dear girl has gotten married without anything making the event special—no church, no new dress, not even her family around—nothing except that she's in love with your brother. *Deep.* And she's asked for this song, so you're going to sing it. Twenty times, if that's what she wants."

Katalin sang it again, displeased with all but perhaps three notes.

She woke in the middle of the night with the song pressing on her. She thought of Róbert and of the danger he was in and of his silence and of her wrecked audition and all that had gone wrong before and after. She tried to push it out of her mind, tried to sleep. But the song kept returning.

The next day after work, she sat down at the piano and began to consider that she might get through the song better if she didn't have to sing it alone. Maybe it could work as a duet. She wrote a harmony using lower thirds and fifths. Quietly she hummed the new part to herself. It was plain and simple, but she liked it well enough, and this small act of creation made her surprisingly happy.

The task now remained to tell the other singer.

THAT EVENING AFTER she put Mari to bed, she reviewed the song a little, combed her hair, and adjusted her barrette. Then she went to the cellar, bringing the song book with her. From the wooden stairs, she called Péter's name. There was no answer.

She wandered toward the space he inhabited under the stairs. Sometimes a light blanket hung here, affording him some privacy, but tonight the blanket had fallen onto the floor. She peered in.

Péter's little room was formed by exterior walls on two sides, the stairs on a third side and overhead, and the fallen blanket on the fourth. On the floor was what served as his bed—a folded blanket with a sheet over it. On top of that, rather carelessly pulled up, lay the comforter from Ildi's parents. A box held Péter's clothes. A small up-ended crate served as a night table, and on it lay a flashlight, a pencil, the music book she had given him, and the book about the Indian named Winnetou. An old train ticket stuck out from the pages as a marker partway through. Péter was doing well just to keep going with the book. The longer she knew him, the more his reading difficulty pained her. He was not unintelligent. Her eyes shifted to the diagonal stair beam where Péter had thumbtacked some papers, and one, she realized, was the note she had written him in the *rathskeller:* YOU ARE SMARTER THAN YOU THINK. Did he really need this reminder that he was capable?

Or maybe he had kept it because it was from her. An inner twinge told her yes. She hadn't looked for his tenderness, or at least she hadn't meant to. But since that day when against all wisdom she had kissed him—even though, oh Lord, it was only on the cheek—she had been aware of a turn in Péter, a heated nerve. And here she was, standing in front of his bed. It frightened her, what loneliness might drive her to do. She backed away to the laundry sink.

Above, the cellar door creaked open. It was Péter, his shirt rumpled and grimy. He smiled and trotted down the stairs when he saw her.

"We have an opportunity," she said. "Let's take a walk and I'll tell you about it."

"Let me wash up first. I'm just home from work, and I'm a mess."

She waited outside the cellar door. When he joined her, he had changed his shirt, and his face shone damp in places from splashing at the sink. They walked out of the building together, wandering west, passing apartment windows with yellowed shades pulled down. It was Saturday night, and clusters of young men laughed and shouted outside the bars. Taxis noised past. Soon the sidewalks would fill with people heading out after the operettas. Katalin gestured north with a corner of the music book. On a quieter side street, she told Péter that Antal and Ildi were *really married* and then had to remind herself that Péter hadn't been aware of the subterfuge. She told him about the celebration coming up and that Ildi wanted her to sing.

"I'd rather not sing by myself," she said, "and I'd like you to do the song with me. It's not hard."

Péter's steps slowed. "How many people?"

"I don't know, thirty or forty, maybe."

"God, that many?"

"It's not hard music," she repeated.

"With thirty or forty people there, it is. Will this be at a fancy restaurant? I don't have a suit. And Ildi asked you to sing it, not me. You're a good singer. I don't know why you think it would improve anything to have me sing it with you."

She had become so accustomed to his kindness that she had not counted on resistance. They were passing a crowd, so she laid her hand on Péter's forearm and hurried him down the street and around an empty corner. In the light of a streetlamp, they stopped.

"I can't do the song alone," she whispered.

"You said it's not hard."

"It won't be hard for you. It's very hard for me."

"Why?"

To give any reason other than Róbert would be a lie. She gazed down at the cobbles and told him the truth, which was that the song was so horribly tangled, messed, and knotted with Róbert and passion and the Rajk troubles and pregnancy. "And maybe there were days I was scared before *that song,* but not even the war scared me the way all this did, because all of a sudden I was pregnant and Róbert was gone and I was not just scared, I was more terrified than I have ever been in my life."

In silence Péter listened, looking at her, his deep-set eyes shadowed under the streetlight.

"And that's when I had to do my audition for music academy," she said. "And I had to sing *that song.* And everything just ... tore apart. I couldn't sing. My performance was an absolute," she flinched but said it anyway, "shame. So if you have wondered why I don't sing much, well, maybe you understand now. Things started and ended with that song."

"I see."

There was a long space of quiet, and Péter looked away from her. "Katalin, I don't know if this is what you want me to say, but I don't like what happened to you, with that man, and I think you deserve much better."

She glanced around, checking again to make sure they were alone. The only passersby were out of earshot. "But I think Róbert got prison," she said.

"And this is the man you're waiting for."

She thought of her unanswered letter. "Yes."

"Does Ildi know about the bad memories? Does she know what she's asking?"

"She knows about what happened. She wrote new words for the song— happier words. She thinks if I just practice it with the new words I can do it. I'm not sure I can. Not alone. That's why I was hoping we could do it as a duet."

He sighed. "Let me hear the song, then."

They turned toward home and she sang very quietly as they walked, *Oh, my beloved, I give you my heart. Know, dearest, that all that I am is entrusted to you.* She looked straight ahead or at the street and did not sing to his face. After she had gone through the melody twice, she stopped in the glow of another streetlight, opened the music book, and sang three times the new part she had written for him. Angled away with his shoulder to her, he tried humming the part and got most of it right.

"That was good," she said. "I think you could do this without too much trouble."

"We'll see."

They walked on, and she sang his part with him to help him learn it. Soon she realized they were a block and a half from home, in front of the drugstore, diagonally across from a vacant lot of rubble and wall fragments. Of any corner in the city, this was the one she most hated.

Those walls, now broken, had once contained her father's ophthalmic office. Her cousin and her aunt had lived above. In 1944 a bomb crushed the building and her aunt, and the embers blew in the wind. A few months later, in the hungriest days of the siege, Antal had come to this corner and carved flesh off a dead horse. The city fell soon afterward. Russian soldiers went on a spree, and this corner stank of vomit and piss. People said girls were raped here.

That was in the past, Katalin told herself now. The fire and sin and stench had died out. This was only a corner with some rubble and a drugstore.

Still, there were shadows, and she drew closer to Péter as they walked.

THE NEXT DAY Péter and Katalin practiced the song in the apartment, first by themselves and then with her mother playing violin. Anya had written a simple violin accompaniment because there would be no piano at the restaurant. Péter was not used to singing with a violin and at first was confused about when to begin or stop. But he caught on. Anya told him he was doing very well, and she led him through each of the entrances several times to strengthen his confidence. Katalin told herself to remember the strategy for Péter's future lessons. After the practice, Katalin went outside with him and they stood together on the walkway, Péter mumbling something about the thirty or forty people.

"Think of it this way," she said, teasing. "After scything without stop for a week, this will seem easy, won't it?"

"No."

"Still, I'm grateful to you, Péter. I owe you a favor. A big one."

His eyebrows rose and he laughed a little. "You know, you can get in trouble making offers like that."

Her face flashed hot. "I mean—"

"You're talking about an honorable favor, of course."

"Well … yes …."

He smiled. "Damn."

She had never heard even the smallest ribaldry from Péter before. Flustered, she laughed back, and it came to her that she trusted him.

Trust was beautiful.

Desirable.

She watched as Péter left down the walkway in his quiet, fluid stride. Still no word from Róbert had come, though she waited daily. These two years had been so long and empty, and she was a woman, not a martyr. There had to be an end to this waiting.

Chapter Fifteen

~~~~~

Under the Sun

W HEN PÉTER ARRIVED in Kőpatak late Monday afternoon, the day was
hot. He headed for the creek pool where his father had said the twins
were swimming. He waded upstream, boots and socks in hand, until he could
hear the twins' splashes and see their wet heads.

"Gyuri!" he called out. "Tibi!"

The boys threw their lank bodies across the water and paddled toward
him, their bare buttocks white under the surface. Péter laid his glasses on the
root of a Russian olive tree and stripped down to his undershorts. Glancing
up and down the creek and through the trees on the bank above, he hesitated.
Then he pulled off his shorts and plunged naked into the chest-deep pool. The
cold water was fluid pleasure as he streaked below its slow-rippling ceiling. He
and his brothers chased and dove in the mottled sunlight under the branches,
the twins spluttering and laughing.

Péter was standing waist-deep in the stream when a female voice teased
from above, "Hello!"

The twins stopped splashing. Péter backed up into the deeper water and
pushed his wet hair off his forehead. Without his glasses his view was blurry,
but he knew it was Ági Kozma, picking her way down the crumbling dirt of
the bank.

"Well," she laughed, "I see three fish for my frying pan. The big fish looks
tasty. I think I'll catch him."

She stooped and gathered up Péter's pile of clothes.

"Put that back," he told her.

"Come and get it."

"Ági," Gyuri cried, "you can't do that!"

"Drop it, Ági!" Péter shouted. "And go away!"

She snorted.

"You're *engaged*," he yelled, frantic now. "Is this what you do when you're going to get married?"

"Good God, Péter. Why don't you just laugh about it like anybody else would?"

She threw the clothes down and climbed back up the bank. Péter waited until she was long gone. The hairs on his arms were stiff with cold when he sent the boys into the trees to dress. Then he had them stand watch at the top of the bank while he pulled his clothes on, fingers trembling. *Goddamn her.*

He told the twins to go home, and when they were well downstream, he walked toward the fields and into the great stretch of grain. This field that now belonged to his family was about the same area as the one they had owned and worked before, eight and a half acres, but subtracting the creek mud, only seven of the new acres had a crop on them. He and his father and the twins would have this harvested before he went home at the end of the week. The family used to dream of having more land than they could harvest.

Péter plucked a head of wheat, a perfect yellow-brown symmetry of bearded seed. He pried out one of the grains and bit it. It crunched, ready for reaping. Shading his eyes with his hand, he looked out over the fields. He wished Katalin could see the poppies and cornflowers among the grain bending in the wind.

On the other side of this field lay the one that had been owned by his family and now belonged to the collective, the People's Bread Farm. The collective, like everyone else, would have to turn in a quota, although a lighter one. Péter had heard that People's Bread actually had more land than they could manage. Their tomato and paprika plots were weedy, the Zölds had said, and some fields lay fallow. Maybe Márton kept badgering Apa not so much because the collective needed land but because it needed strong men with sons. Péter didn't know, but he wondered.

THE NEXT MORNING before dawn, he hitched Zsuzsi to the wagon and loaded in scythes, rakes, whetstones, baling string, gloves, straw hats, lunch satchels, and bottles of water and wine. Mrs. Donáth arrived as Péter was readjusting the harness. Apa had arranged for her to stay with Nagyapa, prepare his meals and help him to the privy if he would let her. The old man was unhappy about missing harvest. Last year he had been able to limp along with Gyuri and Tibi as they bound sheaves.

The work started at sunrise, Péter taking the west border of the field and Apa the east. Péter sharpened the scythe blade, the stone on metal scraping in the dawn, and began swinging the scythe in wide, low arcs. Gyuri walked behind him, gathering the stalks. Across the field, Apa scythed and Tibi gathered. The twins tied the stalks into sheaves and bunched them upright. The sheaves would remain here for a week or two while the grains hardened.

The work went on. Scrape, swing, gather, bend, rise, tie, rake, carry. Again. Again. Again. The sun climbed. Péter mopped his sweating face with his handkerchief. To keep his hands from blistering, he wrapped cloths around the scythe handles.

When their shadows fell directly north and pointed at Eger Mountain, it was noon. Péter and his father and brothers ate the bacon and bread they had packed in their satchels. They watered Zsuzsi. The sun moved west, full and hot. Throughout the afternoon Péter and Gyuri worked silently, mechanically together. Péter had long since stripped his shirt off and was working in his undershirt. He didn't allow Gyuri to go bare-chested. "Sunburn," he warned. Across the narrow field, Apa swung the scythe, his strokes slower than this morning.

They worked until it was too dark to see, and when they finally went home, Nagyapa was waiting up for them. Mrs. Donáth said Nagyapa had eaten well and not complained. Péter drove her home in the wagon, and Apa and the twins fell into their beds. Hours after dark, as Péter finally took Zsuzsi to her stall, he made himself practice singing: "*Caro Mio Ben*" and "Ave Maria." The tones fell heavy from his tongue.

"I'm sorry, Zsuzsi," he said. "I know I sound awful. I'm tired. Good night."

THE NEXT DAY under the sun, Péter saw a lunch wagon roll by for the collective harvesters. Ági Kozma sat in back. In the afternoon, a State car drove past.

It was on Thursday morning that Péter first saw harvesters on the old field he and his father had planted. Jakab Kozma worked amidst the grain with three other men and a small child. Also with two women, familiar somehow, one of them young and the other about Apa's age.

Suddenly recognizing the women, Péter turned away. He did not speak to Gyuri or to Tibi about either the mother or the daughter in the field there. Nor did he speak of them to Apa. Absolutely not to Apa.

IN THE SPRING of 1946, Péter was seventeen, his mother dead a year and a half. His father had been making Saturday trips into the nearby town of Heves. After one of these drives, Apa returned later than usual and that night asked Péter to come into the barn with him. There in the lantern glow, Péter sat down on a straw mound while his father pulled up the milking stool and lit a pipe.

"Péter, I ... ah ... I don't know if you've guessed why I've been driving into Heves."

"For supplies, you said."

"Yes. Well." Apa clasped the pipe's bowl. "There's more. Well, there's a woman I've met. The harness maker introduced me to her. She lost her husband in the war, and ... so ... this has been a hard time for her. Just like it's been hard for me, your mother gone and all. Hard for all of us."

Péter hunched his shoulders in the night chill and picked up a spike of straw.

"This woman from Heves," Apa continued, "she ... she's nice, and hard-working, and I like her. Your grandfather's met her, and he likes her."

"And you want to get married," Péter mumbled.

"Yes, maybe, that is, I want you and the twins to meet her. And I want her to meet you. And also ...." Apa held the pipe still. The smoke spiraled upward. "She has a daughter."

Péter dropped the straw. "How old?"

"Sixteen."

"No."

"Péter, wait—"

"No."

Apa did not force him to come to Heves. He did not bring the woman and the girl to the house for an awkward meeting. But soon after the words in the barn, Apa took Péter to Kőpatak's one café and bought him a raspberry soda. He seemed to keep an eye on the door. A woman whose hair was black with a streak of gray walked in, and she and Apa smiled at each other.

"Anna, come meet my son Péter," he said.

The woman walked toward Péter with a hand outstretched. Péter stood. He thought of his mother. He inclined his head and tried to look this woman in the eye. But behind her someone was following—a girl with arching eyebrows and a tortoiseshell barrette instead of a kerchief. She had a fine figure in her snug dress. He wasn't looking to inspect, but how could he not notice?

So this was the girl who would sleep in his house of males. Her mother would sleep with his father. Péter would step out of the privy and find this girl waiting her turn. She would be there when he dressed in the morning and when he undressed at night. She would be dressing and undressing and washing her smooth female skin. And inevitably, when she moved about the house, he would watch her. He wouldn't really mean to, he would tell himself not to, his father would tell him not to, maybe even she would tell him not to, but it would happen. And she, this stranger, would watch him. That would happen, too.

Now in this moment in the café, the girl stranger walked toward him. Her eyes narrowed and her lips tightened. He muttered good day and looked away. She muttered it back to him. She gave a low huff. He could swear she did.

That night in the barn, Péter told his father he didn't like that haughty girl and she didn't belong here.

"This house is for our family," he said. "She's not in our family."

"Sometimes households change. We would adjust."

"Our family already changed when Mother died. We already adjusted when the Russians moved in. It was horrible."

"Son," Apa pleaded, "the girl's mother is nice. Helpful. I have your two brothers to think about. And myself ... good Lord, I admit it! Try to put yourself in my place."

But Péter could not put himself in his father's place, not if it was that woman's place, not if it was that girl's place.

"I don't want that girl here," he said. "If she moves in, I move out."

The lines of Apa's forehead deepened. "Where would you go?"

"Some other farm. Day labor, I don't know. Maybe early to the army."

His father put his head in his hands.

Several nights later, Apa told Péter that he had spoken with the woman from Heves, and all was ended. Péter turned away, greatly relieved. But every so often he thought of how the woman and his father had smiled at each other, and in the years that followed, Péter edged closer to putting himself in his father's place. That place was very lonely.

THIS WOMAN WHO had once smiled at his father was there now in the old field with her daughter, both of them gathering wheat stalks behind the reapers. A small boy tagged after them. One of the reapers turned and called, and the woman came to him. The woman was strong and trim, and she picked up the child as she walked. Was the child her own, or her daughter's? She laid her hand on the man's elbow and they spoke.

The daughter straightened up with her wheat stalks and looked toward where Péter stood. For one moment they saw each other. He turned and swung the scythe, as his father was doing, alone, at the other side of the field.

AT DUSK, PÉTER and his father and brothers left the fields, walking instead of driving the wagon. Halfway home, a man on a horse approached from behind and caught up with them. The rider, a young man with a square face, was Gábor Szita, the veterinarian who had married Mrs. Donáth's daughter.

"How is Uncle Zsigmond?" he asked, referring to Péter's grandfather in the way almost all the villagers did. "Improving, I hope?"

"Sometimes I think so, sometimes I don't," Apa said.

"I suppose it hasn't been an easy week for any of you," Gábor said. "The boys look tired. Would they like to ride?"

He dismounted. Péter helped him boost Tibi and Gyuri onto the horse, and Gábor led the horse as they walked the darkening road toward home.

It was a long evening, a longer night. Péter's sleep broke when his grandfather called out. Péter went to him because it was his turn to help Nagyapa with the bedpan. When Nagyapa lay back down, he kept saying that he could work in the fields tomorrow and didn't like hanging back like an old woman.

"Shhh, Nagyapa," Péter said, for the Zölds were sleeping in the opposite corner. "Shhh."

On Friday, the harvesting slowed. Apa had developed a cramp in his back and would sometimes pull back and change his stance, grimacing. During breaks, he would take a swig of *pálinka*. The twins complained more. Gyuri said he was going to be a factory worker when he grew up, or a fisherman, or a butcher—anything but a wheat farmer. Tibi kept coming up with reasons to wander off: he had to pee, he wanted water, he wanted something from the wagon. Péter told him to quit shirking or they'd be out here all summer. He felt he was delivering the same lines he kept hearing in the *Szabad Nép* meetings.

On Saturday at noon, he and his father leaned the last sheaves together while Gyuri and Tibi made a final pass with the rakes. Apa rubbed his lower back and looked out over the long stretch of stubble and propped sheaves. "It isn't really a bad crop," he said, "considering the land. Still, who knows what kind of profit there'll be. We'll find out after threshing."

They looked to the next field over, where only half the crop had been harvested so far.

"They're slow over there," Apa said. "I hope to God the collective does better than I think it will. I hear that when collectives don't meet their State quota, other farmers pay."

Péter looked around uneasily. There were too many rumors.

"I want to take some of the crop home," Apa said, "let it cure in the barn, the shed."

Slowly, Péter nodded.

They spent the rest of the day carting home sheaves. The rest of the crop would stay in the fields until threshing. The ones at home they would hand-thresh with their old flails for seed wheat.

"And how much of the crop is going into the root cellar?" Péter asked.

Apa did not answer.

* * *

THE NEXT AFTERNOON, Péter prepared to go back to the city. As he picked the first of the apricots, Apa joined him in the grove. Péter told his father he would not be home the next weekend because he would be singing at a party with his music teacher.

Apa raised his eyebrows, as if impressed, and wished him luck. Although they seldom spoke of women, Apa asked him about this teacher, and if she was young, and if she was married, and if she was pretty. When Péter answered yes, no, yes, Apa wanted to know more.

Péter was reluctant to say more. "She's very kind, Apa," he said at last. "I told her about Mother."

"Ah."

"I'm her only student. Mainly, she works in a nursery. And takes care of her baby."

"She has a baby?"

"Yes, but the father is gone. She thinks the ÁVH took him."

"Holy God. And she invited you to sing with her at this party." Apa rested his elbow on a low apricot branch. "A young, pretty woman is inviting you. And she has a baby and the father is gone. It sounds risky, son."

Péter turned aside and reached for another apricot. His father was a fine one to talk of risk. Péter climbed into the tree for the higher fruit and did not answer.

Chapter Sixteen

Unison

STILL NO LETTER arrived from Róbert, and Katalin stood empty-handed each day at the mailbox. Once she muttered, "Can't he even *write*?" But Mari, in a sudden burst of mangled sound, mimicked the words, consonants indistinct but irritated inflection flawless. This childish echo disheartened Katalin beyond speaking.

And maybe her own anger wasn't even fair. In this prison of a nation there could be countless reasons why Róbert hadn't yet come to her or written. It was a grief to wake up in the middle of the night rehearsing them, but there could be.

MONDAY NIGHT, PÉTER came to the apartment and gave her apricots. Though his face was tanned from the week he had spent working in the sun, he looked tidier than he usually did, less windblown. He'd had his hair cut. When she told him it looked quite nice, he smiled in a self-deprecating way and said the time had come to harvest it. He came again on Tuesday night to practice the song for the party. He had worked on it in Kőpatak, he said, but when he sang it for her, the words were incorrect in two places, and he was getting one of the harmony lines wrong. She would have let him sing the harmony in his own way if it had fit with the melody, but it didn't. When she told him about the errors, he sighed heavily and squeezed his eyes shut.

"We'll fix it," she said. On the piano she played the harmony line once more for him. "Please don't worry. You're an excellent singer."

"That's not what the fellow I work with says. Today I was singing—not even to be heard, just singing to myself—and this Lajos, he's a drunk, says, 'You're going flat, Mr. Opera Star.'"

"So what does a drunk know? I've never heard you sing off-pitch."

"I don't like him," Péter went on. "He's no help with the work. He treats the horses as if they're slaughterhouse nags. And when he called me Mr. Opera Star, I told him to … shut his … mouth."

By the way that Péter clipped his words, it was an easy guess what kind of mouth Péter had told the man he had and how he had told him to shut it.

"Then he gave me a shove, and I shoved him back," Péter confessed, "and the janitor rushed over, and so did this girl who serves lunch, and they pushed us apart. I felt like an idiot. I don't know what's the matter with me. I've always just minded my own business before, I mean, except with my father, I've kept my mouth closed."

"You're a singer. Singers aren't supposed to keep their mouths closed. Not forever. Let's work on the song again. Words first, without singing."

In unison they rehearsed the words by speaking, Péter facing the curtains and Katalin sitting on the piano bench, staring at the keys: "Oh my beloved, here is my heart." It grew awkward. They monotoned through the song several times until he asked if they could just get on with singing it. Then they sang it over and over, with Katalin correcting Péter's harmony.

Afterwards she set the music to "Ave Maria" on the piano and played the first line, but beyond the apartment wall, she heard voices and a cough. The neighbors were close by. Maybe a sacred song wasn't safe, not with the way Péter's voice carried now.

"Just sing it on *á*," she told him.

She whisper-counted the tempo and struck the first note. Facing the tile stove, he sang, beginning just below the midpoint of his range where his voice hit that beautiful roughness. The song lifted, moved, prayed, and opened unto heaven, carried on a single vowel.

THURSDAY NIGHT PÉTER came for another practice session during his usual lesson time. When she asked him if there had been any more problems with the unpleasant man at work, Péter said the man had been absent. That had been happening often, he added.

They rehearsed the song for the reception several times with Katalin's mother and then practiced it more on their own. In the last week and a half, Katalin had sung the song often enough to grow a little bored with it, and she took this as a good sign. Maybe old emotions wouldn't twist the song away. But she admitted to Péter that she was nervous.

"Well, there's something you could try," he said. "I did it in that restaurant where the Gypsy made me sing, and I did it here, when I first started singing for you. I imagined I was behind the plow mare back home." He smiled at her and spread his hands, palms out, recreating the scene. "So that's what you think of. Horse rump, tail swishing ...."

She laughed. "And that's how we get through this love song, by thinking of a horse's rear?"

He shrugged. "If it helps."

THE NIGHT BEFORE the party Mari woke at two a.m., wailing disconsolately from the crib. Katalin went to her daughter and lifted her out. The child thrashed, digging her small fingers into Katalin's shoulders. Katalin swayed, rocking her.

"*Csillagom*," she begged, "my star, go back to sleep."

The child's sobs at last faded, but now she babbled against Katalin's neck. "*Na-ma? An-an?*"

"Your nagymama is asleep with your nagypapa. Antal is asleep with Ildi. Please, Mari, shhh."

But it was half an hour before Mari sank back into sleep. With all rest shattered, Katalin lay tense in her bed as unbidden thoughts of Róbert pressed in on her. Why hadn't he written?

And what good did it do to spend knotted, restless hours thinking of him when he, apparently, couldn't be bothered to think of her? With this bald honesty, she began to cry silently, but the tears only made her cheeks itch. She made herself stop. But still, she could not sleep.

SATURDAY AFTERNOON KATALIN took Mari to a family friend, then rushed home to get ready for the party. Ildi had gone to the beauty salon, something she rarely did, and when she returned home, her hair had been swept up into a French twist, accentuating her regal forehead. She and Katalin took turns with a tube of coral lipstick and a compact of rouge. In her life, Katalin had owned the bourgeois luxury of lipstick only once, rouge only twice. Cosmetics were hard to come by, and these Ildi had purchased from a co-worker with relatives in Austria. Black market makeup.

"I just wish my family could be here today," she said.

For her family was not allowed to leave the confines of their remote eastern village. Ildi was not even sure they knew she was really married. In a static-filled phone call her mother had placed from the village post office, Ildi had told her, meaningfully, how nice it was to wake up next to Antal every morning, but she wasn't sure her mother understood, and Ildi had been afraid to say more, in case the phone was bugged.

"You know something's wrong with your country," Ildi whisper-complained to Katalin, "when you can't tell your family you're married."

Ildi slipped into a blue silk dress she had borrowed. It had been salvaged through the war and had probably changed hands several times, but it still possessed a rare elegance. Katalin owned no suitable dresses except a fitted red one Róbert used to like. She had not worn it since before her pregnancy, and it was tighter through the chest and hips than it used to be.

"You have more shape than you used to," Ildi said. "I think you look gorgeous."

Ildi brushed Katalin's hair and pulled back the front locks with two rhinestone barrettes. Katalin liked the sparkle. But her head was beginning to hurt behind her eyes. Before she left the flat, she swallowed two aspirin tablets from a bottle her father had brought home from the hospital. They were probably the only family in the building who didn't have to stand in line for aspirin.

THE PARTY WAS a dinner event, held midday to give Antal and Ildi the chance to take an overnight train trip as a honeymoon. Katalin's mother had made arrangements with a restaurant on Stalin Avenue. It had been a favorite of Ildi's family before the war, when a shell hole large enough for a bicycle to pass through had been blown into one of the walls. The hole had since been repaired, though the plaster didn't match.

The dinner was to be served in the restaurant's roomy courtyard. A wisteria vine grew in a lush arc over the courtyard side of the doorframe, the blossoms dangling like grapes. The tables in the open air were draped with white cloths and set with vases of cosmos. Umbrellas shaded the tables. Katalin busied herself with handing glasses of white wine to guests as the afternoon sun spilled down. Péter arrived, dressed in the gray suit her father had loaned him for the day. He'd had to cinch in the trousers with his belt.

"*Jó napot*, Katalin," he said. "You … you look … pretty." He was gazing at her in frank admiration. "Where's Mari?"

"It would be too long a day for her. I left her with a friend."

He seemed a little disconcerted by this. "I thought I could help you with her."

He felt like a stray goose here, she guessed. She gave him a glass of wine, and it relieved her for his sake when an older man, a friend of the Brauers named Árpád Kassai, struck up conversation and happened to mention that his father had bred horses.

Péter's eyes lit up. "Draft animals? Pleasure?"

Katalin let them talk and wandered away when they began discussing mares in heat. She found a spot of shade by a stucco wall. Nearby, Ildi and Antal laughed with guests.

Ildi was telling the story of the first time she'd rehearsed music with Antal. "He dropped his music all over the floor … twice. I thought, 'Oh, Lord, if this is what he does in the rehearsal, what's he going to do in the performance?' "

"But in fact I did *not* drop my music in the performance," Antal told them all, eying Ildi teasingly. "I memorized it, proving to this doubter that I was not as ridiculous as she thought."

Katalin felt a small grinding at her right temple. She let a waiter refill her wine glass and sat down with her family for dinner. Cold cherry soup was served, then roast pork. She knew that her father had summarily paid for all the food and drink because the bride's family could not. At the end of dinner, her father stood and toasted the new couple. "Who have been married for about six weeks now," he added, as the family had planned in advance. "And I'd like to remember the Brauer family, too, who unfortunately could not join us today."

The clinking rose and died away. Then Antal stood and raised one hand for quiet.

"From what I gather," he told the group, "some of you were surprised to find out we'd been married. Maybe you've have been wondering why we didn't do this a year or two ago, since we've been friends for so long. But some things are best if they're not rushed." He picked up his wine glass. "Like wine. And music marked *adagio*." He paused. "And love. My grandfather once said that real love grows out of respect and trust. He was right. If I didn't know it then, I know it now. I've always respected Ildikó. There was never any question of respect. Trust, that takes longer, especially—"

Especially now, Katalin thought, but she was afraid for Antal to say it in this city where distrust had spread like influenza.

He seemed to have caught himself. "Naturally trust takes longer. Once I really knew Ildi, there was no question of trust, either."

Antal rested his hand on Ildi's shoulder, and she curled her fingers around his.

"But love's riskier," he told the group, "because you suddenly realize that what happens to her happens to you, too, and the other way around. And to face that, to really face it, and then to say, 'Yes, so be it,'—that is …."

He turned to Ildi and she looked up at him.

"Exhilarating," he said.

He raised his glass in the air. "Here's to this dear woman," he continued, voice quavering, "for loving me. And for waiting while I found the courage to love her back."

Ildi jumped up and threw her arms around his neck. The wine glass fell from his hand, shattering on the table and soaking the cloth. The guests roared and cheered. Antal burst out laughing and lifted another, imaginary glass. "To my wife!"

"Kati! Péter!" Ildi shouted. "Your song."

Katalin signaled to Péter, and they joined her mother near the wisteria vine. Palms sweating, Katalin looked out at the guests and at the exhilarated couple. Ildi grinned at her and brought her hands together, miming applause.

Katalin noticed Péter clenching his hands. She told him in a whisper to think of a horse's rump. He suppressed a laugh, and she nodded to her mother to begin the violin introduction. Very quietly Péter hummed along, as he often did to set himself on pitch.

They began in unison. *Oh my beloved, here is my heart.* She felt the notes pulling within her and heard a low tremble in Péter's opening. She leaned near him, steadying them both. They sang on, dividing the song more smoothly now, Katalin following the melody on the second line and Péter's voice flowing in harmony under it. *Here is my heart, and with joy and gratitude, I receive yours.*

The song approached the apex. There in the heights, pain grasped her temples. This song carried pain. It had always carried pain.

No. Not today. It would carry joy today. She tightened her gut and demanded it. She crescendoed.

But her voice weakened. She pulled in another quick breath. Her throat tensed. Over Péter's harmony her notes wavered, faltered.

Her mother glanced at her over the top of the violin.

Péter touched her fingertips. He lowered his chin, pulled back his shoulders. With a quick intake of breath, he reached up to the melody that had been choking in her throat, and suddenly his voice soared. *Forever, all that I am belongs to you.* He softened then on the last line, finishing the short song as the accompaniment held.

"Do you want to repeat it?" he whispered.

Katalin gave a stunned nod. Her mother improvised an interlude, taking the song back to its beginning as though it had been planned this way all along. When Anya signaled with a bob of her head, Katalin counted out one measure and began to sing again. Péter sang the melody with her on a supporting undercurrent so restrained he barely breathed it. But it was enough. The song swelled, flowing past the pain, flooding over it, free and unstopping. Before its end, Péter quieted, giving the song to her. With what was left within her, she sang three lines solo. He joined her again on the final line. They closed in unison.

The final violin notes lifted, lingered soft as the last kiss of night, and faded. Through the courtyard a hush had fallen. Katalin squeezed Péter's hand. It was shaking.

One of the listeners clapped, and another, and the trickle of applause became a storm.

Antal ran across the courtyard and hugged Katalin, spinning her off her feet. "We've told you a million times you could do this! See?"

He turned to Péter and clasped his shoulder. "Marvelous! And what a perfect rescue."

"It wasn't a rescue."

The man named Árpád Kassai approached her, his hand shading his eyes from the sun. "That was wonderful."

Katalin's hot forehead was throbbing now. She refastened her barrettes, trying to lift her hair away from her face, and wanted to smile but winced instead.

"Thank you," she said.

"I direct a small choir in Buda," he told her, "and it's a very good one, if I may say so. I'd be pleased if you and the young man would audition for it."

"Péter doesn't read music."

"I'm sorry to hear that. I like his voice very much. But in my choir the singers have to be good sight-readers." Mr. Kassai's high forehead wrinkled over the gray scramble of his eyebrows. "I hear that you are well-trained. Would you be interested?"

"I'll have to think about it," she told him. "But thank you."

"Of course." He reached into his breast pocket and handed her a calling card. "Please telephone me if you'd like to sing with us. We may need a soprano section leader in the fall."

His businesslike sincerity moved her. She thanked him again, returned to her table and dropped Mr. Kassai's card into her handbag.

Two violinists and a cellist had begun playing waltz music. Katalin watched Antal and Ildi cavorting and spinning with the music, laughing when they bumped or misstepped. Others danced nearby, the women sweating in their has-been finery and the men throwing off their old jackets. Péter came over to her with his wine glass, and she gestured to the empty chair next to hers.

"You did a fabulous job," she said. "I have to thank you for saving the song."

"I didn't save it." His voice was remarkably at rest. "I just sang it. You sounded beautiful. People keep saying that, especially Antal."

"I still say you saved the song. You're heroic."

He smiled. "Maybe you've had too much to drink."

As they watched the dancers, she asked him if the people in his village danced.

"They used to," he said, "on the square, before the war. My father was a good *verbunkos* dancer once. He knew the moves, the jumping, slapping the boots. But I never learned dancing."

The wine was weaving a slow peace through her. She reached a hand toward him. "Would you like me to show you how to waltz?"

His eyes flitted toward her parents. "Would it be all right?"

"Come."

In an open spot on the pavement, she placed his left hand on her waist and she clasped his right. She tapped the pulse of the waltz on his shoulder—*EGY-kettő-három*, ONE-two-three. He pulsed it back on her waist. She showed him the step of *egy* and the sweeping follow-through on *kettő* and *három*, and he moved with her. On the fourth repetition, their knees collided. They laughed. Under her hand she felt him relax. By the end of the second dance, the music's rhythm seemed to steer him.

But now the wine—or was it the heat, or her headache?—was making her hazy. Her feet seemed a long way from her head. She leaned against Péter's shoulder and his arm tightened around her waist. But the tension in her head wound harder. She stopped and rested against his collar bone.

"I'm not feeling well," she said. "I think I'd better sit down."

"All right," he said, though he seemed reluctant, and he walked her back to her seat.

She crossed her arms on the table top and laid down her head. Péter adjusted the table umbrella over her and sat down with her, his hand on her shoulder. She inched her chair closer to his and waited for the inner knotting to ease, but it did not. Eventually Péter offered to see her home. On the way out, Katalin told her mother why she was leaving and asked her to pick up Mari.

Her mother's eyes wandered to where Péter stood waiting. "And he's walking with you?" she whispered. "Katalin, you shouldn't be playing with that young man's feelings."

"I'm *not*."

Her mother raised her eyebrows. "Remember what you've been through."

ON THE WAY back to the apartment house, she took Péter's arm. It was a slow walk in the heat, and in Jókai Square she sat down on a bench in the shade. Though she did not want to, she thought of Róbert, who was alive and had not written to her and did not know of his daughter. Péter sat beside her. When he put his arm around her, she leaned into him. She did not turn to look up at him, because she wanted him to kiss her, and if she turned to him, he might do it, and if he did, he would not take it lightly. If it happened this time, it would happen another time and another, and he would not be able to let go. And she would still be checking the mailbox.

"Péter," she whispered, "of all the people I've known," she touched his hand and almost could not go on, "you're the one I'm most afraid of hurting."

She felt his arm tense as he drew her closer.

"Why?" he asked. "I don't want you to be afraid."

So she risked it, lifting her eyes to his, and their lips caressed. The touch was gentle, and she would trust herself with no more. As they walked home, she clutched his hand.

COMRADE ERIKA WAS smoking in her doorway when they reached the foyer. The boy Rudi was shooting marbles across the red-brown tile floor. He looked up.

"Someone was trying to find you," he said to Péter. "Some lady."

"That's right," Erika said. "She's waiting for you down at the operetta café. Someone from that village you're from."

"My God," Péter said. "Who was it? What's wrong?"

Erika flicked her cigarette. "I don't know."

Péter turned to Katalin. "I have to leave."

"Yes."

"Are you well enough?"

"Go."

He clasped her hand so hard it almost pinched, and then he turned. Her temples pounded as he jerked the door open and bolted out.

Chapter Seventeen

～～⌒〰⌒～～

Now and in the Hour of Our Death

Péter ran the whole way to the café. At an outdoor table, Mrs. Donáth sat with a half-empty beer glass. When she saw him, she stood and enclosed his hand in her dry fingers. "Péter. Come. Sit down."

He did not sit. "What's the matter?"

"It's your grandfather. He's very sick. His color is bad, his breathing is weak, and so is his heartbeat. There is probably an infection of some kind, but he's been weakening for a long time." She looked at Péter, her round face weary. "He's dying."

"He has good days and bad days," Péter argued. "Maybe—"

"No," she interrupted him gently, "he won't make it this time. Your father didn't want to leave your grandfather's side, but he wanted you to know. Listen, I have to go back on the next train. Why don't you come with me and say goodbye to your grandfather."

His eyes filled, and he wiped at them under his glasses. He mouthed, "Let's go," but there was no sound.

It was dark when they walked through Kőpatak, Péter still in the clothes he had borrowed from Katalin's father. The wind carried the scent of the mown wheat crop. Mrs. Donáth gave him a motherly hug when she said goodbye at the lane to her house, and he went on alone. At his home, his brothers were sitting on the hardened earth of the porch, their faces white in the kerosene light.

"Nagyapa's going to die, Apa says," Gyuri whispered. "He's going to *Istenország.*"

Istenország, God's country. Péter clamped his arms around the twins' narrow shoulders. He wanted to tell the boys that God's country was a good place and their mother was already there. But who really knew what lay beyond the terrifying terrain that their mother had crossed, that their grandfather was crossing now?

The lamplight flickered. Gyuri said the Zölds had gone to the barn to sleep. Péter went inside. In the kitchen, Mrs. Zöld had left sandwiches for the family. Apa was sitting in the dim main room next to Nagyapa's bed, and he beckoned to Péter. On a shelf above the bed, two candles shone.

"Thank God you've come," Apa said. His voice sounded dry and hoarse as though he had been smoking too much.

Péter pulled up a chair and looked at his grandfather's white-gray face and withering body. Nagyapa's chest seemed to have flattened into the sheets. His eyes were open and his breath came in gulps and hisses. Péter touched his grandfather's bony shoulder, and its unnatural coolness startled him.

"*Jó estét*, Nagyapa," he said.

Nagyapa's lips twitched.

"He was in bad pain yesterday," Apa said. "I don't think he is now."

"Nagyapa?" Péter asked.

A small gasp.

"It's me, Péter."

Three chugging breaths.

Time passed—how much, Péter did not know. After a while, Apa went outside with the twins. Nagyapa's breaths grew louder and harsher, like snoring. His head lolled.

"We'll miss you, Nagyapa," Péter said.

Another chug.

"You've always been a good grandfather, even when your leg was hurting."

What else would Nagyapa want to hear—if he could still hear? In recent weeks the old man had been asking him to sing. Péter had always put him off: another day. Now there were no more days.

He sat forward on his chair. What would Katalin tell him to do? Well, breathe.

He drew in a breath and lifted his rib cage: *"Ave Maria, gratia plena ...."* He coughed down the tightness forming in his throat. *"Santa Maria, Mater Dei, ora pro nobis, nobis peccatoribus, nunc et in hora mortis nostrae."* Holy Mary, Mother of God, pray for us sinners, now and in the hour of our death.

Nagyapa's breaths came faster, thinner, rougher.

Over his grandfather's rasping, Péter pushed on with the song. On his left side, his father had returned, smelling of cigarette smoke. On his right, Tibi and Gyuri shuffled close.

"Péter," Apa's voice shuddered, fell, "keep singing."

Péter began the song again. "Ave Maria, gratia plena, Dominus tecum, benedicta ...."

The rasping from the bed stopped. Péter waited, eyes stinging. The world hung silent.

Then, a rattle.

Apa stepped forward, bent over Nagyapa's face, and touched the old man's eyes closed. Péter felt Tibi's shaking arms wrap around him. Gyuri began to cry. Apa pulled Gyuri in, and Péter held Tibi. There where the candlelight bent into the darkness, he and his father stood with the frightened boys, waiting out their crying.

Péter helped Apa wrap Nagyapa's body in one of his bed sheets. They carried the body to the cool of the root cellar, the twins following like confused sheep and carrying the kerosene lamp. Péter and Apa laid the wrapped body on the earth floor next to some boxes of newly picked apricots, then Apa herded the boys toward the stairs.

Péter lit the cellar lantern and told the others to go on back without him. He looked at his grandfather's sheet-wrapped form and blinked back tears. Outside, he could hear Apa talking with the Zölds, who had awakened with the commotion. Péter waited until their voices and footsteps faded away. Even with death lying beside him, a nervous old question rose in him. He pried off the loose boards of the false wall until he had exposed the opening into the low hidden room. With the lantern, he ducked through and hunched over the barrels inside. He lifted a lid on one. It had been empty last time he checked: now it was half-full. Péter lifted another lid. This barrel was almost completely full. So was a third barrel he checked, and a fourth.

So his father had been hand-threshing the sheaves they had carted home last week and left in the barn and the shed. Here was some of next year's seed wheat, or grain for milling with a hand quern, perhaps for selling on the black market. It was contraband, withheld from the State's reckoning. Péter had known with dread that it was here, just as he had known—really, when it came down to it—that his grandfather was dying. If he had been here, he could not have held up death, and he would not have stopped his father from hiding this grain, either. They would not make it through the year if they turned in everything required. Turn it in and starve, or hide it and go to prison. What a choice.

Péter climbed back through the wall and replaced the boards, then overturned a crate and sat with his grandfather. He felt he should pray but was so unused to it. He sat in silence and slowly crossed himself.

Apa. The hidden grain. Gyuri. Tibi. Nagyapa. Péter touched the sheet where it covered his grandfather's face. *God have mercy.*

He wept into his hands.

* * *

IN THE YARD the next morning Péter helped his father build a coffin. As they worked, Apa said that his sister, Teréz, would be coming in on the afternoon train. She lived east of Miskolc, and it had always been a disappointment to Nagyapa and an irritation to Apa that Teréz so seldom visited. The family blamed her husband more than they blamed her.

"Is Uncle Ödön coming?" Péter asked.

"God, I hope not."

They discussed the burial. It would have to be arranged with the priest, who was fairly new in the village and met with State approval. Péter had never been sure how some priests received such tolerance while others were thrown into prison, although he could guess. He and his family had kept their distance from this new man, but they would not bury Nagyapa without a priest. It would be like sending his soul to wander desolate in the other world's darkness.

It was a Sunday, and at about the ending time of the mass, Apa went to the church to speak with the priest. Péter then joined Apa in the cemetery and they chose a plot between two aspens near the grave of Nagyapa's wife, ten years gone, and not far from the grave of Péter's mother. They pulled weeds away from the wood markers and scraped out grit that the wind had blown into the lettering on his mother's: *Margit Tóth Benedek, 12 April 1909–9 November 1944.*

At Apa's request, Péter went to tell the village crier of Nagyapa's death. The crier shouldered the strap of his skin drum, and as Péter walked home, he heard the man drumming in the town square and calling out that Zsigmond Benedek had died and would be buried at noon tomorrow. Péter ran home and helped Apa and the undertaker prepare Nagyapa's body for the laying-out. He felt very tired.

Aunt Teréz arrived that evening, just before supper. For a long time, she sat with her face in her hands in the *tiszta szoba* next to the ornamental bed where Nagyapa lay. Péter and his brothers hung back and did not really greet her until she rose, went into the kitchen, and tied on an apron. She had never been a large woman, but now it struck Péter how spare, even thin, she seemed, how colorless in her brown kerchief over her gray hair. He gave his aunt the customary kiss on each cheek, and with a nod and a flick of his thumb, he prodded the twins to do the same. The Zölds introduced themselves to Aunt Teréz, and Mrs. Zöld helped by washing the accumulated dishes. Aunt Teréz began to cry as she fried the sausage she had brought. She looked tired, too, but Péter couldn't recall a time when she hadn't. She apologized for her husband and daughters not coming. The daughters were busy with their children, she said.

"And Ödön." She spread her hands. "There's his work."

"Of course," Mrs. Zöld said politely.

Péter believed nothing of what Aunt Teréz said about Uncle Ödön's work. If the man had ever done half as much work as his wife did, she wouldn't be such a worn-out scrap of a woman. Thank God the man wasn't here drinking up Apa's *pálinka*, glowering at the twins, and ordering Aunt Teréz around.

Aunt Teréz sighed. "There should be more mourners visiting," she told Apa. "There *will* be more tomorrow, won't there?"

"I expect so," Apa said, "but who knows who will come? The collective's still reaping, the threshing machine's been scheduled. I have to start my field-threshing in a few days, too. The work doesn't stop." Apa rubbed his temple. "Until you die. I suppose our father is finally getting a rest."

THE NEXT MORNING, Péter helped his father slaughter four chickens for the wake. Mrs. Donáth arrived, and she and Aunt Teréz plucked and stewed the chickens with onions and peppers. No one was sure this would be enough, but they didn't want to cook food they couldn't spare for people who wouldn't come.

At noon, a humid pall of clouds spread over the cemetery. Péter stood at the open grave with his family, the priest and a few mourners: Mrs. Donáth along with her husband and their daughter Panni, the widow of the town's former grocer, a few old farmers, and the Zölds, who had come straight from the communal fields. Was this all? Where were the others—the men with whom Nagyapa had harvested and thatched before his leg went bad, friends with whom he'd played cards in the tavern or in barns, families whose weddings and funerals he had attended, neighbors who had crossed paths with him every day of their lives? Where were the Kozmas, for God's sake?

Péter tried to listen to the priest. God was mentioned. Something was said about ashes and dust, and the coffin was lowered into the grave. Apa threw a handful of earth onto the coffin, and the others did the same. Péter, his father and the undertaker picked up shovels and mounded dirt over the grave. Péter thought of all that Nagyapa had lived through: the collapse of the old empire, two wars, the fascists, the communists, gaining land, losing it. After all that, here they were burying him in less than fifteen minutes. Aunt Teréz wept. The twins trembled.

Apa beckoned to Péter. "Could you sing that song?" he whispered. "The one you sang last night."

"Here?"

"Please."

Péter felt suddenly hot and desperately thirsty, his throat raw.

"Please," Apa repeated.

Aunt Teréz was blotting her tears with her handkerchief. Tibi clung to Apa's hand while Gyuri stared at the new grave and sniffled. Péter stood with one hand on his shovel, licked the inside of his mouth, and tried to begin. "*Ave Maria, gratia ....*"

He looked off to the wood marker where yesterday they had pulled away dandelions and long grass: *Margit Tóth Benedek, 12 April 1909–9 November 1944.*

Around him, all was still. He sang, clutching the shovel with the force of every sorrow since the 9th of November, 1944. "*Ora pro nobis peccatoribus.*" *Pray for us sinners.*

Gyuri and Tibi sagged against Apa.

"Pray for us sinners."

Péter bent his head, felt the song flickering, ebbing.

"Pray for—"

The sound cracked, broken as death. There was nothing left. Without voice, Péter leaned on the shovel handle and the wind blew across his face. He put up his hand, shook his head. Someone, perhaps Mrs. Donáth or Mrs. Zöld, whispered the rest of the Latin words.

"Amen," Aunt Teréz breathed.

One by one, the people filed past the grave and told the family that Zsigmond Benedek had been a good man. Apa cleared his throat and tried to thank them. Péter looked at them in mute numbness. The grass rustled and Péter turned.

Tamás Márton and the tall police chief strode toward them. Márton posted himself next to the priest. "We are sorry for your loss," he stated as though reading out an edict.

Péter shifted his eyes to Apa, who gave no answer but to pull the twins closer to him.

"We are sorry," Márton repeated, "but it is time for Ottó and Bori Zöld to return to work."

Márton turned and walked off. The policeman escorted the Zölds as they trudged away. The priest followed, then the others. Mrs. Donáth lingered with Aunt Teréz, and the two women saw the twins home.

Apa squatted on his heels beside the newly mounded grave. "Goodbye," he whispered, and Péter laid his hand on his father's shoulder.

THE PEOPLE WHO had come for the burial also turned up for the wake, and so did some others, like the Kozmas. Aunt Teréz worried that the four stewed chickens wouldn't stretch far enough. Péter carried water to the kitchen for cooking more dumplings, and as he was stoking the fire in the stove, Márton stepped into the kitchen, his boots heavy on the earthen floor. The man's gaze wandered across the pantry door and rose to the loft.

"Apricots out back, I see," he said to Péter. "What are you going to do with them?"

"I'm not sure," Péter hedged.

"The produce cooperative, I suggest."

Márton left the house, and through the doorway, Péter watched him wander among the guests. Mrs. Donáth handed Márton a glass of wine. Apa, seeing Márton, turned and walked in the other direction.

AFTER THE GUESTS had left, Péter prepared to return to Pest, already having missed a day of work without permission. He folded the suit he had borrowed from Katalin's father, which was sweaty and dusty and would have to be cleaned. His muscles ached in exhaustion.

He thought of Katalin, as he had so often in these hard days—her warmth and her dancing and her voice close to his ear. And her kiss. It disquieted him to remember that she'd been afraid of hurting him.

He went to the garden and cut some lavender for her. His mother had once planted it as a narrow sprout, and now it splayed blue and bushy, the only thing that seemed to have thrived since his mother's death. Apa joined him in the garden.

"I really wish you could stay and help with the field-threshing," Apa said at length. "The lavender's for your music teacher, I guess. How did it go, when you sang at that party with her?"

"I got through it without any mistakes. Katalin's singing was very beautiful."

Apa stood silently in his best white shirt, which was soiled on one sleeve by burial dirt.

"It just seems like trouble," Apa finally said, "you getting fond of a ... what are they called now, a *bourgeoise*. Things like that don't usually work; they're too uneven."

Péter trimmed the stalks with his pocket knife. He could scoff at his father's words, but in fact there had never been a day when he wasn't aware of his unevenness with Katalin. The awareness was there whenever he stood next to her piano; it was there when he drank coffee from her china cups, even though they were chipped; it was there when he thought about how to get her father's suit cleaned; it was there when he compared today's chicken stew to the pork dinner served up at Antal's party. It was there when he remembered her soft kiss.

"In the city, everything's mixed up now," he told his father. "It's all mixed up, who's above and who's below. Like the Zölds. They're not rich anymore."

"They certainly aren't."

"Apa, I'm sorry about my singing today."

"It was good singing. The only good thing that's happened all summer."

"But I mean, I'm sorry about breaking down."

"And do you think that is so unforgiveable?" Apa's face was set, and behind him, the dull clouds smeared the sky. "I'll tell you what is unforgiveable. Márton showing up at the burial and telling Zöld and his wife to go back to work before we'd even set the damned shovels aside."

"Apa, Tamás Márton was asking what we were going to do with the apricots. He said we should sell them to the State cooperative."

"Of course he says that. Because the cooperative is always in need, because what they pay isn't worth piss, and what Márton's sorry farm grows isn't worth piss, either." Apa crossed his arms. "I have good apricots. That fruit is mine, I grew it, and I grew it on the shred of land that still belongs to me. I will not sell it for piss."

"Then do *something*, because that man is not going away."

Except for a small twitching under his mustache, Apa stood utterly still. "A horse's prick up his arse."

Chapter Eighteen

~~~

Night Music

THE DAY AFTER Antal's party, Katalin worked in Péter's garden with Mari, pulling weeds away from his cabbages and lettuces. A low worry nagged at her as she remembered Péter dashing out the front door, chasing bad news.

Ildi and Antal returned, high-spirited, from their one-night honeymoon in time to set up chairs for the weekly music gathering. Katalin took goblets from the cupboard and poured Tokaj wine left over from the dinner party. As the guests arrived, she greeted them at the door and offered them a glass. Even Comrade Erika. Katalin watched for Péter, glancing out the tall windows to the street below, unsure what time the train usually brought him back on Sundays.

For the first time since her pregnancy, she sang for the gathered musicians that evening. It was somehow a simple matter: when they asked for the song she had sung at the party, she set down her wine glass and sang—without accompaniment this time, because her mother was out. At the end, the guests clapped and cheered. Katalin thanked them and went to pull Mari away from a guest's purse. Someone asked her where the other singer was, the fellow with the beautiful voice.

"He was called away," Katalin said. She looked toward the window again and glanced at the clock.

MONDAY, PÉTER HAD still not returned. This troubled her; it wasn't like him to be gone on a work day. On Tuesday after work, Katalin checked the mailbox—several letters for her father, none for her—then wandered through the courtyard with Mari. Before she headed upstairs to her flat, she opened the cellar door and called down, "Péter?"

"Pétó?" Mari echoed.

There was no answer.

"I don't think he's here, Marika," Katalin said, and she tried not to dwell on how, sometimes, people simply vanished.

So when she looked out her bedroom window late that night and saw him on the street below, walking into the circle of light at the building's front entrance, she dashed out of the apartment and down the back stairs. She reached the cellar door just as he did. His smile kindled when he saw her, and for a moment she felt unexpectedly shy. The courtyard was empty. She glanced upward, checking for listeners on the balconies, and she and Péter moved out of the light sphere of the cellar door.

"I'm glad to see you," he said softly.

"Did you just now get back?"

"No, last night." Péter looked worn, with his collar unbuttoned and rumpled in the night warmth. "I had to work late tonight to make up for being gone."

"What was the matter, that you had to leave?"

"My grandfather died."

"Ah, nem, Péter, I'm sorry," she said, though she couldn't help a flash of relief that it was not a threat that had pulled Péter away, only a grief. As if grief were ever *only*.

"I should have known this was coming," he said. "The signs were all there."

"We don't usually want to know."

"No."

She let her fingertips brush his wrist. He clasped her hand, and she felt the work-roughened surface of his thumb.

"I sang the 'Ave Maria' for him right before he died," Péter said. "I don't really know if he could hear me by then, but I sang it. And at his burial, too. My father asked me to." Péter's grip on her hand tightened. "But I broke down on *ora pro nobis*."

"If you made it to *ora pro nobis*, you did better than I would have done. How can we sing when it's time to weep?"

He closed his eyes momentarily and nodded. "I think I understand now why it's been so hard for you to sing. After all that's happened to you."

"But I sang Sunday night at the music gathering. I finally did it."

"Good." He smiled. "Very good."

He told her he had brought some things back from Kőpatak. She waited in the warm night shadows while he went downstairs. He returned with a bottle of apricot *pálinka* for Antal and Ildi and a parcel wrapped loosely in paper for her. Katalin eased the paper open and ran her fingers over the fragrant, dusky stalks of lavender.

"It's lovely."

She looked at him, and his eyes were gentle and weary behind his glasses. "Péter," she blurted out, "I'm awfully glad to see you back. I was scared."

Somewhere in the apartments above a mother called to her child; somewhere a radio played. But here between them the night was still. Above the courtyard, the shaft of sky was starless and gray-black.

He touched her hair beside her cheek. "Katalin."

She laid her hand on his shoulder and felt the flow of muscle and bone and life. And then, whether it was he who pulled her close or she who stepped forward, she wasn't sure, but now she stood in his arms against the warm angles of his chest. She touched her finger to his lips, and with a single light pressure on the curve of his neck, she beckoned him and kissed him, a skimming of the lips at first.

But the touch lingered, spinning into another moment and another. With an unpolished tenderness, Péter pressed her to him and kissed her again and then again. Her own heat quickened.

"I'm glad you're back," she whispered.

From above them, she heard voices on a balcony. Katalin made herself remember: any neighbor, any parent, any brother or sister-in-law might be watching. She knew she wasn't ready for their questions about what was happening. She could barely admit it to herself.

"Péter," she whispered, "I think I'd better go back upstairs."

"I wish you didn't have to."

"I know. I'm sorry."

His arms released her, reluctant, and she stepped away. He stopped her with his hand and gave her the bottle of *pálinka*. "Good night, Katalin."

As she climbed the stairs, she turned back three times. He was always watching.

In the apartment, all was quiet, her parents reading in the front room, Mari sleeping, and Antal and Ildi having gone out somewhere. Katalin left the bottle of *pálinka* on the dining table for them. Hands unsteady, she knotted kitchen twine around the lavender stems, then carried the bundle into her bedroom. The night breeze rustled the curtains. Since Mari was asleep, Katalin did not turn on the overhead light, but holding a curtain aside with her elbow, by the glow of a streetlamp she hung the lavender from the rod. She thought of Péter cutting it in the garden of his village home and realized she wasn't sure what to imagine. A small adobe house, most likely. A dirt floor, a crooked stick fence. Sadness shuddered through her as she pictured the poverty of the man she had just kissed.

She undressed and sat down on the bed in her nightgown. The breeze touched her bare arm, and a flush of lonely desire stung hot within her, startling and haunting in its strength. How she wanted to run to him, shake him where he lay in his makeshift bed: *Péter! It's me, Katalin. I don't want to be alone.*

A crazed risk. She had already taken one risk too many when Mari was conceived.

By habit, even by instinct now, her eyes rose to the small photograph of Róbert, though she could barely see it in the dark room. Had she stopped waiting for him? Maybe she had. But what was the point in waiting any longer? She could not go on standing still. Even if she wanted to, her daughter would not. Children moved, they walked, they ran. If she herself kept standing still, her child would leave her behind. Somehow, in some direction, she would have to move, to step, to *go*.

AT THE NURSERY school the next day, the head teacher was absent, and Katalin found herself in charge of the children's lessons and activities. By mid-afternoon she was surprised by how well it was going. She and the children spent extra time singing. There was real ability emerging among the children, especially Erzsi with her joyous sense of rhythm and Zoli with his flawless, shining pitch. Maybe Péter had been like Zoli as a child.

The next day Katalin took her zither. The head teacher had returned, and Katalin asked her if the children could sing for their parents at the end of the day. The woman shrugged yes. So when the parents arrived, Katalin gathered the children in front of the end wall where Stalin's portrait hung.

"Closer together, girls and boys," she told them. "Stand here in front, Zoli."

"Here, Kati *néni*?" the boy asked, straightening like a telephone pole.

"Yes. And you, too, Erzsi, over here. Good."

Katalin sat in a low chair and strummed the zither on her lap. "Like the squirrels in the trees, we are very happy," the boys and girls sang, in an enthusiastic rendition of a communist children's song. The parents gave a light smattering of applause.

"Now let's sing, '*Bújj bújj zöld ág*,' " Katalin told the children.

As they began the simple game song, some of the parents sang along. She and the children then went on to "*Lánc, lánc eszter lánc*" and a few other familiar songs. The parents clapped in delight. Katalin could hear them telling each other how good the children sounded.

At the end, Zoli and his mother were the last to leave. "Thank you," the woman told Katalin. "Every day Zoli talks about you and your music."

Katalin thought about the children and their singing as she rode the tram home with Mari. She felt pleasure in their gains. In Péter's gains, too. Though she had never given much thought to becoming a teacher, it began to make sense now. To do *something* was better than to stand still.

* * *

PÉTER CAME FOR a voice lesson that night. After the lesson, they talked outside the apartment door, and she told him about the children. He listened eagerly to her story, smiling in recognition when she named off the songs. She would have let herself stand close to him and touch his arm if she were sure they wouldn't be seen. He asked her quietly if they could go to the park together on Sunday—"With Mari," he added—and she told him yes.

Afterward, she hesitated to tell her parents of their plans, though: *What are you doing, Katalin?* they would think, even if they didn't say it. *He is a peasant.*

IN THE BOTTOM of a kitchen cupboard, Katalin's family kept small gifts her father's patients gave him as gratuities, before or after, for a job well done: chocolates, brandy, occasionally even something from the West, like French wine. Such things had come in handy when her family in turn needed favors or were at the bottom of an endless wait list. Friday morning before she left for work, Katalin went to the cupboard and slipped a box of Swiss chocolates into her big handbag. After work, with Mari in hand, she stopped by the city's teaching academy.

"I'd like an application for the elementary teaching program," she told the woman at the front desk. "For this fall."

The woman twiddled a pen. "The deadline has come and gone."

Katalin cocked her head and lifted the chocolate box halfway out of her bag. A few minutes later, she left with an application.

Arriving home, she stopped at the foyer mailboxes. She set Mari on her feet, unlocked the family box, and pulled out three long envelopes.

"For your Uncle Antal," she told Mari as she flipped through the mail, "and for your Grandpapa, and ...."

And a letter addressed *Katalin Varga* in a vertical, once-familiar cursive.

"*Jézus,*" she whispered.

She turned the envelope over. Yes. The return address was Mezősárgás.

"Mari!" Katalin ordered, for the child was toddling off. "Come!"

She shoved the mail into her handbag, snatched the little girl up onto her hip again, and took to the stairs. At the door of the flat, she paused to gather her breath, then stepped inside and told Mari to go to Nagymama. In her bedroom, Katalin pushed the door shut and pried open the envelope.

It held a folded sheet of music manuscript paper. She pressed the creases flat. The music sheet had been notated in pencil, double staff, all the way down the page. A piano piece. At the top was written *Nocturne for Katalin Varga,* and near the right margin, very small, she read, *R.Z.—1951.* She turned the paper over. The musical notation filled most of the back page, and beneath it, she found a message:

> My lovely Katalin,
>
> Thank you for your letter and for your unending goodness and loyalty.

Loyalty. She put her hand to her lips and swallowed hard.

> I wrote the enclosed piece for you. Please forgive me. Please understand ....
>
> *Róbert*

That was all.

She retraced his words: "my lovely Katalin ... unending goodness ... loyalty ... forgive me ... please understand ...."

She turned back to the beginning of the music and read through the piece, running a finger under the top notes and humming the melody. It was in a minor key and flowed like a somber dance until, at the apex, it rose into a major scale. This much she could make out, but not the nuances of the chords, and she didn't have the skill to play the piece on the piano. She wanted to ask Ildi but couldn't face the questions that she and then the whole family would raise.

And Péter—good, tender Péter, whom she had kissed. He had every reason to ask questions as well. She had no answers.

LATE THAT NIGHT, she thought of someone who could help, someone for whom this would not be a surprise. The next day after work, she went to Mr. Boros' shop with Mari in her arms and Róbert's music in her bag, arriving just before his closing time. When all the customers had left, Mr. Boros locked the shop and they went to the small back room where a practice piano was kept. Katalin let him look at the music and read Róbert's note.

Mr. Boros sighed. "He says nothing about the child, I see."

"He doesn't know. I haven't told him yet."

Katalin held Mari and stood beside the spinet piano. Mr. Boros touched the keys. Róbert's music rose, twisting into dissonance just momentarily then flowing into harmony again, carried forward inexorably on the bass undercurrent. At the bridge of the piece, where the minor melody became major.

She gasped in recognition.

Four descending notes from *"Caro Mio Ben"* formed the theme Róbert had planted in the song. In the reprise, the theme returned, minor and haunting. A long chord, shifting in the bass, ended the piece. Mr. Boros lifted his foot from the sustaining pedal.

"Play it again," she said. "Please."

He played the piece three more times. Katalin tried to absorb every note, every slur, every pause, while in her arms Mari clutched her yellow blanket and sucked her thumb. The music faded.

"Melancholic, isn't it," Mr. Boros murmured. He turned to look at her. "Katalin, tell him about his daughter."

THE NEXT MORNING, she rose before the summer light. While Mari slept, Katalin tried to write another letter to Róbert, but the words about their daughter would not come. Finally she set the pen aside. She spread out the map again. A thought took hold and grew, and once it had grown she could not ignore it. For good or ill, she would follow it.

She could only hope that Péter would forgive her.

Chapter Nineteen

～ ⌣ ～

Losing

THAT SUNDAY MORNING Péter woke especially early and couldn't go back to sleep. He made himself read for two hours. Later, he prepared for meeting Katalin. He washed at the laundry sink, shaved, combed his recalcitrant hair, and put on his best shirt, which was only a little less frayed at the collar than his others. Yesterday he had even paid Irénke *néni* to iron it, though he hated paying her a single *fillér* since she had usurped Mrs. Kovács' apartment and laundry job. There were times she came in here to do the washing, and he couldn't stand it.

But enough of that. As he buttoned his shirt, he thought of Katalin, the way she had sheltered in his arms that night, with her curved warmth resting against him and her lips pressing his. It had happened so quietly, naturally, like wheat ripening. Yet even now it filled him with a longing deep enough to slay him.

ON THE SUBWAY to the park, he noticed Katalin was not talkative, though he asked her about her zither and her guitar and about the children at the nursery. This dismayed him, being the one coaxing conversation. It was almost a relief when Mari, on his lap, grabbed for his glasses. He pried them gently out of her hand.

"I'm sorry," Katalin said. "She's so inquisitive. And you're so patient with her."

"I like her."

"I know."

They stepped off the subway at Heroes Square, which fronted the park. Péter lifted Mari to show her the bronze Magyar warriors astride their muscular horses. The little girl thrust a finger toward the statues and said, "*Ó!*"

"*Ló?*" he asked her. "Do you see a horse? *Ló?*"

"*Ó!*"

"It's a new word for her," Katalin said.

Katalin's eyes looked strained, but perhaps it was only that she was squinting in the summer glare. For much too short a moment she touched his arm. They headed past the half-ring of statue saints and rebels, across the bridge over the lake's neck, and into the park. They sat on a bench among the trees and let Mari gather twigs and pull on the grass blades. The sun filtered through the branches overhead. Katalin kept glancing from side to side; more than once she seemed about to say something but stopped when other people walked by. He wished he could tell her something that would make her happy.

"I've been reading," he said. "The Indian book."

"Yes?"

"I'm halfway through."

"Good!"

He laid his hand on hers, and for a moment she drew close. "Péter," she whispered, "I have to talk to you about something."

She did not want to discuss it here. Péter hoisted the child onto his shoulders. Though it would be a long way home, they decided not to take the subway and instead walked down a side street.

"I have to apologize," she said, barely above a whisper, as they passed a plaster apartment house. "I shouldn't have kissed you the other night. I'm sorry."

His hands tightened on Mari's ankles. "Why are you sorry?"

"I think—it seems—I'm not really free."

"Are you talking about Mari's father? He's gone!"

"I thought he was. I mean—you're from Heves County, aren't you?"

"Yes, Kőpatak."

"And Mezősárgás is near there, right?"

He scowled in apprehension. "Fifteen, maybe sixteen kilometers away. Why?"

"About a month ago I found out Mari's father is there."

Péter stopped so abruptly that Mari almost fell from his shoulders. Katalin threw her hands up to right the child.

"Keep walking," Katalin urged. "It's true. I was afraid Róbert was dead, or starving in prison somewhere, but I heard he's in Mezősárgás."

"But what's he doing in Mezősárgás? There's nothing there!"

"I don't know. I wrote to him, and at first there was no answer, but …

Péter, I'm sorry! I shouldn't have started encouraging you. I'm so sorry. Day before yesterday, I heard from him."

The sun beat down. Katalin shaded her eyes with her hand and looked up at him. "He sent me some music."

"You sent him a letter, and he sent you *music* back? What kind of an answer is that? My God, Katalin, you told him about Mari, and he didn't say *anything*?"

She took a step back. "He doesn't know about Mari yet."

An old couple was approaching on the sidewalk. Péter tugged at Katalin's shoulder, leading her around a corner onto an empty, narrow lane. He set Mari down on the gritty cobbles, and Katalin gripped the child's hand.

"You didn't tell him?" Péter persisted. "In your letter, you didn't say anything about Mari?"

"No. I wanted to tell him face to face."

"And before you found out he was there, before you wrote to him, he never wrote to you, never came?"

She pressed her lips together and shook her head.

"So how long has this fellow been in Mezősárgás, not visiting you and not writing?"

"I don't know! I don't know any of this. And that's what I have to talk to you about. No, listen, please! I know you don't like this, but I have to see Róbert. I wrote him and asked him if we could meet, but he didn't answer. Péter, stop huffing like that! Who knows what strain he might be under—maybe it's just not safe for him to write to me, I don't know. But I have to talk to him."

"And you want me to take you to Mezősárgás."

"Yes. Please."

Her hair fell alongside her jaw, and she blinked, and she was beautiful, and all this was impossible to endure.

"I'm sorry," she said. "I know this isn't easy for you, but I have to do this. I have to go. He's my baby's father."

"God, don't I know."

"And I thought that maybe next time you go home to Kőpatak, Mari and I could come along. And—I ask, please—if you could help me get to Mezősárgás. I guess we'd probably have to spend the night in Kőpatak with your family."

He stared off at some graffiti on the wall across the narrow street. "And what does *your* family say about this, you going off overnight to the country with me, with someone they hardly know?"

She hesitated. "I haven't told them yet."

"You don't like telling people things, do you? You haven't told Róbert about Mari, you haven't told your family about going to see him—"

"I have reasons!"

"Well, I'm not taking you out of this city without you telling them. They'd be furious with me. And when it comes to that, they'd probably rather go with you themselves. I expect they have some things they'd like to say to this fellow. Where I come from, they would tell him to marry you."

"I know. I don't want them to tell him to."

Her lips compressed, and in this obstinacy, Péter grasped at a thin straw of hope. She didn't want Róbert to be told to marry her. Maybe—please—maybe she didn't really want to marry him.

"I don't want them telling him or me what to do," she said. "This is between Róbert and me."

"And it looks like I'm just the coachman here."

"It isn't like that, Péter!"

If it wasn't like that, he didn't know what to call it. In the distance, traffic rumbled. He looked down at the cobbles, the mortar, anywhere but at her. No. He would tell her no. He wouldn't take her to that bastard in Mezősárgás. Péter lifted the word *no* from within him and turned to her—

But he could not gaze into her eyes, round with worry, and say no.

"If you'll tell your family," he said, "I'll take you. But you should think about something. This fellow should have come back. Damn it, any man worth his own balls—"

"Don't talk to me like that!"

"—would come back! He's not in prison. He could do it if he tried. Because ..." Péter broke off, fighting down the strain in his voice. "Because if it were me, and there was some beautiful girl—like you—and the beautiful girl loved me, I'd come back. I'd do it. Somehow. I'd bribe somebody, I'd fight, I'd crawl, I'd ... I don't know what. But I'd come back. Especially if," he made himself go on, "especially if I had lain with her."

Katalin's chin trembled.

"But this Róbert hasn't come to you," he said. "If you really think you should go to him, all right, I'll take you to Mezősárgás, but it's only because you need a yes or a no."

She lowered her head. He touched her shoulder only for a moment. It troubled him to touch her. On backstreets they walked home without speaking. Even Mari, in Katalin's arms, was silent. At the apartment house door, they stopped, and neither of them reached for the knob.

With his finger Péter slowly traced the crease of her forehead. "Do you still love him?"

She looked down, closed her eyes. "He's my baby's father."

MONDAY AT WORK was unproductive. The press had gone through one of its stoppages, and on the loading dock there was nothing to load. So Péter washed the truck, bucket-carrying the water from a standpipe up the street. The man Lajos Szabó made a few passes over the truck with a wet rag, then sat down on a packing crate and smoked. Péter was past caring whether Lajos worked or smoked. Besides, Lajos didn't look well: his eye sockets were gray.

"Haven't heard you sing today," Lajos suddenly said from his packing crate. "If you wait until there's something to sing about, you'll wait a long time."

"I'm not waiting for something to sing about, I'm washing a truck."

"I used to sing. I used to wash trucks. There's no point."

Péter turned his back.

A little later Lajos was gone. In the lunch line, the serving girl named Dóra asked Péter if Lajos had shown up for work.

"For a while," Péter said. "Looks like he left again."

"That poor idiot."

At the end of the day shift, the droop-shouldered janitor, Ernö Gárdonyi, came to the loading dock and gave Péter a small, beckoning gesture. Something must be up. Péter joined Gárdonyi in the shade of the building next door and kept an eye out for other workers.

"Listen," Gárdonyi said. "I'm sorry to tell you this, but it appears your Uncle Béla is dead."

"What ... how—"

"I saw a cousin of his. She said he was in the prison at Vác. She sent him a letter recently, and it was returned to her with a note on it. 'Unable to receive mail,' it said. I hear that those are the code words when somebody has died."

Péter turned his head aside. When his grandfather had died last week, Péter had known the man was old, and it was time—not a happy time, but maybe somehow the right time. This was all wrong. Béla was certainly not young, but not standing in death's queue, either.

"Was he beaten?" he whispered to Gárdonyi.

"I don't know. We can only hope not. Maybe he got sick. I'm so sorry."

Péter felt his breath shaking.

IN THE MEETING the next morning, Péter sat at a front table across from Dóra and Gárdonyi. Dóra stared down at the table top. Nearby, Mr. Molnár stood before the gathering, shifting his weight.

"I have an unfortunate announcement," he said, and he rubbed his chin. "This regards Lajos Szabó. He died sometime yesterday. His body was found last night."

Nearby a woman gasped. A man swore. Péter's breath hitched. Dead? How could Lajos be dead? Only yesterday he was here, muttering. Holy God, why was everybody dying?

Across the table, Dóra buried her face in her hands, and Ernö Gárdonyi whispered something to her.

The Party rep stepped to Mr. Molnár's side. She looked around the room uncertainly, like an animal out of its territory. "Let's read *Szabad Nép*," she said.

She paced the front of the room. Stopping near Péter, she held the newspaper out to him. "Comrade, the article on the top of page three, please."

His pulse pounded. He couldn't read for all these people. Devil take it, wasn't there any way out of this? What would Katalin do?

"I'm sorry ... sorry, comrade," he said to the Party rep. "I worked with Lajos, and this news has hit me hard. I don't think I can get through the reading."

"It has hit us all hard," the Party rep said, still holding out the paper.

Péter did not move.

Across from him, Dóra pushed herself up from the table. "I'll do it."

She stood in front and read in a resigned monotone. Péter mouthed *thank you* to her, though he wasn't sure she saw it, and he sat there thinking about his dead co-worker and his dead uncle and his dead grandfather and about the fact that he had almost had to read in front of a hundred people and about Katalin wanting to go to Mezősárgás and again about Lajos being dead, and about the last thing Lajos had said to him: *there's no point.*

Gárdonyi was sent to work on the loading dock that day, and Péter asked him about Lajos as they lowered their heads together, checking crates of pages.

"I knew he was sick," Péter said, "but I didn't know he was *that* sick."

"No. He hanged himself. In his flat."

"Mother of God!"

Péter asked Gárdonyi one appalled question after another. He learned that Gárdonyi, Lajos, Dóra, and her mother all lived in the same apartment building. It was Dóra and her mother who had found Lajos' hanging body and ran to summon Gárdonyi.

"*Nem*," Péter breathed, as the desperate scene took shape before him. "If I'd known he was so miserable, I'd have tried to be nicer to him."

"If you had been nicer, he would have done the same thing. Mercy on him. Mercy on all of us."

After work, Péter sang in the boiler room because he didn't want to go home. The apartment house was unbearable now that Katalin had asked him to take her to her old lover. Sometimes he thought of telling her the plan was off, it was a terrible idea, he would not do it; then he would remember her sad confusion, and he would relent. He knew he was supposed to hope that the man would do right by her and marry her, but it was easier to hope that this Róbert would fall under the wheels of a Soviet convoy. Next to the brooms and the paint cans, Péter sang easy songs because his voice was tired, and he slouched more than Katalin would have let him.

When he stepped out of the broom closet, Dóra was standing by the boiler under the dials. She looked at him, neither smiling nor frowning, and held a tray with two forks, two old crockery plates, and an enameled metal bowl full of dumplings. She set the tray on a step stool and dragged two chairs over.

"I like your singing," she said, voice listless. "There was some lunch left over. Here, let's eat. Sorry, there wasn't much gravy left. Horrible day, isn't it, with Lajos dead and all."

Her straight hair hung diagonal over her forehead. Hers was not a soft face, but if she would ever smile she would probably be pretty. When she untied her apron and pulled it off, he had a jarring sense of the girl undressing in front of him. They sat down together, holding their plates, and ate.

Péter said, "Ernö Gárdonyi told me what happened, said that Lajos hanged himself and you found him."

Dóra twiddled her fork among the dumplings. "Yes, Lajos lives upstairs from us. *Lived* upstairs. His girlfriend used to live there too, but then she moved out. Who could blame her, the way he drank? My mother and I started looking in on him a few months back. Last night we knocked on his door, but there was no answer, and I peeked through the kitchen curtains, and there he was," she put her hand to her throat, "on a plumbing pipe. So we had to go get the manager to unlock his apartment."

"And then you went and got Uncle Gárdonyi?"

"Of course." She looked at him, head tilted, as though surprised he would ask. "Naturally."

She crossed her legs, which tapered nicely at the ankles.

"Thank you for reading in my place today," he said.

"You already thanked me." She picked at a dumpling, then set her plate aside. "There's a Party meeting in the lunch room this evening. I guess I'll go. After what happened last night, I just don't want to go home."

Péter nodded, recognizing the feeling.

"You might as well come to the meeting, too," she said.

In a day or two he would have to ask for time off to take Katalin to Mezősárgás. It wouldn't be a bad idea to humor the bosses beforehand by showing up at the meeting. He told Dóra he'd go.

THE MEETING WAS dull. The Party rep talked about Yugoslavia again. Péter tried to look like he cared, but he had nothing against the Yugoslavs: it wasn't they who had killed his mother, taken away his father's land, or gotten Katalin pregnant.

He glanced at Dóra beside him. She was looking at the clock. He found himself lingering on the way her tan skirt draped over her crossed legs, rising and falling on the curve of her thigh. So this was the girl who tended to leave her top buttons undone, the girl who had laughed at him for singing to horses. He had disliked her for it, but maybe it was time to let it go. After all, she was also the girl who had been appearing in the boiler room to listen to him sing and to bring him food. Back in Kőpatak, it was assumed that if a girl fed you, she liked you. He had to admit it was nice to be liked. Besides, she had rescued him during the reading today. And last night the poor girl had found a suicide.

And as for himself, well, he was twenty-two years old, and until these last two weeks, he had never kissed a girl. And now that he had ... oh, Lord, there were some things that could not be forgotten, and they all rushed in upon him as he looked at the drape of Dóra's skirt over her thighs.

DUSK WAS SETTING in as they left the meeting and stopped at a bar. At a rickety table, they drank brandy. He let her do most of the talking. She lived with her mother, she said. Her older sister had married and moved to Csepel, and her father had left the family. Dóra stated this without comment. When she asked Péter where he was from, he told her he was from the plain and left it at that. She then asked him about his sounds in the boiler room.

"Those are voice exercises," he said. "Part of my singing lessons."

"Lessons." She swirled her brandy glass. "What are you hoping for—to sing on the radio?"

It was strange to hear her talk of hoping. He had started the lessons because a girl with a child in her arms had sung with the beauty of the night stars, and her brother with a violin had told him that music speaks. Beauty and speech—maybe that had made him hopeful, but it felt more like hunger.

"I just want to sing better," he said.

"You already sing better than anybody I know."

Somewhere in the dim bar, a radio had been switched on. Clarinet music was pouring out in the style that Katalin called swing. Two couples took to the floor, rocking, twirling and laughing.

"That looks like fun," Dóra said. By now she was on her second brandy.

Péter watched the couples' movements. The dancing didn't look much harder than what he'd done with Katalin at Antal's party. He could probably do it. He sipped his brandy and considered. If he danced badly, who cared, really? If he looked ridiculous, it wasn't death. The others out there didn't look so sharp, either. If he trod on Dóra's feet, that probably didn't matter, as long as she didn't mind, and he guessed she wouldn't, given the brandy.

He turned to Dóra and gestured, shrugging, toward the dance. They stood up, grasped hands and began scooting and stepping, trying to imitate the back-and-forth movement of the others. Péter stayed on the beat. Dóra did not. It was fun, or at least fun enough, considering that she had found a suicide and he had to take Katalin to Mezősárgás.

The music slowed, and Dóra reached around his neck. Her body heated his.

AFTERWARD THEY WALKED along the thoroughfare in the light of the streetlamps and passing taxis, Dóra leaning on his arm. She had grown a little tipsy. He knew by the heaviness of his steps that he'd had more brandy than he needed, too. They turned at a corner and soon reached the backstreet building where Dóra lived. Crossing the courtyard, they passed the trash bins and a pushcart. Where was he supposed to say goodbye to her? At the door of her ground-level apartment, her hand tightened on his arm. She pointed up at a glowing third-floor window.

"That's where Ernö Gárdonyi lives," she said. Her finger moved down the row to a darkened window. "And that's Lajos' flat. God, what a horrible thing."

She began to cry, and he felt helpless. He put his arms around her and touched her head, letting her lean on his shoulder. It was what he would have done for Katalin. Dóra quieted and wiped her eyes with her hand, then pulled her key from her skirt pocket and pressed it into the keyhole.

"Why don't you come in," she said.

From somewhere behind the brandy, he felt unsure. "I don't know, it's getting late."

"Just for a while."

He followed her inside and looked around. They were standing in the kitchen of a small apartment with a spiral ladder-stair to a loft.

"Where is your mother?" he asked cautiously.

"At work. At the hospital. She has an overnight shift."

Here they were, with the mother gone, and Péter could not stop remembering the sweep of Dóra's skirt over her thigh. She enclosed his hand in hers. She told him he was a good singer and a good person. She wished she had been nicer to him when they first met, and she liked dancing with him tonight. He touched her cheek just under her ear. She smiled, something she so rarely did, and drew close. He stroked her side. It seemed impossible not to.

A long kiss, and she caressed his neck, his back, his chest. His blood churned. His arms tightened hard around her and she laughed a little.

"Easy," she whispered. She lifted one pretty finger toward the stairs. "Why don't you stay? My mother won't be home until sometime tomorrow. We can go upstairs. If you want, I mean. And in the morning I'll make breakfast for you."

Tomorrow. Sunrise. Morning. There was not just tonight, there was tomorrow. This blood-heat would wear off. The drinks would wear off. The sun would rise. And when it did, this girl would hardly matter to him.

He stepped back, Dóra's waist between his two hands.

"What's wrong?" she asked.

It would all wear off. Oh, but it hadn't worn off *yet*.

"Péter?"

"I … I don't think I belong here," he said, though his body screamed at him to shut up, grab the girl, and drag her up the stairs before she changed her mind.

She blinked. "I like you," she said. "I like having you here."

"I shouldn't stay," his voice somehow went on. "We shouldn't do this. You don't really want us to. I don't really want us to. I mean, I do, but I don't. Things happen. I have a friend who got pregnant and the man's gone. It's not good. I think I'd better leave now before we … regret …."

"I'm used to regret."

She leaned on his chest and then, very quietly, she began to cry again. He held her, but not as tightly now, and whispered, "Poor girl, poor girl." Gradually his arms gave up her warm flesh until he held only her hand, and then her fingers, and then he let go. He stepped back, and she stepped back, and he went out into the night, alone.

THE NEXT DAY he almost asked Ernö Gárdonyi to stand in the lunch line for him and bring him his noodles and gravy. But in the end, Péter took his place in line, and when he reached the front, he greeted Dóra by name. Their tired eyes met, and though she didn't really smile, she ladled out an oversized portion for him.

AT THE END of the work day, he waited outside Mr. Molnár's office beside a poster of a man with a wrench and a woman with a red flag. *Work is a matter of honor and duty*, the poster said. There was some small, tedious satisfaction in being able to read the sloganeering better than he used to. When Mr. Molnár appeared, Péter asked for Saturday off—"To help a friend, comrade"—and he promised to work late tonight and the next night.

Katalin owed him.

It was almost eleven o'clock when he went home that night. Antal, violin case in hand, was just arriving back from an opera performance. They paused in the foyer together, and Antal said there were a few things his family wanted to know regarding this upcoming trip. Péter had been on his feet for hours, so he sat down on the stairs.

"Last night Katalin told us you'll be helping her see Mari's father," Antal said. "Let's just say we were *surprised* that she even knows where Róbert is. She hadn't said anything about him for so long. And now she says he sent her some music—"

"Seems to me he owes her a damned lot more than music," Péter interrupted him.

"Oh, I agree. But listen, you don't have to do this trip if you don't want to. I can go with her, or my father can. This is our family's responsibility."

Péter rested his elbows on his knees and considered it, but when all was added up, he did not want anyone there who might talk Róbert and Katalin into marrying. "I told her I'd go," he said to Antal, "and I will."

"Katalin said it would probably have to be an overnight trip?"

"Yes," Péter said, "and she and Mari and I will stay with my *family*."

"I trust you, and I told my parents that."

"Thank you," Péter sighed, now acutely relieved that last night he had left Dóra's apartment when he did. "Antal, what do you think? This Róbert, is he any good?"

Antal set the violin case down on a stair. "I only knew him a little. After I found out Kati was pregnant, I asked around about him at the academy. I got mixed reports. Moody. Creative. Insightful. Unreliable. Unconventional. Friends with agitators. And so on." Antal cast a glance at the door of Comrade Erika's apartment. He leaned toward Péter, whispering, "Katalin says this trip to Mezősárgás is her business. But, look … I don't want her in a corner with Róbert! If I were going with her on that trip, I wouldn't let her out of my sight, and that's probably why she's so determined to go with you instead."

"I don't want her alone with him either, but what am I supposed to do?"

"If she asks you to look after Mari, don't do it. You are *not* Mari's nanny. I told her not to take advantage of your kindness."

They said good night, and Péter went to the cellar and washed his face with cold water. Body and mind, he was wound tight as Antal's violin strings, and when he went to his bed, he sat restless on his blankets. The sorrows of this week surrounded him—his grandfather, and his uncle, and Lajos, and the two girls he had kissed. Maybe he would feel better if he sang, but he couldn't. At his grandfather's burial, the music had broken inside him, *ora pro nobis*.

But fragments of that song came to him now, and though he did not sing, he listened. The *Ave* brought Ernö Gárdonyi to his mind, for he strongly suspected the man was a priest the State had thrown out of the pulpit. Péter had been to neither mass nor confession since his mother died. It had seldom mattered to him, but now in this dark, sad place under the stairs he felt the lonely company of his sins. He closed his eyes and recounted the things he would say if Gárdonyi were indeed a priest and if he himself were bold enough:

If I were braver, I would have looked harder for Uncle Béla. I wouldn't have found him, but I would have looked.

And I should have done something different about Lajos. I don't know what, but now he's dead.

Péter rested his head in his palms.

I shouldn't have let my mother go looking for the cow the day she died. I should have looked for the cow myself.

And I should have let my father re-marry when he had the chance.

Then maybe Gárdonyi would ask, "Is there anything else, brother?"

And I love a girl I can't have.

ON HIS LUNCH break the next day, Péter went to the post office and telegrammed Apa: COMING SATURDAY WITH GIRL AND BABY. PLEASE CLEAN HOUSE.

ON SATURDAY MORNING, he and Katalin rode the train with Mari crawling back and forth between their laps. It seemed to Péter that Katalin had taken special pains with her appearance: a softly draping blouse, neatly barretted hair, and white-polished sandals, although he had told her to wear good walking shoes. It stung him, this careful prettiness for another man.

At Háromkeresztes there was an hour-long wait to change trains for Kőpatak, so he showed her the restaurant where he had sung with the young Gypsy named Miklós. The place had not yet opened for the day. On the ride between Háromkeresztes and Kőpatak, Mari fell asleep with her head in Péter's lap and her feet in Katalin's. Péter stroked the little girl's downy hair and prepared Katalin for what she would find, and not find, at his home. He had been putting this off.

"There's no sink," he said, "and no toilet. Not much privacy, either. It's crowded. There's a city couple, like Ildi's parents. And please don't feel bad if my father doesn't say much to you; that's just the way he is."

"I understand."

Outside the window, sunflowers bent their heavy heads in the sun. Behind the spreading fields, the hills pushed up. A stork flew across the sky and came to rest on the wooden lever post of a well.

"It's beautiful here," Katalin said. She looked at him, and it was then that he really noticed the tense pull at the corners of her eyes.

IT WAS EARLY afternoon when they reached Kőpatak. As they walked down the rutted dirt road, he saw her taking in the reed-thatched roofs, the ducks in the drainage ditches, the creaking wagons. He sensed the villagers watching them, the women looking up from their vegetable plots, the men and boys turning their eyes. When they passed the Kozmas' garden, Ági was there, with her full hair bouncing as she waved. "Peti! Look at you, bringing home not just one girl but two!"

He didn't answer, only tugged Katalin to the side of the road as a State car roared past.

The gate posts of his own home had never seemed more crooked and shabby to him than they did now. He could smell the pig sty. And even from here, he knew the garden needed edging. He lifted the latch and opened the gate, shooing a hen away with his foot.

"Mari, look at the hen," Katalin said. "This is where Péter gets the nice eggs he brings us. And the lavender." She turned toward the house. "And the windows look so pretty with the flowers in them."

Surprised, Péter followed her gaze. For the first time since the year of his mother's death, there were potted geraniums in the windowsills. Mrs. Zöld must have put them there. She had probably heard about the telegram he sent Apa. The front door of the house opened, and the twins bounced out in their suspenders and bare feet.

"The baby's here!" Gyuri shouted back through the doorway.

Apa stepped out the door and met them under the eaves. "Son," he said in greeting to Péter.

Turning to Katalin, he inclined his head. She reached out her hand. He clasped it and uttered the old Hungarian welcome, "God brought you."

Chapter Twenty

～～～

The Cowherd

THE CITY WOMAN named Mrs. Zöld had set a midday chicken dinner on the corner table in the *tiszta szoba*. As they all ate together, Katalin had a feeling that her being here was more of an event than she had intended. She held Mari on her lap, helping the child eat, and wondered what these people had been told about her reason for coming. When Tibi asked why she and Péter were going to Mezősárgás, she said that she needed to look for an old friend. Péter's father touched Tibi's wrist as though warning him to ask no more questions, and she guessed the man knew something. Gyuri and Tibi hurried through their food, and soon were leaning near Mari, handing her spoons, grinning when Mari threw them on the floor, making a game of picking them up again.

After the meal, Péter went out to harness the horse and hitch up the wagon. Katalin stayed in the *tiszta szoba,* and Mrs. Zöld helped her diaper Mari and put a clean dress on her. On a shelf over the bed, Katalin saw framed photographs of the sons Mrs. Zöld had mentioned: a young man with a bride, and another young man, grinning, in a driving cap. Knowing the woman was an exile, Katalin told her about Ildi's family.

"Isn't it hard," Katalin asked, "being city people in the country?"

"It's very hard, if you haven't chosen it. The work is hard. And the worry. We're not young, and Ottó's lungs are not the strongest. He had pleurisy when he was a child. We've requested a transfer, but … well, we'll see. We miss the city. We miss our sons. Worst is the worry." Mrs. Zöld looked at her thoughtfully. "And why is it that you've come today?"

Katalin picked up Mari and let the child rest on her shoulder. There was no good reason not to tell the kind woman the truth. She explained briefly about Róbert, then added, "So I guess if I marry him, I'll be a country person, too."

"Adjustments come easier to the young," the woman said. "You're young, you're strong. You could be happy here, if you were here of your own will."

Soon Mrs. Zöld went outside to the well, and Katalin put new little shoes on Mari; she had bought them for the occasion.

"You'll look so pretty for your apuka," Katalin said, speaking from under the tension in her own jaw. "Do you think you can say that when you see him? *A-pu-ka.*"

The child only grinned and pulled off the shoes.

"No, Mari," Katalin sighed. She combed her own hair and put on lipstick she had borrowed from Ildi. Reaching into her bag again for a small metal pillbox, she pinched out two aspirin tablets and swallowed them down.

PÉTER HAD TOLD her it would take an hour or more to reach Mezősárgás. The wagon creaked and jostled over the road. Katalin sat beside Péter on the coach box with Mari on her lap while he held the reins of the black horse. The fields around them were spiked with the stubble of the recent wheat harvest. On their left, the land stretched away flat; to the right, it rose toward the Bükk Hills under a great expanse of sky. She felt the bumping of the wagon in her hip bones. The sun was hot, and she put on the straw hat that Mrs. Zöld had given her to prevent sunburn. Katalin hoped she wouldn't have to wear the plain, unfashionable thing around Róbert.

And Róbert, what did he even look like now? She couldn't picture him tanned and strapping like the farmers here. The young could adjust, Mrs. Zöld had said, if they came here of their own will. *If.*

Mari squirmed and twisted in Katalin's lap. At length, the road turned and Péter pointed ahead toward a village at the foot of a long, low hill. A large house with spreading grounds and a terra-cotta roof dominated the upper end of the village, and fields and vineyards radiated out from it.

"That village is Mezősárgás," he said. "It's about half the size of Kőpatak. It's not much of a place. The Mezősárgás farmers always used to try to sell their produce in Kőpatak or in Heves or Eger. That house on the hill used to be the baron's estate."

"Have you been there?" she asked.

"Not since it was collectivized. Back before then, there were some summers I worked in the fields. My father and I used to do day labor for the baron's field manager. That big house is the headquarters of the communal farm now."

The communal farm. That was the address on Róbert's letter.

"And where do the communal workers live?" she asked.

"Some in the village, some outside of it. Some live in the headquarters. We have the same thing in Kőpatak, just a smaller house. Owner gets thrown out, workers move in."

"So ... maybe ... in that big house .... Does Róbert live there, do you think?"

Péter kept his eyes on the road ahead. "Good chance of it."

"Do you think ... well ... does he have any space of his own?"

Péter's voice tightened: "I wouldn't know."

"Would I ... I mean ... would that be where I'd live? If I married him?"

"I don't know! How would I know what would happen if you got married?"

"I'm sorry," she murmured.

The horse's hooves kicked up the dust of the road. In spite of the bumping, Mari had fallen asleep against Katalin's breast and upper arm. Carefully Katalin shifted the little girl's weight.

"The baron used to have some land near Kőpatak," Péter said. "Before the war, my father used to talk of buying some. Everything was easier before the war. We had more produce to sell, and we had two horses then. We did some carting for other farmers since we had a team. My mother did the milking and sold eggs. It's harder now."

"I'm sorry, Péter. I want better for you."

"I wish things were different for you, too."

She slipped a little closer to him, even though she had been telling herself to stop this tenderness with Péter. It was just that she had grown so used to having him near. She let her hand fall behind him and her fingertips linger on his back.

"I'm not sure what I'm wishing for me," she said.

Péter looked ahead and behind, and with no other traffic close by on the road, he eased the horse to a stop. In the quiet, he touched one lock of her hair. "You don't have to go to Mezősárgás, Kati. You don't have to see him. Please. I'll turn the horse around, take you back to Kőpatak, back to Pest. Back home."

She looked over her shoulder at the way behind them, the reaped fields and the growing provender. She wavered. Róbert had not asked her to come. But in this battered country, a man could be afraid to ask. And Róbert still did not know about the child asleep in her lap.

"We need to keep going," Katalin said. "*I* need to keep going."

Péter sighed, squinted into the distance, and shook the reins.

The land had been slowly rising. Péter turned the wagon onto a crossroad that led into the village of Mezősárgás. It was past mid-afternoon when they approached the old baronial mansion at the base of the hill. The two-story house had a spreading portico and yellow plaster walls that needed paint. Katalin guessed the baron's family must have belonged to the petty gentry, no better. The carved fronds and cherubs on the window frames showed scorches and holes from the war. Maybe some soldiers had been billeted here. Between the center windows hung the Hungarian tricolor with the communist red star in the middle.

"Here we are," Péter said, voice tight. "Headquarters of the Gold Harvest Farm."

Katalin and Péter climbed down from the wagon with Mari. The high wrought-iron gate stood ajar. Inside it, what had once been lawn was now a potato field. A black State car stood in the driveway, and hoes, shovels, and a bicycle leaned against the portico columns. A hefty peasant woman stepped out of the door with a wooden scoop and a bowl and dipped into a burlap bag beside the front door. It hit Katalin that this woman probably knew Róbert. Maybe Róbert even lived here. Katalin told herself to call out to the woman but cowered back. The woman disappeared inside the house.

Péter gestured at the opening in the gate. "Go in," he said.

"Come with me. Please."

They entered the gate and walked to the stone-paved portico. The peasant woman had not closed the door. A fly buzzed out. Katalin stepped up to the entryway, carrying Mari. People here would probably assume Mari was Péter's child. For now, let them.

She peered inside. Directly ahead stretched a large staircase with a threadbare red carpet. In the vestibule near the staircase stood a huge, low liquor cabinet piled with file folders, brandy glasses, a child's doll, and a fedora. To the left was a wide doorway opening into what must be the parlor. Her eyes riveted on one thing: a black lacquered grand piano.

Somewhere a typewriter was clacking. A man about the age of her father, his trousers tucked into his boots, was now trotting down the stairs. Spotting Katalin and Péter, he crossed the vestibule, opened the door wider and stood with his hand on the knob. "What do you want?"

She glanced at Péter. He nodded, prompting her.

"We're trying to find Róbert Zentai," she told the man. "We heard he was here."

The peasant woman they had seen on the portico now came into the vestibule from some back doorway.

"You aren't from around here," the woman said.

"I am," Péter answered. "From Kőpatak."

"What do you want with Zentai?" the man asked.

Katalin was about to give the explanation she had prepared, something about needing to discuss some family business with him, but for better or worse another idea came to her. "We heard he plays piano," she said. "We wanted to talk to him about lessons."

The man raised his eyebrows. "Zentai plays piano?"

"You didn't know?" Katalin asked.

"Never heard him play." The man spoke to the peasant woman over his shoulder. "You know where he is?"

"Cow herding. He's either in the barns or bringing the cows in."

The man led them to a window at the side of the house and pointed out an adobe barn and a cow path. The path led to the pasture, he said, with the road intersecting. Péter nodded as though this was not unfamiliar to him.

"If you wait on the road near the path," the man said, "Zentai will probably be coming home with the cows before long." He smirked. "You can talk to him about all the piano lessons you want."

They thanked the man, went back to the wagon, and drove to a crest in the road. On the other side, the road sloped gently toward a stream that Péter had said continued on to his village. From the crest they could see the cattle path where it bisected the road, a stone's throw away.

"We'll wait here," Péter said.

He tied the horse to a tree trunk nearby and they waited in the shade of an elderberry bush. Katalin fanned herself with the straw hat. They took turns chasing Mari. Péter said very little. After a time, the horse stamped. Péter turned. He heard the hooves before she did.

"The cows," he said.

With Mari in her arms and Péter beside her, Katalin stood behind the elderberry bush, craning her neck to peer around the branches. Below, a long line of cows passed, and behind the last cow walked the cowherd. He wore a dark hat and a khaki shirt with the sleeves rolled up. She could not see his face in the shadow the hat brim made. In one hand he carried a long staff and in the other he lifted a cigarette.

"I don't remember Róbert smoking much," she whispered to Péter.

"Is that him?"

The cowherd was lanky, medium height. Yes, that much she remembered of Róbert. She thought his shoulders had been broader and straighter than this, but maybe he was hunching as he leaned on the stick. The cowherd turned his head, and she saw his lean face and a sandy-brown sideburn.

Pulling back behind the branches, she clutched Péter's arm. "It's him. I'll call to him." She handed Mari to Péter. "Keep her safe."

Róbert had crossed the road and thrown aside his cigarette stub. He followed the cows onto the section of pathway that led across a fallow field toward the barn. Katalin ran into the middle of the road and down the slope a few meters, the dust kicking up around her sandals.

"Róbert," she called, but her voice was no stronger than the swirl of dust.

Róbert and the cows went on in their long file.

She ran down to where the road met the path. There she stopped. Róbert was only a short distance off now, his back to her. She drew a deep breath, felt it anchor her stomach and lift her chest. "Róbert!"

He looked over his shoulder, turned. His staff clattered to the ground. Ahead of him, the cows plodded on. Róbert's lips moved, and she thought he was speaking her name. She walked up the path until she was standing in front of him. She smiled a little. He extended his hands to her. She grasped them; he let go.

"Katalin."

His voice was hoarser than she remembered. He was still handsome but looked older, the shadows at his eyes darker. She reached up and touched his chin, feeling the stubble growth of a day or two.

"Hello, Róbert."

His eyes swept up the road. "You ... how .... Are you alone?"

She hesitated.

"I can't believe you're here," he said. "My God. Is something wrong?"

"No," she said, in spite of these two years.

He looked behind him to where the cows were retreating. "I have to take the animals to the barn."

"I know. I'll wait for you to finish. Please."

A softness flickered in his eyes but retreated before her hopes could rise. He pointed in the direction from which he had come. "I could meet you there in an hour. In the pasture."

"An hour. Good."

She went back to wait with Péter and Mari. After an hour had come and gone, Péter said, "Enough, let's leave," but she shook her head. By her watch, an hour and twenty minutes had passed when she saw Róbert on the path below, heading for the pasture. She dusted off her skirt and smoothed her hair.

"Take Mari with you," Péter said.

"Péter, please keep her for just a little while—"

"You came here to tell that fellow about Mari. I'm not looking after her. I made an agreement with Antal."

"What does Antal have to do with this? Five minutes and I'll come and get her."

"Five minutes, or I'm bringing her down there myself."

Róbert was waiting under an acacia tree in the middle of the pasture. He had changed his shirt and shaved. She wanted to say it was good to see him, but it was suddenly hard to speak; he looked so gaunt and alone under this tree.

"Well," she managed to say, "thank you for the music you wrote for me. It's beautiful."

His face creased. "You think so?"

"You doubt it?"

"I doubt everything."

Róbert took her right hand between both of his and kissed her carefully on the cheek.

She tried to tease him, "That's not how we used to kiss."

He laughed a little and embraced her, and for a moment barely longer than his laugh, she rested against him, feeling the coarse weave of his shirt and the prominence of his collarbone. Then his arms fell away.

"How did you get here?" he asked.

"With a friend from Kőpatak."

"I didn't know you knew anyone from there."

"He's my student."

"You're teaching, then."

"Just Péter. He's my only student."

"And you're attending the Academy?"

"No."

"No?"

"No, I work in a nursery school."

"Ah." He blinked, almost flinched. "And how is Antal?"

"Married." The word came out too sharply.

Róbert looked at her somberly, and it came back to her that even in their good days he had not often smiled.

"And you?" she asked. "What are you doing here?"

"Herding cows. As you can see."

"But … music? You ordered music from Mr. Boros. That's how I knew where to write you. Piano music. Chopin."

He looked around, waiting a long time to answer. "Good intentions."

"Are you singing?"

He spread his hands, indicating the pasture. "I am not inspired."

"But you wrote music—the piece you sent me."

"Yes, a moment's inspiration, remembering the city. Remembering the Danube." He paused. "Remembering you."

She grasped his hand, but it only remained limp in hers, and she knew the five minutes she had promised Péter were up.

"Wait for me," she begged Róbert and ran back across the pasture.

Péter had already begun heading down the hill with Mari. She did not answer his questioning look. Taking Mari into her arms, she retraced her steps, smoothing the girl's dress and her short dark hair, begging her, "You'll give your apuka a pretty smile, let him see what a nice, nice girl you are, won't you, Marika? Yes. Of course." She kept up the patter with her daughter until she stood in front of Róbert; then she dared look at him.

He was utterly still, seeming not even to breathe. "Who is this?"

It was the moment she had rehearsed in her mind for two years. "This is …." She stopped, breathed. "This is Mária Jozefa. Mari is our daughter. Your daughter."

A quiet gasp. "But … only once—"

"I know."

"*Istenem*." Róbert's eyes fastened on Mari's face. His lower lip quivered; he pulled it in. He reached toward Mari but stopped short, turning to Katalin as though for permission.

"It's all right," she said.

"Mari," he murmured.

The little girl touched his reaching finger, then drew back and studied his face from the safety of Katalin's chest.

"She looks like you," he was struggling with his voice, "and like my mother, a little."

His eyes lowered as he watched his daughter, and with that downward lay of the lids Katalin remembered him playing piano, reading, thinking, kissing her. She reached for him and their fingers intertwined on Mari's elbow.

"Róbert," she whispered, "I can't tell you how I've missed you. I've been so worried. Are you all right?"

"Please don't worry."

"But why are you here? Why are you herding cows?"

He dropped his hand. "Why are you working in a nursery?"

"I needed a job."

"We take what we're given, don't we?"

She glanced over the pasture. No one seemed to be around. Except Péter somewhere, a long way off.

"What *happened*?" she whispered.

He looked toward the road. "Who did you come with?"

"I told you. Péter."

"Pétó," Mari said.

Róbert looked at Mari in surprise. "She can speak," he said softly.

"Yes, she has a few words, says the names of people in the family, says Péter's name."

"Who is this Péter?"

"Like I said, he's a friend. My student. Tell me what happened. Please."

Róbert gestured toward the creek. She followed him with Mari, stepping carefully through the willows and down the bank of tree roots and crumbling dirt. At the edge of the shallow stream, she set Mari down and let the child slap the shallow water. With a pocket knife Róbert cut a willow wand and gave it to Mari, pressing her hand between both of his.

"How long have you been here?" she asked.

"Since I was assigned here. Listen, if anyone comes, I'd better do the talking."

"Róbert, what happened?"

He stood with his hands on the hips of his faded trousers.

"Why didn't you answer my letter?" she blurted out.

"But I did."

"You sent music, but there were no answers, none! Where were you? I was frantic! Were you in prison? Just tell me."

He did not speak.

"The ÁVH?" she prompted.

Silently, he nodded.

"They took you, then?"

"Yes. I was trying to get out of the city, to get away, but they ... they knew, or they followed me. Anyway, they found me at the train station. I was trying to go to Veszprém to wait out the ...."

He kept getting stuck, like Péter when she first knew him.

"You were trying to wait out the trouble, yes?" she offered. "The crackdown?"

His shoulders drew in. "Yes, and all of a sudden there they were, clapping handcuffs on me. They took me to their headquarters on the avenue, and they kept asking me about my roommate. 'Where is Gyula Kardos?' 'We know you were one of Gyula Kardos' co-conspirators.' 'Where is he?' 'Where are the other traitors?' I didn't know where the others were. I pretty much knew where Gyula was, but I tried to steer them away from that." He paused, sucked in a breath. "They talked like we were out to topple the whole Rákosi government. If only! But how much power do a bunch of penniless, naïve students really have? None."

He turned away and dug into the earth with the toe of his boot. The creek murmured. A bird called.

"And then?" she asked.

"So then they put me in a cell in the basement of the headquarters. With a Gypsy pickpocket and some poor bastard they said was an embezzler. He said he wasn't. I don't know. Who can believe a damned thing anybody says? So I was in that cell for ... I don't know. It felt like an eternity; maybe it was only a few days. Then they pulled me out for more questioning."

Katalin touched his arm.

"They took me, blindfolded, to a prison. I didn't know where I was. Turned out to be Kistarcsa. They kept asking me about my anti-socialist, reactionary activities. That's what they called it. Middle of the night, no sleep, more questioning. If they didn't like the way I answered, they'd flick cigarette embers at me. Or slug me. That's how they do things. Over and over. They wear you down."

She reached to his cheek and caressed it, remembering in agony the way he used to caress hers. "But you're not broken. You're not, Róbert!"

"Broken, worn down, where's the line in between? They crumble your dignity. Nothing's off limits. I was spat on, pissed on, they sent in women to—"

She held up her hand, shook her head.

"They know everybody's weak spots," he said. "They told me my music was bourgeois, third-rate."

"But you didn't believe that, did you? You can't!"

"After a while, you believe anything." Róbert coughed, trying to steady his voice. "So then one of the officers—maybe it was his job to act human, I don't know—he told me there were just a few things they needed to clarify, and if I'd answer his questions, I could leave. He said there was a communal farm where I could work." Róbert gestured in the direction of the baronial house. "Said there was a house with a piano. Said he'd heard I was an excellent musician. So that was it. After all the shit, that's what did it. A compliment. I told them what they wanted to know."

Katalin didn't ask what he had said, but she had a sad, terrible guess that Gyula Kardos was in a work camp now.

"I'm sorry, Katalin," Róbert said. "You probably wanted to think of me as braver than that."

"If you were braver, maybe you'd be dead by now. For a long time I was afraid you were."

"No. I'm not dead."

"Be glad of it, Róbert."

He looked down at Mari, and they watched their daughter dip her fingers in the creek.

"Do you live at the farm headquarters?" Katalin asked him.

"Yes."

"And you play the piano there," she said, in spite of the fact that the man at the headquarters had never heard him. "Of course you do. You wrote a piece for me."

"No, that little piece was up here," he tapped his skull, "that's all. I can't play piano here. I'm too out of practice. There are too many people around."

"Then you could sing. Right here in the pasture." A sudden exasperation rose in her. "My student would."

Róbert raised his eyebrows. "And what about you? You should be at music academy."

"I had a *baby*."

He nodded, watched Mari, said nothing.

"How long have you been out of prison?" she asked him quietly.

A long silence.

"Since September of '49," he finally said.

"That was almost two years ago."

He did not answer.

"Two years that I heard nothing from you." She pressed on, "Róbert, why didn't you come see me?"

He brushed a straight lock of hair off his forehead and his hand shook. "The city is not safe," he said. "It is too hellish; I don't belong there."

"I would have met you somewhere else if you wanted," she said. "Anywhere. Even if you had just sent a letter, at least I would have known you were alive."

"I was alive, nothing more. I had nothing that someone like you would want. Everything was over."

"Not for me, it wasn't. I have given month after month, night and day, to your daughter!"

"I didn't know, Katalin," he whispered. "I didn't know."

He squatted down beside Mari and touched her shoulder. When Mari looked at him and did not draw away, he picked up a rock and held it out to her. Mari eyed the rock, took it from his palm and tasted it.

"*Nem,*" he chided gently. "Throw it. Like this." He picked up a second rock and tossed it into the creek.

Mari grinned. She swung her arm and the rock plunked into the water in front of them.

"Good girl," Róbert said. "Good …."

His voice gave out. He stood, turned his back, put his face in his hands and wept. Mari watched in confusion, her little mouth trembling, until she threw herself on Katalin's legs. Katalin swept up Mari in her right arm and wrapped her left around Róbert's too-thin back. His shoulders were heaving. Mari buried her face in the curve of Katalin's neck.

"Róbert!" Katalin cried.

"Forgive me," he moaned.

"Not everything is over. Listen! We could start again. We could. The three of us."

He turned to her and said something so muffled and furtive she couldn't make it all out: "I … great evil … never …."

"Róbert, we could—"

Over her lips he pressed two rough fingers, hushing her. "You're stronger without me."

She stood utterly still with her hand on his back. *No,* she wanted to say. *Mari and I need you, Róbert,* she wanted to tell him, but she could not.

"Maybe it would go the other way," she said. "Maybe Mari and I could make you strong."

But he said, "No, Katalin," and in her heart something eased in relief.

She pressed her lips together and refused to cry. "Is there someone else?"

"Why are you asking me this?"

"After bearing your child, I think I deserve to know."

He looked at the ground. "There is a divorcée in the room next to mine. Sometimes, when nights are terrible, I see her. It's a pain killer."

She clasped Mari and turned away, but he had already seen her face.

"Oh, God, Katalin," he cried, "what I've done to you. I'm sorry!"

Mari had begun to whimper and bend in Katalin's arms, wanting the stream again.

"Mari, it's time to go." Katalin positioned her daughter firmly on her hip. Mari fussed, stretching toward the water, but Katalin told her no and turned toward the sloping bank.

"Katalin, wait!"

She did not wait. She stepped onto the bank and the soil fell away under her sandals. Róbert ran after her and vaulted his way up the bank. From above, he reached out, lifted Mari onto the solid ground of the pasture, and held out his hand to Katalin. She grasped a willow branch instead and pulled herself up. At the top, she was about to reach for Mari again but stopped. From her bag she took a pen and a scrap of paper. In case he had not kept her letter, which he probably hadn't, she wrote down her address and telephone number for him. He was, after all, Mari's father. She put the paper into his hand and closed his fingers around it, resting her hands on his one last time. He could write to her or telephone her if he wanted to. Or he could leave it as one more good intention, like the Chopin music.

She gathered Mari into her arms again. "Goodbye, Róbert."

PÉTER RAN DOWN the road to her and immediately wanted to know what Róbert had said, what she had said, what had happened. She told him she just wanted to leave. He asked about it again on the ride home, as the wagon bounced and Katalin's tailbone hurt on the hard seat and Mari shifted and kicked on her lap.

"Later," she told him.

The blouse she had so carefully chosen for this day clung to her, damp with sweat. Her face felt gritty from the dust. Mari began to cry, a pitiful mewling that Katalin might have been able to deal with if she hadn't felt so close to doing the same thing herself.

"Péter, sing. Please. Maybe Mari will stop crying."

"Wouldn't she rather hear you than me?"

"*I* would rather hear you."

The sky's light had cooled, and it was almost evening. Over the creaking of the harness, Péter sang an old lullaby. There in his singing was that beautiful roughness that was like the surface of a deeply pulling river. Mari's cries faltered and she quieted. Katalin rested her own cheek against the child's head and let her eyes close.

"I know you said you'll tell me later what happened," Péter said, "but just tell me one thing now. Will we be going to Mezősárgás again in the morning?"

"No."

She thought he said, "Thank God," although she wasn't sure. They drove on to Kőpatak. Katalin saw that neighbor girl with the full hair, the one who had called him Peti. The girl did not greet Péter this time, only leaned on her porch post and watched.

INSIDE THE HOUSE, Mrs. Zöld brought Katalin bread and cheese and told her she and Mari could rest in the *tiszta szoba*. Katalin laid the child down on the Zölds' bed, and within minutes Mari was asleep. Péter brought in a basin of warm water, gave Katalin a wash cloth and a towel, and told her he was taking the twins down to the creek for an evening swim.

Katalin drew the curtains and made sure the door was closed. She scrubbed her face, then slipped off her blouse and her bra and smoothed the washcloth over the knotted sorrow of her body. She changed into clean clothes and ate most of the bread and cheese, saving some for Mari.

It was quiet here. Through the window drifted the lowing of a cow. She lit the kerosene lamp that hung above the corner table and looked around: earthen floor, whitewashed walls with occasional patches of adobe and straw showing through. Muslin curtains. The house was rough but not squalid. Two photos hung on the wall above the corner table. One, probably from the time of the first great war, showed a soldier in uniform. The other, in a fluted metal frame, was a wedding photo of a peasant couple. The young man in a wide-sleeved shirt and black embroidered vest looked very much like Péter and Tibi. The bride was a round-breasted woman with a heart-shaped face like Gyuri's and eyes that laughed in spite of her formal pose. A few locks of curling hair strayed from under her ornate headpiece.

A knock sounded on the door of the *tiszta szoba*.

"Come in," she called.

Péter's father entered and hung his brimmed hat on a peg near the door. Seeing Mari asleep on the bed, he crossed the room tiptoe to where Katalin stood in front of the photo.

"My wife," he said.

"She's pretty."

"She sang nice."

"Yes, Péter told me."

Jancsi Benedek shifted his stance. "Thank you for teaching Péter."

"It's my pleasure."

He ran his hand over his brow, leaving a faint streak of dust, and seemed unsure whether to go on. "Did you find who you were looking for in Mezősárgás?"

"Yes," she said, and stopped herself from adding *and no*.

MRS. ZÖLD'S HUSBAND came home that evening from a long day in the fields, and in spite of his weariness, he told Katalin he was glad to meet a singer from the city. After a late supper, the twins played hide and seek with Mari, taking turns hiding or carrying Mari around to look for the other brother. Gyuri tried taking Mari into a hiding place with him, but Mari laughed and shrieked and gave everything away.

Later, while Péter held Mari, Katalin read aloud from the book Péter had brought about the Indian named Winnetou. The twins sat on either side of her at the table. Katalin traced her finger under the words as she read, giving a nod of approval to the twins when they began to follow along. It seemed Tibi squinted. Page after page, they went on. The Zölds sat on the bench of the clay oven, the woman mending and the man simply listening, elbows on his knees. Péter's father had pulled up a chair and was resoling a shoe. Now and then, he asked a question about the story. He wanted to know when it happened. And whether these Indians were good horsemen. Like the old Magyars.

When it was late, the twins climbed the ladder to the loft, where they had spread their mats for the night. Péter and his father made a straw bed in the kitchen for Katalin and Mari, covering it with sheets and an old feather comforter. Katalin tucked Mari between the sheets.

After everyone else had gone to bed, she went outside to the porch with Péter, and they sat together under the eaves. The night breeze carried a scent of animals and their dung. This bothered her less than she would have guessed; it smelled of things growing. A half-moon shone.

"Thank you for reading to my brothers," Péter said.

"You were listening, too."

"We all were. Back in Pest I found some more books in the cellar. I want to read them, but they have so many words. One's about animal husbandry. The other is by that writer, what's his name—a street near your house is named after him."

"Jókai. Do you want me to help you with the books?"

"You wouldn't mind?"

"After all you've done, how could I mind? And besides, I still owe you a favor for helping me sing at Antal's party."

He laughed a little. Maybe he was remembering, as she was, the day he had astonished her with some teasing about what that favor might be. She missed the light-heartedness between them.

In the quiet of the night, she told him what had happened in Mezősárgás. Róbert had been in prison, she told him. She said that the *bastards*—a word she almost never used—had worn him down, and he informed on a friend, and he wasn't in prison long. She didn't want Péter to say again that Róbert should have bribed or fought to return to her. Péter didn't. He listened to it all, and at the end he asked, "What about Mari? Is he going to help? Is he going to pay?"

"I didn't ask him to. I think he has nothing now. Just *nothing*. It was hard, really hard, seeing him the way he is now—worn out and thin and not playing piano and not singing and not doing anything but watching cows. Not even wanting anything. It's so horrible, Péter, everything about him is not this, not that, just *not*. And then today down by the stream he looked at this beautiful little girl and realized she's *his*, and there was a glimmer of life in him and he started to cry. But that was the end of it. No more. He turned to me and said, 'You're stronger without me.' "

Her voice weakened and she forced out the last words. "And I couldn't disagree."

"*Jaj*, Kati."

"Péter, Róbert's sleeping with someone. He said it's a pain killer."

Péter grimaced. "Whose pain?"

"I know that doesn't surprise you," she said. "I should have seen it from the beginning, I should never have—"

"Katalin, you talk like this is all your fault! 'I should have.' 'I shouldn't have.' But he's the one who didn't come back, didn't answer your letter. He's the one in somebody else's bed. Isn't it time you blamed *him*?"

Her throat began to ache. "I do."

She hung her head and cried. Péter held her around her shoulders, tightening his grasp when she shook, smoothing her hair back when it fell into her face, wiping tears off her cheek with his finger, easing up on his hold when she began to quiet, but not letting her go.

"Kati, please forget him."

"Róbert changed my whole life. There's no leaving that behind."

"No, but ..." the rough undertones of his voice hovered in the night, "but I wish you would let someone else love you."

She sat very still. "The 'someone else' would have to love Mari, too."

"That isn't hard."

"I can't answer you, Péter," she whispered.

The stars were spattered white against the night sky. The breeze stirred. At length Péter stood and held out his hands, helped her to her feet, and opened the door of the house. In the kitchen, he lit a candle and set it on the shelf above the water jar. He said "Sleep well" in the flickering light, and for one moment she squeezed his hand. He then stepped into the pantry and she watched the door close behind him.

KATALIN DID NOT know what time it was when she awoke on the straw bed, but the light at the window was not dawn. She sat up, the straw crunching under her. Mari turned in her sleep. Katalin rose, crept across the kitchen to the window beside the door and pushed back the curtain. Outside on the road shone the steady double glow of a parked car's headlights. A smaller circle of light moved near the barn. A flashlight. Now another: two flashlights. The spheres of light traveled across the ground, elongated, lifted to the house, and lit on her.

She jerked away from the window. "Péter!" she screamed. "*Péter!*"

Chapter Twenty-One

⌒⌒⌒

Darkness

SOMEONE HAD YELLED his name. Péter pushed himself up from sleep.
Somewhere a strange light was moving.

"Péter!"

It was Katalin. He threw aside his covers, yanked his trousers on, and
grabbed his glasses. "Apa!"

Apa shoved back his blankets. "God," he choked.

Péter tore into the kitchen. Apa followed in his nightshirt. Katalin, in her
nightgown, clutched Mari in her arms. The twins were shouting from the
loft. The Zölds rushed out from the *tiszta szoba,* knotting their bathrobe ties
around their waists.

Péter opened the front door barely wide enough to look out. In the yard,
two flashlight beams parted like searchlights, one shining on the barn, the
other roving the road. In the white glow, Péter saw a State car and a wagon
with two horses. He stood aside so his father could look.

The twins clambered down the loft ladder. Apa pulled them by the wrist
to the door of the *tiszta szoba.* "Tibi, Gyuri, go sit at the table," he ordered. "If
I go out, don't follow, and if these men come in, don't say anything!"

"You, too," Péter told Katalin. "Take Mari."

She gripped his arm. "The police?"

"It has to be."

Apa turned to Mr. Zöld. "Make them stay in the house. I'm going out
there." He made for the pantry to dress, slamming the door.

Péter ran outside, shoeless and shirtless, to get there before Apa and his
fury did. In the dark yard, a cricket sang its grating song. Péter could only see
one flashlight beam now, and it turned and glared in his face.

"What are you doing?" demanded a thin voice behind the light. Péter recognized it, the deputy of the Kőpatak police.

"I've come out to see what's the matter," Péter answered.

"Where's your father?"

"In the house. Getting dressed."

From the direction of the barn, a gunshot cracked and the report split the night. The door of the house banged open.

"Péter!" Apa shouted from the porch. "Péter!"

"I'm here!"

The flashlight beam turned to Apa and trailed him as he ran to Péter's side. Péter stood with his father in its ghostly halo, feeling like a cornered animal. He did not know what that gun had been aiming for. Next door, a light had come on in the Kozmas' window.

The beam turned and shone on the barn. "Come," the voice of the police deputy said, "both of you."

The deputy led them around to the back. Péter could hear the animals shuffling restlessly inside the barn. The light beam pointed down the steps into the root cellar. The door stood ajar, shattered at the latch. Péter now understood: the gunshot had blown off the lock. From within, something thudded and clattered. Boards dropping. The false wall.

It was only a minute ago that he had heard the shot. He suddenly grasped that the police hadn't wasted time prodding for loose boards. Someone had tipped them off.

Péter stepped through the injured door with his father in front of him and the flashlight following like a gun muzzle. They crowded into the low underground room among the sacks of potatoes and ropes of sausage. A kerosene lantern had been lit. Two men were tugging boards out of the back wall and pitching them onto the floor: Tamás Márton and the chief of police.

Márton dropped a board and nodded toward the gap in the wall. "Shine that light in here," he told the deputy.

The deputy turned his light, illuminating the barrels of grain in the crawl space. Márton lowered his head, climbed through the opening, and lifted a lid on one of the barrels.

"Here's the grain Benedek owes," Márton called. "Said he couldn't meet his quota. Couldn't pay his taxes."

Péter glanced at his father. Apa's eyes darted and his lips compressed under his mustache. In his haste, he had buttoned his shirt crooked.

Márton bent through the opening again and joined the rest of them in the cellar's front area. "It's a crime against the people to hoard produce, Benedek." He lit a cigarette. "These men can arrest you."

The chief of police crossed his arms. The smaller, bald-pated deputy looked at the floor.

"Why have you been hoarding that wheat?" the chief asked Apa.

"I was not hoarding it. My family was eating it."

"And do you always hide food you're not hoarding?" Márton flung aside the spent match. "That makes it hard to get at, doesn't it?"

Except for a faltering in his breath, Apa made no answer. Péter eyed the billy club and the pistol on the chief's belt and nudged his father's elbow.

"Well, doesn't it?" the chief asked.

Apa did not speak.

"Comrades," Péter said, fighting back a rising panic, "we're just storing the grain."

"Well hidden," the chief said.

"No, no, it's just storage down here." Péter grasped for anything that might win some sympathy. "We hid produce during the war when the German fascists were stealing from us. That's when my family started using that space there. But now it's just storage."

Márton waved his cigarette impatiently. "Peti, you can hardly expect us to believe that. Your father hasn't paid his taxes, hasn't given a thought to the economic plan, hasn't given a Gypsy's damn about the warnings we've given him."

Apa stepped toward Márton. "I have children to feed, and another crop to sow," he spat out. "And if you have something to say about me, you can say it to *me,* not to my son."

"What's the point in saying anything to you? You don't listen, you don't answer, and if you did answer, it would be nothing but lies—"

Apa grabbed Márton's shoulders and shook him. The cigarette stub flew out of Márton's hand.

The chief stepped closer and set his hand on his billy club.

"Apa, let go!" Péter cried.

"Benedek, stop!" shouted the deputy.

But Apa did not let go.

Péter clasped Apa's wrists, bore down with his thumbs on the pulse veins until he felt Apa's hands go limp. He pulled him away from Márton.

"We're sorry," Péter said, jaw clamping.

No! Loosen your jaw.

He sucked in a low breath, lowered his chin, and met Márton's eyes. "My father meant no harm, comrade. As he said, he has children to feed."

"Other people feed their children *and* pay their taxes."

"Other people," Apa flung back, "are not taxed in blood like I am!"

The chief clenched Apa's arm and twisted it behind his back.

"If he owes," Péter shouted, "I'll pull out the rest of the boards for you, and you can take what he owes. Let him go! *Please.*"

The police chief loosened his grip but did not let go. The deputy positioned himself at Apa's other side. Apa glared at the men.

Márton jerked his thumb over his shoulder at the gap in the wall. "Let's finish this," he told the other two. "And you," he added, turning to Péter, "help carry the barrels out to the wagon."

The police chief stood watch next to Apa. Péter, Márton and the deputy pulled boards out of the wall until they had opened a hole large enough to drag the barrels out. One by one they pushed the barrels up the steps, rolled them across the yard and up a wooden ramp into the wagon. There were eleven barrels in all, some heavier and fuller than others. After the eighth barrel, Márton, sweating and grunting, waved his hand and said, "That's enough for now."

Péter waited in the yard and looked anxiously toward the house. He could see Katalin silhouetted in the kitchen window. He was relieved that she had dressed; he didn't want these wolves to see her in her nightgown.

The two policemen escorted Apa across the yard. The deputy tripped and stumbled against Apa. "Sorry there," he muttered.

"Go inside," the chief ordered Péter and his father, "and leave the door open."

Katalin, the children, and the Zölds had clustered stiff as broomsticks in the kitchen next to the straw mattress. Tibi began to say something, but Apa waved his hand, commanding him to be silent. Katalin looked Péter's way, her eyes dark and round with worry. The deputy entered and took up guard duty just inside the door. No one spoke.

Márton and the police chief stepped in. The chief held a clipboard. His gaze wandered to the loft above, returned to the huddled group. He scribbled something on his paperwork.

"The family I know," he said. "The class aliens I know." His eyes lingered on Katalin, and he snickered. "But who's the dame?"

Péter moved closer to her. "She's from Pest, and she's my music teacher."

"Well." The chief raised a brow. "Nice lessons, eh?"

At his sides Péter's fists clenched. He felt Katalin touch his hand.

"They're *singing* lessons," she told the man firmly. "And Péter is talented."

Tamás Márton gestured toward the clipboard and spoke to the chief. "That's probably in the notes. He does take lessons. Those two and the baby were in Mezősárgás today, stopped in at the collective there."

Péter's gut knotted. How much did these people know? Had his whole life and Katalin's been noted and filed?

"So, Comrade Music Teacher from Pest," the chief said, eying Katalin, "why were you in Mezősárgás?"

"Leave her alone," Apa told him. "You came here to see me."

"So we did," Tamás Márton said.

For the next hour and a half, the deputy kept cover over Apa, even following him to the privy and back, while Márton and the chief searched the house. They climbed the loft ladder, and Péter could hear them crossing and recrossing the floor overhead, sorting through sacks and crates. The men took bottles and jars from the pantry. In the kitchen they found the shopping cash in the chipped beer stein. The chief stuffed it in his pocket. He told Apa it would be considered as a very partial payment of his tax debt. The men also found the key to the root cellar, although it was of no use now that they had shot the lock off. In the *tiszta szoba* they threw open drawers and cabinets and pulled blankets off the bed. They informed the family that in the morning they would come back for the rest of the grain and for the four piglets and five chickens that were owed to the people.

And they would also take the horse.

"Not the horse!" Péter said.

The twins sat down on the floor and cried, which set Mari to sobbing on Katalin's neck. The men squatted beside the old steamer trunk in the *tiszta szoba* and riffled through the colorful skirts and aprons.

"Please," Apa implored, "those belonged to my wife."

The chief snorted and closed the trunk. He grabbed the one good picture frame off the wall. Opening the back of it, he tossed the wedding photograph onto the floor.

"Sentimental memorabilia," he said. "The frame will go into the State coffers."

Apa walked into the room, picked up the photo off the dirt floor, set it on the corner table and turned hard eyes on the chief and Márton.

Márton told Apa, "You may pack now."

"Pack?"

"You will be taken to an undisclosed location," the chief said, "for hoarding and for non-payment of taxes."

Apa did not move, only glared at the two men and the deputy, who still stood sentry by the front door. "And for how long?" Apa asked.

"That isn't known at this time," the chief said. "Take some clothes and your razor if you want it. And don't waste time." The chief turned to Péter. "You. Go get a shovel."

"But why—"

"*Go.*" The chief stepped to the door, threw it open, and clicked the flashlight on. "I'm watching."

The chief stood in the doorway and shone the beam across the yard.

Péter made his way numbly to the shed. He lifted the shovel, this instrument that had buried his mother and grandfather, and slung it across his bare shoulder.

"Hurry up!" the chief shouted.

Péter ran back, rested the shovel against the doorframe of the house, and went into the kitchen. The chief trailed him in. There the deputy still kept the twins, the Zölds, Katalin and Mari corralled.

From the *tiszta szoba*, Apa trudged into the kitchen with the one suitcase the family owned. The chief took it from him and handed it to the deputy. The chief then pulled Apa's hands behind his back, snapped handcuffs onto his wrists, and pushed him toward the front door.

"No!" Péter planted himself in front of the open door and spread his hands and feet into the corners. "Stop!"

"Move," the chief commanded.

"Peti," the deputy said, "get out of the way."

"No!"

Márton checked his wristwatch and turned to the chief. "We're all tired; let's get this done."

The chief drew out his billy club and raised it.

"Péter!" Katalin shouted.

"Move," the deputy said, almost begging.

"Péter, move!" Apa ordered. "*Come here!*"

Péter ducked. The club grazed the side of his face, burning it, blasting pain through the cheekbone. He staggered away from the door and threw his arm around his father's shoulders.

"Look out for your brothers," Apa hissed in his ear. "Do whatever you have to. Now, for God's sake, stand aside."

Péter stepped back, his cheek throbbing. The chief pushed Apa through the door and the deputy followed. Tamás Márton stood in the doorway and faced the rest of them. "We'll see you later," he warned, and he turned and left, slamming the door.

Péter threw the door open again and ran to the front gate. His brothers panted after him. Pitching the shovel into the wagon, Márton climbed onto the drive seat, shouted to the horses, and reined them onto the road.

The deputy opened the door of the State car and Apa, handcuffed, sank onto the back seat. As the chief and the deputy climbed into the car and turned the ignition, Apa peered out the rear window. For half a second and for an eternity, his eyes locked on Péter's. Then the dome light went out, the car sped away, and Apa was gone.

* * *

No one slept. When the sun came up, Péter put on his shoes and shirt and fed the animals. His cheek blared pain. Returning to the house, he sat down on the bench at the *tiszta szoba* table, which had been stripped of its tablecloth, and let his fingers wander over the two objects that had been left there, chucked aside as sentimental and bourgeois: his parents' wedding picture and the Winnetou book. The twins scrabbled their way onto the bench with him, Tibi pressing his face against Péter's shoulder and Gyuri slumping across the table. Mr. Zöld sat silently by the clay oven. Katalin paced the room with Mari in her arms. From the ransacked loft overhead, Péter could hear the creaking footsteps of Mrs. Zöld as she surveyed the damage.

"What's going to happen to Apa?" Gyuri asked after a long time.

"He'll come back," Mr. Zöld said.

It was a kind attempt and Péter wanted to tell his brothers that of course that was right, but he could not say it.

"People don't always come back," Tibi said.

"Your father will try," Katalin told Tibi.

This—that their father would try—was one thing Péter didn't doubt. In this certainty, he found the strength to coax the boys to the barn for their belated chores. It was while they were pitching fresh straw into the stalls that the State came for the three remaining barrels of grain, and into their wagon they also wrestled four resistant piglets and half the Benedeks' chickens. They left behind the old cow, who was no longer a plentiful milker, the sow, and some piglets and hens, if they didn't return for them later. Péter and his brothers walked out into the yard to watch.

Last, the State workers led the mare out of the barn. Gyuri turned horrified eyes to Péter. Tibi tried to bolt after the horse.

Péter gripped their collars. "Stay here," he ordered.

"But they can't take Zsuzsi!" Tibi said.

"Do you want them to hit you the way they hit me last night?"

They stood without speaking as the lead man made notes on his clipboard and another worker tried to tie Zsuzsi to the back of the wagon. The mare pulled back against the rope.

"Watch out!" Péter shouted. "The horse bites."

Ten minutes later the horse, the wagon, and its cargo were gone.

A little later in the morning, he and Katalin in their exhaustion tried to decide what should be done, but the only obvious thing was that the children needed sleep. Péter and Katalin sat on the edge of the Zölds' bed in the *tiszta szoba* and made the children lie down. The Zölds had gone out somewhere. Mari burrowed between the twins and sucked her thumb while Katalin read from the Winnetou book. Eventually all three children fell asleep. Katalin closed the book and leaned her head against Péter's collarbone. He held her hard.

"Péter, what are we going to do?" she whispered.

"I have to go to the police station. My father didn't take his winter coat. Stay with the children. Gyuri and Tibi are scared. If they wake up, tell them I'll come back."

"But what if the police don't let you come back?"

"All I'm doing is taking them a coat."

"They'll probably just keep it."

"It's too shabby for them to keep."

"If you have to go, try to talk to that short man. I don't think he liked being brutal. Not like the others did."

He told her he would try. This was a Sunday, and he thought the deputy usually manned the station on Sundays. Péter took his father's coat, and on his way across the yard, he noticed a small mound of spilled grain, hardly enough to grind for a single loaf. He squatted down and sifted a few of the precious seeds between his fingers.

He reached into the pockets of the coat, checking for holes. One pocket was worn through, but the other was whole and strong. Péter scooped some of the grain in his cupped hand and emptied it into the pocket. He wanted to fill the entire pocket, but no, a bulge could be too noticeable, too likely to be searched out. This handful would have to be enough for Apa to find, to touch, to chew. Maybe to hope. Péter carried the coat back to the house.

"Do you know how to sew?" he asked Katalin.

"A little."

Péter climbed the ladder to the pillaged loft and found his mother's old sewing basket. He brought it to Katalin, and in the light of a front window, she threaded a needle and sewed a false bottom into the pocket over the smattering of grain. At his request she sewed loosely so his father could undo the stitches. Péter's cheek throbbed and his stomach twitched, for here they were, hiding grain again, but—sweet Christ—who knew when he would be able to send his father another message?

"It was our seed wheat," he told her as she sewed, and her brown eyes looked at him, full and sad.

THE POLICE STATION was housed in the same adobe building as the post office, served by the one electrical line that came into Kőpatak. It was known throughout the village that the town's two telephones were located here and in the post office, accessible to each other and to the ÁVH network. When Péter entered the police station, he saw the telephone on a desk near a long row of file cabinets, in front of a wall with the usual portraits of Stalin and Rákosi.

He saw no one around except the two dictators. Beyond the files and down a short hallway, Péter knew, were two jail cells. Maybe his father was in one of them, pacing like a caged animal as he waited to be taken to the undisclosed location.

"Hello?" Péter called out.

"Go sit in the waiting room, Peti Benedek," the deputy's voice called back. "I'll see you when I can."

Péter sat down in one of the three hard chairs between the door and the desk and waited with Apa's coat on his lap. The deputy padded around behind the counter, pecking something out on a typewriter, using the telephone to tell somebody that the business with the economic saboteur had been attended to last night. Péter waited. Half an hour had gone by, according to the clock near Stalin and Rákosi, when the deputy called him to the desk. The man was unshaven and visibly tired.

"What do you need?" the deputy asked brusquely. "If you've come to see your father, that can't be done. He isn't here."

"Where is he?"

"That information cannot be given out at this time."

"When can it be given out?"

"That is not in my hands."

"How long will he be gone?"

The deputy shrugged. "Undetermined at this time."

"Comrade, I have two little brothers! They have no mother, and they need their father!"

"I am aware of that, Peti, and your father should have considered it more. What are you doing with an overcoat on a warm day like this?"

"My father didn't take it with him. I want him to have it. In case he's still gone when the weather changes. If you could tell me where he's going—"

The man rested his elbow on the desk and put his forehead on the heel of his hand. "That can't be done. I already told you that."

"Then could you … could *somebody* please see that he gets it?"

"It's summer."

"Summer won't last."

The deputy sighed, opened a desk drawer, and pulled out a roll of masking tape and a pen. In block letters on the tape he wrote *Benedek*. Péter handed him the coat, and the man stuck the tape onto the collar and threw the coat in a box under Rákosi.

"What's that box for?" Péter asked.

"Outbound." The deputy rose from his desk. "I'm going home. It was a goddamned night and now it's a goddamned day. I hope we can send your father his goddamned coat." He steered Péter toward the door and whispered fiercely, "I'm sorry for you and your brothers, and I'll do what I can to see that you don't get thrown out of your house, but keep your goddamned mouth shut about it."

They walked out the door just as the chief of police was coming in. The deputy told him in passing that all was in order, no emergencies. Péter stepped quickly away.

He ran across the square to where Katalin and the children were sitting on the patchy grass beneath the monument to the Great War. Katalin stood up, visibly relieved, and curled her hand into the crook of his elbow. Péter glanced around and saw passersby looking their way.

By the time they reached home, he was sure that news of the night raid had spread. Villagers who didn't live on this stretch of the road wandered by, passing the gate in silence. The Kozmas watched from the fence.

About an hour later, a knock sounded at the door. Péter opened it cautiously. On the doorstep stood Panni, the daughter of Mrs. Donáth, with her little girl and her husband, Gábor, the young veterinarian. Gábor carried a bulky package wrapped in brown paper. Péter beckoned them inside and introduced them to Katalin. In spite of all that had happened, Panni smiled when she found out Katalin was his voice teacher.

"We heard Péter sing at his grandfather's funeral," she said. "I wish we had such lovely music more often in Kőpatak."

Panni's daughter and Mari gazed at each other curiously. Katalin and Panni took the children into the *tiszta szoba* to play while Gábor and Péter stayed in the kitchen. Gábor set the package down on the iron top of the cook stove, which had been cold all day. "A ham," he said, indicating the package, "from Panni's parents. Please don't talk about it ...." He lifted a hand toward the door, *out there.*

"My God, so kind," Péter murmured.

Gábor squinted at Péter's sore cheek. "Did *they* do that?"

Péter nodded.

"Despicable," Gábor whispered. "Do you need anything for the pain?"

"Katalin gave me some aspirin, but there's hardly any left."

"I'll bring some more. And if there's anything else we can help with, we'll try."

"But isn't it risky for your job?" Péter asked. He had heard that much of Gábor's work came from the communal farms in the area.

"It's not as risky for me as you'd think. There aren't many people with my training around here. I'm harder to replace. Tell me, did they take your mare?"

"Yes."

"I'll try to see that she's well cared for."

Péter closed his eyes in weary gratitude. "Thank you."

* * *

He had no choice. After the visitors left, Péter told Katalin he couldn't return to the city with her. He was going to have to stay with the twins for the time being and make some kind of plan. The strain on her face was unbearable to him as she told him that she understood, she agreed. He held Mari for her as she packed her overnight bag and said goodbye to Gyuri and Tibi.

"Help your older brother," she told the twins. "Do you understand?"

The boys nodded.

"I'm very serious about that," she said, her voice uneven, and she hugged them.

As late afternoon clouds gathered, Péter walked her to the train stop. She asked him if there was anything he needed her to do back in the city, and he told her it would be a relief to him if she would stop in at the print shop tomorrow and let his boss know that he wasn't simply skipping work. "His name is Frigyes Molnár. Tell him ... oh, God, I don't know, tell him an emergency has come up. I hope he doesn't ask you questions. Have him give the message to Ernö Gárdonyi, too."

"Frigyes Molnár, Ernö Gárdonyi," she repeated.

"Say I'll be back in a few days."

"But will you?"

"I hope so." He gazed into her brown eyes and was wrenched by her worry. "I really hope so."

At the train stop, he raised the lever arm to hoist the signal flag and they waited for the train, alone on the platform except for Mari. Katalin set the child down next to her and held her hand. Péter touched Katalin's hair. She leaned on his chest, and when he put his arms around her, she lifted her face to his. He kissed her, softly questioning; she pressed close and let her lips linger on his. Afterward, she looked at him and with one finger touched his cheek next to the bruise.

"Oh, Péter," she whispered, "I hate to leave you here like this."

From the east came a rumbling. He held her tightly and kissed her again, longer this time and with a great longing sorrow, but the train screeched into place at the platform. Then there was nothing he could do but see her to the train door, help her in, and hand her luggage and her daughter up to her. He said goodbye to Mari, but his voice broke when he said it to Katalin. The train chuffed away. He lifted his hand, in case she could see him out the window. But he could not see her, and in desolation he watched the train disappear.

Chapter Twenty-Two

～～

What We Would Have Done If We Weren't Waiting

A s Katalin rode the train between Kőpatak and Háromkeresztes, the memories tore her: Róbert's hunched shoulders, the glare, the pounding, Jancsi Benedek in handcuffs, the children's cries, Péter's beaten cheek, and at the end, his anguished kiss. Tonight Péter would be trying to console his brothers while listening for State cars. She put her hand to her mouth and shut her eyes.

The train pulled into Háromkeresztes. It would be a two-hour wait for the Budapest connection. She couldn't bear to sit in this station where cigarette butts littered the floor and Stalin and Rákosi watched from the wall. Gathering Mari into her arms, she followed the road that she and Péter had taken together yesterday—was it only *yesterday?*—to the restaurant where he had first met Miklós.

From outside the old wood door, she heard a violin teasing. The music slid in a glissade so dramatic, so full of pathos, it could only be Miklós. She pulled the door open and there he stood with his violin. She'd not seen him in six years, and he was a man now, no longer a shadow wedged between boyhood and manhood. His oily hair tossed as he played. Behind him, another Gypsy hammered away on a cimbalom. Mari swayed in fascination. Katalin sat down at a back table.

The room smelled of broth and peppers. Naming the exhausted emptiness within her "hunger," Katalin ordered soup and bread and wine, and as she was tearing the bread into pieces for Mari, Miklós glanced in their direction. Katalin smiled. His face above the violin puckered in puzzlement, then broke into an astonished grin. He ended his song and sidled between the tables over to her. "Katalin Varga?"

"Yes. Hello, Miklós."

"It's been so long. And the baby is yours?"

"Yes. Mária."

"Pretty little thing. Who is her lucky apuka?"

"He and I are not together now."

"Ah. The way life is."

Miklós swept away with his violin but he raised a finger, signaling her that he would come back. After playing a romping *csárdas* and a Serbian folk song, he returned to her table and sat down. She pulled a few forints out of her bag and pushed them toward him as a tip. "Kissing your hand," he said, "I thank you."

He stuffed the money into the lining of his black vest. His eyes, she noticed, no longer shifted constantly as they had at the end of the war. Still, the years had weathered him, as they had weathered Róbert. And weathered her.

"How is your brother?" Miklós was asking. "Is he still playing violin?"

"Oh, yes." She flicked a smile. "And I'm glad you are, too."

"Can't stop. It's my bread and cigarettes. What are you doing here?"

"I'm on my way home from Kőpatak. And Mezősárgás."

Miklós lifted his black eyebrows questioningly, but she only tore off another morsel of bread for Mari.

"So you have a daughter now," he said.

"Yes. And you? Do you have any children?"

"Two. Boys. One here and one in Miskolc. But I don't tell that story when I'm sober. I hope you still sing."

How tired she felt after last night. Mari had begun to fidget, and Katalin shifted the child on her lap.

"Miklós, do you remember someone named Péter Benedek? He told me he came in here once last spring, and you were playing, and you talked him into singing in front of everybody, and then afterward you told him where I live. Remember him?"

"Yes! A poor, shy bastard with a voice like the holy angels. And he came and found you?"

"He did. And now I'm giving him voice lessons. He's … he's a friend."

Miklós dusted his hands in delight. "Good, good, I sent you business, and maybe more, yes? *Sej,* why don't you sing something? With Joska and me. Come."

Mari made a sudden lunge for Katalin's spoon. Katalin wrested it out of her hand. "My daughter's restless and I'm exhausted," she said. "It's been a terrible weekend and I'm not going to sing."

"You sang during the war. What's more terrible than that?"

During the war she had held out hope, because some day the war would end. Now the war was over, but what was there to hope for?

"During the war I was a child," she said.

Miklós leaned across the table toward her. "In the city ... do you sing there?"

"Well, I'm giving Péter voice lessons."

"But do you *sing?*"

"A little."

"No. 'A little' music is not enough for you. Enough for some people, maybe, but not for you. And not for that shy fellow, and not for your brother, and not for me. If I didn't have my violin, I'd be dead in here." He thumped his finger on his chest over his heart. Then he stood and turned the finger toward her own heart and said vehemently, as if swearing, "Live or die."

SHE WANTED TO live, to let breath and blood into that poor organ to which Miklós had pointed, to scrape together joy and ardor and even anguish if that was what it took, and to live. On the train between Háromkeresztes and Budapest, she began to sing. It started with a quiet children's song to keep Mari happy.

"Új kenyér, új kenyér," she sang.

When she finished, the man beside her said, "My little boy sings that song, too."

"Sing it again," said the young girl sitting across from her.

Katalin sang it a little louder. Then the girl's mother wanted another song. This was awkward, entertaining an audience of train passengers, but there were worse things than awkwardness. She sang "*Madárka, Madárka,*" hurting with the memory of Péter's first voice lesson. When people across the aisle wanted more songs, she went on to a slow dance song from Péter's county, and then to an Italian song she had learned from her mother.

The conductor, in the middle of his rounds, looked at her and nodded her on. He took tickets without speaking and set his finger to his lips when others spoke. Passengers from farther back in the train car inched forward in the aisle. "Do you know '*A Magyarokhoz*'?" "Can you sing Mimi's aria from *La Bohème*?" they asked. "What about Schubert's *Romanza*?" She managed. It was not a peak performance. But it was the best she could do after leaving Kőpatak, and Róbert, and Péter.

Clasping Mari on her lap, Katalin tightened her belly, loosened her bone-weary jaw, and kept on singing.

THE NEXT DAY she dropped off Mari in the infants' room forty-five minutes before her normally scheduled shift, then walked the two blocks up the street to the print shop where Péter worked. After some inquiries, she found Frigyes Molnár on the stairwell, and by some fortune better than anything she'd come to expect, the man named Ernö Gárdonyi was with him, leaning bent-shouldered on the handle of a mop. She told them that there had been an emergency in Péter's family.

"Another emergency?" Mr. Molnár asked. "Only a few weeks ago, he was gone to bury his grandfather. Before that he was gone for harvest."

"Yes, comrade," she said. "But we all have our hard times, don't we? This must be Péter's."

"Benedek's honest," Ernö Gárdonyi said to Mr. Molnár.

A straight-haired girl in a kitchen apron had descended the stairs and now stood uninvited among them. "It's true," the girl said to Mr. Molnár. "I don't think Péter knows how to lie."

Katalin was pretty sure Péter did know how and would do so if he had to, but he probably wasn't good at it, and that scared her.

The man named Gárdonyi turned to her. "And you? Are you his relative? Friend?"

"A friend," Katalin said. "He's my voice student."

"Yes, he talked about voice lessons," the girl mused.

Katalin felt an unbidden pang. This girl seemed to know Péter. Katalin didn't want the girl to know him like she herself did.

"Is he all right?" the girl asked.

Katalin did not know what was safe to say. "I think so," she said, though what she really meant was *Oh, my God, I hope so.* The man with the crooked shoulders nodded.

THAT DAY AT the nursery school she grouped the children into a small choir formation and spent extra time leading them through every song she had ever taught them. They sang the scale over and over, crouching down on low *do* and rising on each note until they stretched for the ceiling on high *do.* She showed the children how to expand their rib cages, open their mouths as if yawning, and place their tongues behind their bottom teeth.

"It's good to practice singing so we can sound our best," she told the children. "I have a friend who loves singing so much that he found a little closet to practice in at work, right there with the brooms and the mops."

"At my house there's a broom," Zoli said earnestly. "I can practice with the broom."

"Good," Katalin laughed. She would have to tell Péter.

If she could. If he came back. She tightened her belly and braced herself against another wave of fear.

She had to sing.

"Again," she told the children. "One more time on our *do re mi fa*."

That evening, on the way home from work, Katalin stopped at the pharmacy and stood in line for toilet paper, Mari in her arms. She still hated this corner. There had been one night when its memories of fire, puke, and rapes weren't quite as hard-edged, but she'd been with Péter that night, and now he wasn't here.

Ahead of her in line, a man in a flat, back-sloping cap was stepping up to the counter. She recoiled, recognizing the cap. Here was the ÁVH, asking for shaving cream. Just as they had asked for music students like Róbert, and old laundresses like Mrs. Kovács, and farmers like Péter's father. The shop door opened and Comrade Erika and her sister stepped to the end of the queue. Katalin felt surrounded.

When she reached home, she went to the cellar to see if Péter had come back. He hadn't. She told herself that this was only Monday, and of course it was too soon for him to have come back yet. Still, after supper, she checked again.

Her family kept asking about the weekend in Mezősárgás and Kőpatak. After Mari was in bed that night, she sat down with them in the main room while the phonograph played, and she told them about Róbert: prison, informing, cow herding, thinness, the woman in the next room, the grand piano he wasn't playing.

"He said I'd be better off without him." Katalin gripped the arm of the sofa and made herself go on, "And he's right."

On the phonograph a Mozart flute concerto played as the family bent close to her.

"Do you want me to pursue this at all, Kati?" her father asked. "I could hire a lawyer and try to get you some child support."

Katalin shook her head. She brushed away a tear that had pooled but not spilled. "Saturday night, the police showed up at Péter's house and took away his father."

Her family gasped, swore, asked questions, listened. She told them everything, and she did not hold back.

THAT NIGHT IN the bedroom as Mari slept, Katalin stood holding Róbert's photograph under the small lamp on the bureau. She looked again at the once-beloved angles and shadows of his face. She would go on loving those contours as over the years she saw them in Mari's face. From the top of the bureau, she lifted the music Róbert had sent her after she had waited for so long. She sounded the melody again in her mind and reread his message scrawled beneath the last staff: *Forgive me.*

She would be forgiving Róbert for the rest of her life.

Katalin refolded the music. She slipped it back in the envelope from Mezősárgás, and between its folds she placed Róbert's photograph. Quietly she opened the top drawer of her bureau and laid the envelope face down under some scarves. Maybe, a long time from now, she would practice Róbert's piece on the piano until she could play it reasonably well. Possibly she would teach it to Mari. Someday, most likely, she would give the photo to Mari. And she would tell the girl what there was to tell about her father.

Forgive him, Mari.

THE NEXT MORNING before work, Katalin went to the cellar to see if maybe in the night Péter had come home, but he had not. After work that evening she went with Mari to the cellar again, but he had not returned during the day, either. She missed Péter as she helped Mari climb back up the stairs. She missed him throughout the evening as she looked down on his courtyard garden, and as she heard her mother singing folk songs to Mari, and as the breeze twisted the lavender bunch hanging from the curtain rod in her bedroom. Sometimes she heard footsteps on the street below and she hurried to the window, but she saw only strangers.

Here she was, once again waiting for a man to return, knowing more starkly than ever that not all returns were possible.

For a long time she stood at the window with her daughter in her arms. "Sometimes we just have to go on, Mari," she said quietly, "and do what we would have done if we weren't waiting for things to get better."

She turned, and two pieces of paper on the bureau caught her eye. One was the application for teacher's college, still uncompleted. The other was the calling card of Árpád Kassai, the man who had asked her to audition for his choir. She knew she should call him. *Music. Live or die*, Miklós would have said.

She wished she could talk to Péter about all this. She looked out the window for him again, checked the cellar for him again, and waited forlornly in the foyer, as though it would do any good. And although she had told herself not to dwell on it, she remembered his last kiss, and that made everything harder still.

But she pulled herself back to the apartment and telephoned Árpád Kassai.

Chapter Twenty-Three

Solo

For Péter it felt like another funeral. Here he was in Kőpatak instead of Pest on a Monday morning, having to make sudden arrangements for a person now gone, and trying to think of who might need to be notified. Had his father agreed to do day labor for anyone? Did he owe anyone money? Péter guessed he'd be hearing about it soon enough if his father had obligations. It would serve no purpose to go around knocking on doors.

But one person he had to notify was Aunt Teréz. Péter took some of the aspirin the veterinarian had given him for the pain in his cheek, and he pondered the safest wording for a telegram. At the post office, he ordered a message saying JANCSI GONE. DO NOT KNOW HOW LONG. Aunt Teréz would understand Apa was on no holiday.

Later that day, he received a reply back from her: DO YOU NEED HELP. He certainly did. With his job in Pest, what was he going to do about the twins? But if he asked Aunt Teréz for help, she would want to take the boys to stay with her east of Miskolc. He couldn't stand the thought of them there in the same house as Uncle Ödön and the bottle he kept at his elbow. No, Péter would rather ask the Zölds for help. They were here anyway. But how much could he reasonably ask of these hard-put people? The question of his brothers nagged at him day and night and interrupted every thought of returning to the city.

On Tuesday, Péter walked the property, taking stock of what was left, trying to calculate it out. The house had not been taken from them, at least not yet. He wasn't sure why. Maybe the ÁVH, who had sent the Zölds here, couldn't figure out where else to put the class aliens. Or it was possible, with many people leaving for the city now, that no one really wanted the house.

Or ... what was it the police deputy had said? That he hoped the family wouldn't get goddamned thrown out? Could it be that the squat, wilted man was somehow trying to stop things from getting worse? With all his ragged heart, Péter wished it, but it seemed that people who tried to stop things usually got run over.

He walked back to the garden plot and looked over the cabbages, melons, vegetables, and potatoes. The family had planted more potatoes than usual this past spring, and Péter was glad of it, now that the grain was gone. He turned to the apricot trees that still belonged to them. Next year he could distill more *pálinka* from the fruit and make some money selling it on the black market, if he dared. Or maybe the bottles of pálinka would come in handy for bribes ....

This couldn't go on.

He paced to the pigsty and into the barn. They had the sow, and the remaining five piglets were growing fast. Four of the pigs they could sell, and the other they could butcher in winter. They still had the cow, too, though she didn't produce much. And nine hens pecked in the yard—the State hadn't returned for them. The family would eat. They would manage through the winter, he guessed—if he was careful, and if the Zölds pitched in. Péter didn't know how much they were paid or what their arrangement with Apa had been.

He walked to the front gate and onto the dirt road. Following it out of town, he crossed the bridge over the stream and walked along the end of the field they had harvested last month. Apa had plowed it after wheat harvest and had planted it with provender. The new shoots were making a good start. Their cow, at least, would eat. They could sell some of the extra fodder if the State didn't appropriate it.

He stepped out into the field and plucked one of the shoots. Maybe not even this small crop would still be theirs to sell by the time it was mown. And next year? The State had taken their horse. How would they plow? With their hands? The State had taken their seed grain. How could there be a next year with nothing to sow? And Apa, gone. Péter's hand choked the provender shoot as he pictured his father behind barbed wire, bony and lice-bitten, holding his shovel.

Everything that had happened Saturday night came crowding into Péter's mind—the flashlights, the gun, the false wall boards hitting the floor. He didn't doubt for a moment that the authorities had known where to look for the grain. What had happened that let the secret out? When Nagyapa died and the family put his body in the root cellar, had they been careless with the lock? Maybe during the wake, during the tears, even during the burial, someone had stopped in here and noticed a board askew. Or the twins—had they seen it? Maybe they had pulled a board aside, and fascinated with a secret, prattled about it with other boys at the creek or in the square. The news could have worked its way through the whisper chain and back to the Party.

Péter tried to think of those who could have seen the wheat or heard about it. And who then had passed the word on to the police? To know was one thing, but to tell was another. Who had an old score to settle? There could be any number of men around town that Apa had once offended. A pain tightened at the base of Péter's neck as he acknowledged this. But maybe it wasn't hatred, just the rampant desperation. Who didn't need some favor from above? Someone might have bartered off Apa for lower taxes or a raise in pay. Or a passport, for God's sake. People would do anything for a passport. Or they would give others away to get prison doors opened. Like Katalin's old lover had.

Favors. Ági needed some. She wanted an apartment on Csepel Island so she could get married. Péter remembered her saying so to Tamás Márton under the eaves one night.

And the Zölds. They had a son in some miserable military camp. If by snitching they had a chance to bring their son home, wouldn't they take it? Wouldn't anybody?

The provender shoot fell from his hand.

FOR SUPPER THAT evening, Péter and his brothers and the Zölds ate the ham that the young veterinarian had brought, which they had also eaten last night, and this morning, and at midday. There was no bread to go with it. Péter had sent the twins to the bakery that morning, but the woman at the counter had told them there was no bread left. Later Gyuri had seen someone walk out of the bakery with a loaf. The twins, upset, had recounted this to Péter when they came home, and that evening over the breadless supper they brought it up again.

"Don't say anything more about it," Péter warned them. "It's best not to complain."

"But that lady at the bakery lied to us!" Tibi insisted.

Péter waved his hand to stop him. "Enough," he said. How he disliked this, stepping into the place of their father. "Finish your supper. Then go water the garden, both of you."

The boys sulked but obeyed. Péter stayed at the corner table, knowing he had to talk with the Zölds. This would be much easier if it weren't for the monstrous thought that had occurred to him in the field today.

But it was Mrs. Zöld who spoke first, in that motherly voice of hers. "What do you think should be done now?" she asked Péter. "Will you go back to the city?"

These two were gazing directly at him. He looked for a furtive shifting of their eyes or some kind of guilty smile, but they only seemed to be waiting for his reply.

"My job is there," he said, "in Pest."

"But what about Tibi and Gyuri?" she asked.

"I got a telegram from my aunt," Péter said. "She asked if I want help. I haven't answered her yet. I could ask her to help with my brothers, but …." He glanced in the direction of the door, where his brothers had gone, where his father had left, where all the trouble had come in.

"Do the boys like your aunt?" Mrs. Zöld asked.

"They don't really know her. But they *don't* like her husband, and neither do I."

"As I remember, your father doesn't either," Mr. Zöld said.

Péter fingered the chipped edge of his painted plate, one of the few remaining pieces of what had been his mother's favorite crockery. The time had come to ask the Zölds the great favor he needed from them, but this afternoon's doubt was pounding through him. He slammed his palm on the table and blurted out, "Did you tell the police about the hidden wheat?"

Their faces puckered in a sting of hurt and confusion.

"No," the man said.

"Your father was good to us," Mrs. Zöld said. "And anyway, we didn't know about the grain, not until the police arrived."

If they were lying, they certainly did it convincingly. With all that was in him, Péter needed to believe them. "I'm sorry," he said, "but everything is so bad, and I don't know what to think."

"We understand that," the woman said. "It's bad for us, too."

From outside on the road, he could hear the clatter of a horse wagon, and from the direction of the barn, Tibi's voice.

"I have to go back to the city," he said to the Zölds. "I don't want my aunt and uncle in charge of my brothers. I don't want the boys to have to leave their home. I'll try to come home from the city as much as I can, but could you please look after the twins when I'm not around?"

"Péter," the man sighed, "there's something we need to tell you. Bori and I have put in a request to go live with my brother near Kalocsa."

"Ottó had to see a doctor about chest pain recently," Mrs. Zöld explained. "The farm work here has been very difficult for him. The doctor wrote a medical request to have him transferred."

"And that works?" Péter asked. "You put in a medical request, and you can move?"

Mr. Zöld shrugged. "Sometimes, so they say. Presumably dead bodies don't serve the economic plan very well. But we don't know when permission to move will come through. If it ever does."

"Certainly we can help you with Gyuri and Tibi until we move," Mrs. Zöld told Péter, laying her hand on his forearm. "And we will, if you'd like us to. But I'm sure the boys would much rather have you with them, Péter. They don't know us like they know you. They don't love us like they love you. You're their brother. You're their family."

Péter pulled off his glasses, rubbed his stinging eyes, and rested his forehead in his hands. "I know," was all he could say. "I know."

HE DID KNOW it, and that knowledge cut him whenever he struggled through reading the rest of the Winnetou book to the twins, or when he woke at night hearing Gyuri cry, or when Tibi shadowed behind him all day long, barely leaving him any peace, or when neither of the boys would fall asleep unless he was nearby. Wednesday night, Tibi wet the bed. Two hours later, Gyuri woke with a nightmare. Thursday Péter sent a reply telegram to Aunt Teréz, MANAGING FOR NOW THANKS, although he wasn't managing very well.

He sent a telegram to Katalin, too—CANNOT COME TO LESSON—though surely she knew. WANT TO COME SOON, he added, and surely she would know that, too. But she couldn't know how deeply, how painfully he wished it. There was so much more he wanted to tell her: *Save my spot in the cellar. I'm coming back. Wait for me. I'll be there soon.* But a bleak certainty was growing, stronger each hour, of what he had to do instead. And he would have to do it soon, before the authorities did it for him and made him pay.

After the boys were asleep that night, he sat outside under the eaves, leaving the door a little ajar in case Tibi or Gyuri called to him. Christ in heaven, if only Apa would somehow—*somehow*—appear at the front gate. How had Apa managed this, day after day, night after night, year after year since Péter's mother died? How had Apa looked after the crops and the animals and especially the children, who needed more than he had in his emptied heart?

Péter thought of the woman from Heves that Apa would have married if he himself had not stood against it. How might things have turned out if Apa had a woman now? She might have spoken sense to him. He might have listened, might have taken fewer chances. He might still be here, a happier man.

Péter watched as an owl beat its wings across the night. He felt his father's loneliness like a wound, now that he bore his own harrowing loneliness for Katalin. Very quietly he began singing the song she had taught him—*Oh, my beloved.* But he had learned it as a duet, with her, and as he sang it now by himself, here where the night breeze carried trouble and sorrow, he felt completely alone.

PERHAPS, UNDERNEATH IT all, Péter had long known what things would actually come to. On Saturday he took a slow walk across the bridge over the stream, past the trees where his mother had died. He looked toward the higher land, the better land that for a time too short had belonged to his family. There he and Nagyapa and Apa and Zsuzsi had labored, and there even the twins and his mother had helped with harvest. Closer in lay the new field that had yielded this year's wheat and was now offering up provender. The field had been faithful. It had done the best it could. Upper field and lower, it was all beautiful land. He told himself it would always be beautiful, no matter who worked it, no matter which horses or even which tractor drew the plow. Its crop would always feed people, no matter who harvested.

Péter raised his hand to his brow, shielding his eyes from the afternoon sun, and after a long last look, he turned back to town. On the dirt road, he repeated to himself the words he had been preparing. He walked into the town square to the big house that used to belong to the richest farmer in town and now housed the headquarters of the People's Bread Farm. He set his hand to the gate latch, paused, and entered.

A child was picking dandelions in the yard. She glanced up at him. When he said good day, she only stared. Péter walked on toward the house and a chicken flapped out of the way. He thought of last Saturday—how impossible it seemed, that it was only a week ago—when he and Katalin had knocked on the old baronial door of the communal farm headquarters in Mezősárgás. He told himself that if they had spoken with the comrades there, he could do it here. He tried to smooth his hair.

On the porch, a woman stood at a work table knifing apart a newly plucked chicken. Péter recognized her as the mother of one of the boys he had gone to school with long ago. He would have greeted her by name if he could remember it and if his tongue had not felt so tight.

The action of her knife paused. "Peti Benedek," she said without smiling. "What do you want?"

"I need to see Comrade Márton."

"Why?"

"Please, is he here?"

She sighed and put down her knife. With the one hand that was not bloody she opened the door and called in. "Jancsi Benedek's eldest boy here to see Tamás."

Through the open doorway, Péter peered into this house where the communal workers came and went and where some of them now lived. The place was like the farm headquarters in Mezősárgás—muddy boots in the entryway, old hats hanging on pegs, farm tools where they didn't belong.

The door opened wider and Tamás Márton stood there, his colorless hair falling like straw over his forehead. He gave no greeting, only waved Péter in. Péter followed him into what had probably once been a bedroom. It was an office now, as messy as Mr. Molnár's back in Pest. On one wall hung a blackboard with names written on it and numbers scribbled beside each. Márton shut the door, gestured toward a straight-backed chair for Péter, and reached for a vodka bottle. He splashed some of the liquid into two shot glasses, handed one to Péter, and sat down behind the heaped-up desk.

"So you helped your, eh, music teacher get to Mezősárgás to see her old … *friend.*" Márton rubbed his hand across the birthmark under his eye. "Nice of you. And how did that go?"

"She went home," Péter said warily. "I haven't spoken with her since Sunday."

"After quite a goodbye kiss at the train platform, I hear." The ends of Márton's mustache rose as he gave something of a smile. "We're all enjoying this. The shyest boy in the village brings home a looker from the city."

Péter gripped his glass and pressed his lips together.

"You might as well know," Márton went on, "or *she* might as well know, Róbert Zentai is leaving Mezősárgás. Going off to work somewhere else—I can't remember where. Near an aunt or a cousin or so forth. If your girlfriend needs to track him down because of the baby, our office could find out where he's going."

Péter's mouth went dry. How much did these people know about him, about Katalin? Márton drained his glass and set it, empty, on a stack of papers on the desk.

"So," Márton said, "I didn't send for you. You came here. What do you want?"

"When is my father coming back?"

"I don't know. I hear that you asked the same question at the police station. We aren't trying to make things any harder on you than necessary." Márton riffled through a few of the papers on his desk. "But I don't have to tell you your father was sabotaging the economic plan. The State is required to protect the people from saboteurs."

Péter had expected no other answer, really, but still the blood rose and pounded hot in his face and hands. Márton glanced at his wristwatch, something that Péter had never owned, and probably something few of the comrades out in the fields had ever owned, either.

"Is there anything else?" Márton asked.

"Yes." Péter held the vodka glass in his right hand and set his left hand in his lap. He thought of his brothers and all that he had lost, all that he stood yet to lose. Lowering his chin, he pulled a breath deep into his chest as he had done many times at the brink of a difficult line of song. "I want to join the collective farm."

Márton tipped his head to one side, frowning slightly. "Oh?"

"Yes, comrade."

"After all the reactionary resistance your father put up, why do you want to join?"

Péter's hand tightened on the shot glass.

Careful. Tighten only your belly. Loosen your hand. Loosen your jaw. Pretend you're behind a horse, remember? If you can sing to a horse's rear end, you can speak here.

Péter lifted the glass to his lips, willing the movement to be smooth, and let a few drops fall on his tongue. He set the glass, still mostly full, on the floor beside him. "I want to join," he said, "because I'm a farmer."

"What of that? So is everyone else around here."

Péter's neck tensed as he saw Márton smirk. The man was probably waiting for a desperate apology, but Péter had a feeling that desperation would work no better than anything else. No, he would go on with the words he had made himself rehearse on the road, and in his chores, and in the night when his brothers' crying woke him.

"I'm a good worker, a good farmer," he said. "I'm fast with a scythe."

Márton leaned over the desk and rested his chin on his palm.

"And I'm strong, I have endurance," Péter said, his voice steadying a little. "That's not a boast, comrade, it's just the way it is. I can put in longer harvest days than almost anybody I know. And my brothers know how to hoe and milk and tie sheaves. They're good workers, at least when they work with me. They're strong boys, and someday they'll be strong men."

Márton regarded him with one eyebrow raised.

"And the mare, the one that you ...." Pulse throbbing, Péter stopped himself from saying *the one you took*. "The one we used to use, that the collective uses now. I hear the communal farmers don't like working with her—they say she bites. Well, sometimes she does. But I know her. I can work with her. In the city I sometimes drive a team. I'm used to horses. I've never met a horse I couldn't manage."

In the humblest tone he could summon, Péter added, "I would help to make the communal farm productive. I mean, even more productive than it already is."

Márton rose from his chair. He crossed to the window and stood for a long time looking out onto the square. "And what about your land?" he asked. "The field by the stream?"

It was going to come to this; Péter had known it, and he had told himself that for the sake of Gyuri and Tibi he would not leave this place until he had said it. He swallowed. "The land," he said, "would be collective property."

Márton gave a laugh that was half grunt. "Your father would be furious."

Péter did not deny it, nor did he tell Márton that he was furious, too. "I am of age," he answered, "and my father is not here."

"You know this will have to be approved by the farm members."

"I know," Péter said. But he was certain the farm members would not dare to disagree with Márton, the Party rep: the game was won or lost here.

Péter played his last card. "I think I could boost worker morale, comrade. I am a singer. People like singing."

"And you think it makes a difference?"

"It has for me."

Márton looked up at the ceiling as though calculating; he pulled in his lips and slowly nodded.

As HE LEFT the collective headquarters, Péter saw the young veterinarian across the square. He called to Gábor, and when they stood close enough to speak without being overheard, Péter told him he had just talked with Márton. "I asked to join. If you could please speak in my favor …."

"Of course." Gábor gave him a somber, sympathetic look. Aloud, he changed the subject. "I'll probably be delivering a foal tonight or tomorrow. Small mare, large foal, so it might be difficult, and my assistant is ill. People say you're calm around horses. Would you be able to help?"

"Yes."

"Good, then. If there's a knock on your door in the middle of the night, don't be afraid. It's only me."

Péter smiled painfully. "Thanks."

HIS BROTHERS WERE playing marbles under the eaves when he reached home. They ran and met him at the gate. Tibi shouted something about a big party coming up in the village, a wedding. Péter couldn't imagine himself caring, and neither could he imagine himself being invited.

"It's Ági," Gyuri said. "She's getting married and moving to Csepel. There was a big list of people who wanted apartments, and she thought she'd have to wait and wait, but then she got one."

"She got an apartment," Péter repeated, and instinctively he looked toward the cellar under the barn, where the barrels were now emptied of seed grain.

That evening he asked the twins if they had known about the false wall before the night raid. They said yes, they had found it while playing in the cellar. "After we buried Nagyapa," Tibi said.

"Did you tell anybody?" Péter asked.

"I didn't," Gyuri said quickly.

"I didn't either," Tibi said. "Well … just Ági, I mean."

"Tibi!" Péter shouted, and his hand rose to cuff the boy.

Tibi stood flinching, eyes wide.

But what good would it do to chastise his brother now? No, he couldn't add guilt to the fear and grief that already was this poor child's inheritance. Péter shook his head, lowered his arm, and draped it over Tibi's shoulder. He would not speak to the twins of Ági and the seed wheat until they were men. No, not even then. He walked with the boys into the house and said nothing at all. There had already been too many words these last few days—to Tibi, to the Zölds, and worst, to Márton.

Still, he had to talk to one more person, and those words would be most difficult of all.

Chapter Twenty-Four

~⌣~

If

IT HAD NOW been more than a week since Katalin had seen Péter. He had telegrammed her last week to say he couldn't make his voice lesson, which she had assumed anyway. Still, she clung to this thread of hope: at least as of the moment he had sent the message, the authorities had not jailed him or carried him off. She went to the post office to telegram back. There was so much she wanted to say and ask, but Stalin and Rákosi were watching from the walls. All she dared write was MISS YOU—which she did, much more than she could tell him. She walked slowly home.

Comrade Erika informed her that if Péter Benedek was not coming back, then his junk needed to be cleared out. On a Wednesday night, when he had been gone a week and a half, Katalin went to the cellar with the intention of moving Péter's belongings into her family's storage room. But when she looked around his little cave under the stairs—at his clothes, the packing crate upended as a night table, the music book she'd given him, other books he'd found, the comforter from Ildi's family—she could not move him out. She wanted to wait at least a few more days.

Her eyes wandered to the note she had written to him, YOU ARE SMARTER THAN YOU THINK. So many messages had passed between them: a laugh, a brush of the fingertips, a lift of the brow while singing. A kiss, especially that last one at the Kőpatak train platform, with all its grieving ardor.

Tonight he would be lying on his mat in Kőpatak, worrying about raising his brothers without their father, in the same way that she herself had agonized every night of Mari's life. He would be dreading State cars and midnight poundings on the door. She wanted to lie down beside him there and kiss his hot forehead, to press him close, to murmur to him that he was stronger than the hatred around him, to tell him he was not alone, to hear him tell her that she was not alone, either. In the darkness, his rough but gentle voice would speak her name, and just for a moment their fear would ease.

ON WEDNESDAY EVENING, she left Mari with her parents and took the tram across the river to Buda. From the tram stop, she walked west and north through a neighborhood that the war had ground into rubble. In the six and a half years since then, some replacement buildings had been thrown together, the corners already sagging and the paint on their façades already cracking and chipping. She checked the address she'd been given and headed for a flat-roofed beige construction with a bust of Lenin over the metal double doors. It was the new State-funded *kulturház* of the neighborhood.

In the plain lobby, Árpád Kassai stood waiting for her. He bowed his balding head as he kissed her hand in the old, gentlemanly way. Mr. Kassai pushed open a door, which jammed at first, and they crossed what seemed to be a dance floor. He led her to an upright piano near the stage at the other end of the room.

"I'm very glad you decided to audition for the choir," he said.

He sat down on the piano bench and played several inversions of the C major chord. As Katalin stood at the bass end of the piano, Mr. Kassai told her he would like to check her range and sounded a middle C as the starting pitch. He took her through ascending patterns, then descending. It was like the lessons with Péter.

After some tight opening notes, she relaxed. Mr. Kassai played the supporting chords and nodded as he listened. She sang upward, carrying off a high A without straining, managing a high B-flat. At B she shook her head, wistfully remembering when she could sing C confidently.

"The higher notes will grow," the man assured her. "Your middle and upper-middle notes are beautiful. Let's see how you do with sight-singing."

He handed her a sheet of choir music and she read through it silently, tapping the rhythm with one finger on the top of the piano. It was not easy music, but neither was it as difficult as what she used to sing with her mother.

"Sing the soprano line, please," Mr. Kassai said. "I'll play the chords of the accompaniment. Here is your starting pitch."

She began to sing. Though she focused more on accuracy than tone, the song's range was comfortably within her own, and the notes felt natural and strong. Mr. Kassai kept nodding.

"Your skill is impressive," he said at the end. "You learned all this from your mother?"

"Yes."

"Not from classes?"

"No."

"You didn't want to go to academy like your brother?"

"Well, but I have a daughter now and …" she paused, and the conviction settled into her. "And I want to work with children."

"I wish you success with that, then. Go where you're needed. But I'd like to have you in the choir while you're available. Sometimes we need soloists. Are you interested in solos?"

"Possibly."

"May I hear you sing something? What about the lovely song you sang with that young man at your brother's party?"

That lovely song. For so long it had carried jagged memories of Róbert; now it carried memories of Péter. She almost told Mr. Kassai no—

Live or die.

"I'll have to sing it *a cappella*," she said, "if that's all right."

"Of course."

Mr. Kassai sat waiting on the piano bench. Katalin played the song's opening chord to derive the pitch. From behind her, she thought she heard a door opening with a rush of street noise, but she shut her eyes and listened only to the piano's dissolving tones. She straightened, drew in a low, quiet breath, faced the stage, and began to sing. The song lifted and spread, filling the vacant room, seeping into the empty places inside her with its beauty. Something told her this was the best she had sung in a long time. She felt neither pride nor fear; she simply sang, because it was in her to sing, and somehow, to sing was to live.

"Lovely, good," Mr. Kassai said when she finished. "Yes."

At the back of the room someone clapped. Katalin turned. Gasped. There in the doorway—smiling, hair windblown—stood Péter.

"What a singer!" he shouted.

"It seems you're called elsewhere," Mr. Kassai said to Katalin. "Very good audition. Rehearsal is next Monday night at six thirty. Here."

"I'll come."

She hurried across the room to Péter, and as she drew close, she noticed the strain behind his smile, the shadows under his eyes. She stepped into the lobby with him, and he let the door bang shut behind them. She touched his shoulder. He pulled her in and held her tightly.

"I've been so worried," she whispered. "Has your father come home?"

He touched his lips in a signal for her to wait. The bruise on his cheek had faded to a yellow discoloration. They walked out the main door and crossed the street, turning toward the river.

"How did you know to find me here?" she asked.

"I went to your flat. Your mother told me where you were. I saw Mari there. She ran to me so excited—'Pétó! Pétó!' "

"Yes, she says your name every time she sees your garden."

Katalin wanted to blurt out a thousand questions, but she made herself wait until she felt it was safe to tell her. She took his arm. The breeze carried a caress of early autumn as the last spread of daylight faded over the battered rooftops.

"I have a little news," she said. "I'm applying for teachers' college."

He turned to her and his tired eyes lifted. "That *is* news. You'll be good at teaching. I wish you were Tibi's teacher."

"I haven't finished applying yet. But the time has come."

"I may have to do something like that, too. The veterinarian in Kőpatak said I should take technical classes. Agronomy, animal husbandry. He said I could do some of the classes by correspondence."

Katalin pictured him laboring over the assignments, just as he had labored over improving his reading. She knew he seldom felt self-confident. Yet in spite of his own frustration and embarrassment, he had accomplished more than either of them would have guessed.

"The course work," she said, "you can do it."

He laughed wearily. "You always say that."

"Do you think you'll take the courses?"

"I haven't had time to think."

He looked around, craning his neck. They shouldered past other pedestrians on Alagút Street and followed the busy arterial into a tunnel that passed under Castle Hill. In the dim orange light of the tunnel's walkway, they stopped, and Péter positioned himself between her and the road.

He spoke low, close to her ear. "My father has not come back. And no word from him. No information."

She gripped his arm.

"I have to go back to Kőpatak tonight," he said. "To stay. Today I went to the print shop and said goodbyes, and tonight," he was struggling with his voice, "I have to say goodbye to you, too."

"Not yet," she whispered. "No. No, stay here."

A sudden torment crossed his face. "I can't leave my brothers. I'm all they have left."

"Bring them."

"They couldn't handle the change. Not after all they've been through. Especially Tibi."

"But maybe your father will come back." She was suddenly pleading. "We can hope for that, can't we?"

"I try to hope for it. But I can't plan on it, can't wait for it."

She remembered him trudging to the police station with his father's winter coat the day after the arrest. Péter had admitted from the beginning what he could not expect. She, on the other hand, had waited for Róbert day after day for two lost years.

"You're realistic," she told him, words breaking.

"I don't have any choice. And there's something else." He stood very close to her and spoke in a voice no louder than a lover's: "Kati, I joined the collective farm. I gave up the rest of my father's land. The State would have taken it sooner or later, and I had to get the pressure off my family. Can you understand this? Please?"

She looked into his shadowed face and nodded. "I know. I've learned. Some fights you can win and some you can't. I respect you for knowing the difference."

Péter sighed with a relief so palpable it almost seemed he would buckle. "I had to go and talk to the Party secretary about it. Tamás Márton. He was one of those three who came."

Katalin thought back on that unutterable night. Yes, she recalled the man: the birthmark under his eye, the terrible coolness with which he checked his wristwatch as Péter was slammed in the face.

"Oh, Péter."

"I tightened my belly like you always said in voice lessons, and I told him how much help I would be and what a hard worker I am, on and on, la la la."

"You did what you had to." She grasped his hand. "I'm sorry it came to that. So sorry."

They walked on along the eerily lit tile wall of the tunnel. A bus rumbled past. They followed the walkway onto the Chain Bridge, and where the walkway veered at the bridge's east tower, they stopped. They leaned on the railing, watching the barges in the churning water below, and she rested against his side. He pulled her closer.

"I don't want to say goodbye," she told him.

Under the dark, arching night he kissed her, long and deep, and their warmth mingled.

"Péter …." She stepped back and looked at him. How could she tell him all that she needed to say? Where to even begin?

"You've done so many hard things," she said. "And …."

He waited, touched her cheek.

"When you took me to see Róbert," she said. "I know that was hard for you."

His eyes flicked down. "Very hard."

"But thank you for doing it. I had to go."

"Have you heard from him?"

"No. And I won't."

"You know that?"

"It's what he's been showing me all along. You knew it. But I didn't want to see it."

Péter put his hand on her arm and was quiet.

"And if Róbert ever comes looking for me," she said, "I won't go with him. I know that now from visiting him. You helped me see what kind of man he was."

Péter nodded. "God knows I'm relieved to hear that."

"I'm sad for Mari, not having a father," Katalin said, "But I've had enough."

"You've had too much."

They stood hand in hand at the railing, and Péter watched the waves below. It was a long time before he spoke. "I wish Mari were mine." He looked at her. "I wish you were, too."

Her fingers tightened on his hand, and she felt her chin trembling. "What are you saying?"

"I love you. But you already knew that."

In his eyes, a world of anguish was reflected. Katalin put her arms around him. Yes, she had known it, but it had been a gift too frightening to open.

"I wish I had more to give you," he said. "I wish I could marry you and keep you and love you and provide for you and Mari. But I have less now than I ever had, nothing but two scared brothers and a job on a communal farm."

Katalin felt hot tears forming. "You want to marry me?"

"Yes."

"And you want to raise Mari?"

"Yes."

She leaned against him and wept.

"Katalin, I'm sorry! If this is too much, if I shouldn't have said all this, I'm sorry."

"Is this even possible? For us to marry?"

Péter cupped her chin in his hand and lifted her face. "Do you want it to be possible?"

His sudden hope seemed too much to bear. Wiping her tears, she looked up beyond the bridge chains to where the night sky flung out over the broken hopes of the city and of Kőpatak and of this whole aching world.

"How could it even be?" she asked.

"Oh, Lord, Katalin, if you're willing, I'd do anything to make it possible. Listen. Gyuri and Tibi and I, we aren't starving. We still have some animals and our garden lot and the apricot trees." His words spilled faster now. "And those classes the veterinarian told me about, those would help, maybe get me more pay from the collective. I'd do it, I'd take the classes. We could manage. Maybe you could teach in the Kőpatak school."

"But the program I'm applying for, it takes two years."

"I'll wait. If I could just keep on seeing you, I could wait."

Her hand gripped his. What would it mean to follow Péter to the *puszta*? The sweat, the cold, the relentless work—was that what she wanted?

Yet only a few weeks ago, she would have pledged herself to a cowherd on the *puszta* if he'd had the courage and loyalty to marry her. Róbert wasn't strong enough for it, she knew now. But Péter was.

Katalin looked down into the dark, brooding water, and a thought shook her. "What if you're taken away?" she asked Péter. "Like your father."

"Then take Mari and come back here to your family. And please bring my brothers. But I don't think that's going to happen. The collective already has the land. What they really need now is my work. I'll do everything I can to keep us all safe. We can do this, Katalin. We can make this work. If you want to. If," he traced his finger over her damp cheek, hesitating, "if you can love me."

"I'm afraid to say yes and I can't bear to say no. I have to think."

He murmured that he understood. She did not doubt it. She stroked the curling tangle of his hair, and his eyes softened in pleasure, beautiful under the expanse of night.

"Thank you," she said, "for asking so much of me."

He kissed her again as the river rippled below.

"I'll wait," he told her.

VERY LATE THAT night she saw him off at the train station. It was a hard goodbye. All through the next day at the nursery school she thought of him, and in the afternoon little Zoli asked her what the matter was. She said a special friend had gone away and that made her sad.

She stayed up late that night finishing her application for teachers' college. People said it was an advantage, in applying for anything, to be a peasant or a proletarian worker. Katalin wasn't either one, but after long deliberation, she wrote on the application, "I would be interested in teaching in a peasant village." To take an interest in a peasant village was not necessarily to marry into it. The next day, Friday, she carried the application to the college's admissions desk. She was late with it, she knew, so she took along a bottle of Italian Chianti from her father's stash of gratuities.

"Just in case not all the classes are completely full," she said with a smile to the desk clerk, and she handed over both the application and the Chianti.

SHE HAD SAID nothing to her parents about going to college, and she'd made only short remarks about it to Antal and Ildi. Ever since she met Róbert, she'd told her family so little. It had been a time of hiding. Péter had seen it in her. "You don't like telling people things, do you?" he'd once asked her, voice straining in anger. She thought of his words as she waited for the tram home from the college. Péter had always told her the truth.

That night at supper, she told her family the truth. When the conversation around the table hit a lull, she said there was news. She shifted on her chair and started with the easiest: she wanted to join a choir. In Buda. Directed by Mr. Kassai. And if they could look after Mari while she went to rehearsals, she'd appreciate it.

Her mother studied her thoughtfully. "All right."

Mari rocked side to side in her high chair. Katalin laid a quieting hand on the child and spooned a few noodles onto the high-chair tray. The family sat waiting.

"And today I applied to teachers' college," she said. "Late, I know, but I hope I'm accepted anyway."

Ildi and Antal leaned toward her, eyebrows raised.

"Well," her mother said, "this is a little sudden."

Her father set down his fork and knife. " 'Sudden' is the way our daughter does things. Katalin, have you thought this through?"

"Yes. I like children. I like teaching. I know I should have taken this step sooner, but I kept waiting …." She stopped, not wanting to say what they all knew, that she'd been waiting for Róbert.

"I think it's a good decision," Ildi said. "Kati will be a good teacher."

Katalin looked at Ildi in gratitude and rose to clear plates from the table. She tried to answer their questions, telling them that she didn't know what her chances were, but if the program accepted her, the State would pay the cost, and there would be child care for Mari.

"I wish you'd told us about this sooner," her father said, "but at least you're thinking of your future. Finally."

Her mother began pouring tea. Mari had eaten her fill and was now dropping noodles onto the floor. Katalin washed her daughter's face and hands with a cloth and lifted her down from the table. It was time to tell the family the rest. She tightened her lips to keep them from trembling.

"There's something else," she said.

Her mother paused with the tea pot.

Katalin sat down. "Péter Benedek asked me to marry him."

"What?" Antal asked, and Ildi gasped.

Her parents shot glances at each other. Her mother put down the pot. "Oh, Katalin, you didn't say yes, did you?"

"I said maybe. He said he'd wait for me."

All around the table, their questions exploded. What about school? How would they get by? Did she have any idea what she was getting into? Did he?

"My God, Katalin, that's a very hard life," her father said. "A peasant village on the *puszta*, the work, the pressures—"

"I know. I've thought about that. Many times." Katalin steadied her voice. "But I'm an unmarried mother, and that isn't easy, either. Péter's a good man. The best. And if a good man wants to marry me and raise Mari, that's no small thing."

Her mother sank into her chair, put her head in her hands. "And do you love him?"

"I haven't let myself say yes. Only maybe. But I trust him."

"So do I," Antal said.

"But that place where he lives is not safe," her mother argued. "Think what happened to Péter's father."

"Yes, I've thought about that," Katalin said. "Over and over. I was there when it happened, and I can't quit remembering it." She looked down at her daughter, playing on the floor with a wooden spoon. "But here in the city? Mari's father was arrested. Ildi's family was dragged off. People have been shot. Raped. Pest may be home, but it isn't safe. Just familiar."

"I don't think there's any such thing as 'safe' anymore," Antal said. He reached for Ildi's hand. "Sometimes we have to choose our risks. And then hope to be strong."

"That's what Péter and I are finding out," Katalin said.

SHE ATTENDED THE opera that night, as she had done in the days before Mari, before Róbert, before her failed audition. The opera was *Madama Butterfly* and Antal was playing in the orchestra. Katalin sat with Ildi in the far balcony and let the music sweep over her. The lead soprano was striking to look at, and her voice was so perfect, so lyrical, that in some moments Katalin held her breath.

Yes, perfect. The woman was the kind of singer people used to say Katalin would become. Katalin closed her eyes. If things had turned out differently, if she'd gone to music academy, if she'd kept studying, if she'd devoted herself and worked relentlessly, maybe this would have become her life—singing Puccini, an orchestra beneath her, a chorus behind her.

The stage, an audience, accolades. Glamor.

"The singer's incredible," she whispered to Ildi.

"And miserable," Ildi whispered back. "Antal says her third marriage is falling apart."

"Oh, no."

Katalin listened to the diva in quiet sympathy. Maybe the weight of such a life was more than the singer could bear. Did she ever long for the mundane stability of ordinary work? Did she envy women—like teachers—who went home and closed their doors?

And those other women onstage in the chorus, had they fared much better than the soprano? Were they married? Did they wish they were home tucking their children in bed? Katalin thought of Mari. And these nights at the opera were so long. When did the women arrive home? Impossibly late? Didn't they miss making love with their husbands? She couldn't help thinking of Péter, and she suddenly ached for his touch, the feel of his body close to hers. It was growing harder and harder to be content without him.

The opera went on in all its heartbreaking pathos as Madama Butterfly waited and waited for the man who had abandoned her. Butterfly gave herself up. Katalin bowed her head with sorrow that Butterfly had killed herself for an unworthy man.

AFTER THE OPERA, she joined Ildi and Antal for a cup of espresso at a coffee house across the avenue. They sat at an outdoor table. Katalin crossed her arms in the cool night and looked out at the loud, electrical city that had been her home all her life. Tonight in Kőpatak the stars would be out. Péter would be sleeping, and in a few hours he would rise before the sun to begin his work. How tired he must be. If she married him, she would take on some of the work herself, maybe the garden. It wouldn't be easy, but it had been so long since anything was.

"Katalin." Antal's voice across the table interrupted her thoughts. "That was a shock you dropped on us at supper. Are you really going to marry Péter?"

She looked at her brother and his wife, sitting close together in the night chill. "I've only said maybe."

"I did that with Ildi," Antal said. "A person can only say 'maybe' for a while."

"I know," Katalin said.

"It must have been hard for him to ask you to marry him," Ildi said. "He seems so shy."

"But shyness isn't the same as fear."

Katalin bit her lip, remembering Péter asking her for voice lessons in spite of his shyness. She remembered him standing beside the piano, making himself sing out. She remembered him sitting under the light bulb in the basement, making himself read. She was there the night of his father's arrest. She knew how his parentless brothers needed him, and she knew that when he had to, he'd done what his father couldn't and gave up the family land.

"He's strong," she said, "and he's been so kind to Mari and me."

Ildi leaned against Antal's shoulder and smiled. "Well, I can tell you from experience, kindness is sexy. Irresistible."

Antal laughed a little. Katalin felt her cheeks go warm. She lifted her cup and smiled. Antal winked at her.

THE NEXT EVENING, a Saturday, she wandered down to the basement after Mari was asleep. On the night when Péter came back and left again, she had helped him clear his belongings out of the cellar. Now his makeshift quarters seemed so empty. Yet in his haste and distraction, he had forgotten to take the comforter Ildi's family had given him.

Katalin stepped closer and peered into his space under the stairs. A note was still thumbtacked on a post. She knelt and unpinned the message she'd once written to him, YOU ARE SMARTER THAN YOU THINK. She stuffed the note into her pocket. With a lonely ache, she gathered up the comforter and carried it upstairs to her bedroom.

Since Mari was asleep, Katalin turned on only the desk lamp. The room was fragrant with the lavender Péter had given her in the summer, still hanging in a dried bunch from her curtain rod. She pulled the note from her pocket and laid it on the bed. Beside it and around it, she set out other things she had collected to take to Kőpatak: pencils, paper, and another Winnetou book for Gyuri and Tibi. A music book to give to Panni, the veterinarian's nice wife. Just knowing that Panni and Gábor were there eased some of Katalin's fears for Péter. To the pile, she added two books Péter had found in the basement and said he wanted, a Mór Jókai novel and a book about the care of animals.

Katalin ran her hand over the frayed cover of the novel. She would help Péter read it. In Kőpatak they would sit together with the book spread open on the *tiszta szoba* table, and Mari would climb onto their laps. Péter would welcome Mari. Not every man would welcome someone else's child, but Péter was kind.

And kindness, as Ildi said, was irresistible.

Next to the growing pile on the bed, Katalin set the folded comforter. The nights would turn colder, and Péter would need it. In time, so would she. She knew it now, as she fingered the soft cotton. Within herself, in a place deeper than every fear, she let the truth settle: *I love Péter.* This was what she wanted—to share the nights and days with him and trust him with the years.

From the crib, her daughter's breath rose and fell as rhythmically as music. Katalin listened while the night deepened. Then she turned, sat down at her desk and wrote a letter.

> Dear Róbert,
>   Our beautiful daughter is a year and a half old now and constantly growing. It's good that she met you, even if only once. But she didn't know to say goodbye to you, so I am saying it for her now. There is a

good man who will be her father. I release you.
I pray you are strong and in some way happy.

Katalin

Her parents and Ildi and Antal had all gone out, and the apartment was empty. Katalin carried the letter into the front room and burned it in the tile stove, watching as it turned to embers. The goodbye would rise with the smoke into the night sky. There would be nights in Kőpatak when she would watch Péter stoke the fire in the clay oven, and she would remember this moment, this choice of the heart.

Sunday morning, very early, she bundled the comforter tightly with twine and crammed it into a large market bag. The books and other items she packed into a rucksack. She woke Mari, dressed her, and handed her a bottle of milk. Then Katalin shrugged the rucksack onto her back. Slinging the bag over her shoulder, she anchored Mari on her hip and headed for the train.

THE EARLY AUTUMN sun shone full as she walked up the Kőpatak road to Péter's house. She passed the neighboring houses and saw him hoeing his front garden.

He looked up. "Katalin!" Pitching the hoe aside, he ran to the gate and threw it open. "Is everything all right?"

"Yes." She set Mari down beside the gate and dropped the rucksack and the bag.

He touched her face. "I can't believe you're here."

She swallowed down the ache that came to her throat. Oh, the words she'd held back, like songs she couldn't sing.

"Péter," she blurted, "there were things I couldn't say because I was afraid. I couldn't tell you I love you, but I do."

She heard the quick intake of his breath. She clutched his hand in her trembling fingers and went on, "I was afraid that if I really wanted something, I would never have it. So I couldn't tell you that I want to marry you. But I do."

"You're saying yes?"

"Yes."

He searched her face, his lips parted in astonished wonder. "Oh, Kati." He pulled her close. "My brave woman."

At their feet, Mari reached up. Péter lifted the child. Katalin rested against Péter's chest and let her gaze wander over this world that would become hers: the barn, the house with the eaves hanging low over the porch, the garden, where the summer's cucumber vines still curled and some cabbages had not yet been pulled up. A swallow flitted by. In the road, a wagon clattered past them.

Somewhere Tibi and Gyuri were off doing chores. Somewhere the family's cow grazed. In the fields that used to be Péter's, the winter wheat would soon be sown, and in an office somewhere, someone was scheduling Péter's work on the communal farm. Somewhere the police were making rounds. Her arms tightened around Péter. The morning sun flooded down.

"Yes," she repeated.

Chapter Twenty-Five

~⌒⌣⌒~

The Train to Kőpatak
Two years later, October 1953

IN THE TRAIN, the man bent forward on his wooden seat, stretching the small of his back and shifting his weight. His back complained far more now after these two years of shoveling in Hortobágy. He rubbed his lower spine and let out a groan, but silenced himself when he saw the peasant woman in the facing seat watching him. She grimaced.

"Sorry," he muttered, knowing how he must look, and smell, to the woman and her child. He had not had a haircut in six months. This morning, as best he could, he had washed himself with a bucket of cold water, but his clothes had not been laundered in a month.

The woman grunted. Then she pulled an apple from a basket, and without a word she leaned over and handed it to him.

"Thank you," he breathed. Earlier in his life he would have added politely, "God repay you for it," but he had not heard mention of God in a long time.

Against the smooth peel of the yellow-red fruit, his own fingers looked cracked and old. Was he an old man now? He had never been one before. Never mind. He lifted the apple and bit into it, off-center in his mouth to avoid a hurting tooth. His thirsting tongue savored the wet sweetness. When he had eaten all the fruit's meat, he nibbled the core clean, spit the seeds into his hand and slipped them into the pocket of his shabby winter coat. One didn't throw away seeds. Two years ago, he had found seed grain in the pocket of this coat. He had rationed it out to himself during the first hungry winter, allowing himself a few kernels a day. In them, he tasted home and hope. A little of the grain he had saved for the spring, and he planted it in a sunny spot between the embankment where he worked and the long, musty barn where he slept. When other men walked by his tiny crop, they sometimes plucked and ate of it, but he never really begrudged them the gleaning. He would have done the same.

It was late October, and he was glad to be leaving Hortobágy before winter. He looked out the train window onto the stubbled fields strewn with mulch. Not far off, he recognized a broken sweep well, still unrepaired, and he knew he was within a few kilometers of Kőpatak. In his lap his hands sweated. At the camp they had all been told to expect nothing— *"Nothing!"*—when they were released.

What would he return to? Did he have a home? Who would be living now in the house with the clay oven, where the apricot trees grew? Were his boys there? The twins? And his good eldest son who had filled the coat pocket with seed wheat? Every day, every hour of these twenty-six months, he had thought of his sons with longing and terror, and every night in the drafty barn he had crossed himself and whispered their names.

In the shaking train now, he lifted his hand halfway to his forehead, moved it barely right, barely left. *Tibi, Gyuri, Péter.*

AT THE KŐPATAK platform, Jancsi Benedek stepped down from the train carefully so as not to twist his stiff back. Holding his satchel, he walked into town on the dusty road. The houses of Kőpatak looked trimmer and more pleasant than he remembered, if only because they weren't Hortobágy barns. He glanced at the communal farm headquarters and the police station, not knowing who might be looking back. The flag of the People's Republic still hung outside the headquarters. He turned away, squinting in disapproval. Not that he had expected differently, but in some desperate way, he had hoped. For Stalin had at last died—may God torment his soul—and his ass-kisser, Rákosi, had been shoved aside and replaced by a man named Imre Nagy. People said Nagy was a reasonable communist, less fond of human misery. Jancsi Benedek didn't know. But he was out of Hortobágy.

It was a Saturday. A crowd had assembled in the Kőpatak market square, the men in dark jackets and the women in kerchiefs. Jancsi stayed behind the crowd, reluctant for anyone to see him and ask where he had been these two years. Somewhere, children were singing. He moved beside an elm tree on a slight knoll in the square, and as the crowd shifted a little, he saw the singers. About a dozen small girls and boys in autumn jackets stood clustered near the central war memorial, singing and watching the directions of a young woman whose back was turned to him. She squatted, apparently to avoid blocking the view of those watching the children. The youngsters sounded good. Surprisingly good. The song was one his wife used to sing. Wondering if he knew any of the children, he looked at each face. They would have been mere cubs when he left, but yes: some had the eyes, noses, and chins of families he had known all his life.

The song slowed as it ended, and the children repeated the last line. Three little girls in the front row stepped forward hand in hand, the smallest one dark-haired and very young. These girls sang the last words again, and even the voice of the youngest was strong and sweet. Jancsi Benedek felt a soft, unexpected pleasure. The crowd clapped. Someone whistled.

Jancsi moved closer to the ring of listeners and stood beside a family he didn't recognize. Perhaps they had come in from somewhere else for market day. Or perhaps this village he used to call home had strangers in it now. He peered again through gaps in the crowd at the singers. Two older boys stepped in with the children at the back of the cluster. The boys were lanky but broad-shouldered and beginning to sprout man-height, one of them darker with a heart-shaped face, the other paler and wearing glasses ....

Gyuri and Tibi.

Jancsi raised his hand to his trembling mouth and blinked away the blurring in his eyes.

From somewhere at the front of the crowd, a young man walked forward to join the singers. It was his eldest son, fully a man now, Jancsi saw. Péter stopped to speak to the little dark-haired girl who had sung, then turned when the young woman directing the group called his name. She said something to him that Jancsi didn't hear. Péter nodded to her and took his place with the twins at the back.

Overcome, Jancsi told the strangers beside him, "Those are my sons. Those three."

The eyes of the strangers flitted over him. The woman sidled closer to the man she was with and grasped the hand of one of her children.

The director now joined the group of singers, stood to the side of the children and announced the final song. She was pretty and wore no kerchief and seemed somehow familiar. The young woman looked at the singers, waiting until she had the attention of them all, then turned to the audience. By herself she sang the opening line, her voice warm and pure as sunlight breaking. She lifted her hand, and the children sang the next few lines with her.

His sons entered the song. Listening, Jancsi caught his breath. The twins were growing into their manhood voices. They leaned close to Péter, following him on the song's lower current. It was a simple song, one that a penniless swineherd could have played on a pipe, but Jancsi could imagine no more beautiful sound than this. When the music ended, the crowd burst into applause. People in front began moving. He stood on tiptoe.

And suddenly Péter saw him. Péter's mouth fell open. He grabbed his brothers by the shoulders, turned them, pointed. The three pushed through the crowd. An arm's length from him, they stopped, and he felt their eyes take in his gray gauntness. Then, beginning with Péter, they threw their toughened arms around him.

"Péter," he rasped. "Tibi, let me look at you. Gyuri. My God."

The twins bounced, laughed, tugged at his elbows, shouted. Jancsi felt his back cramp. He hoped they didn't see him wince.

But Péter was watching, and he took Jancsi's satchel. "Are you well, Apa?"

"Well enough."

"Good, then ..." Péter's voice choked off and he laid his hand on Jancsi's shoulder. "You're home. I can't believe it." Péter turned. "Katalin!" he called over his shoulder. "Mari!"

Around them a circle of onlookers had formed. Children stared, women gasped, and men exclaimed, "It's Benedek!"

But on the outer rim of the circle, Tamás Márton crossed his arms. Jancsi looked away.

The young choir director now pushed her way forward, leading the dark-haired child by the hand. Next to Péter she stopped, and Péter took the little girl into his arms.

"Apa," Péter said, "you remember Katalin, my voice teacher." He smiled. "My wife."

"Father," Katalin said. She gazed at him in astonishment and clasped his right hand in both of hers. "Welcome home."

Jancsi nodded his thanks. The child in Péter's arms looked at him, her large eyes blinking. She leaned close to Péter's ear, and Jancsi heard her ask, "Apuka, who is he?"

"This is your grandfather, the one we told you about," Péter answered her. "The one who was gone."

The child cocked her head and a dimple rose on her cheek. She almost smiled at Jancsi. He had grown unaccustomed to smiling. He almost smiled back.

On the way home, he walked with Péter and the little girl while the twins and the young woman went on ahead. Jancsi was tired, his gait dragging, and he was conscious of needing the same patience from Péter that the child did. Péter called the child Mari. Jancsi remembered now, in the last chaotic hours before he was taken, that there had been a baby here named Mari.

"Your wife's daughter," he said to Péter.

"Her daughter, yes. And my daughter."

"The man in Mezősárgás didn't claim her, then?"

"Not enough to make a difference. But I'm glad to have her."

At the gate of his house, the twins were waiting. Jancsi followed as they showed him through the yard and the barn. He counted eight chickens, not as many as there once had been, but they were healthy birds, and after the desolation of Hortobágy, this was a gift.

The milk cow had grown old and the family'd had her butchered, Gyuri said, but Péter had managed to buy a heifer that would soon be mature enough to mate. Jancsi nodded. The mare's barn stall stood empty, and Tibi said she had gone to the collective farm, but Péter and the veterinarian saw to it that she was well fed. From what the twins said about the garden and the apricot trees, Jancsi guessed they were producing about the same as usual—no more, but also no less—and this, too, was a gift.

After this the twins led him into the house. On the floor lay a Turkish carpet Katalin had brought from the city. A zither stood propped in the corner, and Tibi said Katalin had been teaching him to play it.

"Good," Jancsi said. "Everything … good …." He wanted to say more but could not speak.

THE OCTOBER EVENING was cool, but winter's harshness had not yet arrived, and at dusk Jancsi and Péter sat under the eaves in their coats. As the kerosene lantern glowed, Péter sharpened his pocket knife on a whetstone. He spoke of what had happened these last two years. Gyuri and Tibi had just started seventh grade. Gyuri was doing very well and they were all proud of him. School was harder for Tibi, but he had glasses now. Katalin had arranged that.

"She helps him with his schoolwork," Péter said, stroking the blade over the stone. "She's been helping me, too. I'm taking *tehnikum* classes in animal husbandry. She goes through the readings with me. Sometimes, when I have questions, I ask the veterinarian. Maybe you remember him—he's married to Mrs. Donáth's daughter Panni."

"Yes. I remember."

"I'm grateful for that family," Péter said. "Not all the Kőpatak women welcomed Katalin, but Panni and her mother did. The others, well, they're learning to respect her. Because their children like her. She started that little choir, and she's the new kindergarten teacher. Our daughter's three and a half. Year after next, she'll be in Kati's class."

"And what about that city couple?" Jancsi asked.

"The Zölds? They moved to Kalocsa not long after you left. They have family there."

"And how long have you been married, son?"

"Only a few months. It was August, after harvest. Before Katalin started teaching."

"There's so much I've missed."

Jancsi pulled a cigarette from his threadbare shirt pocket. The middle finger of his right hand was bent slightly askew where a camp guard had struck him with a rifle butt, and he had difficulty lighting the match. Péter leaned over and helped him.

"Apa," Péter asked quietly, "where were you?"

Jancsi thought of the grim expanse of marsh and mud where he'd lived among former shopkeepers, cobblers, and landowners, although some like himself had barely owned enough land to stand on.

"They told us not to tell," he said to Péter.

"Not even to your family?"

"That's what they said."

Jancsi looked at this son, who had sent him his coat and kept the garden growing and kept the twins from starving, this son whom he trusted when he trusted no one else in the world.

"Keep this quiet," he whispered. "I was at Hortobágy. The drainage projects."

Péter shook his head.

"Were other men from around here taken?" Jancsi asked.

"We heard about some being taken from Heves and from Mezőkövesd, but we didn't know where they went. Then we heard that one from Heves had come back. I went to Heves to ask that man if he'd met you, but he said no. He'd been in the Mátra mines, and when he started talking about men who died, I thought ..." Péter stopped. "Oh, God, Apa ...."

"Just tell me, are you safe, you and the twins and your wife and the child?"

"I've done everything I can to make it that way."

"Is Márton still the Party secretary?"

"Yes. And still president of the collective. And now the head of the town council."

Jancsi's gut wrenched and he threw aside his cigarette.

"But we're pretty much left alone, at least for now," Péter said. "We're managing. I do field labor and I sometimes drive a team. Sometimes I help the veterinarian. I'm taking those classes and hoping we have some kind of a future. The twins work in the fields with me, and Katalin teaches, and among us we have enough to eat. And you'll eat, too."

Péter stopped sharpening the knife and his hands became absolutely still.

"Apa," he said, "I joined the collective. I gave up the land. I'm sorry. Very sorry."

Jancsi put up his hand, stopping him. "You gave it up before they took it by force. I should have done that. While I was in Hortobágy, every day—no, every minute—I feared for you and the twins." His voice had gone hoarse. "But now I come home and find you strong. And the twins are tall. And you have a good woman and a little girl. How could I have hoped for so much?"

Péter let out his breath and rested his forehead in his hands. Jancsi reached over, laying his hand on Péter's muscular shoulder. He felt his son's shoulder loosen, as though laying down a load two years heavy.

Chapter Twenty-Six

Evensong

Tibi and Gyuri had carried buckets of water from the well into the kitchen, and Katalin had heated the water on the cook stove. Péter now poured it into the large metal bathing tub that he had bought when Katalin moved here to marry him. After he had ushered everyone else out of the kitchen, he helped his father into the tub. Apa pulled in a sharp breath and winced when he bent his back. Péter steadied him at the elbow. There was a recent welt on Apa's wrist; Péter asked his father about it but did not press him when he gave no answer.

After the bath, Péter gave Apa a clean nightshirt. Apa put it on; then, leaning against the ladder to the loft, he drank the milk Katalin had left for him. Péter was not sure where his father should sleep, so he began explaining the current arrangement: the twins in the loft for now, Mari in a trundle bed in the corner of the *tiszta szoba,* and he and Katalin in the bigger bed in the opposite corner.

"So the bed is being used, then," Apa said.

To Péter it seemed so long ago now, those years when by peasant tradition they had left the bed decorative and unused, prettily made up and piled with linens and pillows for guests who did not come. Until the Russians arrived. And then the Zölds.

"Yes, the bed's used," Péter said. "It was empty for a while when the Zölds moved out. But then Katalin came, and she thought it was a perfectly good bed." He laughed a little. "So I had a pretty bride saying to me, 'Péter, let's use the bed,' and I wasn't in a mood to say no."

"Who would be? No, just give me a mat in the pantry, and I'll be much more comfortable than I've been for two years."

The twins spread a good layer of straw on the pantry floor, laid down a mat for Apa, and set blankets at the foot. Péter stood by as Apa eased carefully onto the mat, holding the small of his back. When Apa had pulled up the blankets, the family gathered in the pantry doorway to wish him good rest. Mari had been watching her new grandfather silently all evening, but now she stood between Péter and Katalin and whispered that she wanted to talk to him.

"Go on, then," Katalin urged her.

The child knelt on the straw in her nightgown. "Good night, Nagyapa," she said softly.

At last Péter saw his father truly smile. He understood his father's pleasure, for Péter remembered the first time Mari had called him Apuka.

THE TWINS HAD gone to their mats in the loft. Mari had been tucked into her trundle bed. Péter had turned out the light, the one electrical bulb that had recently been installed in the *tiszta szoba*. After Mari was asleep, Péter carried a candle into the opposite corner and set it on a shelf above the bed. Katalin followed. They sat down on the bed and he told her how relieved he was to see his father home, alive. He did not use many words for it, but he did not have to. She touched a curl above his left ear and told him yes, she knew.

"Another male in your crowded house," he teased her gently.

"I'm glad he's back, Péter."

They spoke in hushed voices because of Mari in the corner. They had learned to make love almost soundlessly, too. The candle on the shelf flickered as Katalin drew back the comforter. It was a little ragged these days, so they kept it covered with a quilt his mother had embroidered. Péter watched the beautiful quiet of his wife's movements. In spite of all that had broken upon them and could yet break, she had found peace here with him. Last month she had told him so, here in this bed, in the calm after their love.

On the dresser tonight she had set a pan of warm water. "When I heated it for your father, I saved some for us," she said.

He smiled at her.

They undressed. She dipped a cloth into the water and smoothed it over her own flesh, then tenderly over his. Somewhere outside the window, a nightingale called, a small trill of song. On some nights dogs barked or a State car engine rumbled on the road, but tonight there was music. The candle's sheen lit the slope of Katalin's shoulder, the curve of her breast. This was his joy and consolation: the good, pulsing mystery that was her body and soul. She slipped under the coverlet, and he blew out the candle.

Notes

Chapter 5

A szegény raboknak szabadulására ....
For the freedom of the poor prisoners ....

Words to this song, *"Fölszállott a Páva,"* are by the Hungarian poet Endre Ady. English translation as given in the jacket notes of the CD *The Choral Music of Kodály 3* by Hungaroton Classic recordings. The melody is a traditional Hungarian folksong, and it was arranged into choral variations by Hungarian composer Zoltán Kodály.

Chapter 12

Duna, vized miért olyan keserü?
Danube, why are your waters so bitter?

From the traditional Hungarian song, *"Bécs várostól, nyugatról keletre ...."* English translation from the notes of the CD *Verbunkos* by the Hungarian State Folk Ensemble, 2004.

Photo by Chip Van Gilder

CONNIE HAMPTON CONNALLY has loved music and the written word all her life, and many of her adult years she's spent working in those fields as well. She holds a BA in English from the University of Washington and an MFA in creative writing from Antioch University. She's published magazine stories and newspaper articles, worked as an editor, and taught high school English and elementary music.

Through teaching music, she discovered the work of Hungarian composer Zoltán Kodály, who uplifted his nation through decades of war, fascism and communism. Ms. Connally couldn't resist this theme of beauty amidst hardship. She wrote *The Songs We Hide* as a result, and she is currently writing another novel set in Hungary.

Ms. Connally and her husband make their home in Tacoma, Washington. They travel frequently, since two of their three adult sons live on other continents. Because of her family and her characters, Ms. Connally has set her heart—and often her feet—in faraway places.

Find her on the web at:

www.ConnieHamptonConnally.com.

Discussion Questions
for Book Groups

1. What rights and choices do we have that the characters in The Songs We Hide do not? What individual rights do you believe should be steadfastly protected by a government, and under what circumstances (if any) should a government limit those rights?

2. In The Songs We Hide, loneliness is a recurring theme. Who is lonely in the story, and why? How has the cultural and political environment brought loneliness on the characters, and how have they brought it on themselves?

3. To what extent are Péter and Katalin each distrustful of others in the beginning? What builds trust between them? What causes you to trust or distrust a person?

4. What does music add to the characters' lives? To the story?

5. Does Péter's growth as a singer change him, and if so, how? How have you grown personally by developing your talents?

6. What do you think drew Katalin to Róbert? Do you think the relationship was doomed from the beginning? What does Katalin learn through her painful experience with Róbert?

7. Antal initially enters into a "paper marriage" with Ildi so that she won't have to leave the city, and it is only later that they commit to real marriage. What are the different reasons people marry, and which do you feel are most valid?

8. In an episode from Péter's past, we see that when he was a teenager he opposed his father's wishes to remarry. Do you believe Péter was wrong in the stance that he took? How well do you think teenagers usually understand their parents' feelings, and vice versa?

9. How is Péter's life made more difficult by Jancsi, his father? Do you find yourself blaming Jancsi or sympathizing with him?

Made in the USA
San Bernardino, CA
25 April 2018